Frances Brown was born in Emsworth, on the Hampshire/Sussex border, at a time when her parents were just settling down from their life on the road. Her mother was descended from generations of fairground travellers and her father came from a circus family. The first person in her family ever to have a full education, Frances attended Chichester, Petersfield and Slough grammar schools before reading History at the University of London and then training as a teacher at Sussex University. Frances Brown is married and lives in Malvern, Worcs.

The Other Sister

Frances Brown

HEADLINE

First published in 1992
by HEADLINE BOOK PUBLISHING PLC

First published in paperback in 1993
by HEADLINE BOOK PUBLISHING PLC

10 9 8 7 6 5 4 3 2 1

ISBN 0 7472 3953 3

Printed and bound in Great Britain by
HarperCollins Manufacturing, Glasgow

HEADLINE BOOK PUBLISHING PLC
Headline House
79 Great Titchfield Street
London W1P 7FN

For my son, Daniel

Chapter 1
December 1883

Steffi leapt up and instinctively stretched out his arms – whether to grab her or fend her off he wasn't sure. Reacting from shock, unable to make sense of this crazy thing that was happening.

The argument, the shouting, the crack of a whip and now – Amy rushing past him, cradling her face in hands that were already streaked bright red by blood streaming through her fingers. Like mulberry juice, he thought.

And a moment later he hated himself for not catching hold of her and trying to do something to help. But the screaming confused him. Rosa's screaming. And the general pandemonium that broke out as Amy fled from the circus ring.

'Amy! Amy, my babe! Quick, stop her, someone! She's hurt.' Her mother's voice echoing as she ran after the girl. And then Rosa at his side, screaming with terror before sobbing that she'd seen her sister's eye hanging out.

'No. No, Rosa. I'm sure it can't be that bad,' he whispered, in an effort to soothe her while at the same time trying to expunge the horror from his mind.

But what on earth had gone wrong? Steffi felt a desperate need to work out exactly what had happened, shift the shattered pieces of the afternoon back into a sensible pattern, put the clock back to a time before the world came to disaster.

That stroll along to the theatre with his father after lunch, for example. Everything had been fine then. No hint of trouble. Levic in an unusually good mood as he talked about the new barebacking act he was working on with the girls' mother.

'But why,' Steffi had wanted to know, 'do you have to do tricks on horseback, Pa? Why can't you just stick to clowning?'

'Because I'm not *just* a clown. I'm an artiste, Steffi. And an artiste never stops learning,' Levic said.

1

'But Ma said that what you and Dorina are doing is dangerous,' he had objected.

His father laughed at that.

'What's so funny?' Steffi asked.

'The thought of a tightrope walker trying to tell an equestrienne that her act is dangerous,' Levic chuckled.

'Oh, but I don't think she'd say it to Dorina . . .' Steffi had stammered, fearing lest he had misrepresented his mother. For what Mirella had actually said was that Levic was 'playing with fire' by getting involved with Dorina's act, and Steffi was not exactly sure what she meant.

His father was right though. It was funny for Mirella to worry about two people turning somersaults off horseback when she herself every night walked a slender thread of rope through the air sixty feet above spectators' heads without, it seemed, thinking anything of it. But there again, Mirella had been walking her tightrope for what amounted to a life-time – well, Steffi's life-time at least. For his mother had told him how she had had to interrupt her career twelve years ago when he was born.

He loved to listen to her talking about the past. About how she had been working with savage lions in her uncle's menagerie show when she had first met Levic and been attracted to the famous clown. Of how, some time later, Levic had left her and travelled to America where he earned even greater renown before returning and sweeping her off her feet with a proposal of marriage.

But Steffi was not surprised by such an outcome. He found it impossible to believe that anyone could have resisted the charms of his beautiful mama, especially once they saw her dancing along her rope in a silver sequinned dress, flowing black hair cascading over her shoulders.

Steffi had heard Levic's angry mutter as they entered Apsley's this afternoon to find the arena already occupied by the theatre's owner, Arnold Foreman. The old man was supervising his two granddaughters as they went through their usual limbering up routine – back-bends, bringing head up between legs, picking up a handkerchief backward with their teeth, lying on the ground and coiling their bodies around their heads like snakes – but he was quick to respond to the signs of Levic's displeasure.

'Okay, old son. We're just finishing off now. I know you and Dorina have first call on the ring today,' he called out.

2

'That's right. We have,' Levic said, scowling around for his partner.

'If you're looking for my daughter, she's out back, getting the horses ready,' Arnold volunteered. 'That's why I took the opportunity of putting these two young madams through their paces.'

At which remark, the two sisters brought their extraordinary contortions to an end and scrambled to their feet.

'We're not madams. We're misses,' Rosa panted, her face flushing pink right up to the roots of her blonde hair.

She was a chubby girl, almost exactly the same age as Steffi, and he had felt curiously excited, seeing her like that, with her grey eyes huge and glistening, and her chest heaving up and down with the strain of so much exertion.

'I thought we're supposed to be called "Mamselles" now we're on the programme,' Amy piped up.

A year younger than Rosa, and with a pretty, pert face and cheeky smile, she had always been Steffi's special friend, so he was quick to agree with her. 'Yes. "Mesdemoiselles Rosa and Amy – Queens of the Globe" – that's how your grandad introduces your act. But I don't suppose you can hear the announcement when you're waiting in the wings, can you?'

'Not clearly, 'cos we're too busy keeping our balance and getting ready to come in on time.'

'Speak for yourself,' Rosa interrupted. 'I don't need to concentrate that much any more. I'm sure I could walk a blooming globe in my sleep.'

'Good,' said her grandfather. 'Then go and fetch one and show us how it's done.'

'Oh, not now!' she groaned. 'I thought you said we could finish early and go with Steffi to the park, if his mother will take us.'

'Yes, you did, Grandpa,' Amy added.

'And remember what you said about Mammy and Levic needing to practise.'

'That's right,' the younger girl said, clasping hold of her grandfather's arm and mischievously peering up at him. 'So we'd better not take up any more time in the ring.'

'See what I mean? A proper pair of madams who order me about as if they own the place,' Arnold Foreman grumbled, shaking his nearly-bald head. 'But that don't mean to say they can have all their own way.'

Whereupon he led the girls, still protesting, up on to the

3

stage to finish their practice while Steffi watched, envying their skill and their whole lucky existence. For, unlike Steffi, Rosa and Amy were not rationed to spending brief holidays at Apsley's. They lived here in this famous London amphitheatre and in the bosom of their family all the year round. Unlike him, at the end of the school holidays, they never had to pack their bags, take leave of their parents and go back into the world on their own.

Mind you, there was no denying that, young as they were, they had to work hard for their living.

Which was what Steffi had been thinking as he sat in the stalls and watched the sisters roll out the big red and gold globes and mount them, one apiece. Then, with arms outstretched, start to take the tiny steps which set each one in motion. Round they trundled, slowly round the stage in a carefully guided circle – despite their protests, clearly loving this part of their practice and regarding it as play.

And Steffi had been so absorbed that he had spared scarcely a glance for what was taking place in the ring. In fact, he only grew aware that something was amiss when he caught sight of the girls' father, Matty, clambering over the ring fence and heard him shouting.

Yes, now that he thought about it, that was when he had registered the first sign of trouble, even though he had not understood what was happening.

One minute there was Rosa and Amy, balancing on their globes, being taught how to roll them up a gentle incline, while in the ring Steffi's father and the girls' mother were putting their horse through its paces. Everything peaceful, nothing untoward. And then all of a sudden hell started to break loose.

'Whoa, boy! Whoa!' Levic yelled, reining in Black Chieftain as the horse reared in response to Matty's sudden shout, causing Levic almost to lose balance.

'Whooa! Whooa!' Matty repeated, his voice sounding strangely slurred.

'Matty! Get out of the ring! Can't you see we're working?' Dorina scolded, as if speaking to a naughty child.

'Och, aye. I can see you're both at it as usual,' her husband grinned.

'Go away, then.'

'Why?'

'Because we're busy,' Dorina snapped.

4

'Och, aye, always busy, busy, busy.'

'You've been drinking man,' Arnold roared from the stage.

'Och, aye. You're right.'

'Haven't I made it clear I won't tolerate drunkenness on my premises?'

'Aye.'

'So, take yourself off and dry out,' Arnold roared again.

'Dry oot? Och, no. Not today, the Sabbath. It's me day off. Ye canna tell me what to do today, Arnold. I do what I like. And where I like. And who I like. And . . .'

'You're drunk, man. Go and sleep it off, for heaven's sake,' Levic had said, quickly dismounting.

'Sleep, ye say? What, in an empty bed? Why, that's no good to a raw-blooded Scot. Which is why I've come to fetch me wife.'

Matty lurched towards Dorina who was standing motionless, her face ashen.

'Shush! Don't say such things in front of the girls,' she whispered.

'The girls?' He twisted round and stared glassy-eyed at his daughters who were just following Arnold down from the stage. 'Och, aye. My own two wee lassies with their gramps as usual. More slaves to serve the Emperor, eh? Well, catch 'em young and break their spirit before it grows too strong, that's my advice, Arnold.'

'What's he mean, Grandpa?' Rosa wailed, burying her head in the old man's coat. 'Why's Daddy talking like that?'

Amy said nothing, simply looked up at her father with a puzzled expression on her pretty face.

Then, obviously aware of Arnold's mounting fury, Levic had tried to intervene. Clutching hold of Matty's sleeve to steer both him and the horse back to the stable, he muttered, 'Come on, let's you and I step outside for some fresh air, Matty.'

'Tak' yer hands off me, yer bastard,' the drunkard started to yell as he wriggled from Levic's grasp. 'I'm not stepping anywhere with you, you whoremonger. Just because you think you can have your way with my . . .'

'Shut up!'

Matty visibly jumped as Arnold roared.

Steffi jumped too, his gaze riveted on the old man as he thrust Rosa and Amy aside and stood snarling at their father.

'It's all right, Dad,' Dorina started to say. But she was

5

interrupted by Arnold, now speaking to Matty in an icy whisper.

'I've warned you before to watch your language, my lad. You blaspheme in front of my daughter or grandchildren again, and I'll bloody well make you pay. D'yer hear me?'

Even Steffi listening from the other side of the ring recognised the edge of danger in the quiet voice, but it was lost on Matty.

'You? You stupid old bugger, what can you . . . ?'

Suddenly there was a horsewhip in Arnold's hand and a warning scream.

'NO! You mustn't hit my daddy!'

And a little body flashed between the two men and a bright face turned to protest again just as the whip lashed out.

And there was a moment when Steffi saw Amy's flesh sliced open like fresh fruit under a knife before she covered her face with her hands and ran past him out of the ring. And he did nothing to stop her. Stood paralysed by the shock of what he had seen until brought to his senses by Rosa's screaming.

Chapter 2

This time as he packed his trunk and got ready to leave Stangate Street, Steffi found himself eager to return to the haven of his great-grandmother's house in Aldershot – even if it meant the beginning of a new term. School and all the bullying he had to put up with there was bad enough. But just now Apsley's was worse and he could not wait to get away from the place.

What if Amy really had lost her eye in that awful fight yesterday? She was still in hospital and no one seemed to know how badly she was hurt. Her face still covered in bandages, Mirella said, and not even her own mother allowed in to see her. And it was all the fault of stupid Matty coming in drunk like that and then Mr Foreman losing his temper and striking out with the whip . . .

But this sort of thing was always happening at Apsley's. Whips and wild animals, guns and accidents and people getting hurt. It was a cruel place, and he was glad to be leaving it – especially as his mother was coming home with him.

'Ready, Steffi?'

It was a bitter January morning and Mirella was already dressed in her travelling outfit – a green costume with fur-trimmed cape and bonnet. But she was not looking her best, with her eyes swollen as if she had lain awake all night. Or been crying.

Was she also feeling upset by what had happened to Amy? And was that the reason she had been so short with his father over breakfast this morning? 'Yes. Just coming,' he called, struggling with the buckle on the lid of his box.

'Come on, then. Quickly. Your father's holding the cab.'

Then there was a perfunctory leave-taking during which Steffi had the uncomfortable feeling that his father's thoughts were elsewhere.

'Goodbye, Stefan. Work hard at school, remember.'

A last, whispered exchange between his parents in which he caught Levic's words: 'But you know that's all nonsense, my dear.' Then Mirella turned away with a flounce of her head and directed the cab-driver to be off.

Within minutes they had turned the corner into Westminster Bridge Road and were passing Apsley's. Despite his feelings, Steffi found himself taking in every detail of the building as if afraid of never seeing it again.

Apsley's – the name had filled him with dismay the first time he heard it mentioned as a little boy, conjuring up some massive grey castle with dungeons into which his parents were magicked at Christmas and held prisoner for weeks on end by a wicked wizard called Pantomime.

He remembered standing at the garden gate, thumb in mouth and clutching his cloth rabbit, watching and waiting for Mirella and Levic to be off.

In fact, when he looked back, that seemed to be how Steffi spent half his childhood. Watching and waiting for his parents to be off. Or to reappear.

'Bye, bye, darling. Now, you be good while we're gone.'

His mother's words wafting over him together with the spicy scent of her long, black hair as she swept him up in her arms to say goodbye.

Leaving him devastated. Not knowing when he would see her again. Not sure if he would ever see her again, despite all Gran Liddy's reassurances.

'Bye, bye, darling. Now, remember what I said, and be a good boy.'

Apsley's – he recalled his first visit to the place when he was about five or six years old.

'Guess where I'm taking you tomorrow, Steffi,' Liddy had murmured, and he could tell from her expression that it had to be further than the canal or Laffan's Plain.

'I don't know.'

'London.'

'In a train?'

'Yes, in one of the big trains.'

'Why?'

'Well, just think. Who do we know who's in London at the moment?'

And his heart had started to beat very fast.

8

'I don't know.'

'Yes, you do. Of course, you do, Steffi. Who would you like to see most in all the world?'

And he had started to say, 'My mammy . . .' but the words somehow got stuck and he had to fall back again on, 'I don't know.'

At which point Liddy sighed with impatience and started to detail the whole of the forthcoming treat.

By train to London and hackney cab to Westminster Bridge Road in time for the matinée performance of 'Harlequin St George and the Dragon' (whatever that was) at Apsley's.

'And just fancy, Steffi. You'll be able to see your papa in his clown costume doing all sorts of tricks. And your mammy walking on her tightrope. You'd like that, wouldn't you?'

He nodded.

'You'll be amazed to see how clever they are.'

He nodded, frowning this time. He did not want to see how clever they were. He just wanted to see them.

Mind you, he felt a fizz of excitement when, having arrived in the grey windswept street and peering up at a big ordinary-looking building, he caught sight of huge posters on which two names stood out from all the rest: Madame Mirella the Miraculous Rope-dancer and Levic, King of Clowns.

Fancy! His mammy and daddy – and all these people come to watch them too, he thought, as he stumbled through the doors and was immediately swamped by a sea of frowsty coats which threatened to drown him and Liddy before they reached the top of the interminable steps leading to their 'box'. Which turned out not to be a box at all, but a tiny room like a train compartment with seats facing all one way.

And then hours of waiting again. But that did not really matter now there was so much to see and hear all around him.

His initial disappointment at not sitting downstairs close to the circle in front of the stage was soon overcome when he scrambled on to a seat at the front of the box and realised how much better it was to have an overview of everything – and everyone!

'Well, what do you think of Apsley's?' Liddy asked.

'It's big,' was all he managed to say.

Never before had he seen so many people. Like a show in themselves, yelling and pushing and shoving each other into seats, tossing peel and toffee wrappers into the arena.

9

He sat mesmerised by the bright gaslight, the noise and the smells – sawdust and oranges and that peculiar sharp odour that horses and wild animals exude – until the plush velvet on his chair prickled through his trousers and made the skin behind his knees itch.

Eventually, though – having twice counted the chandeliers and then the individual lustres on the one hanging nearest their box – he had grown tired of all the waiting, nodded off and missed the start of the show.

'Stefan, do you realise who that is?' Liddy was suddenly prodding him and whispering in his ear.

'Who?' he asked, blinking with bewilderment.

'The man in the clown costume.'

'No?'

'That's your papa.'

'No!'

Staring now in amazement. Papa? That funny-looking man couldn't be his papa, could it? Then glancing round to see everyone laughing and feeling horribly self-conscious to have a papa that people kept laughing at.

But he felt altogther different when, with a fanfare of trumpets, Mirella entered the arena. Hearing the people around him sigh as, in her shiny costume glittering all over with sequins, she skipped lightly into the spotlight and proceeded to climb a tall, tall ladder stretching right up into the roof of the building.

'That's my mummy!' he whispered, scarcely able to believe what he was seeing. His gaze following so intently that he felt as if he were climbing every step of the way with her, arriving breathless at the top and then shutting his eyes as she prepared to move out onto the thin rope.

But he knew that she crossed and re-crossed the arena because he occasionally squinted through his fingers and saw. Most of the time, though, he sat with his eyes shut tight, not daring to look in case she should topple and fall.

Mirella on the high rope, the thunderous applause evoked by her performance, the cheers and guffaws which greeted Levic whenever he bounced into the circle squealing 'Well, boys and girls, here we are again!', Levic's acrobatics and conjuring tricks, dancing and singing – these together with the other artistes and the pantomime which followed – all, like some gigantic kaleidoscope, revolved in Steffi's memory to form one

10

bright picture after another to bring back that first never-to-be-forgotten visit to Apsley's.

But no picture remained in his mind with greater effect than his first sight of the two little girls.

They came in just before the pantomime started, as part of the grand finale of the circus scenes – riding in a miniature chariot drawn by a tiny, pure white pony, dressed as warrior maidens, with Amy holding the reins and Rosa clutching an oval shield with her other arm stuck out in rigid salute. Steffi thought they looked terribly impressive, but felt sorry for the pony.

'Is that a proper horse or just a baby?' he asked Liddy.

'A proper horse. A fully-grown Shetland.'

'Well, I never knew a horse could be that small. I bet he finds it hard work pulling all that weight.'

'Yes, I expect he does.'

'So why doesn't someone make those girls get out and walk?'

At the time Liddy laughed instead of answering, but to his embarrassment repeated his question to the girls themselves when they were introduced to them after the show.

'Get out and walk?' Rosa exclaimed, 'Oh, no. It's much more fun when we can ride into the ring, isn't it Amy?'

Steffi was struck by the way the younger girl's gingery curls bounced up and down as she vigorously nodded her head in agreement.

'Anyway,' Rosa continued, 'there's no need to worry about Sheltie. Circus ponies like doing what they're trained to do, don't they, Amy?'

This time the younger girl nodded less vigorously and her green eyes, when they looked up, seemed to be questioning her sister's wisdom.

'How can you tell what animals like doing?' Steffi found himself asking, genuinely interested.

'Because my grandad's their trainer and he knows,' Rosa said airily.

At the time Steffi was impressed by this answer. After all, the chubby, fair-haired girl sounded so certain and he supposed she ought to know what she was talking about because she had been born in the circus and lived there all her life. Whereas he was only a visitor.

But as he grew to know her better, he realised that Rosa often said the first thing that came into her head. And although

11

her imperious manner seemed to invite contradiction, few – apart from her little sister – ever dared take up the challenge.

Not that Amy was much better, mind. In fact, she had proved every bit as bad as her sister when it came to leading him into mischief in the early days.

Those early days! They seemed so long ago now, but it was only three years since Steffi had started joining his parents regularly at Apsley's, arriving a few days after Christmas to give them time to settle into the show's routine, and staying till the end of his school holidays.

'Now, look, Steffi. I want you to try to keep away from Dorina's girls while you're here,' his mother had cautioned the first time they set out to walk the short distance from his family's digs in Stangate Street to the theatre.

'Why?'

'Because they're trouble.'

'Trouble?' he had asked, immediately interested.

'Yes. Spoilt out of their silly little heads, both of them. Which is their grandfather's fault. Arnold dotes on them and turns a blind eye to their capers.'

'You mean they're naughty?' Steffi said, with the superiority of a nine-year-old boy who considered himself to have grown beyond such behaviour.

'I mean they like to cause mischief,' Mirella said. 'And when they do, it's usually others who cop for the blame. Understand?'

'I think so,' he said.

'Well, remember what I say, then.'

And he had cause to remember her warning later that day.

Being Sunday there was no scheduled show, but the theatre was still bustling with activity as carpenters repaired sets, and artistes rehearsed or made alterations to their costumes. As soon as they arrived Mirella rushed off to bag one of the sewing machines in the wardrobe-room, leaving Steffi to make himself useful in the painters' workshop sloshing blue colour over a backcloth that had been damaged the previous evening. But after a while the fumes from the turpentine caught at his throat and he had to excuse himself and go outside for some fresh air.

He found his way downstairs and eventually out on to the pavement, but on his return stood perplexed in front of a wide stone staircase and a tunnel-shaped passage, not sure which one would lead him back.

'You're lost, aren't you?'

He looked up and saw the fair-haired girl bounding down the stairs towards him, followed by her sister.

'No, not really. I'm just going back to the painters' workshop. And I know I have to go up some stairs, but these don't look like the ones I came down.'

'They're probably not, then. This is *our* staircase and it leads to our grandfather's rooms,' she announced airily.

'Yes, but . . .' the smaller girl tried to butt in, but her voice was drowned out by Rosa who went on to inform him that her grandfather's rooms were private and he hated people to trespass near them.

'Oh, but I didn't mean to . . .' Steffi began to say before his words were cut short.

'What's your name?' Rosa demanded.

'Stefan.'

'You mean Stephen,' she corrected.

'No. It's Stefan,' he insisted, 'but most people call me Steffi.'

'Steffi? That sounds as stupid as Stefan. We don't know anyone called that, do we, Amy?'

Her tone implied that if they did not know another Steffi then there must be something wrong with the name, so he was grateful when the younger girl piped up with, 'No, but I think it's nice.'

He immediately decided that, of the two sisters, he preferred Amy, because she spoke more quietly and her little pointed face and greenish-blue eyes put him in mind of a pixie.

'We've seen you before, haven't we?' Rosa said next. 'You're Mirella and Levic's son. I heard my mother say you were coming on a visit. Why don't you live with your parents all the time?'

'Because I have to go to school,' Steffi replied defensively.

'You could go to school in London. Or have a tutor like we do.'

'But my ma and pa don't stay in London all the time. They tour around the country in the summer.'

'Oh.'

'Why don't they take you with them?'

He turned to look at Amy who had now taken up the questioning.

'Because they're too busy. And anyway I've got a great-granny who looks after me and she's got a big house where she'd be lonely if I wasn't there.'

13

'Oh,' Amy said, apparently satisfied.

'I bet her house isn't nearly as big as Apsley's,' Rosa said, returning to the fray.

'No, of course it isn't. It's only a house, not a theatre,' he explained.

'Well, our grandfather owns all this place and it's much bigger than you think.'

'Is it?' he said, looking around, remembering the immense structure that had loomed up as he and Mirella approached the building from outside this morning.

'Yes, it is. So if you're trying to get back to the workshops and you don't want to get lost, you'd better follow us.'

So saying, she clutched Amy's arm, pulled her close and whispered something in her ear. The smaller girl stood frowning as she considered for a moment and then her green eyes lit up and she nodded.

'Yes, come on,' she urged. 'We'll show you the way back to the workshops.'

Grateful, he followed the pair into the tunnel-shaped passage which was dark even though it was daytime.

'I don't remember coming along here,' he muttered.

'No, you probably came down the backstairs. But don't worry, we'll take you the quick way,' Rosa said, nudging Amy. 'Only don't make too much noise,' she added, 'because we're going past the ring doors and there's a rehearsal going on.'

'Right,' he whispered back.

To start with he tried to take note of where they were walking so that he would know the proper route next time, but it was so dark in the tunnel that he soon lost his bearings. As far as he could see there was a veritable maze of tunnels in the place so he was glad to have the girls with him as guides.

'Where are we now?' he asked as they emerged into a long cobbled yard with what looked like carriage-huts and store-sheds on either side.

'These are the elephant houses,' explained Rosa, 'so I advise you not to go too close.'

'Why?' he asked, stopping in his tracks.

'Because,' she declared solemnly, 'elephants are very dangerous. They go mad if they smell the blood of a stranger and start to stampede and smash everything down in their effort to get at him.'

'Really?' Steffi exclaimed. 'But then how is it they can perform in the ring and . . .'

'Shush! We can't talk here,' Rosa cautioned. 'It's too risky.'

He stared at the huge doors, puzzled. Were elephants that aggressive? Something did not add up in what Rosa said and he wanted to question her further, but she and Amy were already striding onwards. He was just thinking that it seemed to be taking him a lot longer to get back to the paintshop this quick way than it had the other when the girls paused in front of a stout black-painted door. After a brief glance round, Rosa opened it and beckoned him to follow them through.

He thought it was odd when he found himself confronted with a flight of steps leading downwards, but the girls seemed to know perfectly well where they were going so he gritted his teeth and followed them down into a rambling, dusty, ramshackle world illuminated only by dimly burning gas-jets set in cages. It took a few minutes for his eyes to grow accustomed to the fitful light and recognise the ghostly, louring shapes surrounding them. They were old props, discarded scenery and other stage junk.

'Where are we now?' he whispered.

'Under the stage,' Amy whispered back.

Then he realised he had been tricked.

'This isn't a quick way to the painters' shop,' he muttered. 'Why did you bring me down here?'

By way of reply both girls broke into frenzied laughter.

'I told you,' Rosa spluttered. 'I told you he'd fall for it. Boys are so stupid. He didn't even notice we were going in the opposite direction.'

'Yes, I did,' Steffi stammered. 'I thought we were going wrong, but I decided to wait and see where you'd lead me.'

'No, you didn't. You thought you were going to the painters' shop all the time. We fooled you,' Rosa hissed.

'You didn't,' he fibbed. 'I knew all along where you were leading me and I wanted to come down here.'

'You didn't. You're lying,' she said, her voice beginning to rise hysterically.

'Shush!' Now it was Amy's turn to sound the caution. 'Don't shout, Rosa. We don't want anyone to know we're down here.'

'Why? Aren't you allowed?' Steffi asked, remembering what Mirella had said about the girls and their propensity for mischief.

'Of course we are. We're allowed to go anywhere in this place,' Rosa declared. 'It's just you who shouldn't come down because you're not even in the company. Still, now you're here, Amy and me will show you round if you like.'

The offer was made so disdainfully that he felt like turning on his heel and immediately making his way back upstairs. He was furious with the girls for playing such a trick. Still, the place was interesting so he decided to stay a while longer and explore.

'All right,' he agreed, following them deeper into the warren.

Somewhere up ahead – or was it round to their left? – he could hear something that sounded like water lapping against stone and he stopped, feeling terribly unsure.

'Where's that water coming from?' he asked. 'We're not heading towards the river, are we?'

Rosa laughed.

'No, it's the river coming up here to get us,' she whispered.

'No, really. I want to know, where's the water coming from?' Steffi demanded, having visions of them all being suddenly whooshed away by some subterranean current of the Thames.

'Don't worry. Rosa's only kidding. What you can hear is the water in the wells that the scenery drops into under the stage. The river's always getting in and filling them up so that the sets get swamped.'

'Oh.'

Amy's explanation did little to reassure him. Now, to his anxiety about being swept away by a tidal wave he added the fear of falling into some deep well and being left there to drown. Perhaps he should turn back, and insist that the two girls come with him.

'Crikey! What's that?'

His blood froze as the sound reached him – the hollow, echoing roar of some beast. Not a horse or a dog, but – yes, he could swear to it – a lion. Somewhere in the darkness ahead there was a lion. Or lions.

Involuntarily his arm shot out and grabbed Amy's.

'We can't go that way. We've got to get out of here. Quick!'

'Why?'

'Because I think there's lions . . .' Suddenly he realised how stupid it sounded. 'I mean, that noise . . .'

'Of course there's lions. They're kept down here in the base-ment. But they're all in cages, unless one or two have managed

16

to escape again,' Rosa said, turning to see how he would take this announcement. 'Why, you're not frightened of lions, are you?'

His pride struggled with his sense of self-preservation and won a narrow victory.

'No, not really,' he stammered. 'It's just that . . . Look, are you sure you're supposed to be down here?'

'Of course. Amy and me are allowed to do what we like in this place, aren't we, Amy?'

'Yes,' Amy said stoutly, 'and our friends can do what they like too. So if anyone here tries to tell you off, say you're our friend and they'll soon leave off.'

'Thanks, I'll remember that,' he mumbled.

Chapter 3

'Name?'

'Eh?'

'What's your name, sonny?'

Steffi had jumped. He was not used to being shouted at. Besides, he found the continual hustle and bustle all round him quite overwhelming and life at Apsley's so different from the tranquil routine at Liddy's house that by the end of his second day he had begun to feel dazed.

'Stefan,' he murmured, anxiously glancing up into the face of Arnold Foreman to see if he looked as cross as he sounded.

He did.

Dark eyes glittered beneath brows that were so very black that Steffi immediately remembered Rosa telling him how her grandfather used dye on them and his goatee every day in an effort to disguise his age. It was obviously true. Steffi could see dark, gingery streaks above the main outline of both brows, and – yes, along the sideburns as well. Which made him wonder about the thin rim of hair round the bald head dome . . .

'Something wrong?'

'Oh, no.'

'Smut on my face or something?'

Arnold Foreman brushed his fingers over his cheek.

'No, no. It's fine, sir,' Steffi stuttered.

'Right. Well, "Stefan" you said. Levic's boy, eh?'

'Yes, sir.'

'And up here for a couple of weeks, eh?'

'Ye-es.'

Steffi held his breath. Surely Mr Foreman was not about to send him packing because of yesterday's little adventure into the cellars? After all, no real harm had come of it . . .

'Making yourself useful, are you?'

Steffi nodded, aware that Arnold Foreman was scrutinising him with gimlet eyes.

'I hear you've been hanging around the workshops. That's good. You can learn a lot up there. Pays to be handy in this life.'

'Yes, sir.' Steffi began to breathe more easily again.

'And my granddaughters tell me you're dying to have a go in the ring.'

'Eh?'

All he'd said was that he wished he lived in a circus so that he wouldn't have to go back to school after Christmas. Then Rosa and Amy had quizzed him about tumbling tricks and he had boasted a bit about the things his father had taught him while he was doing his own limbering up exercises in the meadow behind Liddy's house. Nothing special. Only hand-stands, cartwheels and flip-flaps. And Steffi had to admit he wasn't much good at those. Certainly nowhere so good as his father who had castigated him for being useless; too stiff and tense to make any sort of acrobat.

'Well, I don't mind you having a go,' Arnold Foreman said. 'Plenty of scope for another youngster in the opening spectacle. Can you turn a cartwheel and do a flip-flap?'

Steffi nodded.

'What am I thinking of? You're Levic's son, so of course you can! Right, then. Go up to wardrobe and get fitted with a costume. Tell them I sent you.'

Steffi turned away. There seemed no point in trying to explain, because as the son of Levic and Mirella it was assumed he was capable of great things. Besides, he had no wish to give satisfaction to those cocky girls by admitting how useless he was.

He could hear a busy clatter as he mounted the stairs and, when he entered the wardrobe-room, was glad to see Mirella seated at one of the sewing-machines pushing a mound of pink satin under its needle. Sidling up, he told her what Mr Foreman had suggested.

'Good idea. Why not?' was her response.

'But I have to go home soon,' he remonstrated.

'Never mind. It will be good experience for you.'

'And I shan't be able to do anything properly. You know how Papa's always trying to teach me things I can't manage.'

'Don't worry,' she said complacently. 'There'll be far too much going on for anyone to notice you. Arnold wants you in the arena just to swell the numbers, so all you've got to do is look good, smile and throw kisses to the crowd. You can manage that, can't you?'

'Throw kisses?' he repeated dubiously.

In the event his first appearance in the ring proved less of an ordeal than he had feared. In fact he found it fun. Especially when handed a sword and kitted out in a soldier's uniform to play a part in the final spectacle – an authentic re-enactment of the Battle of Waterloo with real cannons being fired and horses and camels and elephants charging around the arena.

With this as his reward he did not mind spending hours in rehearsal, picking up some elementary dance routines and basic ground tumbling, and doing things he would never have dreamed of attempting ordinarily.

But that was the thing about Apsley's. He kept finding himself doing the unexpected because there were so many strange things going on all the time.

He got used to roaming amongst magical landscapes and rubbing shoulders with exotic beasts and men in weird make-up and wonderful costumes. Contortionists suddenly collapsing on the floor in front of him and, before he knew it, coiling their feet around their necks. Dwarves and giants. Men who climbed each other to make a pyramid. One who did a head-stand on the top of an enormously high slender pole which itself was balanced on the forehead of his partner.

Cowboys, Indians, oriental potentates and slaves, pygmies and grotesques – so many wonders before his eyes while at the same time his ears were bombarded by the ringmaster's yells, animals clattering in and out of the arena, and the band blasting its numbers.

The pace was hectic. Life was frantic.

With no time to worry about anything, Steffi simply got on with what was necessary and lost himself in a new identity. He became part of the show, a member of the troupe.

'Hey, Steffi! Come up into the box with us!'

Rosa, having already changed into her next costume, issued her usual summons.

Steffi picked up his sword and followed. He loved watching the pantomime from the fourth-tier box reserved for the use of the children after they had finished their opening scenes and were waiting to take part in the final spectacle.

'We've got some oranges and nuts to eat,' Amy confided as they made their way upstairs, trying not to make too much noise as they passed the doors of boxes occupied by the public.

Once inside their eyrie, however, they abandoned restraint and settled down to have a good time just like all the other members of the audience. Except that Rosa and Amy were a good deal more fidgety than most because they had seen the show so very many times before, there was no novelty left in it for them.

'Have a nut?' offered Amy, shoving a paper bag under Steffi's nose.

'Thanks,' he murmured, taking the hazel but making no attempt to crack its shell. His attention was rivetted on the sensational ascent of Sinbad who was just being seized and carried off in the claws of the Great Roc, the drama being heightened by a prolonged roll on the drums.

The band was situated in the pit just below their box so Steffi enjoyed the benefit of being able to look down on the drummer as he delivered this strenuous tattoo, noticing how the effort brought beads of sweat out on the man's shiny, bald pate.

'Bet you couldn't hit it,' Amy said.

'Hit what?' he asked mechanically, still entranced by the soaring aloft of the huge bird.

'His head, of course. With the hazel nut,' she added, smiling.

It wasn't his idea. He would have been happy to sit there all night enjoying the pantomime had not Amy urged him to join in the game in a way he found impossible to resist.

'Look, you aim your nut at his drum, and I'll try to drop mine on his head. Come on, it's a dare!'

When both nuts missed, Rosa had a go. Hers missed too. Then, once they realised it wasn't so easy, all three of them were swept away by the urgency of their mission and began to rain down missiles until eventually several struck home – on the poor drummer's head as well as his instrument.

Honour satisfied, Steffi's attention was drawn back to the Grand Transformation Scene which was taking place on the stage, and again he became so engrossed that before the end of the pantomime he had all but forgotten the part he had played in the assault on the drummer. So he was all the more surprised when, having scuttled down to join the ranks of the

French Army for the final spectacle, he found this last scene proved but the prelude to his own Waterloo.

The battle was over. He had played his part, brandishing his short sword, screaming his blood-curdling oaths as loudly as the rest while the cannons roared and horses reared and red and green flares lit up the scene of mayhem and carnage.

Then the audience had taken up the struggle, fighting each other to get out of the theatre while the actors retired to their rest.

'Hey, lad. Here a minute!'

Steffi guessed the man was calling him although the words were hard to grasp because the chap had such a struggle with his teeth when he talked. Then, as he approached, he recognised the fat, round face of the drummer, but it was too late to beat a retreat.

'Yes?' he asked dubiously.

'I've got a bone to pick with you, laddie. You bin sitting up in the top box with them little gals, ain't yer?'

Steffi nodded.

'And you bin tormenting us by flinging down nuts, ain't yer?'

'No,' Steffi's voice whispered while his head treacherously nodded in agreement with his accuser.

'Well, you better watch it, mate. I don't like little boys who torment people and I've got a special way of dealing with 'em. Get me?'

He grabbed hold of Steffi's ear, dragging him halfway across the stage before releasing him.

'Look, I'm sorry but I didn't mean . . .' Steffi started to explain, but the drummer did not stay to listen. After rattling his teeth and making an odd growling noise, he turned on his heel and waddled quickly off into the wings.

For a moment Steffi stood there, relieved to have been let off thus lightly when the man had looked so angry. Not that he had not had just cause, but perhaps he realised that Rosa and Amy were as much to blame and . . .

'E-ee-i-ow!'

Steffi heard his own yell disappearing above his head as he fell.

Whereas the moment before he had been standing on firm ground, the earth had suddenly opened up and sucked him down into darkness and he fell through space until he juddered to a halt in total blackness.

'Help! Help me, someone!' he screamed.

But his voice echoed as if through a vast hollow cavern, terrifyingly empty. Where was everyone? What on earth had happened? Had there been some terrible explosion? Was this the end of the world?

After scrambling to his feet, it took him a moment to work it out.

He must have been standing on one of the traps when the drummer went into the wings and released the catch. So he had plunged into the basement under the stage amidst that warren of passages he had previously explored with Rosa and Amy. The only difference being that there had been gaslights then to illumine the way and now the place was in utter darkness.

Still, if he kept his head he should be able to find his way out without too much difficulty. All he needed was to get his bearings – he knew he was somewhere under the prompt side of the stage – and then feel his way along this tunnel to the nearest staircase.

The trouble was, the tunnel stretched in both directions and he had no idea which led where.

He was suddenly alerted to the fact that he was not alone when from one direction came the sound of a coughing grunt. But his delight at the prospect of company was short-lived once the noise was repeated. It did not sound like a man coughing. In fact he knew it wasn't a man coughing, because it was the same noise that had made him so scared last time he was down here. What he was hearing was the sound of lions.

Now the last thing he wanted to do was go anywhere near the lions, so he turned in the opposite direction and stumbled along that way, not stopping to work out that he had to pass by the animal cages to reach the exit.

For what seemed like hours but was probably little more than ten minutes he shuffled along, fighting a mounting tide of panic as the blackness of the passage refused to dissolve into the shape of a door or staircase. Coming to a stop eventually with his heart pounding as he heard ahead of him the sound of water softly lapping against the sides of one of those deep wells into which the stage-sets were lowered.

That was the moment he came closest to panic.

'Steffi! Steffi!'

For a moment he thought the voice was coming out of the

ground – a water-sprite or mermaid come up from the well to lure him to a watery grave.

'Gran! Gra-an!' he found himself sobbing instinctively for the person who had cared for him all through childhood. But it was not she who answered.

'Steffi, are you there?'

It was his mother. Mirella had come to look for him and was somewhere out there in the darkness calling. Thank God! Now he would be all right.

'Mammy! I'm here.'

'Where?'

'Under the stage. I fell down one of the traps and I can't find my way out.'

'Don't worry, my love. Just keep still and stay exactly where you are. I'll soon get you up.'

In next to no time he became aware of the sound of footsteps echoing close by, a door opening, and the glow of an approaching lamp.

'Well, you can't say I didn't warn you about those two little madams,' Mirella had chided once they were back in Stangate Street and he was getting ready for bed.

Steffi hung his head, expecting a telling-off.

But not a bit of it! Instead, his mother began to chuckle.

'Aiming nuts at the drummer's head, indeed! That's the sort of trick I would have got up to at your age.'

Then to his great delight Mirella had sat on his bed talking to him well into the night – telling him about her sister Cassie and the fun they used to have when they were little, talking about her family, how she had run away from her first job as a scullery maid when she was only fifteen and joined her uncle's travelling menagerie show. Chatting about anything and everything that came to mind.

He could hardly remember her ever talking to him like that before, talking just for the sake of talking, talking well into the night – with him never thinking to ask her where Levic had got to.

And yet, when Steffi looked back, he wondered why his father was not there that night. Who or what had caused him to stay out so late.

No such thoughts troubled him at the time, though. He

had been too busy basking in the warmth of Mirella's affection, glad for once not to have to compete for her attention.

So it had certainly never occurred to him to suppose that his mother might have been clinging to his company that night because she was lonely. Even then.

Chapter 4

'Steffi, are you warm enough?'

'Yes, thanks.'

'Why not take your scarf off then, now we're settled?'

'All right.'

Mirella watched him unwind the navy muffler from his neck and tug it loose from the top of his coat before folding and resting it on his box beside him on the seat.

'We were lucky to find an empty compartment, weren't we?'

'Yes,' she replied.

'I thought I might have to put my box in the luggage van.'

'Yes,' she said again.

'There's lots of soldiers in the next carriage,' Steffi observed, hanging his head out of the window and looking up the train towards the engine.

'Is there?'

'Yes. Lots.'

'Mind your eyes once we start moving, Steffi. We don't want any more accidents.'

The words were out before she realised.

Steffi immediately pulled his head back from the window.

'Like Amy's, you mean? But she'll still see all right, won't she, Ma?'

'Of course she will. It was only one eye damaged and, please God, that won't be so bad as they fear, once the bandages come off.'

'Oh, I hope it isn't,' Steffi groaned, sinking back into his seat and taking no more notice of the engine even once its whistle began to shriek and the train's wheels to slip and judder into motion.

Mirella cursed herself for reminding him of yesterday's disaster. Bad enough that she had to take him back to Aldershot before there was any definite news of Amy, but worse travelling with him in her present mood. For she was finding it hard to be sociable this morning – even with Steffi. Her mind was in such turmoil.

Still, it was not Steffi's fault, she reminded herself, looking up to smile reassurance at him. Only to find herself instinctively recoiling from what she saw.

Fortunately, Steffi in the opposite corner of the compartment was unaware of her reaction. Gazing out of the window, lost in his own thoughts, untroubled by the fact that in profile he was the image of his father.

A thin, pale face with high forehead and swept back waves of black hair, slightly hooked nose and a determined chin – she could almost see the black silky moustache that would grow in a few years' time to make him look even more like Levic. Except that Steffi possessed eyes that were not brown and restless like Levic's, but gentle blue.

She breathed out a sigh. Somehow it was important to have found this distinctive feature in Steffi which marked him out from his father. She dreaded to think of Steffi inheriting anything like the same restlessness that made Levic's life a torment to himself – and anyone who managed to get close to him.

She shut her eyes, doubting for a moment whether she had ever achieved that feat – of getting close to her husband. Or whether she was, as she feared, still married to a total stranger.

This business with Dorina, for instance. Could there be any truth in Matty's assertions?

She bit her lip, trying to envisage the scene that had led up to Amy's accident yesterday. She'd heard enough to know that whatever happened, it must have been very upsetting for Steffi. Matty had been drunk, of course. She was careful to stress that fact to Steffi in her effort to dispel any doubts sown in his mind about his father. Although, looking at him now, wrapt in his contemplation of the flying landscape, she decided that at twelve he was still too innocent to understand the implications of what Matty had said.

But was there any truth in his allegations? she asked herself again. And flinched, aware that she could no longer afford to ignore the situation brewing between Levic and Dorina. Although Levic insisted that his interest in Matty's wife was purely platonic, Dorina might well put a different interpretation on his behaviour.

Mirella bit her lip again. This time with annoyance. As far as she was concerned this was no new story. Just another chapter in an old one.

All their married life she had had to live with the fact that Levic was attracted to other women. Though unsure how far he allowed his little fancies to go, she had always tried to give him the benefit of the doubt. To take him at his word when he assured her that his deeds lagged well behind the sweet courtesies he liked to accord the fairer sex.

'Look, my dear. You mustn't forget I was born Hungarian, even though I left my country at such a tender age,' he would say.

'I don't see what that has to do with anything,' she protested.

'Well, it does. It explains why I don't share the *sang-froid* of your typical Englishman,' he said, slicking down the end of his silky moustache as if to draw attention to his foreign looks.

'I'm not talking about *sang-froid* I'm talking about fidelity, Levic.'

'Of course you are, my darling. But that's not in question. You know I am and always will be completely faithful to you.'

'So what about the way you were philandering with that dancer?'

'Oh, come on, Mirella.' Now he would pour his soul into his eyes. 'You know me better than that.'

'Yes, but others . . .'

'Never mind about others. For me there are no others. Just you and me – you must believe that.'

'Yes, but . . .'

'No "buts", my darling,' he whispered, pulling her into his arms and covering her mouth with his lips to stifle her objections.

And it worked, damn him. Nearly every time he succeeded in kissing and charming her into compliance.

But maybe there was something in what he said. Perhaps it was no more than a difference in social custom that caused so much friction between them.

'In my country,' he had once exclaimed, 'romance is a national pastime.'

'What do you mean by that?' she demanded.

29

'A national pastime,' he repeated complacently. 'Like horse-racing is with the English.'

'I don't see the connection.'

'Well, think of it this way. Just as you would rarely see an Englishman pass a useful horse without patting its rump, so one of my countrymen would naturally show his appreciation of a fine woman by . . .'

'Yes?'

'Well . . .' he chose his words carefully, '. . . some similar courtesy.'

'Courtesy? Is that what you call it? I'd call it something a lot shorter – like lust!'

'Lust?' he had repeated, as if the word were unfamiliar to him. 'Oh, no, my dear. There you are referring to a different animal entirely.'

'Am I?'

'Of course you are, my love. But it's a natural mistake for a woman to make, so I forgive you.'

Then he had pulled a series of comic faces which dissolved her anger into so much laughter that, looking back, she could not decide whether anything he had said was meant to be taken seriously.

Which did not mean to say, she reminded herself, that this present relationship between Levic and Dorina was not becoming fraught with problems – for everyone.

Take today, for instance. Sunday – so no performances at Apsley's. The one possible day of the week for her and Levic to be alone together. Or with their family.

Surely it had not been too much to expect of him that he spend this one day with her and Steffi? So little to ask, that he take time off to see his son back to Aldershot. Especially as it meant so much to Steffi.

But no. Levic had other plans. Preferred to spend the day in the company of Dorina. Had arranged to go with her to buy a new horse, he said.

Well, of course, it was true that he and Dorina needed another horse for their riding act, Mirella had no doubt about that. And Levic had shown her the notice in the *Era* that mentioned the imminent arrival of Hugue's Continental Circus at Tilbury en route for Scotland.

'They're shedding some of their livestock and I know they've got three or four horses that might fit our bill,' he said.

'So why not go and look at them during the week?' she suggested. 'Go one morning and be back in plenty of time for the two o'clock performance.'

'No. I'm afraid it's got to be Sunday, because they'll be shifting the loads on to rail almost immediately.'

'Let Dorina take care of it then. If she thinks it's so important to buy a new horse that she can put her mind to it at a time like this, when she's got a little girl lying injured in the hospital. Besides, they're her horses.'

'But she needs a second opinion,' Levic said, ignoring the remark about Amy.

'Why not take Matty with her then?'

'She will. Oh, I thought you knew that. Matty will be there as well,' Levic said, as if that made the situation more acceptable.

It didn't. It made things worse. He might just as well have admitted that she would have more cause for concern if he and Dorina were going off for a jaunt on their own.

'So why not leave them to it?'

Levic heaved a sigh.

'You know Matty, my dear. A better judge of booze than horseflesh.'

His words brought the sort of smile to his lips that reminded Mirella of his jest about women, and she was left wondering about what kind of filly he had in mind when he spoke of horseflesh.

Levic was standing, one foot resting on the blocks forming a temporary ring fence, watching the Hugue personnel putting the various animals they had on offer through their paces.

'Well, what do you think, the chestnut or the white?' Matty mumbled, keeping his cigarette in the corner of his mouth.

'I'm not sure. I like the white,' Levic said, studying the big percheron, 'but it's up to Dorina. She knows what she's looking for.'

'Nae doubt,' Matty murmured.

'Which would you take?' Levic asked him.

'Me? Och, it doesn't matter what I think. But if you really want to know, I'd take the white. He's definitely best.'

'Why do you say that?'

'More cooperative.'

'But the chestnut looks stronger,' Levic mused.

31

'Aye, and the chestnut's steadier. But Dorina will tak' the white.'

'You think so?'

'Aye. She'll go for the white, because he'll be more willing. It's so obvious, she could cut the cackle and settle it.'

'You can't blame her for wanting to be sure though. This horse is very important to her.'

'Oh, aye. She's always saying her act is only as good as the horse she rides and the clown who partners her.'

'Well, it's nice to know that I'm put on a par with the horses,' Levic said lightly while scrutinising Matty for signs that the little sandy-haired Scot was trying to send him up.

'Aye,' Matty agreed. 'You should consider that an honour, because she rates her bloody horses a lot higher than me . . .'

'Oh come on, Matty, every marriage has its ups and downs. Why, even Mirella and I . . .'

'That's different, laddie. You and your missus live to your own lights without a tyrant breathing down your necks all the time – dictating how you live, where you go, what you do.'

Withdrawing what was now a dog-end from his mouth, Matty held it between finger and thumb regarding it with disgust before letting it fall and grinding it under his boot.

'Arnold, you mean.'

'Of course I mean Arnold. The doting grandfather with the whip.'

'It was an accident, Matty. No one was more shocked than Arnold at what happened.'

'Shocked! What's the good of being shocked when you've landed a poor wee lass in the Infirmary?'

To change the subject, Levic hooked out his pocket watch and registered the time before remarking, 'I wonder what's keeping Dorina. She said she'd only be gone a few minutes.'

As if to answer, at that moment Dorina rode in astride the percheron, now properly saddled, and the pair of them circled first at a trot and then in the steady gallop used in the ballerina act.

Levic squinted so that he could focus on the pair. There was no doubt about it. Dorina with her bright eyes, flushed cheeks, and breast gently heaving, looked splendid on the white horse.

'What do you think?' she called, reining in, bringing the horse to a standstill.

'His back and legs are good,' Matty volunteered, 'and he looks intelligent.'

'Yes,' she agreed, patting his neck, 'but I'd be lucky to find another horse like Black Chieftain. He hardly needed any training. Just seemed to know immediately what I was thinking and be prepared to do it.'

'Like me, poor sod,' Matty mumbled.

'What do you think, Levic?' she called.

'He looks splendid,' he said, concentrating now on the horse. 'The right age. The right build and colour. So, if you think he's got the right temperament, all we've got to do is settle on the right price.'

'Exactly.'

'Will you and Matty take care of that, or do you want my help?'

He leapt forward to offer her support as she sprang down from the saddle and she murmured in a low voice, 'No, you and I should do the negotiating. Matty's useless at that sort of thing and we don't want to end up paying more than we have to. Do we, old chap?' she crooned, nuzzling her blonde head against the horse's muzzle.

Levic found it odd going home to the empty rooms in Stangate Street. After growing used to Steffi hanging around all the time lately, he was looking forward to having Mirella to himself for once. To talk over the events of the day with her, tell her about the bargain they had managed to pull off.

Apropos of which, he felt annoyed about one thing – the way Matty had slunk off and left him and Dorina to bring the new horse back on their own. He had obviously taken umbrage at Dorina's suggestion that Levic should handle the money side of the business. So typical of the fellow! Ready to take offence at nothing. Dorina was quite right not to pander to his tantrums.

Not that Mirella would see it that way, he thought, pausing in the midst of pouring his tea. She would say that poor Matty was being driven into a corner by his domineering father-in-law and it was up to his wife to help him out. She would forbear to say that it surely behoved others like Levic not to interfere while the couple solved their problems.

Such a view made sense. Except that in this instance he did not think Mirella was right. It was Dorina who was hard done by, having to put up with Matty's ridiculous behaviour. In fact, she needed friendship more than anyone he knew – especially in view of her exceptional talent.

It would be a crime to stand by and see an artiste like Dorina brought low by the jealous antics of her nondescript husband.

You see, he found himself arguing in his head with Mirella, she's not like you. Not so strong-minded, so she needs a lot of support from the people around her.

He shut his eyes and conjured up the vision of Dorina as he had seen her this morning on the white horse, straight-backed and her breasts rising and falling as she cantered round the ring. Yes, a fine artiste. And a fine figure of a woman.

He pulled himself up with a start. It was dangerous to begin thinking like that, especially when Mirella was not around to take his mind off things. Which reminded him, bed tonight was going to be pretty cheerless without her. Damn!

Still, there was nothing to be done about it, so he might as well fill in the time by working out details of that new trick he had in mind for his riding act with Dorina.

He was planning to somersault from the back of one galloping horse to land on another. A dangerous trick. He knew that. Vital therefore to work out every move carefully before he attempted anything.

Chapter 5

'Lord, I'm tired.'

'I can see that,' Levic said as Mirella collapsed into a low chair, letting her head flop against its back and shutting her eyes.

He dreaded to think what the time was. Already Tuesday he guessed, before checking his watch to confirm that it was indeed past midnight. And they had only just got back from the theatre after giving two performances. No wonder Mirella looked worn out. He knew she shouldn't have taken on so much, but she would insist on going all that way to Aldershot with Steffi and then racing back for today's double showing.

'Well, you just take it easy while I put the kettle on for a hot drink and then we'll go to bed.'

'Lovely,' she sighed, 'if I can summon up the strength to crawl into it.'

'No need. I'll carry you,' he offered.

Her mouth gaped in a wide yawn.

'You might have to.'

He felt a surge of warmth in his stomach. He had missed her and it was good to have her back. Apart from anything else there was so much he had to tell her. About the new horse, for example. And Matty's infuriating behaviour.

He started to launch into his account.

'Wait a minute, Levic,' she interrupted him. 'Don't you want to know about Steffi?'

'What about him?' he said, put out.

'Steffi. You know, Steffi . . . our son? You said goodbye to him yesterday. Don't you want to know how he settled in when he got back to Liddy's?'

'Yes, of course I do. But wait until I finish telling you . . .'

'He didn't seem very happy,' she persisted.

'Why not?'

'I don't know. That incident with Amy upset him. And then there's school.'

'Oh, I shouldn't worry your head about that. All boys . . .'

'But we're not talking about all boys. We're talking about Steffi and I don't like seeing him unhappy,' she said querulously.

'Nor do I. But, since there's nothing we can do about it, I see no point . . .'

'Blast you, Levic!'

'Me?' he spluttered, trying to work out what he had said to make her so angry.

'Yes, you. You don't give a damn about Steffi.'

'Come on, Mirella. You know that's not true,' he shushed, leaning over and kissing the top of her head. 'It's just that you're tired and need a good night's sleep.'

'I may be tired but what I said was true. You don't give a damn about Steffi and I wish I knew why. It's not natural. I mean, you of all people, Levic – growing up without a father – surely you want your own son to grow up differently?'

Suddenly he felt as weary as Mirella looked.

'Believe me, Steffi *is* growing up differently,' he mumbled. 'He has a mother and father who make sure he's cared for properly.'

'But that's not all a son needs,' she protested.

'It's more than I got.'

'Yes, but that was different. If your father died so soon after you were born, you can't blame him for neglecting you.'

'I didn't say I blamed him.'

'Well, your mother then. Are you saying she never looked after you properly?'

He thought he detected a note of contempt in Mirella's voice.

'No,' he muttered. 'I'm saying I don't want to talk about it.'

'But . . .'

'Let's forget the drink and go to bed,' he urged.

Mirella sighed impatiently.

'Bed. That's always the way out for you! Bed or work. You bury yourself in one or the other to avoid facing up to anything that hurts. But not this time. I'm not letting you hide from the fact that Steffi's unhappy.'

'Okay, so Steffi's unhappy. But there's nothing I can do about that tonight, is there?'

'God, I don't know what your mother ever did to you, but it

must have been bad to make you so unfeeling towards your own child,' Mirella muttered as she rose from the chair.

She shouldn't have said it. Suddenly he was trembling and wanting to strike out at her. Slap his hand across her face, smash his fist against her head. Abruptly he turned and made for the door. Once there, in a carefully controlled voice, he whispered, 'Don't you ever speak about my mother like that again. Do you hear me?'

'Levic, I didn't mean . . .'

'You know nothing about it, Mirella. Nothing. Nobody does.'

'Where are you going?'

'Out.'

'But it's late. Don't go now, Levic. Please . . .'

He heard her voice tail away as he strode into the night. He knew he could not trust himself to stay.

He walked very fast. Then faster. Stretching his muscles, sending his blood coursing round his body, forcing his lungs to fill until his chest heaved with the strain and he had eventually to relax the pace a little. He walked blind for the first half hour, only dimly aware of marching up Stangate Street, passing Apsley's and St Thomas's Hospital and then striking eastwards along the bank of the river to reach Blackfriars Bridge. Only then did his vision begin to clear and his mind rid itself of crazy impulses.

The streets were deserted apart from an occasional cab rattling over cobbles to take some late reveller home. For a moment he considered flagging one down and going home himself, but thought better of it. For, peering through the swirling yellow-grey fog at a familiar landmark, he began to recognise where his footsteps were leading and to overcome his resistance to visiting the place again.

As he walked, in his mind he returned to these streets as they were thirty years ago and he, not the grown-up Levic of today, but the little boy who lived here then. A poor scrap of a lad who had felt more at home in these streets than in the dingy room behind the biscuit bakehouse where he slept and kept his few belongings.

Duff's premises had been situated in a narrow road off Shepherdess Walk – called Goswell Street, if his memory served him right. Was the place still there? he wondered. Probably not, after all this time and the amount of development which had recently taken place around Hoxton.

And old Duff must be long since dead and gone, Levic thought, summoning up a picture of a stout man with a round red face, always in his shirt-sleeves and wearing a short white apron.

His mother had worked as a pastry cook for Duff and after she died Duff had taken the four-year-old Levic into his home to save him from the Workhouse. Which was kind of him, because Levic was completely on his own, his widowed mother having left all her family behind in Hungary. On the other hand, it was probably no mere altruism, for Duff soon saw in the lad a useful pair of legs for running errands and hands for carrying trays full of biscuits into the local taverns. Then, later, Levic had found himself employed on heavier jobs such as fetching fuel and stoking up fires for the ovens.

But whenever he could, he escaped into the streets – not because he was work-shy, but because he felt so bad when trapped indoors for any length of time.

Levic cast his mind back to these streets as he remembered them: black and slippery, shining with rain, and sometimes full of swirling grey mist that drifted in front of shops and clung to street lamps as if afraid of the otherwise all-encompassing dark. And the din: the shouts and raucous singing, barrel organs churning, horses' hooves clattering over the cobbles and carts being trundled by. Carts full of fruit and vegetables, and old clothes and bits of furniture, coal or milk. And the water cart that used to sprinkle the roads in summer to lay the dust.

In his mind's eye he saw himself struggling to carry a heap of spicy biscuits on a tray almost too big for his little arms to reach from side to side. And when he tried to visualise what he had looked like – because his head had always been bowed over some load he was carrying, the first things that came to mind were his boots. Brown boots, battered and tied with string, with their tongues hanging out. But lucky to have them when there were so many without. Children who ran barefoot begging in the streets and no proper job to go to.

No, he had been lucky on several counts. Working in the bakery meant there were broken biscuits to eat. And when he delivered to the music halls, their patrons often took pity on so skinny a lad and stood him on a table to watch him drink ale or eat up some crusty bit of mutton pie left on a dish.

So it was not hunger that troubled him, but something much worse – fear. Though only a little boy, he had lived through such fear that its shadow always dogged him, always lay in wait at the back of his mind ready to pounce and tear out his throat. And the only way he knew of keeping that fear at bay was to stay on the move, to run from anything that might remind him of the night his mother died. To run and run and run.

'There he goes! Off again, little flibbertigibbet,' people used to joke about his obsession.

'Didn't your mother ever teach you to walk, young fellow?'

'Where's the fire?'

Levic, the man of the world, smiled when he remembered the jibes. He could afford to now. But not then. Then he hated to be reminded of his mother. But the trouble was, no matter how successful he was at avoiding her during the day, at night she would creep into his dreams and stare into his eyes, grieving to see him so shabby. He would hear her adjuring him in her native tongue.

'We were used to better things than this in our own country, Levic. Never forget that, my little one. You come from a good family and must never forget your breeding. Remember you were born the son of a gentleman and always act accordingly.'

Levic's smile died away as her words echoed back over the years. He did not want to hear his mother's voice. He dared not let her slightest breath fall on him again.

By Jove, the old Eagle Tavern. Now here was a place that hadn't changed at all.

He peered into the pleasure gardens along its side. Dark and deserted at this hour, but he could still make out the oriental turrets and huge gas lamps that fascinated him when he delivered his biscuits here as a boy. A magical place to him then, this and the Albert Saloon where crowds gathered for the concerts and displays of rope-dancing and wrestling. In fact he owed a great deal to those wrestling matches, for once they were finished he used to fall on the soft heaps of tan bark left over from the ring and have a wonderful time doing cartwheels, handsprings and flip-flaps through them. And it was there that someone spotted what he was up to and launched him into his profession by arranging for him to appear as a tumbler in the Rodney Head Music Hall in Whitechapel.

Was that the cause of his row with Duff? He couldn't say now.

All he knew was that soon after this he was tying up a few things in a bundle and setting out to make his fortune.

And what age was he? Ten years old. Two years younger than Steffi. So what right had Mirella to say that he neglected his son? Had he not seen to it that Steffi enjoyed every advantage that he himself had lacked? A comfortable, secure home and a decent education.

He swallowed hard. A secure home and a decent education – yes, that's what he wanted for his son. For Steffi. For he had always been determined to do what was right by the lad. Which made it all the more unfair when Mirella accused him of not showing proper feelings. After all, there was no doubt in his mind that he loved the boy, even if there were times when he found his presence in the household irritating.

In the evenings after the show, for instance. Although tired, Levic and Mirella usually followed their own pleasant routine of hot drinks and a bite of supper in front of the fire, and a quiet chat before turning in. But all that was spoilt when Steffi was there, because he tended to monopolise Mirella's attention, keeping her talking and laughing in the kitchen until Levic wondered whether she was ever coming to bed.

Not that he was jealous of his own son. Of course not. But he just wished the boy could be more self-sufficient when he came to stay with them and take up less of his mother's time. Moreover, if he was honest, he did fear that Mirella would end up spoiling the boy and for that reason took a harsher line with Steffi than he might otherwise have done.

After all, the most important thing he could do for his son was teach him how to be a man, and you did not learn that lesson without sustaining a few knocks – as he himself had found out at a very tender age.

After leaving Duff's, he had found his first job at Greenwich Fair where he was taken on by Talbot's Circus and taught to do more tumbling tricks and juggling and trapeze work. But there were many times when, if he had only had enough strength, he would have crawled back to the bakery and begged to be taken in again. Such as when the job with Talbot's ended so disastrously.

'Go on, Levic. Dare you to try some tricks on the new trapezist's equipment,' the older lads challenged him.

'All right, then.'

He clambered aloft and fixed a pair of slings over his top

boots to save himself if he fell. Then the other boys gave the trapeze a good swing and he turned a successful somersault on it.

'Hurrah!' his pals cheered.

They made him feel so good.

'Now try the throw-out,' one of them shouted.

Eager to please, he whirled himself head downwards and – to his utter amazement – kept falling until he crashed into a row of seats. Whereupon, looking up, he surveyed among the stars his boots dangling in the air, still safely attached to the slings.

The sound of the other lads' laughter followed him into oblivion.

Sadly Mr Talbot did not appreciate the joke and sacked him. For the next few weeks Levic hardly knew where he was or what he was doing, being only dimly aware of long nights spent curled up under hedges and days scrounging food. He owed his survival to the Sibley brothers who took him under their wing.

With Tosh and Bran Sibley he walked from fair to fair giving acrobatic displays at villages on the way. They travelled light, carrying no tent and finding their audiences on commons or in public houses – preferably the latter so that they had less far to go to spend their takings. He stayed with them just one season, picking up new tricks but not their taste for liquor.

After that his memory became a kaleidoscope of engagements with small travelling troupes and shows until his first big break came with Manley's Circus who took him on as clown to the rope. After travelling with them throughout England he returned to London for a winter engagement at the Surrey in Southwark Bridge Road – the only music hall in the capital at that time to employ acrobats.

But he did remember how in one moment the world opened up for him when Cineselli's Circus approached him with an offer to tour Spain and Portugal. Madrid, Cadiz, Lisbon, Badajoz, Cordoba – he appeared in all of them and for years rarely returned to England because there was nothing and nobody here to come back to. In fact, there was no one to go back to anywhere – which was the way he liked it.

But wherever he was, he seldom lacked the pleasure of female company.

Levic smiled as he remembered Cordoba and the Spanish girl whose brother threatened him with a knife. The violence had served, if anything, to whet his ardour until the girl herself had blunted it again by talking about priests and marriage, despite the fact that he had made it abundantly clear from the start that he was not the marrying sort.

Then he had promptly fallen into the same trap with Leila, the German trapeze artiste whom he met while they were both performing with Circus Renz in Berlin. A lovely girl, blonde and blue-eyed – not unlike Dorina, he suddenly realised, stopping to think about the girl for a moment. Although more petite.

He used to stand in amazement when Leila did her act, thrilled by her skill and daring. Later, when he got to know her better, he discovered that her daring was no more than an act and her mind that of a conventional lass who happened to work in a circus. That what she really longed for was the chance to give up her trapeze and settle down with a '*guten Mann*' and have '*eine grosse Familie*'.

Leila could have no idea what horror her words inspired. A family? Not if he had anything to do with it! There was nothing for him to do but up sticks and leave before he became further embroiled.

And that was what had brought him back to England and that fateful engagement at the Agricultural Hall where he met Mirella.

Everything changed when he met Mirella.

Sixteen at the time, and a wild-eyed passionate little creature with an air of desperation that he found immediately appealing. So different from anyone else he had known. That, together with the fact that she was beautiful, hit him straight away. He was fascinated by her unpredictability, sensing in her a kindred spirit who shared his values and would be as loth as he to give up her freedom in return for some conventional relationship.

But had he been short-changed, he wondered, now that he found himself married to this mother of his child who kept trying to nag him into her own image of a proper father? Still, even though something in Mirella had undoubtedly changed with Steffi's birth, he had no regrets about marrying her. Far from it. He knew he still loved her. And he loved Steffi, so . . .

Suddenly he was holding his breath and his muscles had tensed as if in response to danger. He felt a desperate need to run away from this place. To run and run until he fetched up somewhere else, anywhere – so long as it was miles away from this hateful place where he used to live in the days before Duff took him in. He was standing in front of the very house. And down there – behind that black basement window was the room where his mother had died.

With an effort he pulled himself together, turned on his heel and strode back towards Westminster.

A mistake, a mistake, he kept repeating to himself. Always a mistake to wander in the past. The only thing to do is concentrate on the present, make plans for the future. Keep busy.

The new horse, for instance. There's a challenge. I'm looking forward to working with that new white horse and Dorina.

Desperately he crammed his mind with images of himself supporting Dorina as she pirouetted on the backs of the two horses, and then of himself doing a backward somersault from one horse to the other as they cantered round the ring. Black to white, or maybe white to black – it all depended on how they shaped up when they started working together.

Arriving back at Stangate Street, he noticed the sky already growing light. He prayed Mirella had not been lying awake all this time. Poor girl, it wasn't her fault that he had gone stomping off into the night. She was simply the victim of his frailty; proof that one always hurt most the people one loved best.

My God! No! No. Now he found himself picturing Mirella and seeing not her face but the dimly-remembered face of his mother.

He shut his eyes, but the apparition refused to go away – and he was haunted by the ghostly form of a woman who was neither Mirella nor his mother, but shared the features of both so that he could not separate one from the other. The long black wavy hair and dark eyes, remote and full of pain – was this his mother or Mirella?

He was no longer sure.

But at least he knew that the screaming and dinning in his head belonged to the past and had nothing to do with this silent house and the wife he felt desperate to clasp in his arms.

Chapter 6

'But I *must* go! I promised Steffi.'

'Go next week then,' Levic muttered, keeping his features wooden while he combed his silky moustache into place.

'No, it must be today. I can't let Steffi down when he's expecting me. Or rather – us,' she corrected herself, trying not to show her anger.

It really wasn't fair. Levic knew what great store she set on these visits to Steffi and surely it wasn't asking too much of him to spend one day with the family?

'Well, you'd better go then,' he said, still tweaking his damn' moustache. 'But remember what happened last time and don't get yourself overtired.'

'But I don't want to go on my own. I want you to come as well.'

Levic waved his comb in a gesture of impatience.

'Look, Mirella, I've already told you why I can't. I have work to do here.'

'Oh, yes. Your work!' she growled.

'Well, White Prince can't train himself and it's vital for us to work him in with Black Chieftain as quickly as possible.'

'I know that, but surely one day off wouldn't hurt?'

'Not normally.' He spoke slowly, as if explaining to a child. 'But I have to stay here this weekend because, as you know, Sunday is the only day Dorrie and I can have the ring long enough to start the training properly.'

It was useless to argue. She knew Levic would not come with her. Still, at least nothing he said would put her off going on her own.

Not that he was making much effort to try and dissuade her, she thought.

Levic recognised the set look on his wife's face and tried to charm her anger away. But for once he could not be bothered to find the right words before Mirella climbed into the cab and was whisked off to Waterloo Station.

He waited just long enough to see the hansom turn the corner of Stangate Street and then spun on his heel and strode off to Apsley's, his mood not altogether happy, it being beyond him why Mirella felt the need to go all that way every other weekend. After all, there was nothing wrong with Steffi and he was being well looked after. Which was more than could be said for himself at the moment when the house, especially at night, was so cheerless when she was away.

Still, she would be back tomorrow and he had plenty to occupy his mind in the meantime.

Black Chieftain and White Prince, galloping around the ring, head to croup. If he stood on Black Chieftain's rump and sprang backwards, twirling in the air, he should be able to land on White Prince. It was a trick he had seen done in Berlin by an equestrian who bounced from horse-to-horse, ground-to-horse, horse-to-ground in a demonic display that had left Levic breathless with excitement. And desperate to have a go at it himself.

As he entered the ring, he saw Dorina already going through her routine with White Prince, so he moved quietly round the edge of the ring fence to join the little group of spectators standing in the pit.

'Good morning, Monsieur – and Mesdemoiselles,' he murmured, acknowledging the presence of Dorina's little daughters with a formal bow that caused the eldest to giggle but the younger one to look away.

'Hello, Mr Levic. Amy and me are going to watch some of your practice before Gramps takes us out riding in the park,' Rosa announced.

'Is that so?' he asked, politely looking to her sister for confirmation. But Amy kept her head well down, refusing to meet his gaze.

He immediately understood the reason for her embarrassment. She was trying to hide her face. That poor little face marked by a livid scar that ran across her left eye like some opened out horse shoe which had lost its store of luck. And he longed to find words to reassure her but like all the other people about her decided that the less said the better.

'Well,' he breezed, to cover the awkwardness, 'I suggest you keep your eyes fixed on your mama if you want to learn about riding. Don't you agree, Arnold?'

'I certainly do. There's no more beautiful horsewoman than my Dorina, even though I do say it myself.'

Looking at her, at that moment simply riding the new horse around the ring without attempting anything fancy, Levic needed no further convincing. Horse and rider moving so gracefully together. White Prince with his wonderfully smooth gait – the most important quality needed in a rosinback.

'Ye-es,' he sighed.

'Yep. That white was a good buy,' Arnold said, squinting at the horse. 'He's going to look grand linked with Black Chieftain while you and Dorina do your pas-dee-durr.'

'Ye-es,' Levic sighed again as he imagined himself straddling the two horses and supporting the fair Dorina while she did her dance.

'I'm going to bring in Chieftain now,' she called. 'I'll lead him behind Prince so you can see them in line, okay?'

She was obviously happy, and her mood provided all that was needed to lift his own spirits completely. Everything was happening in a way that confirmed his growing confidence that he would succeed in pulling off the grand trick he had in mind.

On her next entrance he examined both horses intently, studying the rise and fall of their haunches as they circled the ring. Yes, he was sure it could be done – a backward somersault, taking off from one horse and landing on the back of the one behind. Taking off from steady Black Chieftain and landing on White Prince.

As far as he knew, such a trick had never before been done at Apsley's. About thirty years ago an American, Mr Aymar, had amazed audiences here by throwing a backward somersault feet to feet on the same horse, but Levic wanted to improve on that. And with Dorina's help, he felt sure he could do it.

'So why not give up clowning and become a proper equestrian?' Mirella had asked when he told her of his plans.

'Because I don't want to be riding horses for the rest of my life,' he had tried to explain.

'Then why not stick to clowning? That's something you do really well and it doesn't require you to break your neck,' she declared.

Mirella of all people! She who found her delight in walking a rope suspended a hundred feet above the ground! He had expected more understanding from her than that. She should have known he could never resist trying something new –

simply because it *was* new and would bring him face to face with something different in himself. Although illogical, this was an inner imperative as far as he was concerned. An inner imperative – and not, as Mirella had once stupidly suggested, another of his running away strategies.

'Last time round,' Dorina yelled.

He narrowed his eyes to watch the two horses making their way out. One white, one black. Light followed by darkness; the day by night. Like Dorina and Mirella, he suddenly thought, pleased with the notion. And in his mind seeing himself somersaulting from one to the other – and landing on his feet!

After such a productive morning, the afternoon hung heavy about him once he came back to Stangate Street. The trouble was, he was not used to having any length of time to himself these days. He and Mirella did nearly everything together and there was always so much to do even on those Sundays not reserved for visits to Steffi. Letters to write, endless chores attached to keeping costumes and equipment in top condition. But, if he did have a spare moment, one of the things he loved best was to take up pencil and paper and sit working out the details for some new trick.

So winter afternoons often found him and Mirella sitting on either side of the fire, she sewing and he doodling diagrams. And as far as he was concerned there was no nicer way to spend a Sunday afternoon – unless it was to lie in bed and make love.

He shut his eyes and basked in delicious daydreams: he and Mirella taking their pleasure. No performance to prepare for, plenty of time to be together and enjoy each other.

There had been too few of those sort of afternoons lately – partly because of her visits to Aldershot, partly his preoccupation with the new act. This afternoon, however, would have been a perfect opportunity once his practice was over.

Damn Mirella for not being here when he wanted her! He hated being at a loose end.

He could go for a walk, of course. Except that the rain which had driven Arnold and the girls back from the park early was still sheeting down on to the pavements outside, and from the window everything looked cold and grey.

He half-regretted turning down Dorina's invitation to eat lunch with her family. But the prospect of Matty's boorish behaviour, especially after he had spent most of his morning in the company of a bottle, was unendurable. Besides, apart from his professional work with Dorina, he had been trying to give Arnold's family a wide berth since that ugly incident involving the whip and Matty's sulky reaction to the purchase of the horse a few weeks back.

Moving over to the grate to poke the smouldering fire into more life, he eased off his boots, threw himself on the sofa and drew up an occasional table to rest his diagrams on. Since the afternoon was empty, he might as well try to fill it with something worthwhile. He would give some more thought to the riding trick.

Okay, so it had taken him months and months of practice to achieve that first backward somersault on Black Chieftain's back, but nowadays he managed one nearly every time – leaping up so that the horse carried him forward and landed him less than two inches behind his take-off point. And with every leap he felt himself gaining in confidence and grace – able to leap higher, turn a tighter circle in the air, then spread his feet wider and bend his knees so that he could land with ease.

Of course there were times when he failed to make a perfect leap. But even then all was not lost, because he had learnt how to use his legs to adjust the spin. Tucking them in to increase his speed. Pushing them out to slow himself down.

Yes, he could now claim to have mastered this, one of the most difficult of equestrian feats. To have transferred all he had learnt over the years as a ground acrobat to that tiny, heaving, slippery, ever moving platform that was Black Chieftain's back. Circling above the ring like a planet. Coming down to earth only to launch himself into orbit again the next moment.

He had mastered it.

But now a further challenge was presenting itself: the possibility of somersaulting from the back of one horse to another.

Levic leaned forward over the table, picked up his pencil and selected a clean sheet of paper. What would be needed to attempt such a trick? To start with, the horses would have to be trained to move in perfect unison with each other.

Like so! he thought, roughly sketching the two horses galloping nose to tail. Then, at the right moment, he would spring up into the air, high enough to do a complete flip.

Like so! he decided, putting a series of dots to describe the arc his body would make from Black Chieftain, over White

Prince's head before coming to land on his feet on the latter's back.

Yes, it could work. It really could.

With mounting excitement he began to elaborate on the drawing, adding a sketch of his own body caught twisting in mid-flight. He'd have to wait until exactly the right moment when all his nerves and muscles were in complete harmony with the movements of both horses.

Yes. He could feel what that would be like. Then he'd spring, twisting in the air, waiting for that split-second when, still upside-down, he'd see White Prince and begin to feel with his toes for his back and then straighten up with the rise of his haunches.

Right, he thought, so the key to success, as always, will be absolute precision of movement. Well, he could train his body for that, and use the mechanic until he was confident.

But would he be able to rely completely on the horses? Yes. The answer was immediate and reassuring. Yes. Dorina said she could train them to canter at an even gait. And, if Dorina said so, it could certainly be done.

Hmmm!

He sighed with satisfaction, picturing their triumph. The trick would cause a sensation. No doubt about that.

He seized a fresh piece of paper and started another sketch.

Must land gracefully – so! While Dorina, dressed in that fetching silver outfit of hers, would be in centre ring to work the horses and lead the applause when he achieved the climax.

Now he held the two sketches in his hands and in his imagination re-enacted all the movements that would link one with the other, this time hearing the cheers of the spectators and sensing their satisfaction.

It was so thrilling that he longed to share his excitement with someone. Anyone who would understand. Mirella, perhaps. Or Dorina. Or someone else. But he couldn't think of anyone else.

For a moment he considered putting on his coat and going back to Apsley's to see Dorina. He dismissed the idea, reluctant to intrude on scenes of family bliss. But he desperately wanted her to see these sketches. And bring the horses into the ring for another practice.

Wait a minute, though. What if . . . ?

Perusing the sketches again, he began to see other possibilities. The position of the horses, for instance. What if they did not gallop nose to rump, but neck to flank? That would give him a shorter distance to somersault, even if it didn't look so good.

He started to sketch the two horses again, this time with White Prince in the foreground, appearing to gain on steady Black Chieftain.

No. That made it too complicated. Because if the horses did not gallop in strict file, he would have to move sideways as well as backwards once he jumped . . .

'Yes?' he called out absentmindedly.

The hammering on his door came again.

Still clutching his drawings, he rose to answer it. 'Yes?' he repeated, before realising who was standing there. 'My goodness, it's you!'

'Levic, I had to come. I must talk to you. Is it all right? I mean, I'm not disturbing you?'

'Dorina for goodness' sake, come along in before you drown.' Ushering her in, he noticed that apart from being wet she was as breathless as if she had run all the way from Apsley's. And she had obviously not bothered to secure the hood of her cloak properly because water was trickling off her hair down her face. 'No, no. Don't say anything until you've taken off these wet things and warmed yourself by the fire.'

She was staring wildly and seemed to need all her wits to bring her breathing back to normal. So, settling her in an armchair close to the fire, he fetched them both some brandy.

'Tell me what's upset you, Dorrie?'

She looked up, her grey eyes large and brimming with misery – not at all the Dorina he was used to. No longer fully in command and completely in control of what she was doing, but struggling to hold back tears. And her face as white as a page in his notebook.

'I've had the most terrible row,' she faltered.

'With Matty?'

'Yes, Matty.' She spat out the name like some vile taste. 'Oh, Levic, I can't stand much more.'

'Did he hurt you?'

'No. Not really.'

He noticed the waver in her voice that suggested she was inclined to say more.

'You're sure?' he pressed her gently.

'No. I don't think he really hurt me,' Dorina protested, pushing back her sleeve to examine the dull red patch that had appeared on her arm where someone had recently gripped too tightly.

'The brute!' Levic muttered.

'No, no. It's really nothing,' Dorina murmured, attempting a brave smile.

'That will turn into a nasty bruise. A gentleman would know better.'

He felt genuinely angry. Matty was a small man, not quite so tall as Dorina, but that was no excuse. Although, if he was honest there were times when even he himself might have . . . But he had no wish to get involved in any dispute between man and wife.

'Still, I'm sure Matty didn't mean to hurt you,' he added in an attempt to mollify.

'Oh, but he did. He grabbed hold of me so hard I couldn't breathe and there was one moment I thought he was going to go for my throat.'

'Matty?' Levic tried not to sound incredulous.

'Yes, Matty. Oh, you don't know what he's like, Levic, when he's in drink.'

'I think I do,' he said, remembering the pathetic figure Matty usually cut after he'd had a few.

'Like a savage animal,' she declared. 'Trying to maul me about as if . . . well, as if I've got no self-respect.'

'And that's what he was trying to do this afternoon, maul you around?' Levic prompted, deciding it might be easier to console her once he got the whole picture.

'Yes,' she shuddered. Then gulped her brandy and fell to spluttering, her eyelids fluttering as a violent quiver passed through her body. 'Oooh, that's better.'

'Good. It will warm you up.'

'Yep. That's what I need, warming up,' she sighed, her head dropping back to expose an expanse of naked throat.

'So where was your father when Matty tried to . . . well, let's say, offended you in that way?'

'Dad? Oh, he'd taken the girls off to see his sister in Islington. He often does that on a Sunday afternoon.'

'I see. So you and Matty were on your own and . . .' Suddenly at a loss for words, he found himself gazing at her naked throat and wanting to kiss such vulnerable flesh. But he quickly pulled himself together. 'And where is he now?' he asked.

'Who?'

'Matty.'

'God knows.'

'He didn't follow you?'

She brought up her head sharply, snorting with contempt.

'He was in no fit state to follow anyone.'

'I see. So he doesn't know you're here?'

'Good lord, no. He'll think I've gone chasing off to Islington, if he thinks anything at all.'

'That's all right then.' Levic felt relieved. The last thing he wanted was a scene on his own doorstep. 'Have another drink,' he said, as she gulped down the last of her brandy and made another grimace.

'Thanks.' This time, after he poured, she sat back in her armchair, rolling the glass between the palms of her hands, staring morosely at the swirling liquid.

'Don't worry, my love,' he said. 'It will all blow over, you'll see.'

'No. I don't want it to blow over. I won't go on with that man, Levic. I just can't bear him to touch me any more.'

He felt like saying, 'I'm not surprised.' He had never understood what could have drawn a girl like Dorina to Matty in the first place – unless it was the attraction of forbidden fruit. Indeed, Levic had heard it whispered in the company that Dorina had run off with the humble juggler only after Arnold had broken up a more promising relationship with words to the effect that the man had not yet been born who was good enough for his daughter.

'But let's face it, Dorina,' Levic chose to say instead, 'Matty sober is a very different proposition from Matty drunk. What you've got to work out is how to wean him off the bottle.'

'Oh, he's always liked his tipple,' she muttered.

'But it's grown to be rather more than that of late, hasn't it, Dorrie?' he ventured, wondering if she was aware of the extent of the problem.

'Yes. Yes, I s'pose so. But then . . . well, he's got his reasons. Drowning his sorrows, as they say.'

Levic sighed with impatience, uncomfortable with the father confessor role Dorina was putting on him.

'No, there's no excuse for a man like Matty. He's got nothing to be sorrowful about. A darn good wife, beautiful kids, his profession. What more . . .'

'He gets agitated about Dad. Feels he's being undermined all the time.' Her voice was beginning to sound slightly slurred.

'But what does he expect, for heaven's sake? Everything handed to him on a plate? I mean, it's up to him to make a stand . . .'

'Quite. Which is what I tell him. "If you were a man," I say . . . But he hates that. Me telling him he's not a proper man. But you wouldn't let people walk over you like he does, would you, Levic?' she said, her big grey eyes imploring him not to contradict.

'No. I wouldn't.'

'That's because you're a proper man,' she smiled.

He nodded, feeling again that he did not want to contradict.

Then, to his horror, her expression changed. The smile crumpled and her face flushed pink from the throat upwards as she began to sob.

'Oh, come on, love,' he whispered, stretching out his hand to pat hers. 'It can't be that bad.'

He liked the feel of her flesh under his and the knowledge that he was managing to comfort her; liked the feel of her cheek as she lowered her head to nuzzle against his hand, her breath warm on his skin and her eyes doe-like as they gazed up at him.

He stretched out his other hand to stroke her hair. It was still damp, the colour and texture of oyster silk under his fingers. And when she started kissing his hand, nuzzling and kissing it and murmuring, 'I knew you'd understand,' he was pleased to hear her sounding happier, for he liked to make women happy.

'Dorina, my love,' he whispered into her hair, 'I think you're very beautiful.'

'Hmmm,' she sighed.

'But that doesn't give me the right to take advantage of this situation. And I don't intend to,' he added, as if to countervail the ache in his loins and the force of his desire, which was starting to swell and to throb and demand that he take her.

'No,' she crooned. 'I know you'd never take advantage of me, Levic. That's why I feel so safe with you. And why . . . oh, Levic, I do like you.' She pushed up her face and suddenly her lips were on his and she was sucking him into her.

Of course he could have stopped, he knew that. Poor girl was three sheets to the wind and not altogether aware what she was doing. But he didn't stop, because he wanted to kiss her and felt it could do no harm – so long as it went no further.

Then they slid on to the floor, their lips still joined, and arms around each other. Her skin was as smooth as he had always imagined and her flesh soft and yielding, smelling of musk and the sweet hay she fed to her horses. Her body was bigger and softer than Mirella's, more like the lass he had known in Germany that time. Yes, Leila's skin had had this delicious soft feel to it as well, he remembered, sliding his hand along and up her leg until he was fondling her thigh and hearing her sigh with pleasure.

Now he knew there was no holding back, not for anything. This is what he had been missing lately, this voluptuous enjoyment of a woman. Clean and natural, no cloying emotion. Just taking his pleasure, breaking loose, finding . . . yes, with each thrust . . . the confirmation of his power. There, and there, and there . . . again and again until – my God, how good that felt.

He slumped down on top of her completely happy until he remembered that this was Dorina he was holding in his arms. Not his Mirella, but Dorina.

Still, if in those last moments he had forgotten this fact, that wasn't his fault. After all, it should have been Mirella. And would have been, had she chosen to be here . . .

On the other hand . . . My God! She'd go wild when she found out.

He and Dorina – how could he ever explain? Well, he couldn't, so he mustn't even try. And then, so long as Mirella never found out, everything would be all right.

A myriad such thoughts coursed through his mind as he continued to caress Dorina, stroking and kissing her neck and her throat and whispering endearments, completing the rituals of love-making – not needing to consider too much what he was doing because it was all second nature to him. He had always known instinctively how to please women, had always felt very happy to endulge them.

He did not feel happy at the moment, though. He felt distinctly worried.

All those daydreams about Dorina, imagining how it would feel to make love to her. Then to have the fruit handed to him on a plate, as it were, and to find it tasted every bit as good as he had imagined, but – and here was the rub – no better.

He had made love to her. And now it was over, he was left despondent and thinking about Mirella.

Still, no time to worry about her now. At the moment it was Dorina he had in his arms and he must act honourably towards her. He owed her that much.

'Hmm, you are beautiful,' he breathed, making the first delicate moves to disengage himself. Only to find her strong arms immediately tugging him back into her embrace.

Twisting round to see her face, he was met by a completely languorous look, her lips sagging slightly open, her cheeks softly flushed, and her eyes as unfocussed as grey marshy mist. Meeting his gaze, she gave him a slow wanton smile that he found horrifying, and he suddenly wanted to be done with the affair, tidy the whole thing away quickly.

As gently as possible he pulled away, stood up, and started to set his clothing straight, conscious all the while that Dorina, far from making any such move, was still lying prone trying to transfix him in that lascivious stare.

'Come on,' he chivvied, 'time to set ourselves to rights. You tidy yourself up while I make us some tea – and then I think we'd better talk.'

He deliberately kept his tone light, unsure how to proceed without hurting Dorina's pride. After all, they had to continue working together, so they must leave no emotional entanglements, no misunderstandings to spoil things. Luckily it was in both their interests – in everyone's interests, in fact – to cover up what had happened and find a way to continue exactly as before.

She was sitting up, shaking back her hair and slowly starting (thank God) to do up the buttons on her bodice.

'Levic, how long have you been wanting to do that?' she murmured.

'Oh, from the first moment I clapped eyes on you,' he said, recognising this to be no more than the truth. 'But in this life, my love, one has to accept that one can't always do what one wants.'

There, that was a good way to lead into the subject of their future relationship. He must put it to her that, although it would undoubtedly hurt him much more than it hurt her never to have this sort of thing happen again, nevertheless for the sake of all those around them – her children, her father, Matty – they must both make that sacrifice.

'I know, Levic. Which makes it all the more wonderful that you and I have come together at last.'

'Eh?'

'Oh, Levic. Don't you feel as if you've been waiting for this moment all your life?'

He nodded his head, waiting for her to finish so that he could say his piece.

'And now we've come together, you and I,' she rushed on, 'we'll stay together, won't we? And not let anyone else come between us. Not ever.'

Chapter 7

'Hey, have you seen this?' Levic asked, rustling the pages of a letter.

'No?'

'It's from my very good friend, the Hero of Niagara himself.'

'Blondin, you mean?' Mirella said. 'But I thought he was in Australia.' She distinctly remembered reading an account of the tightrope walker's tumultuous reception in Sydney in last week's *Era*.

'Nearly right. He's actually moved on to New Zealand now.'

'And he's written to you from there?'

'Yes. Posted in Dunedin,' he said, checking the envelope. 'It seems he's there with Nelson's Circus at the moment – making a fortune while the racing carnival's on.'

'I bet.'

'And more than seven thousand paid to see his farewell performance in Auckland. Then nearly as many in Wellington.'

'I see what you mean.'

'Well, it makes you think, doesn't it?'

'Think what?'

'Whether we're wise to stay with this outfit.'

'Foreman's?'

'Yes. Just lately I've been wondering whether we shouldn't leave Arnold and go out on our own again. Possibly abroad.'

'Abroad?' For her the word always carried with it difficult undertones. 'But what about Steffi?'

'We could take him with us.'

'You mean it?'

'Yes, if necessary. He's old enough to benefit from it now.'

'You're saying that you'd really like to quit Foreman's then?' she asked, taken aback by this sudden change of heart on Levic's part.

'That's right,' he said unequivocally. 'Not immediately, of course. This summer's already bespoke and I wouldn't dream of letting Arnold down. Besides, there's the new act – I must perfect that before we leave.'

'Oh.'

'But come next winter, my love, that will be the time for us to make our move.'

'Good.'

'Yes,' he sighed. 'I for one feel more than ready for it.'

As he walked off, letter in hand, Mirella smiled to herself, happy that the situation between her and Levic was so much better now than it had been. Indeed, it was hard to imagine why, less than a month ago, she had been feeling so desperate.

That Sunday, for instance, when she had gone off to see Steffi on her own. She had felt so angry with Levic for putting his own interests before the family's that she had even been tempted to stay on in Aldershot indefinitely, to stay with Steffi at the cost of her marriage. That's how unhappy she had been feeling. Then.

And maybe Levic had realised it too. Because since that same weekend he had scarcely been able to do enough to please her. Had confessed how lonely he had felt without her and readily promised not to let anything stand in the way of going with her to see Steffi in future.

Not that they would be able to make such visits for very much longer. For after Easter they would be out on the road again and journeying down into the West Country, moving further and further away from Steffi. Still, she would write him lots of letters to keep him posted and he could come and stay with them during his summer holidays. That would give him something to look forward to.

Poor Steffi. She gathered from something Liddy said that he was having a hard time at school at the moment. Not from the master, but the other boys. From military families for the most part, they tended to pick on anyone with a different background, especially someone like Steffi who tended to walk off with the academic laurels, she told herself proudly.

But that was not the only cloud on the horizon. Dorina and Matty's situation was still casting its shadow over the company and it was impossible to ignore the strained atmosphere between the couple. Matty, drinking as heavily as ever, was sometimes so drunk that he was incapable of performing in the ring. Once or twice Mirella had tried to talk to him about the problem, but got nowhere. And Levic was probably right when he refused to get involved. Hadn't he always said it was folly to meddle between a man and his wife?

When Levic said that the summer was already bespoke he was thinking about the series of Monster Fêtes that Arnold Foreman's company was about to stage all round the country. Each to be massively advertised in the press and then launched with a great street parade which, Pied Piper fashion, would lead people back to a showground where their senses would be drowned in spectacle – there would be exotic races involving elephants, camels, ostriches, Roman chariots; open-air acrobatic performances; and, of course, Madame Mirella on her high wire.

Levic found it hard to conceal his disdain for what he called 'Foreman's Monstrosities', seeing in them nothing less than a travesty of true circus. But knowing how much Mirella loved an opportunity to walk her tightrope in the open air, he bit back his frustration and prepared himself to take advantage of the fact that, with so many performers working outside, at least the big tent was less in demand and he could get on with his equestrian practice.

And he was making headway. White Prince, although not quite so steady as Black Chieftain, had shaped up well and some days Levic felt the backward somersault coming almost within reach. Standing on Chieftain's broad back, sensing the horse's flesh and sinews through his thin slippers, rising and falling with the steady gait, poised, ready to spring, knowing that when all the conditions were right he would succeed in doing it.

When all the conditions were right . . . The trouble was, although he had every detail worked out and his own body in perfect trim, it was the horses that were letting him down.

He would spring with what he calculated to be flawless precision, twisting smartly in the air – only to find his feet slipping down White Prince's rump. And he would be desperately trying to grab hair before the mechanic yanked him and bounced him to a safe but ungainly landing in the sawdust.

Yes, there was no doubt about it. The horses were letting him down.

But it was no use blaming them. It was Dorina's fault. Either she was not concentrating on getting the horses to canter in unison, or she was sending him the wrong signals. In either case, what was clear was that, despite all her training, she was allowing personal feelings to get in the way of her professionalism. And, with so much at stake, that was unforgivable. They both knew that.

He frowned. How to remedy the situation? that was the problem. Whatever he did, he must avoid any repetition of those dreadful scenes endured at Apsley's before he'd persuaded her to pull a veil over their indiscretion and continue their partnership as it had existed before.

He shut his eyes. If there was one thing he couldn't stand, it was emotional scenes with women.

'But if you love me, like you say you do,' Dorina had pleaded, her face pale and eyes red-rimmed from weeping, 'then surely you must tell Mirella . . .'

'No, I can't do that. It would hurt her too much.'

'But carrying on like this is hurting me.'

'I know, my dear. But we really have no choice.'

'Yes, we do. We could run away together, Levic.'

'What, and leave the horses?' he had almost said – substituting quickly, 'No, not when there's children involved. It wouldn't be right.'

She had paused then, her grey eyes opaque and staring.

'I know. Don't think I haven't worried about my girls.'

'There you are then.'

'But perhaps we could send for them. Later, I mean . . .'

This was getting ridiculous and he searched around in his mind for words to quench her fantasies.

'No, Dorina. No matter how I feel about you, I can never leave my wife and son.'

'So, it's Steffi who's holding you?' she had said, grabbing at such a thin straw that he had not the heart to prise it from her.

'If you like. A man owes something to his son and I couldn't bear to hand on a name I'd disgraced.'

She had started to laugh then, hysterically. And he'd been frightened in case the grooms heard and came running into the stables to see what was happening.

'Don't, Dorina. Please. I know how you feel, and I'm sorry. But we've got to get over this.'

'No, Levic. You don't know how I feel. You couldn't, and still do this to me.'

'Look, Dorina, I'm trying to tell you, we have no choice,' he'd said despairingly.

'But I love you. I love you,' she kept pleading. 'And I thought you loved me.'

'Yes, well, I do,' he said, at the same time cursing the weakness which had embroiled him with someone so close to home.

Only after several such scenes in which he alternately threatened and cajoled did he finally succeed in making her see sense. That there was no way they could be together – in the fullest sense – once the show was out on the road. Tents had ears and wagons had eyes. They both knew the score. Besides, they had their act to develop, the double act which meant so much to both of them, which yoked them together more securely than any more conventional tie.

And the strange thing was, he meant it.

'Dorina,' he said, 'don't you see? I'm asking you for something that no other woman on earth can give me. And I know I have no right to expect such a sacrifice, but I'm asking you to make it simply because you are the person you are and you say you love me.'

'You *know* I love you,' she moaned.

'Yes, I know you do. That's why I'm asking you to do things my way.'

'All right then.'

'Good girl.'

'And when we come to the end of the season?' she implored.

'Ah. We'll have to wait and see. But who knows? Maybe by then things will be different.'

'How?'

'God knows.'

'And Matty? How am I supposed to carry on with him all through the summer?'

'Just as you've done before,' he urged quickly.

She groaned.

'No, I mean it, Dorina. You've got to school yourself to go back to normal until we've had a chance to make longer term plans. And meanwhile we put the act first. You agree on that, don't you?'

'Yes. If that's what you want.'

That was exactly what he wanted, but was not getting. After making a brave start and putting all her former zeal into their practice sessions, in recent days Dorina's attention had seemed to waver and she had been far less cooperative. Neither was she looking her best – appearing pale and dispirited, as if eating her heart out again. So, for the sake of the act, he would have to brace himself to sort out the situation before it got any worse.

Coming across her unexpectedly in the stable tent when most of the other women, including Mirella, had gone into Bristol for shopping gave him the opportunity.

'Hello, my love. Look, is there somewhere we can go?' he started to say – only to be stopped in his tracks by her radiant smile.

'Levic.'

'My goodness, that's better, Dorrie.'

'What do you mean?' she said, continuing to smile.

'Seeing you look happy again, I was beginning to feel worried.'

'About me?'

'Yes, of course.'

'Well, there's no need.'

'No, I can see that. But what's happened?'

'Happened?' she echoed, still drinking him in with her big, grey eyes. There was something very disturbing in her dreamy expression.

'So you didn't go into town with the other women, then?' he asked, suddenly desperate to break the silence.

'No,' was all she said.

He put down the galvanised bucket he was carrying and straightened up to meet her gaze. Her grey eyes, fathomless as the ocean, stared back at him.

'What is it, Dorrie? Why are you looking at me like that?'

'I've got something to tell you.'

Instinctively he glanced around to make sure there was no one to overhear.

'Something . . . private?'

'Not as far as I'm concerned. I don't care if the whole world hears what I'm going to say.'

'That's all right then,' he said, breathing more freely.

She tossed back her head.

'Is it, Levic?'

Now her expression had him really worried.

'Come on, Dorrie. Tell me what's on your mind.'

'Right, but before I do, I want to remind you of something you said a few weeks back.'

'What?'

She paused before shutting her eyes and starting to recite what sounded like a well-learnt litany. 'You said that you loved me but you couldn't leave your wife because of your son.'

'And your daughters.'

'Right. You made it clear that we had to put the children's interest before our own.'

'Yes.'

'And I went along with that as best I could. I really tried, Levic. Business as usual, that's what you said you wanted, and that's what I tried to give you. Business as usual. The show must go on and all that rubbish.'

'No, Dorrie. Not rubbish.' He felt quite hurt.

'Yes, Levic. All that seems like rubbish when something real happens.'

'Such as?'

'Such as when I find myself expecting.'

'Expecting?' The word echoed meaninglessly in his ears.

'Yes. Expecting a baby, Levic. Your baby,' she announced triumphantly.

Now he pulled himself together.

'Look, Dorrie, we can't talk here. Come over to the wagon. Mirella's out, so we can talk there in peace.'

She smiled weakly.

'All right. So long as Mirella's out. We don't want to do anything to embarrass *her*, do we?'

His mind worked overtime as they strolled across the tober towards the yellow and green wagon that he and Mirella had bought for the travelling season.

Dorina pregnant? No, Dorina *saying* she was pregnant. It was almost certainly a mistake. They'd only been together that once. Unless . . . yes, of course. There was always Matty.

'Right,' he declared briskly, as soon as she sat down in Mirella's chair. 'You'd better tell me . . .'

'I've told you.'

'You said you think you're expecting.'

'No. I said I *am*.'

'But that's not possible, Dorina. Not when we only came together that once.'

65

'Of course it is.'

'No, no. Be sensible. If you really are with child, then it must be Matty's.'

'No, Levic. Why won't you believe me? I'm expecting your child. I know I am.'

'But, but . . .' he thought wildly. 'Are you sure? I mean, are you sure there's going to be a child?'

'Oh, yes. Quite sure.'

'Does Matty know?'

'Not yet.'

'So, when? How long before it's born?'

'About five months. I reckon early November.'

'Oh, my God!'

'Oh, Levic, isn't there some part of you that's pleased?'

He longed to give her the reassurance she craved. Poor Dorina, sitting there looking as if her figure were already softening under the long, embroidered apron she was wearing over her skirt. Oh, God. It was probably all true then.

'So you don't want it?' she said in a small voice.

'No, it's not that.'

'Or me,' she went on. 'You see, I thought when you mentioned your duty to Steffi, well . . . I thought maybe you'd feel different towards me if I had your child, but it seems . . .' Fat tears began to roll down her face. 'Levic, I love you,' she whimpered.

'Yes. I know you keep saying that, but . . .' Now that the first wave of shock was receding, his mind was grappling with all the possible consequences. How many people would be affected by this cataclysm? Poor Dorina, of course. And Mirella (my God, Mirella!). Matty. And Arnold. The children. So many people's lives about to be turned upside down unless . . .

'Listen, Dorina. Everything's going to be all right.'

'You mean . . . ?' Her face lit up.

'I mean that you can count on me to stand by you, no matter what. But first of all, look at me and listen carefully. You've got to stay calm and not do anything rash, do you understand?'

She nodded.

Chapter 8

Mirella returned from Bristol full of the joys of early summer. It was unusual for her to go shopping for clothes but this coming event required her to wear something more stylish – and, yes, more substantial – than her wardrobe contained. And since Arnold Foreman had agreed to pay for the outfit, she decided to go to the best dress-maker in town. After all, if she was supposed to be a French countess then it was important, not only to look, but to feel like a countess. And she could not do that in something run up for her by the circus costume department.

A French countess . . . well, she could envisage what such a person would wear if entertaining in her own drawing room, or attending a ball, or taking a turn in the park. But what on earth, Mirella wondered, did the well-dressed young countess wear nowadays – to go up in a balloon?

She hugged herself at the notion. This was the sort of adventure she loved. She could never be like her sister Cassie and give up showbusiness to settle down to something safe like millinery.

As usual the idea had sprung from Arnold Foreman, ever anxious to dream up new schemes to attract publicity. He had already tapped the current craze for watching balloon ascents by hiring the intrepid Captain Ewens to take his 'Venus' aloft from several tobers. Now he wanted to weave more drama into such events. So, instead of just the aeronaut soaring aloft, he would carry an exotic passenger – someone famous, perhaps. Or, in the absence of the genuine article, some notable character invented by Arnold.

Hence the story of the tragic widow. Poor young woman – so beautiful, so wealthy, so sad. No trace of a smile had appeared on her lips since her husband, Count Beaunouvel, had been tragically drowned at sea during the French war. Recently, however, entranced by the sight of the balloon 'Venus' floating through the sky, she had offered its captain a diamond ring from her finger if he would allow her to join him in his next aerial flight.

Such a romantic assignation – but not exactly solitary. For advertisements had already enticed several thousands to buy tickets to watch the couple's ascent from Bedminster cricket ground in early June.

'There, I've arranged everything,' Mirella announced triumphantly, dumping her packages on the table in the wagon and flinging herself down on a chair to ease off her shoes.

There was no reaction from Levic.

'Did you hear what I said? I think I've managed everything. I'm collecting the costume on Friday evening. The woman said she'd have it finished by then. And what do you think? I settled on a riding habit in black velvet – you know, the sort of thing Dorina wears for haute ecole in the ring, and I think it's going to look just right. Can you imagine?'

'Yes. It sounds fine,' Levic mumbled.

'And I'm going to have a silk topper swathed with a length of black voile. And a very full skirt with a matching bodice edged with satin braid. With the bodice coming down – here!' she declared, standing up and gesturing at her lower midriff. 'Do look, Levic. It will come down to a point – here! Like a Tudor costume, see? But with a high stand-up collar. And I'll wear a brooch at my throat. Something rich but tasteful. Well, what do you think? Levic! Are you listening? Tell me what you think then.'

She flopped back on to the chair.

'I told you. It sounds fine.'

'Is that all you can say? It's taken me all morning to do this. I've had to buy new petticoats and gloves and boots, but I'm sure they're going to be worth it because the design of the riding habit . . . Levic, is something wrong?'

She stopped, suddenly aware how her voice seemed to be echoing as if talking to herself in an empty wagon. She peered at Levic, sitting just a couple of feet from her, apparently deaf to everything she had just said.

'What? Nothing wrong,' he muttered. 'Go on. You were just telling me you've decided to wear something black.'

'Yes, but I also said . . . oh, forget it! I can see you're not interested.'

She felt acutely disappointed. She had come home so pleased with her morning's work, longing to share her triumph with Levic, so sure he would be impressed by her choices, and here he was – utterly indifferent. Still, she thought, he was against the whole idea of the Monster Fête. That was probably the cause of his bad mood. Unless there was something else bothering him, such as . . . Yes, of course.

'Levic,' she ventured, 'I think I know what's on your mind and there's really no need for you to worry about me.' Seeing him visibly jump, she hastened to add: 'It will be all right. I promise you it will.'

'Mirella!' Slowly he shook his head while at the same time keeping his gaze fixed on her imploringly. 'Mirella, what can I say?'

'Nothing. There's nothing *to* say. I know how you feel about Saturday, but I can't give it up, Levic. Not now. I just can't. All I can say is, I have absolute faith in Captain Ewens and I know he won't take any risks. On the other hand, I can't bear to see you worried like this, so if it's any consolation I won't commit myself to anything in future that you think is dangerous.'

She was pleased to see the effect of her words. Levic's face had noticeably brightened.

'Your balloon trip,' he muttered. Then, quickly, as if the words cost him a great effort: 'Yes, well, naturally I don't like the idea of your going up in a balloon. But if that's what you want to do, then of course you must do it. I shan't try to stop you.'

She leant forward and flung her arms round his neck.

'Thank you, love. Believe me, I'd never have taken it on if I'd known how much it would worry you.'

Levic said no more on the subject, and Mirella, suspecting from his quiet mood that he was trying to disguise his anxiety, decided that the less fuss she made about Saturday's event the better. Nevertheless, as the day drew near, she found it increasingly difficult to suppress her excitement.

'Yes, yes. This will make an excellent launch site,' Captain Ewens announced, surveying the cricket field. 'We'll take off just over there, using the trees as a wind-break.'

Mirella looked admiringly at the tall, rugged aeronaut. He was certainly striking – with his sun-bleached hair and curly reddish beard that put her in mind of a young Viking, except that he was dressed, not in skins, but a belted tweed travelling suit. She was trying to assess his age – probably in his early thirties, she guessed – when he turned and asked: 'Are you sure you've got a head for heights?'

'If I haven't, I'd better find myself another profession,' she laughed. 'Didn't Mr Foreman tell you I'm a rope-dancer?'

'Of course, of course. How stupid of me!' he said, rapping his hand against his forehead. 'Well, we shouldn't have any trouble once we're air-borne then. In fact, I make bold enough to suggest you're the type who'll be over the moon with the experience. You're not at all worried about our enterprise, are you?' he asked, his mood suddenly serious.

'Good lord, no. I've seen lots of balloons taking off – at Crystal Palace and Cremorne and various pleasure gardens – and I've always envied the people going up in them, so to have this chance today is wonderful. I only hope I make a good passenger and don't do anything daft or get in your way.'

'Don't worry, you won't do that. I'm only too pleased to have your company,' he said, his blue eyes twinkling as if he meant it.

At last it was time for take off. The crowds had gathered and 'Venus' had been inflated with hydrogen gas until she was full and round and tugging at her anchor to be away. Mirella, dressed in her sombre finery and accorded all the respect due to her assumed rank, was driven out to the balloon in Arnold Foreman's private carriage.

'Here, I almost forgot. Better take this now!' he whispered, prodding his fingers into his waistcoat pocket and extracting the ring.

'Oh, right. I'd better put it on straight away, so let's hope it fits. Ah, yes. A little loose, but I think it will stay on.' Mirella slid the ring on to her middle finger and squinted at it appreciatively. 'It looks good. A bit too glittery, otherwise it could pass as real.'

'It *is* real,' he hissed. 'And worth a mint. So make sure the bugger hands it back as soon as the show's over.'

Climbing on to a little step-ladder, she jumped down into the wickerwork basket, landing next to the bags of ballast and being steadied by several pairs of hands, including Levic's.

'Now, take care, my love,' he whispered, and there was something about his tone that made her feel uneasy. She

70

looked into his face, struck by its unusual pallor. Dear Levic, fancy his being worried by a simple adventure like this. He never reacted so badly to her rope-walking and that was often much more risky. She had done her best to reassure him, but these last few days he had been pale and tense and not sleeping well, at times appearing to be on the point of saying something, but biting it back. Still, if he had been tempted to dissuade her from making this ascent, she was glad he had avoided presenting any sort of ultimatum.

'Of course,' she replied, surreptitiously squeezing his hand, careful not to betray more obvious signs of affection in front of newspapermen and the crowd.

The panorama as they rose took her breath away. Usually when she mounted aloft she looked down on a world little bigger than a circle bisected by her rope. Now, as the trees dropped away and the waving figures diminished, she found herself surveying everything stretching to the horizon: small clustering villages, farms nestling in valleys, stately houses standing proud on prominent hill tops, and shining ribbons of rivers threading their way through the fields.

Used as she was to the silence of the rope, the silence of the sky surrounding them still astounded her. Apart from the creaking of the basket, there was only the silence – a silence which, she was glad to realise, Captain Ewens appreciated too.

'You see,' he confided after a good few minutes, 'how magical it is up here. You watch – the higher we go, the more our perspective will change until we gain completely new slants on the world.'

'Yes, I know what you mean,' Mirella sighed. 'It's so peaceful up here. As if everything's slowing down to a more natural pace and making me realise how much I fill my life with unnecessary rush all the time.'

'Yes,' he agreed, 'we all do that.'

'Not up here though,' she said dreamily.

'No, not up here. That's what I like about ballooning. It gives you time to enjoy the world without feeling the need to influence things all the time.'

'But you have to study the air-currents, don't you?'

'Yes. But there's little we can do to influence even our direction. Up here our destiny is written on the wind.'

'And how do we tell which way the wind is blowing?' she asked, gazing up into the empty sky above.

'By looking down at the world we've just escaped from. Look, there! You see the smoke coming from those chimneys? That tells you which way the wind is blowing. And the washing on that clothes' line, look. And you might notice the breeze rippling over fields of corn or waves on lakes.'

'Yes, I see what you mean.'

She stared, fascinated by the balloon's distorted shadow floating across a meadow below, feeling at peace with all the world.

Everything down there looked so . . . right.

She pictured Levic, trying to pick up his thoughts as he stood in one of those distant fields below watching her drift gradually out of sight.

And Steffi, what on earth would he make of seeing his mother floating in the sky? He'd no doubt be jumping up and down with excitement. And, oh! she so wished he could be down there waiting for her when she landed.

Together – she, Levic and Steffi, that's how she wanted it to be when she landed. They must come together as a family without wasting more precious time. It was so obvious. Everything was very clear when seen from this height and perspective. Everything seemed easy when she was moving on the wind and meeting no resistance.

Suddenly the atmosphere began to change, the air becoming colder, cleaner and thinner, the shadows on the ground below gradually losing contrast until the whole landscape took on a shrouded, hazy appearance and the basket was swallowed up in cloud. Mirella had moments of doubt. What if something was going wrong – an accident, an almighty explosion followed by the sensation of plunging to her death? Levic, Steffi – never to see them again. No, not possible. Neither life nor death could be that cruel.

'Are you okay?'

The sound of Captain Ewens' voice, distorted and amplified by the clammy mist, startled her but she was grateful for the warm touch of his hand on her arm.

'Yes. Fine.'

'We'll be through this lot in a moment and then you'll probably need your veil to protect your eyes.'

He was right. Emerging above the low cloud layer, she found

herself suddenly dazzled as the mass of white foam reflected the sun's brilliance back into the deep blue.

'Oh, this is so beautiful,' she breathed.

'Like you, my dear,' Captain Ewens purred, dropping his former light bantering tone.

A moment later and he had his arm about her shoulders drawing her towards him.

'How dare you!' she snarled, struggling to get free.

'Easily, my dear. What harm is there in a kiss when there's no one to see? Besides, normal rules don't apply when you're up in the sky with a fellow, dependent on him and his balloon to get you safely down,' he chuckled.

Mirella was too angry to feel frightened by his words.

'You touch me and you'll regret it.'

'Come now, what's so special about you that you can't be kissed, eh? You're not a real countess, remember. Only a circus artiste, so don't feign airs and graces with me.'

His tone had turned sour, and when he made another attempt to press his lips on hers she kicked out with her boot, catching him on the shin and sending him lurching backwards.

'Why, you little spitfire! You can't do that sort of thing up here,' he yelled. 'Remember where you are.'

'And you remember where you'll be when you get down,' she warned. 'It won't be that easy to explain how you lost your passenger.'

Whereupon, ignoring the jerking and juddering of the basket, she started to climb up on to its edge.

'Get down!' he yelled. 'Before you bring us to grief.'

'You've already done that,' she retorted.

'Get down, you crazy woman.'

'Not till you've apologised.'

'But I didn't do anything. You didn't give me chance.'

'Apologise,' she screamed. 'You insulted me and ruined this lovely flight. You'll apologise or go back down without me. I'm not joking.'

'All right, all right. I apologise. Now calm down and help me get this balloon back into balance, for Christ's sake.'

She smiled to herself then, and stood with her back to him, aware of his panicky breathing as he worked to restore stability.

Soon they were plunging downwards again, enveloped in a haze of crystals which shimmered and sparkled before fusing into a damp, cold mist. Then the first blurry colours of the countryside became visible and she knew they were returning to earth.

Landing was far worse than coming down with a bump. First she was jolted out of her senses while the basket was dragged across the ground and then, once the rip cord had been pulled and the balloon collapsed, she found herself ignominiously rolled on to the grass like a rag doll tipped out of a toy-box.

There was only one compensation. As she stood recovering her breath and trying to get her bearings, she recognised that among the group of figures on horseback rushing to greet her was Levic.

Chapter 9

'But what am I going to do, Levic? What am I going to do?' She was quite distraught, her dark eyes wide and staring.

'Nothing,' he said.

'I can't just do nothing. You don't understand. He trusted me and I let him down.'

'Oh, come on. Don't be so melodramatic. It's not that bad.'

'It is!'

'Nonsense. You've got things completely out of perspective. The important thing is, you're back safe in my arms and that's all that matters. The rest can go to blazes.'

'No,' she moaned, 'it's all very well for you to say that. You're not the one with the problem.'

Mirella was right, of course. And he was probably wrong to dismiss the matter so lightly.

'Come on, let's go through the situation again then. You say you definitely had the ring on your finger when you climbed into the basket?'

'Yes.'

'Sure?'

'Yes. It was a bit loose even on my middle finger, so I kept touching it with my thumb to make sure it was there.'

'Right. So, if it fell off during the flight, you'd expect it to turn up in the bottom of the basket.'

'But it definitely wasn't there. Captain Ewens and I searched thoroughly after we landed.'

'Yes, I saw you.'

Levic remembered his annoyance when, after all his exertions as a member of the recovery crew, he arrived at the spot where the balloon came down only to find that Mirella, after her initial delight at seeing him, refused to leave the scene before she had mounted a search for some damn' ring.

'You see, I only noticed it had gone when I had to present it to the Captain.'

'But none of that mattered by then. You didn't forget you were shamming, did you?'

'Of course not. But when I saw you, I thought there might have been some newspapermen with you so I wanted to be ready.'

'Okay, so you looked at your hand and the ring wasn't there. What did you do then?'

'I looked on the ground. Then I told Captain Ewens because, like you, I thought it was bound to be in the basket and I didn't want that moved before I'd a chance to search it properly.'

'But it wasn't.'

'No,' she wailed, 'and the only thing I can think is that it fell out of the balloon in mid-flight, which means we'll never find it.'

'Oh, come on, that's hardly likely, is it? Not unless you were waving your hand frantically over the edge, or doing something equally stupid. And you weren't, were you?' he asked, surprised to see her look suddenly sheepish.

'No.'

She did not sound very sure.

'Well,' he said, 'there is another possibility. Ewens could have pocketed it after it fell off your finger.'

'No, I don't think he'd do anything like that. In fact,' she slowly admitted, 'I'm pretty sure now that the ring could have dropped overboard when we were way up above the clouds, because there was a moment when I was sort of . . . waving my arms about . . .'

'Yes, I can imagine you getting excited about being so high,' he agreed, happy to think the mystery solved. 'Besides, I agree with you. Captain Ewens is too much of a gentleman to stoop to thieving, even if tempted by a diamond ring.'

'Ye-es,' she said cautiously.

Unfortunately Mirella continued to fret about the ring, demanding to know what he thought it was worth and how they were ever going to raise the money to pay for its replacement.

'The worst thing is,' she muttered, 'it may well have had enormous sentimental value for Arnold – something that used to be worn by his wife possibly – and then no amount of money will compensate for its loss.'

'In that case, you just remind him whose idea it was to send you up in a ruddy balloon wearing his precious diamond. As you know, I was against the idea from the start. Circus is circus and, if done properly, should be enough in itself to attract people without throwing in all these cheap-jack tricks.'

'But it was a good stunt.'

'True,' he agreed, trying to cheer her up. 'And Arnold is so pleased with the way you carried it off he might well overlook the fact that the ring has been lost. In fact, he might even have forgotten he gave it to you.'

'Hmm, fine chance of that. He doesn't hand out diamond rings every day.'

At that moment the pony and trap carrying them back to Bedminster turned in at the cricket field, bringing their conversation to an end. While Mirella slipped off to change her costume to avoid being recognised as the spurious countess, Levic wandered over to the stable tent to check on the horses – in a way glad of this latest drama because, though upsetting for Mirella, it gave him an excuse to put off telling her about Dorina.

Oh my God, that was a situation which did not bear thinking about!

He had promised Dorina that he would tell Mirella at the first opportunity. Not before the balloon flight, of course. That would have been too cruel, with Mirella so elated about the project, but afterwards . . . And now it was afterwards, and Mirella was so worried about losing the ring that he could not bring himself to upset her further. Besides, he needed more time to think.

Surely it would be better for everyone concerned if Dorina presented the child to the world as her husband's? If only Matty could be persuaded to agree, of course. But why should he? Why would any man consent to that sort of arrangement? Unless . . . Unless he could be convinced that it was in his own best interests. Or those of his family!

Now there was an idea! Matty might be drunk half the time, but he was a fond father who would want to protect his daughters. So if Levic took him aside – went out with him for a quiet drink, perhaps – and confessed the awful truth, he could then put it to Matty, man to man, that it was up to him to avoid a scandal.

It would be bloody hard trying to explain, of course. God

knows how he would react. But once Levic got round to stressing what harm the exposure of their mother's adultery would do to Rosa and Amy, this might persuade Matty to hush the matter up.

It seemed a forlorn hope, but anything was worth a try.

The big tent was up – striped red and white like a huge humbug dropped on Hereford race-course – and the parade about to start.

Mirella jumped down the wagon steps, with one hand struggling to fix a comb in her hair to keep it from straggling from under her gilded helmet. It was one of those days when everything was rush. She had done some washing this morning – for once they had pulled on to a tober where there was enough space for the lines to be strung at a discreet distance from the tent. She had also been into the town for shopping. But that had left barely enough time for her and Levic to snatch a bite to eat before getting ready for the Parade.

'Levic,' she called, 'are you coming? The wagons are in line and nearly everyone's out there – except for the band, of course. God only knows where they've got to again. Levic, I said, are you coming?'

It was unlike him to lag behind.

Normally Levic would be first man out, checking the carriages and bandwagon to make sure all was spick and span, helping to wind up the tableau wagon and bolt its upper tiers in place so that she herself would have a secure perch in the parade.

His mood was strange today, though. He had hardly exchanged more than a dozen words with her over lunch. It could be that he was sickening for something, or perhaps Matty had upset him. Because, now she came to think about it, Levic had been looking grey about the gills when he came home after drinking with him in the Market Tavern last night. And as for Matty! Well, three sheets to the wind wasn't in it – he'd been seven seas and nine oceans under!

The parade was not a great success. Quite a few people stood along Grandstand Road, cheering their progress, but by the time they reached the city proper, the grey skies had dissolved into a thin drizzle which put a complete damper on proceedings.

Mirella, stuck up high on her throne as Britannia flanked by a lion and a lamb, hugged her cloak round her shoulders trying to cover as much of her flimsy robe as possible, while at the same time aware how irritable the animals were growing. Not the lion so much. Dear old Felix was too dozy to be bothered by a little rain, but the ram currently being used to impersonate the lamb hated the wet and kept working off his temper by butting his horns into her knee until she felt like poking him back with her trident.

It was a relief when, just as they were approaching the cathedral square, a downpour signalled the moment to abandon the struggle and make for home.

'Well, that was a bloomin' washout,' she called to Levic who, in clown costume, had been riding back-to-front on a pony most of the way but now turned around so that he could speed back to the tober.

'Yes, King Parney reigns today all right. Are you okay up there, or do you want me to help you down?'

'No,' she yelled, 'I'll sit it out till we get back. But don't you linger. Go on ahead and get changed.'

'No,' he shouted, peering anxiously up at her. 'I'm going to keep pace with you.'

'But there's no point in our both getting wet,' she remonstrated.

Taking not a blind bit of notice, he dropped back to follow the tableau until it reached the racecourse. Then he rushed ahead to organise the tentmen to come and wind down her platform so that she could descend without delay.

Once back in the wagon she lost no time in undressing and draping her sodden costume along the mantelpiece in the hope of getting it dry.

'A-a-a-tchoo!'

'So that's it. You *have* got a cold. I thought you weren't looking too well this morning.'

'No, it's not a proper cold,' Levic said. 'It's just the damp creeping into my bones. I'll be all right once I get warm.'

'Well, pull all these wet things off then,' she suggested, tugging at his breeches.

'I can't. They've stuck to me,' he muttered.

'What do you mean? Oh, come on, stop clowning around,' she laughed, slipping her hands round his waist and easing the damp cloth away from his skin.

79

'See? They are stuck and I'm going to need you to ease them off me,' he whispered, pulling her close and showering her hair with kisses. She felt his hands sliding downwards caressing her, pressing her against him so that she could feel the hardness struggling to thrust into her.

'Levic, I must get out of the rest of my wet things.'

'Yes, all of them,' he readily agreed, his hands fumbling with the fastenings on her petticoats, threatening to rip them. For a moment they drew apart to skin off their underclothes. Then she, shivering, let him half-lift her into the bed and cuddle his heat into her body.

'My beautiful darling, I love you, I love you,' he murmured into her ear, as his hands smoothed and stroked her skin, moving from her throat to her breasts to her buttocks and then into her, fondling and caressing until she yearned for him.

'Levic, I love you,' she sighed.

He came right into her then, pulling back and plunging, pulling and plunging – until everything in her seemed to rise and ride with him.

'Oh, Levic.' Nuzzled comfortably against him, her limbs entwining his body as easily as if it was her own, loving the feel of his sweat on her skin, his breath on her face, she realised how he must have smudged her with his greasepaint. 'Do you realise, you've still got your make-up on?'

'Yes, I know I have,' he said, frowning.

'Well, it doesn't matter. I can wash off all the marks.'

'Yes.'

He sounded quite down-hearted.

'I mean, even on the sheets. I can get it all off, so don't worry about it,' she urged.

'I'm not worried about the sheets. I was thinking about us, Mirella.'

'Yes?'

'And . . . and . . . there's something I want to say.'

'Go on then,' she crooned, snuggling up closer.

'What I want to say is . . . Well, before I say it, I want to say something else.'

'Yes?'

'And that is . . . I love you.'

'And I love you,' she sighed.

'Then whatever happens, we must hold on to each other, Mirella. We must never let anything come between us, do you hear?' His grip on her arm became so tight, it was painful, but she did not have the heart to protest.

'Of course not, Levic, but what . . .'

Before she could finish her question, there was a hammering on the wagon door, and a man's voice shouting, 'Levic? Are you there?'

'Yes,' he answered, already halfway out of bed and grabbing his trousers. 'I'm here. What is it?'

'And your missus?'

'Yes, she's just changing into some dry clothes, else I'd let you in. What is it, Jerry?' he asked, recognising the voice of one of the grooms.

'Mr Foreman wants you. Over in the big tent.'

'Does it have to be right now?'

'Yep, as soon as you can make it.'

'Why, what's up?'

'Search me. All I know is, he's got something to say, and wants you over there pronto.'

'Yes, but . . .'

Mirella knew it was no use Levic's trying to find out more, because she heard Jerry's boots clattering down the steps as he stomped away. Besides, she could guess what this summons was about.

'Oh, God, what am I going to say to him, Levic?' she groaned, sliding out of bed to drag some fresh clothes out of a locker.

'There's no need for you to say anything. In fact, there's no need for you to come over at all,' he said. 'Just leave it to me to see what Arnold wants.'

'I think I know what he wants. He's remembered that blasted ring.'

'No, I don't think it's that,' Levic said, obviously trying to calm her fears. 'You stay where you are, and I'll tell him you're still drying your hair after the storm.'

'No, don't do that. I'd rather face him and get it over with. Anyway, I don't think it's fair to involve you in my problems.'

'Don't be silly. Remember what I was saying before Jerry interrupted: no matter what happens, we face the music together, you and I. You do agree about that, don't you, Mirella?'

'Yes, but I don't want you to get into trouble on my account,' she said, his unwavering support making her all the more determined to sort the situation out before it caused them both further anxiety.

The rain had cleared now but to reach the big tent they had to press past her forgotten line of washing and the sight of all their clothes drooping and dripping did nothing to lift her spirits.

'Here's Levic and Mirella. Good, that's nearly everyone now!' Arnold exclaimed as they entered the tent and found to their surprise practically the whole company assembled there. 'Come on, you two. Help yourselves to a bloody drink. I want glasses filled for my announcement, and after the soaking you all got this afternoon I thought now was as good a time to make it as any. Two birds with one stone then: celebration and medication, see?'

He was dressed in his usual black frock coat and brandished a bottle of something expensive, and by the way his eyes shone, his cheeks and bald pate glowed and his chest was puffed out, presented a picture of self-satisfaction.

Thank God, Mirella thought, this can't have anything to do with the ring.

'Right, now you're all gathered, I want you to hear our good news. Dorina, my love, and Matty . . . Wait a minute, where's Matty? Come on, son, don't be shy. You've been through this before. Remember how we wetted the heads of the first two as soon as we knew they were on their way, and this time – with the help of the Lord! –' he murmured, casting his gaze up into the big top as if challenging an artiste to give anything less than his best '– it will be a boy. I feel it in my bones. So, I'm asking you now, ladies and gentlemen, please raise your glasses and drink to the health of my darling daughter Dorina, and to Matty, of course, and to my future grandchild, probable heir to Foreman's circus.'

'To Dorina and Matty!'

Mirella joined in the toast, surprised at this public announcement of a condition usually regarded as too delicate to be the subject of polite conversation. But then the Foremans were famous for their attempts to ape royalty.

Dorina did not seem too happy, though. Her eyes looked as bleary as if she had sobbed herself to sleep last night. And maybe she had. For now Mirella came to think of it, Matty must have been a trial when he arrived home with Levic. In fact . . . Of course! Now it was clear why they had both drunk so much. They had been celebrating!

Funny that Levic had not mentioned the baby, though! But

that just showed how little interest men took in such things – except as an excuse for a drink.

'Poor Dorina doesn't look very happy,' she murmured to Levic. 'Do you think she's worried about her horses? I mean, I suppose she'll have to give up working them, won't she?'

'Probably,' he grunted, giving her a further clue to his silence of the night before.

Poor Levic! The horses meant so much to him too, and he depended on Dorina to help work them. Still, he would soon get over his disappointment and it surely *was* good news that Dorina was with child, even though the two people most concerned seemed not yet convinced. Indeed, Dorina was looking sick and weary of the whole business, and as for Matty – his expression had her foxed. She had often seen him glassy-eyed after a heavy drinking session, but at the moment he looked like an animal brought to bay.

Which reminded her.

'Levic, do you think I ought to go and confess?'

'Confess what?'

'About the ring, of course.'

'The ring?' he repeated, having apparently forgotten all about it.

'Yes, Arnold's diamond ring. I know now might not be the best moment, but if I don't tell him soon the worry will make me ill.'

'If he cuts up rough it will leave you more worried,' he muttered, his attention elsewhere.

She would have argued further had not Dorina suddenly appeared. Smiling, Mirella moved forward to hug and congratulate her, only to find herself kept at arm's length.

'Yes, well, I'm glad you're pleased at the announcement,' Dorina said, avoiding Mirella's eyes and fixing a strange stare on Levic.

Ah, she realises how disappointed Levic feels about the horses, Mirella concluded, leaving them to have a private discussion, as both seemed to want to talk.

Now should she or shouldn't she? It was such a difficult decision.

There was Arnold, standing with his back against one of the quarter-poles, puffing on a huge cigar, enjoying his triumph. Surely it would be criminal to spoil his mood? And yet there was always some good reason to put off the evil moment – the packing up, the journey, the build-up, the show. In fact there never was a perfect moment to present bad news.

'Arnold,' she ventured.

'Come on, my lady, drink up.' He took his cigar out of his mouth and beamed at her. 'I heard you got drenched on the bloody tableau, but I know you're too much of a trouper to complain. Still, I appreciate your spirit, Mirella. A thing like that don't go unnoticed on my show, you know.'

'Thank you, Arnold,' she muttered, playing for time by adding, 'and I want to say how pleased I am with Dorina's news.'

'Yes,' he smirked, studying the solid ash rimming his cigar.

She took a deep breath. Now was as good a moment as any.

'Arnold,' she stuttered, 'there's something I've got to say.'

'No, don't tell me,' he said, squinting anxiously at her. 'You've gone and done it too. Blast! It will be bad enough losing my equestrienne without my bloody rope-dancer as well.'

'No, no. It's not that.'

'No? Thank God! Phew! You gave me a nasty turn, I don't mind telling you. So what is it then, Mirella?'

Too late to change her mind, she blurted out how she had lost the ring.

When she finished, Arnold Foreman stood looking completely nonplussed. Obviously holding his temper in check, he gazed into her eyes and calmly asked 'So what do you intend to do about it, my dear?'

She had to swallow hard before making her reply.

'There's not much I can do except apologise and offer to pay for it. I mean, I don't know how much it was worth, but I'll raise the money somehow.'

'Yes, I'll expect you to pay for it,' he declared. 'Every bloody penny it cost.'

His tone annoyed her. It was as if he doubted her ability to make full reparation. Well, she would show him.

'In fact, I was about to suggest,' his tinny voice continued, 'that I hold back your wages – and Levic's as well – until the debt has been cleared.'

She felt her cheeks beginning to flare, but pride forbade her to protest.

'All right,' she muttered grimly. 'But how much are we talking about to settle the debt?'

'Hmm!' He drew on his cigar, squeezing his eyes shut so that he could concentrate on the calculation.

'A tanner?' he suggested at last.

'No, I mean seriously, what was the ring worth?'

'Well, that's difficult,' he explained. 'You see, I paid a man a bob for it three weeks ago and I don't know what the rates of depreciation are for brass and paste.'

'Brass and paste! But you said . . .'

'Just brass and paste, my dear. You don't think I'd trust a bloody scoundrel like Ewens with anything really precious, do you?'

'You entrusted him with me,' she glowered.

Chapter 10

Steffi could hardly contain his excitement. He was on his way to join his parents, to spend six whole weeks – the length of his summer holidays – travelling with them. And as the carrier's cart trundled along the dusty roads towards Oxford he took little notice of the scenery, his mind being too busy with thoughts of what he might find at the end of the journey.

'Ah, there she is!' the carrier mumbled without taking the pipe from his mouth. 'There's your circus, lad!'

'Where?'

'Over there, look. See the big tent?'

'Oh, yes.'

He tried not to show his disappointment. Built up in the corner of a field near the railway station, it did not look nearly as impressive as Mirella had led him to expect.

Once he had been deposited with his luggage outside the gate and begun to walk across, however, the big top grew with every step he took until he was forced to stop and stare at it in wonder.

Its sides were striped pink and white like seaside candy and it had a red top with a flag fluttering from its pinnacle. But what really impressed him was the showfront, a huge glossy painting stretching over the entrance picturing a lady walking a rope high above the tree-tops while a bevy of clowns and exotic animals – elephants, camels, zebras and horses cavorted below. Steffi liked that, especially as the rope-dancer bore more than a passing resemblance to Mirella.

But mingled with his excitement at this discovery was the return of all his old doubts. This world that existed under the banner of 'Foreman's Grand Royal Circus' made him feel suddenly very small and excluded. So much so that if in those first moments he could have turned and run back to Liddy, he would have done so. But, as he reminded himself, Liddy would not be at home. She had gone on her holidays too and was spending the summer with Mirella's parents in Windsor.

Besides, the carrier's cart had already disappeared up the road.

'Steffi, Stef-fi!'

He spun round to see his mother emerge from a yellow wagon and come rushing to greet him. She must have been on the lookout even though Liddy had not been able to provide her with the exact time of his arrival.

Steffi took several steps towards her before brought to a halt by a sudden roaring noise from the tent – a blare of music so loud it seemed as if the whole structure was about to tear itself from its moorings and float away on the sound.

So that's where everyone is, he thought, having been puzzled by the empty tober. He longed to rush into the tent and see what was happening, but his mother clearly had other plans.

'So here you are at last! Did you have a nice journey?' She flung her arms around him and hugged him tight. 'Come on, let me carry one of those bags.'

'No, they're not heavy.'

Too late. She had already seized one.

'That's our wagon. Over there, look. Hungry?' She gave him no chance to mention the enormous packed lunch Liddy had insisted on giving him for the road. 'I hope so, because I've got a huge tea waiting. Oh, Steffi, you've grown so big I hardly recognised you,' she said, her eyes devouring him.

Mirella, he was glad to see, looked exactly the same as he remembered – with her long black hair piled up in curls on her head and wearing a beautiful flowing gown over her costume.

Goodness! So she must either just have come down from her tightrope or be about to do her act! Now he felt dreadful for having arrived at the wrong time.

'Are you in the middle of the show?' he asked, whispering as if afraid even out here he might be accused of getting in the way and disturbing the performance.

'Yes. It's the three o'clock, but nearly over now.'

'So that's why there's no one about.'

'That's right. Everyone's out back, getting ready for the finale.'

By now they had walked to the rear of the tent where most of the wagons were parked. Here several people in costume were milling around in the backyard behind a smaller tent which was linked to the big top and he could hear harness jingling and lots of shuffling and snuffling of animals. Mirella took no notice of this, but led him to the yellow wagon and threw open the door.

'Have you done your act?' he asked anxiously.

'Yes. Mine was in the first half. So all I've got to do now is the finale. And I might give that a miss. After all, it's not every day my favourite son comes to stay, is it?'

He hid his embarrassment by glancing round the caravan. This was the first time he had seen it and he was fascinated by all the shiny mirrors on the panels and the brass angels holding up the oil lamps. And he liked the vase of white marguerites on the mantelpiece above the stove. For some strange reason they reminded him of Apsley's and prompted him to ask: 'Are the girls here?'

'The girls?'

'Yes. Rosa and Amy. I wondered if they'd be spending their holidays here too.'

'Not the whole holidays, but they are down at the moment for a couple of days. Arrived yesterday.'

'But only for two days?' He could not keep the disappointment from his voice.

'Yes. Just for Rosa's birthday.'

'I didn't know it was her birthday.'

'You would have done if you'd been near Arnold during these past few weeks,' Mirella laughed. 'He's bought her something special, you see, and plans to make a grand presentation of it after the show tonight.'

'What has he bought her?'

'Ah, now that would be telling,' his mother teased.

Steffi was half-excited, half-disappointed at the news. He had been so looking forward to seeing the sisters again, but a couple of days – that gave them no time at all!

'Did Rosa and Amy know I was coming today?' he asked.

'Oh, yes. They were hanging about the gate all morning until Dorina called them in to help with the horses.'

Hearing this made Steffi feel better. It was nice to think the girls were as keen to see him as he them. And even if they did have only a few hours together, they could use them to explore the tober and make plans for future, possibly longer visits.

'So where are they now?' he asked, craning his neck to peer out of the caravan window.

'Watching the show I should think. Why? Do you want to go and join them?'

As his mother spoke, there came a burst of band music from the big tent and another roar from the crowd.

'Come on, let's go over then,' Mirella smiled. 'I can see you're dying to see what's happening.'

Of course his mother was right and it was with a sense of growing excitement that he followed her through the artistes' entrance and sank down on the nearest bench. There was a clown in the ring doing some juggling, but Steffi spared him scarcely a glance once Mirella had pointed out two dim figures sitting in the front row and whispered: 'There they are! That's Rosa and Amy!'

'Poor you, fancy having to stay here all summer.' Rosa immediately started to commiserate with him after the show.

'I wouldn't mind. It could be fun,' Amy murmured in a quiet voice which her sister ignored.

'I know I'd just *hate* it,' Rosa continued.

'But why?' Steffi asked, puzzled by the older girl's tone.

'Because I'd get so *bored*.'

'Oh, I'm sure you wouldn't. There's lots of games we could play, like . . .

Rosa shot him a withering look.

'I'm not a child any more, you know,' she said. 'I'm thirteen.'

'Only just,' he protested, smarting under her rebuff. 'Besides, when I said "games", I didn't mean kids' games.'

'What did you mean then?' Rosa asked, examining her fingernails.

'Well, I suppose I meant . . .' Steffi paused, trying to think how best to describe what he had in mind to someone already thirteen.

'We could explore all the new places and muck around with the animals,' Amy suggested excitedly.

And Steffi was about to applaud these ideas when he caught sight of Rosa's expression and quickly checked his enthusiasm.

'No, that sort of thing would be too childish,' he announced, uncomfortably aware of the effect his words were having on Amy, who was quite crestfallen.

He was amazed by how much Rosa had changed since Christmas. She seemed so suddenly grown up – taller and less podgy and her mouth much redder than it used to be. Steffi

90

admired the way she looked though, and wanted to hear what Rosa liked doing for fun, but was afraid to ask in case she snubbed him.

As for Amy, he had not known how to look her in the face when they met and kept his eyes averted whenever they talked so that he would not hurt her by appearing to stare at her scar.

'Rosa, come up here, will you? And you, Amy. Time to get ready!' Dorina's voice interrupted their discussion.

'We'd better go,' Rosa said, 'Ma's promised to do my hair in a special style for this evening. And I've got a lovely new riding outfit to wear. Pink with a gorgeous silk topper to match . . .'

'Rosa! Are you coming, or aren't you?' Dorina called again, sounding cross.

'Come on. Ma's waiting,' Amy urged. 'And there's something she wants to tell us, remember? See you this evening, Steffi.'

'Oh, yes,' Steffi replied, without turning his eyes from Rosa. 'I'll be there.'

'Good. Then you can see me in my new outfit,' Rosa promised with a smile which left him feeling that he had been invited to a feast.

Once the girls had disappeared into their parents' wagon, time hung heavily on his hands until Mirella suggested a walk to the local confectioners to buy chocolates.

'If we say they're for someone's birthday, they'll wrap them nicely,' she said.

'Oh, yes. Rosa would like that,' he enthused.

'And we'll buy some for Amy as well.'

'But it's not her birthday,' he said without thinking.

'No, but I don't want her to feel left out, especially at the moment.'

'Why?'

'You saw Dorina, didn't you?'

'Yes.'

'And didn't you notice anything?' Mirella asked, peering at him under raised eyebrows.

He tried to picture Dorina as he had last seen her, clad in voluminous skirts and apron, standing on her wagon steps to call the girls. 'No,' he replied.

Mirella shook her head and tut-tutted, 'Well, I suppose that just goes to show.'

'Show what?' he asked, growing impatient.

'How little you youngsters see. I thought you'd be bound to notice that Mrs Scott is expecting another child.'

He looked at his mother with astonishment. Mrs Scott – Dorina – expecting another child! How was he supposed to know a thing like that? Should he have been able to tell from the expression on her face, or something? His mother went on to explain, 'That's why she looks so plump.'

'I see,' Steffi mumbled. 'I didn't even notice she was.'

'No, nor did the girls apparently. But Dorina intends to tell them about it this afternoon – which is why I'm talking to you now, so you don't get to hear it from them in the wrong way. Do you understand?'

He nodded in an effort to cover his confusion rather than to signify assent. 'Do you think Rosa and Amy will be pleased with the news?' he asked at last, thinking how *he* would love to have a baby brother or sister.

Mirella sighed. 'Who knows? If it's a boy, it might upset Rosa, because as the eldest girl she's had everything her own way up till now. On the other hand, Amy stands to lose her place as baby of the family whether it's a boy or girl.'

'I don't think she'd mind that,' Steffi said.

'Probably not. But you can never tell how youngsters will react to things,' Mirella said ominously.

And Steffi had cause to remember her words that evening in the midst of Rosa's birthday celebrations.

Just before the show ended, Arnold Foreman entered the ring and held up his hand for silence.

'Ladies and Gentlemen, boys and girls,' he announced in his squeaky voice, 'on behalf of the company of Foreman's Grand Royal Circus I wish to thank you for your patronage and share with you a special secret. Today is my granddaughter Rosa's thirteenth birthday.'

At this point Arnold smiled and spun round holding up his hand in a gesture which commanded a round of clapping, and Steffi, sitting next to Rosa, heard her gasp and murmur, 'Oh my! Do you think everyone knows it's me?'

Then, as the band struck up with the appropriate tune and the whole audience began to sing 'Happy Birthday' Arnold came over to where she was sitting and beckoned.

Rosa shook her head modestly before leaping up and proceeding to the centre of the ring where she stood looking delightfully demure in her new pink outfit. Whereupon there came a fanfare and in was led a splendid grey stallion.

As if on cue, Rosa swept her arms around her grandfather's neck and kissed him before being helped on to the back of her new horse. As she rode it twice around the ring to the cheers of the crowd, Steffi turned to Amy to say, 'What a wonderful surprise! Or do you think she guessed?' But the words stuck in his throat when he saw Amy leaning forward over the barrier with her head tilted to one side, lips slightly apart, and eyes full of yearning. 'Oh,' she was murmuring, 'isn't Rosa lucky? I'd love a horse like that!'

Then the show was over, but not the fun.

As soon as the tent was cleared of jossers, the company re-assembled to drink Rosa's health and continue the celebrations. There was music and a wooden floor laid down for dancing. A huge cake was carried in and presented to Rosa, who now sat holding court like a queen. Shyly Steffi took his chocolates up to her.

'Ooh, lovely,' she cooed, immediately tearing open their wrapping. 'Amy bought me chocolates too.'

'Where is she, by the way?' he asked, remembering the other present he had to give.

'Who?'

'Amy.'

'She's gone back with Ma, who's not feeling well.'

Intent on delivering his gift, Steffi strode straight across to the Scotts' living wagon. At the top of the steps he paused and was about to tap on the open door when he heard Amy's voice imploring, 'Don't cry, Ma. I'm sure there's no reason for you to be upset.'

Peering over the lower half of the door he glimpsed Dorina sitting in an armchair looking bleakly at her daughter, who was kneeling in front of her.

'In fact, I can't think of anything nicer than having a little baby in the family,' Amy was saying in a soothing voice.

Whereupon Dorina started to sob again and Steffi crept away, embarrassed by what he had seen.

Next morning the girls left for London on the early train without giving him a chance to ask why their mother had been so upset the night before – and without even giving him the chance to give Amy her chocolates.

* * *

After that Steffi settled into the routine of a travelling circus and life in his parents' wagon.

For something which looked so small on the outside, it was surprisingly big within, differing from most wagons by having its door positioned at the side rather than at the front where the shafts were fixed. This had enabled Levic to build in a separate bedroom for himself and Mirella – a bedroom which was just that, with no space for anything but a bed and tiny closet for their clothes.

Steffi slept in a bunk bed at the opposite end of the wagon, closed off from the rest of the world by wooden shutters to form a space like a ship's cabin. It even had its own small porthole giving a view of the tober so that he could lie in his bed in the morning and squint through the curtains to watch the earliest risers drinking tea, feeding the animals, inspecting the guys or performing one of their myriad tasks.

For he soon discovered that, just as at Apsley's, everyone on the tober was expected to make themselves useful – except that on a circus tober it proved much more difficult to find his bearings. It was such a busy, shouting, turbulent sort of place – full of men in rolled-up shirtsleeves yelling at one other, for the most part cheerfully enough but sometimes angry and using words new to Steffi. But what was worse, everyone out there seemed to know exactly what they were doing and worked with such fury that his own efforts to help caused more trouble than they were worth. Like when he tried to hand a pole to one of the tentmen who cursed him for getting in the way.

Fortunately, when he tried carrying buckets of water and loads of hay for the grooms, they were more appreciative so he began to confine himself to helping with the animals, especially Dorina's horses. And what was even more gratifying was that Levic encouraged him to help out in his own practice sessions.

'Look, Steffi, do you want to make yourself really useful?'

'Yes.'

'Come over to the tent then, and let me show you something.'

'What?'

'The mechanic.'

'The what?'

'The mechanic. Don't you know what that is?'

'No.'

'Well, I'm sure you would have seen one at Apsley's. It's a

kind of safety device I use when I'm practising some new riding trick.'

'Oh, yes. Of course,' Steffi puffed, lengthening his stride in an effort to keep up with his father's spritely gait as they made their way across the damp grass. 'I'd just forgotten what it was called.'

As soon as they entered the tent, Levic dragged out the mechanic, erected its central post and gave a trial push to its pivoting arm which carried a pulley and rope round the ring.

'Do you know how to work this?'

'Ye-es,' Steffi replied doubtfully, hoping Levic was not about to pin the harness on him and try to teach him some trick riding.

'Good. Well, come over here and let me show you properly and then you can help me practice.'

Steffi did as he was bid, sighing with relief.

'Right. In a moment I'm going to fasten this end of the rope to my belt, see? But I want you to hold tight to the other end. Got it?'

'Yes.'

'Okay. Try it. Hold that end tight, and then push the arm of the mechanic round the ring making sure you always keep the pulley well above the horse's quarters.'

'Like this?'

'That's right. Good lad, you're getting the idea. And now, if I do happen to slip, you should be able to take my weight.'

'And stop you hurting yourself?' Steffi asked, aware of the enormous responsibility and praying that he would manage it properly.

'That's right. But no need to look so worried. I shan't do anything hazardous till you know what you're doing.'

Steffi felt slightly more reassured.

'You won't be trying that backward flip you were telling me about?'

'No, certainly not. That needs Dorina to work the horses. I can't do that unless she's here.'

'I see,' Steffi said, recalling now how Levic had stressed that the two horses had to canter in exact unison before he could somersault from one to the other.

Once into the practice session, Steffi forgot his fears and found that what he was doing became fun. Concentrating on holding tight to the rope and pushing the wooden bar round the ring, he found himself completely absorbed in the act, almost as if he were doing the tricks himself. It could be him doing that single-knee balance, for instance – extending his left leg in a smooth arc from his body, foot outstretched – minutely adjusting his position to fit the rhythm of White Prince's gait, the rise and fall of his haunches. Yes, he could feel what you had to do and almost wished it was he who was doing it.

He was aware that someone had come in and was standing just behind him. It was tempting to look round to see who it was, but he was determined not to take his mind off the job in hand until Levic had safely dismounted.

'What do you think you're doing?'

Her voice made him jump so that he almost let go of the bar. Turning his head, he saw Dorina there looking cross.

'I'm helping,' he murmured.

'But that's my job you're doing,' she snapped.

'No. My father asked me . . .' he started to say. But, clearly uninterested, she was already looking past him towards Levic. 'Why is your son doing my job?'

Levic quickly dismounted and came over to her.

'He's just handling the mechanic.'

'I can see that. But you know I like doing that for you.'

'Yes, of course. But perhaps it's not such a good idea in the present circumstances,' Levic said solemnly, while giving her a strange glance which seemed to sweep down from her face towards her shoes.

Which drew Steffi's attention to the fact that, as his mother had said, Dorina had grown terribly plump and was moving around awkwardly as if ill at ease with her extra weight. He knew this must have something to do with the baby that was due to be born quite soon, but he could not understand why the prospect should make her so bad-tempered.

For Dorina certainly was bad-tempered, especially with Steffi, behaving altogether as if she resented his presence at Levic's practice sessions and was jealous of any attention his father gave him. Most odd, he thought. But only when he mentioned Rosa and Amy and met with such a rude rebuff did he think he had solved the mystery. His being there obviously reminded her of her daughters whom she badly missed.

That, Steffi thought, would account for her attitude.

* * *

Levic did his best to ease the strain between Dorina and Steffi, but with little success.

'It's not Steffi's fault,' he muttered during one of the furtive exchanges which had taken the place of their old friendly conversations.

'What isn't?'

'Our unhappy situation.'

'I know it isn't.'

'Well, you shouldn't take it out on him then,' he said – and was immediately sorry when he saw her face. She was not looking at all well, pale and drawn, and he had noticed how lethargic she had grown of late. 'I'm sorry, Dorina. I know what a trial this is for you.'

'Oh, Levic.'

She held out her hand but, aware of possible unseen eyes, he avoided her touch.

'No, Dorina. We must be careful.'

'Then perhaps we should avoid any sort of contact.'

'What do you mean?'

'I mean it might be better if I stopped having anything to do with you. I just . . . I just find it so hard, Levic,' she pleaded.

'But what about the horses? You know I still need your help,' he spluttered.

She stared at him in silence.

'I'm sorry. I now that sounds callous, but you did agree, Dorrie . . .'

'*You* need *my* help,' she said eventually through clenched teeth. 'My God, Levic, you've got a nerve!'

'Okay. I know it sounds selfish, but the trick's nearly there now. And with Steffi taking the strain on the mechanic . . . well, I thought it wasn't asking too much for you to work the horses. There's no one else I can ask,' he finished lamely.

She sighed. 'All right. If it means so much to you, I'll carry on with it. But while I do, remember I'm carrying this for you too.' She laid her hand on her stomach.

'I know, Dorrie.'

'All right, so long as you remember,' she said bitterly.

'Of course I remember. Don't you think it's every bit as hard for me as for you? But I see no point in going over and over the situation now that we've decided – all of us, me, you, Matty – how we're going to handle things.'

97

'Yes. I must grant you that, you and Matty got it nicely sorted out.'

He hoped to God she wasn't about to start the old argument again. They had already gone through it so many times. And when all was said and done, what could he do but promise Matty that he would quit the show and make sure that he and Mirella were well clear of the scene before Dorina's baby was born? The fact that this suited his own plans was mere co-incidence. He had promised it in order to win Matty's coopera-tion. Which seemed the least he could do. In fact, at the time he had offered to go immediately and it was only Dorina's insistence that such a course, besides threatening everyone's livelihood, might provoke awkward questions, that had made him agree to stay until the end of the season.

So it was no good Dorina putting all the blame on him for this present awkwardness. In some ways it was the result of her own determination to hold on to him as long as possible. But it suited him in so far as it gave him the opportunity to perfect the trick that he had for so long set his heart on.

Nevertheless it was a high price to pay. For in the two months since he had stood under the big top listening to Arnold's announcement, every day that passed had been purgatory. He could hardly wait to get away from Foreman's, and as far as he was concerned the sooner he mastered the backward somersault trick the better.

'Okay, son, haul it away now.'

'What, the mechanic?' Steffi said.

'Yes.'

'No, Levic. You're not ready yet,' Dorina was quick to inter-vene.

'If I'm not now, I'll never be,' he gasped.

'You're wrong. It's too soon to dispense with the mechanic.'

'You worry too much,' he reassured her. 'Yes, okay, Steffi. Take it away now.'

'Perhaps, but . . .' Her voice was beginning to sound petulant.

'Look, there was nothing wrong with that last leap, was there?' She shook her head.

'Thanks to you keeping the horses together, it went perfectly and I had no problem landing.'

'Yes, I have to admit it looked good, but . . .'

'There you are then.'

'So why not try another one like that?' she insisted.

'No. I shan't improve until I dispense with the mechanic and feel I'm leaping for real.'

'You might be right,' she said doubtfully.

'I am. Believe me.'

He was hurt by the way she glared at Steffi as the lad obediently cleared all the safety gear from the ring, but he was not prepared to take issue with her over that again. There were more important things to think about.

'But I don't understand why you have to be in such a rush, Levic.'

He sighed, keeping his eyes averted so he would not meet her dispirited gaze.

'Look,' she tried again, 'at the moment you're making a good leap nine times out of ten. But it's that tenth one that worries me, because without the mechanic that's the one that could prove lethal.'

'Shush!' he cautioned, alarmed in case Steffi heard.

'No, I won't shush,' she retorted.

'All right, all right. We both know there's a certain amount of risk attached to this trick, which is precisely why few attempt it.'

'There you are then.'

'But we're not going to fail. We've done our work well, you . . . and . . . I,' he said, stretching out the last words slowly and at the same time smiling at her. 'So, trust me – and let's go for it. Together, eh?'

'Put like that,' she smiled back, 'what choice do I have?'

Just for a moment he experienced doubt. Not for himself. He had no doubt about his own ability to pull it off. But what about Dorina? Was it right to put her through this sort of stress? He was aware too of Steffi's anxious face as he returned to watch from the ringside.

But there was really no time to reconsider. After preparing for this moment for months and months, he knew he had no more than a few weeks left with these particular horses.

So it had to be now.

Dorina, either convinced or simply tired of arguing, fetched the rosin and began to rub more on to the backs of Black Chieftain and White Prince, all the while she worked, talking to the horses in words that remained inaudible to Levic.

'Ready?' he called, eager to take advantage of the fact that they still had the ring to themselves.

'If you're sure you are,' Dorina said.

'I'm sure.'

He watched her put the horses through their paces. Now that they had started, everything else slowed down. There was no need for any hurry. In fact it was important for him to take his time to study their gait as the horses circled the ring one behind the other. Concentrating on the rise and fall of their haunches, registering and almost unconsciously regulating his own breathing until it harmonised with their rhythm.

Yes.

Steady now.

Stea – dy!

He and they – rising . . . and . . . falling – cantering round the ring.

He was ready.

Slowly he stepped up to Black Chieftain and patted his rump as he cantered by. Then, turned smartly round and, changing his step, ran across the centre and made his leap, landing on the horse as it was completing its course round half the ring.

Standing on reliable Black Chieftain's broad back now, both arms outstretched until he found his balance, then held loosely at his sides while he concentrated again on the rhythm, feeling the solid flesh through the thin skin of his slippers and letting it pulse through him. Into his muscles. Into his blood. Into his sinews. Until he and the horse were moving as one, he and Black Chieftain. Such a reliable partner, and easy to take his qualities for granted.

On the other hand, he felt he had never quite got the measure of the newer horse which, although a beautiful match and quick to learn, still occasionally proved capricious.

Once when he had complained that White Prince had let him down and would never come up to Black Chieftain's standard, Dorina had leapt to the animal's defence.

'It's not White Prince's fault. Remember, when it comes to training horses, the beast is always right and it's you who are wrong.'

Her words came back to him as he rode round the ring concentrating his energies for the vital spring. What she meant was that it was no good for him to synchronise with one horse and then expect the other to fit into this pre-existing harmony. Both horses had their own rhythms and it was up to him to synchronise with both. The trouble was, so often when he seemed close to achieving this, the white horse started to be awkward and spoilt things.

Still, no time to worry about that now. It was up to Dorina to have the horses galloping round in unison. All he had to concentrate on was choosing the right moment to spring. The absence of the safety harness gave him a heady sense of freedom.

This must be my masterpiece, even if I only manage it once, he thought, glad that his son was there as witness.

He sprang. Leaping higher than ever before. Felt himself moving through the air. Moving and twirling – so fast and yet with time opening out so that it more than kept pace, giving him the sensation of an infinitely slow dreamlike flight in which he had all the time in the world to turn and find his way down on to White Prince.

This was the moment. This was what he had been working for and planning for months, practising until he knew every move instinctively . . . so it was immediately obvious that he had sprung too high!

Just in time he remembered what he must do to ensure a safe landing, and opened out the somersault. Felt his toes making contact with White Prince, started to brace against his left leg far back on the haunches to protect himself from falling backwards.

But it was already too late.

Somehow he had missed his timing and his foot was slipping, slithering down the horse's flank and he was crashing to the ground.

Where someone's screaming pursued him into the blackness.

Chapter 11

Papa, wake up – please wake up, Steffi silently pleaded. Opposite him, across the hospital bed, his mother was holding Levic's hand apparently trying to tug him back into consciousness, her voice breaking as she muttered the same message.

'Come on, Levic. Wake up! You've got to wake up – for my sake.'

And Steffi wanted to cry for her anguish but, knowing that would not help, he sat quietly waiting and praying for his father to come back to himself.

For people did come round from this sort of sleep. He knew that, having seen several soldiers drop down in the midst of some grand review staged on Laffan's plain one hot summer's day. And they had soon recovered. They had dropped to the ground in a dead faint – but not died, he kept telling himself. So there was no reason why Levic should not open his eyes any moment and come back to his old self.

Except that time was ticking by and he had been lying like this for hours and hours, a humped mound in the bed with a corpse-white face and bandaged head.

Please, Papa, wake up, he continued to plead soundlessly, and talk to us properly.

For Levic had not been lying in silence all this time. There had been moments when his body had suddenly shaken and writhed and he kept muttering odd, urgent words which made no sense. But the sounds always had Mirella jumping up from her chair and putting her face next to his to whisper, 'Yes, come on, my love. Open your eyes. I'm here, waiting for you.' And once or twice his eyelids had seemed to flutter in response before he fell back into coma.

'Oh, Steffi . . .'

'It's all right. He'll be all right, Ma,' he stammered, rushing to comfort her as she burst into sobs.

'I'm sorry, Steffi. I'm trying to be strong but . . . but . . . oh, Steffi, if anything happened to him, I couldn't . . . I don't know how I'd . . .'

'Don't, Ma. He's going to be all right. I know he is. The doctor said he'd be all right once he came round, didn't he?'

'Yes, but it's taking so long.'

'I know, Ma, but . . . Look! Don't you think he's beginning to look better?'

'How?'

'His face has got a bit more colour,' Steffi said, trying to encourage her.

'You think so?'

'Yes. Yes, I do,' he declared.

'Tell me again, Steffi – what happened exactly when he fell?'

'But I've already told you, Ma.'

He could not bear to go over it all again. After telling the men who had come running into the big tent on hearing Dorina's screams, telling Mirella and Mr Foreman, then repeating it for the doctor's benefit once they had brought Levic to the Infirmary, Steffi still felt sick when he thought about the accident. Wanted to forget how he had stood helplessly by as his father tottered and fell. Wanted to blot out the sound of Dorina's screaming as she rushed towards Levic and then herself collapsed with shock.

'But why wasn't he using the safety harness?' Mirella protested for the umpteenth time. 'What on earth was he thinking of? I'd have thought Dorina would have had more sense than to . . .'

'Dorina?'

With one accord Steffi and Mirella gazed at the figure in the bed.

'Dorina . . .' Levic muttered again.

'He must have heard me,' Mirella announced joyfully, lowering her face to Levic's. 'Levic? Levic, my love, can you hear what I'm saying?'

'Dorina.' he whispered, opening his eyes.

'No, not Dorina. It's me, silly,' Mirella said, smiling happily as she turned to Steffi. 'He's calling me Dorina because he thinks he's still in the ring.'

'Aaargh, my head,' Levic groaned as he lifted his hand to touch the cloth bandage. 'Where am I?'

'In the Infirmary,' Mirella explained. 'And everything's all right, my love. But don't move. Not yet at least. You've got to lie still.'

'Mirella?' he queried, gazing blankly.

'Yes, you idiot!' she said fondly. 'It's me – Mirella, your wife. And here's Steffi, look! Waiting to have a word with you.'

'Hello, Pa,' Steffi said, smiling into amber-flecked brown eyes that immediately lit up and beamed warmly back at him.

'Hello, son.'

After that it was a matter of taking things very slowly and calmly as Mirella and Steffi took it in turns to explain exactly where he was and how he had been brought here.

'So what is it?' he groaned. 'I've busted the leg, haven't I? I must have because . . . Aaagh! Christ! I've never known such pain!'

'Well, don't move,' Mirella said quickly. 'Yes, the leg's broken, but that's not serious. At least it won't be, if you'll take it easy and lie back and rest.'

'Not much choice,' Levic muttered, closing his eyes and sinking back against the pillows. 'The trouble is, I don't really remember what happened.' Suddenly the dark eyes shot open. 'Wait a minute! I was riding the horses, wasn't I? Yes, riding round the ring and . . .'

'Look, it's over now, so don't worry about it. All you've got to do is rest until you're better.'

'But what else have I done? Where's the doctor? I must speak to him.' Stretching out an arm as if to pull himself up, the effort caused him such agony that he sank back with a loud groan.

Steffi was shocked. He had never seen his father give way to pain before, somehow never imagined he could.

'Don't, Papa,' he protested. 'Ma's right. You mustn't try to move. The doctor said.'

'So tell me exactly what I've done,' Levic demanded.

'Nothing that won't mend, my love.' Now Mirella was smiling reassurance and speaking, Steffi thought, in a too obviously bright voice. 'You've broken your leg – as you guessed. Collected some bad bruises in places where no one should see them. And got a bit of a dent in your head where it hit the ground – which is why you've been out for the count for so long. And why you shouldn't talk so much now.'

'Christ!'

'It's all right, Levic. Everything will mend,' she whispered, placing her cheek next to his. 'We've been lucky this time.'

'Lucky, you say! But I failed. Muffed it. After practising that trick for months and months and then, when I had the chance to pull it off properly, what did I do?' Levic paused before muttering through clenched teeth. 'I fouled it up good and proper.'

'But you'll be able to try it again when you're better.' Steffi was only trying to cheer him up, so was quite unprepared for his father's violent response.

'When I'm better? Don't you realise I've broken my bloody leg? That means I'll be laid up for weeks!'

'Yes, but . . .'

'And there's still a month of the show to run and then there's the winter to get through. Who do you think's going to take me on when I'm hopping around on crutches, eh?'

'Shush! You're talking nonsense,' Mirella broke in.

'It's not nonsense. I've been so bloody stupid.'

'Of course you haven't. You took a calculated risk which this time went wrong. It could have happened to anyone, so stop blaming yourself and think how lucky you are it didn't turn out worse. I certainly consider myself lucky,' Mirella whispered, leaning over to kiss him on the mouth.

Feeling uncomfortably in the way, Steffi stood back and let his gaze wander round the rest of the ward, smiling shyly at strangers in their beds, while his parents huddled close and spoke quietly together. It was only when he and Mirella were outside that he asked the question which had been vexing him ever since Levic had come round.

'Ma, do you think we should have told him about Dorina?'

'No, not yet. It would only worry him.'

'I know, but . . . well, he might be angry when he finds out.'

'Angry?'

'Yes, because we didn't tell him.'

'I see what you mean, but there's no point in saying anything till we find out how she is.'

'But it was funny, her just keeling over like that, wasn't it? I mean, I was there and I didn't see her get hurt.'

Steffi felt really puzzled. He knew some women were liable to faint at the least little shock but was amazed when Dorina was whisked off to the Infirmary. It didn't seem right when it was Levic who'd had the accident.

'Well, she has to be very careful in her condition,' Mirella said.

106

From which Steffi deduced that Dorina's trouble was connected with that baby she was still expecting.

He looked at his mother. There were so many questions he was burning to ask, but now was clearly not the time.

'Look Steffi, I think we should pop over to the other wing and see Dorina before we go home. She'll be glad to hear Levic's okay.'

Steffi was pleased with this suggestion. It would be nice to take Dorina some good news and – who knows? – maybe the baby had been born by now and he might be one of the first to see it. He had never seen a very young baby before.

They had to march up and down staircases and through endless dank corridors before reaching the other wing of the hospital and by that time his enthusiasm had been dulled by the sickly stench of the place. Not that it was any worse than in the men's wing, but now that his anxiety had lessened his senses were growing more intolerant and he had to battle against a heaving stomach.

'I want to know how Mrs Scott from the circus is getting on,' Mirella said, accosting a nurse in a grubby apron.

'Relation of yourn?'

'Yes. My sister.'

Steffi was surprised to hear his mother lie so readily.

'Right. Well, you can go in then.'

'How is she?' Mirella asked, clutching Steffi's arm to pull him along with her.

'Middling, I suppose you'd say. I mean, she ain't lost it yet but it's fifty-fifty . . .' The woman pursed her lips and joggled her hand to show how delicately the balance hung.

'Can't you do anything?'

'Only make her comf'table till Nature takes its course.'

'But there must be something more . . .'

'Look, missus, don't you start. I've had enough of that sort of talk from your father. "I don't care what it costs, I want the best bloody doctoring there is for my gal. She's a Foreman and carrying my grandchild and I'll hold everyone here personally responsible if anything happens, d'yer hear?" Raving like a mad man he was.'

'Well, naturally he's upset. And is he still with her?'

'No. I sent 'em both packing, him and 'er 'usband. I mean, you're a married woman, so you know what it's like. A man does the damage and then starts mewling like a babe when it all goes wrong,' she growled, shaking her head at Steffi. 'I've no patience with 'em, not me.'

'So she's not allowed visitors?' Mirella asked, looking at her watch. 'Okay, well, in that case . . .'

'No, I didn't say that. I don't mind you going in for a few minutes. Sisters is different,' she declared before bustling off.

'Come on then,' Mirella said, clutching tight hold of Steffi's hand as if sensing his reluctance to go into that little room. 'It's all right. It's only Dorina, remember.'

He clung to her words as he looked at the strange woman lying semi-comatose against the pillows, her yellow face and eyes staring glassily into space. Dorina. Of course it was Dorina. But he wouldn't have recognised her.

'Hello, Dorina. How do you feel?' Mirella said cheerfully, as she moved up to the bed.

There was no answer, not even a flicker of interest in the grey eyes. Steffi was shocked. He had not expected this.

'I think they must have given her laudanum or something,' Mirella whispered to him before raising her voice to call, 'Dorina, can you hear me?' When again there was no response, she stretched out her hand to smoothe back the hair from Dorina's face, resting it for a moment on her forehead. 'She's very hot.'

This time her words provoked some reaction. Dorina turned and glared at her.

'What are you doing here?' she snarled.

'Come to see you, of course,' Mirella smiled. 'We were in the hospital, you see.'

'You've no right to be here. They shouldn't have let you in.'

'Oh, but we came up with Papa,' Steffi started to say, wanting to tell her how much better Levic was. But Dorina shot him such a poisonous look that he fell silent.

'I suppose you've come to crow,' she muttered, turning back to Mirella and fixing her with a crazy stare. 'Well, I don't care. I don't care about anything any more, now he's dead.'

Steffi was mystified, but decided it was better to keep quiet and leave his mother to do the talking.

'Now, you mustn't speak like that, Dorina. The baby's still all right. I've spoken to the nurse and she says as long as you stay here and rest, there's no reason why you shouldn't carry it to the full term and have a normal birth.'

108

'I told you, I don't care about the baby. I don't care about anything now Levic's dead.'

Levic dead? Steffi flinched at the words. Then relaxed. So that was why Dorina was so upset. He thought back to the scene in the ring when Dorina had watched Levic fall. She must have assumed he'd been killed. Oh, well, Mirella would soon put her right.

'No, love. Levic's not dead,' he heard his mother saying. 'He's getting along fine.'

But her remark failed to produce the desired effect.

'You're lying,' Dorina moaned. 'I was there. I saw it. Oh, God, I saw it.' She shut her eyes but tears immediately seeped under her lashes and streamed down her face.

'No, Dorina, no! You may have seen him fall but he wasn't killed. He's lying here in this very hospital and apart from a broken leg and a bump on his head, he's fine.'

'Not dead? He's not dead? You're sure?' Dorina cried in a strangled voice.

'Of course I am. I've just been talking to him. In fact, we've both been sitting with him all afternoon, haven't we, Steffi?' she said, throwing him a meaningful look that he interpreted as a caution not to mention that they had been waiting for Levic to come round.

Steffi nodded.

'So,' Mirella continued, 'what I want to know is, is there anything you'd like me to bring . . .'

'NO! NO! NO!' Dorina was suddenly screaming.

'Dorina, it's all right,' Mirella soothed, beginning to back away from the bed.

'NO! NO!' Dorina continued to screech. 'You've no right to go near him, do you hear? I'm telling you and your son, stay away from him!'

'Stay away from Levic?'

'Yes. Stay away, because he's *mine*!'

Eyes blazing in a face straining away from her pillows – that was the last sight Steffi had of Dorina as his mother bundled him from the room.

'What was she talking about?' he asked as they made their way out of the hospital.

'Nothing that could make any sense.'

'But what did she mean about staying away from Papa?'

'Nothing, Steffi. Poor Dorina was delirious and didn't know what she was saying.'

'But why . . .'

'It's no good asking why. When someone's delirious they tend to say the first thing that comes into their head. So the best thing to do is forget about it. Dorina will be completely different next time you see her and won't even remember those crazy things she said just now.'

'I see,' Steffi said without feeling altogether reassured.

Back on the tober, Steffi was amazed when Mirella insisted on going over to the big tent and immediately started to check her tightrope, pulleys, couplings and guys.

'But you won't be performing this evening, will you?' he demanded.

'Of course I will.'

'But you can't. Not after what you've just been through.'

'Why not?'

'Because Dad could have died today,' he said, choking on the words.

'I know that,' she said quietly. 'But what happens down here, won't affect my performance up there.'

'But it might,' he pleaded, dreading the thought of another accident.

'Don't worry. I can promise you it won't,' she said.

They were interrupted before he could argue any further.

'How is he then?' the voice of Arnold Foreman barked as he came into the arena.

'Not too bad, thank you,' Mirella replied stiffly – as if she, like Steffi, found it hard to forgive those harsh words Arnold had uttered against Levic in the aftermath of the accident.

'Good.'

'He's come round, thank God. But the leg's broken and he'll have to stay put for a while.'

'Broken, eh? Thought as much,' Arnold said gruffly. 'I'm sorry, my dear. That's going to hold you both back a bit.' He put out his hand and squeezed her arm. 'But don't worry, he'll pull through.'

'Yes. I know. And . . . and thanks, Arnold.'

'That's all right. Must stand together at a time like this, eh?' he said briskly. 'And if I spoke hasty this morning, it was just the shock, you know. Finding my girl in that state, well . . .

110

Don't suppose you heard anything at the hospital, did you? I didn't want to leave her there, but there was this old battle-axe who . . .'

'Yes. We went in to see Dorina before we came home and she seemed fine, didn't she, Steffi?'

Taken aback, he nodded.

'Thank God,' Arnold sighed. 'You see, that nurse told us she badly needed rest and . . . Hell, Mirella! You know how these things can go.'

'Yes, but I also know it's no good worrying. How's Matty taking it, by the way?' she asked, looking around as if expecting to see him.

'Hmm, how you might expect – with a little bit of help from his friend.'

Steffi was glad to hear that until Mirella destroyed his illusions by saying, 'Oh dear! I suppose you mean his friend who lives in a bottle?'

'The same,' Arnold snorted. 'But I don't want to talk about it. I've got enough on my plate getting this show off the ground tonight, what with my best artiste out of action. And I don't suppose you feel up to the mark, do you?'

'Yes, I'm perfectly able to go on.'

'What, just as usual?'

She nodded.

'Phew! That makes things easier. Well done, my dear,' he declared, before turning to Steffi to say, 'And that's what I call a real trouper, my lad.'

'Well, remember I had a good teacher in Levic,' Mirella murmured.

That evening Steffi stood below and watched the knight in shining armour climb up the ladder. Not real armour, of course. The chain mail had been knitted from silver thread to allow complete freedom of movement to arms and legs. Nevertheless, with the glittering gilt breastplate and plumed helmet, the effect was stunning.

Now, tiny but still impressive, the figure had reached the high platform and was pausing to remove the white crusader's cloak before grasping a long balancing pole decorated with coloured pennons and stepping out on to the tightrope.

There was no safety net and Steffi knew the act was dangerous. But even though watching made him feel quite

111

sick, he could not take his eyes off the little figure in the roof of the tent.

Up and down the length of the rope and now back on the platform and starting to remove the plumed helmet . . . He waited for the usual gasp of astonishment from the audience as Mirella shook out her long black hair and revealed that she was a woman. Madame Mirella. His mother. So tiny and remote up there. Dancing in a world of her own.

Remembering Levic and the events of the day, Steffi had to admire his mother's ability to distance herself from anxieties.

Now he watched as she stepped to the middle and crouched to balance the pole carefully across the rope, leaving it there while she sat and slowly slid backwards until her body was hanging upside down, held by the crook of her legs.

Suddenly the band stopped playing and the audience seemed to hold its breath as she swung above their heads. For one terrible moment he feared she had got stuck, but then as the band struck up her familiar tune she quickly righted herself, reclaimed her pole and skipped off the rope.

As she stood blowing kisses in acknowledgement of the tumultuous applause, Madame Mirella looked so happy and carefree that Steffi fell to wondering whether anyone else existed for her when she was walking along her high rope.

Chapter 12

Steffi slept heavily that night despite himself. But looking at his mother next morning, it was clear she had not enjoyed much rest and the strain was beginning to show in her white face and dark-ringed eyes.

'Oh dear, look at me forgetting,' she muttered after placing three mugs on the table and quickly putting one back.

'It's all right, I'll pour,' Steffi urged, leaping up to fetch the teapot from the stove where it was keeping warm.

'Thanks, love. I could do with that. I wonder what sort of night your poor father's had. Better than mine, I hope. I couldn't stop my mind going over and over again what happened yesterday.'

'Why don't you go back to bed then, and let me bring you some breakfast?'

She refused to entertain his suggestion.

'No, no. I'm going up to the hospital in a minute to see how he is.'

'You must eat something first, though,' he insisted, pushing the first piece of toasted bread over to her.

'No, you have it. I'm not hungry.'

'Ma, please. You must eat.'

'Oh, very well then,' she agreed, pulling it off the long-handled fork and dropping it on to her plate.

'It will be the last show today, won't it?' Steffi asked, harpooning another slice.

'Yes, the last one here.'

'So what will we do then? Will Mr Foreman have to go on to Marlow as planned?'

'I really don't know. He might decide to cut short the tour and head for home, if Dorina can be moved.'

'Can he do that?'

'Without a good clown to hold things together he doesn't have much choice. You saw how the house was last night: dead without Levic.'

'Yes, I know what you mean. But what will we do? We can't just go away and leave Pa, can we? Ouch!' he muttered, sucking at his scorched fingers.

'Of course not, but . . . Careful! That's still hot. What we might do is take Levic back to Aldershot until he's recovered.'

'And let Gran look after him. Oh, yes, that's a brilliant idea,' he agreed. 'People say she's better than a doctor with all her cures.'

'That's right. But I can't make any decision until I see how he is. Which is why I want you to eat up and take a message over to Matty for me.'

'What sort of message?' Steffi asked, cramming a crust into his mouth.

'Ask him if he's going up to see Dorina this morning. And if so, will he give us a lift? We might as well go together.'

'Okay.'

But Matty was not at home eating breakfast when Steffi called. Nor was he with Mr Foreman, whose wagon was similarly silent and empty. So Steffi wandered over to the big tent, expecting to find them there.

It did occur to him that the tober was unusually quiet this morning, the animals unnaturally still.

Normally by this time the ground would be bustling with grooms carrying buckets, sounds of whistling, shouts or clanging from somewhere. But not today. Today he could almost hear the vapour rising off the canvas as the sun made its pale appearance.

He was tempted to suppose the place deserted until, on hearing voices, he entered the stable tent and found the men all talking together in a huddle. Suddenly he froze.

'Here's Steffi,' one of them was whispering. 'Wonder how his ma's taken the news.'

His mind raced, trying to imagine what they could be talking about.

'Has something happened?' he asked.

The men looked from one to another for a spokesman.

'Why's everything so quiet this morning?' Steffi prompted.

'You bain't 'eard then?' Jig, the lamp-man, croaked.

'Heard what?' Steffi's mouth had gone dry and he felt his heart contract with fear lest the man should start mentioning Levic.

114

'About Miss Dorina . . . I mean, Mrs . . . oh, dang me, what does it matter!'

'Why, what's happened to her?' Steffi asked, his chest now swelling with relief.

It was Jerry, one of the grooms, who explained.

'Mrs Scott took a turn for the worse last night and the hospital's put her on the danger list.'

'Oh dear! Then I'd better go and tell my mother.'

'Yes, Mirella should know even though she's got enough on her plate already, poor woman. Tell her,' he added, 'that the Guv'nor got the message first thing this morning and drove straight up to the hospital with Matty. She'll certainly want to know,' he muttered, turning back to the other men.

As soon as she heard, Mirella went over to the tent herself to glean more information and arrange for Jerry to drive her and Steffi up to the hospital in the cart used for collecting stores.

'God love us, how we're gonner get through this day I don't know,' Jerry growled, shaking his head as they pulled up outside.

'Well, let's hope things aren't as bad as they seem,' Mirella said. 'In any case, what I suggest is you wait here while Steffi and I go in, and then I can send him out to you with the latest news.'

Once again that nauseous hospital smell of boiled fish and carbolic and blocked drains clutched at Steffi's throat and made his gorge rise as soon as he entered the building.

'What does it mean when someone's put on the danger list, Ma?'

'It means they're afraid she might not recover.'

He tried to make sense of this bleak answer as he stumbled after his mother along the grey corridors leading up to the women's wards and Dorina's private room. Not recover? But that meant die. Rosa and Amy's mother might be about to die, and they were completely unaware of the situation.

He suddenly pictured their misery. Rosa with her big grey eyes filling with tears and her voice choked with sobs, inconsolable. Amy running away to lick her wounds in secret like some injured animal. Oh God, he'd do anything to stop it happening to them! But there was nothing he could do.

'Ma, can't they . . .'

Before he had a chance to frame the question, they had

115

rounded a corner and come upon Matty – sitting slumped on a bench, apparently keeping vigil outside his wife's room.

'How is she, Mat?' Mirella whispered.

Grey-faced and bleary-eyed, he just stared at her, making no attempt to reply.

'It's bad then?' Mirella stammered. 'Oh, Mat! I'm so sorry.'

Matty's face started to contort in a way that made Steffi fear he was about to burst into tears. Not that he could blame the man. He felt like crying too.

But Matty did not cry. Instead his face seemed to twist with fury into a demon mask with lips that slit just wide enough to announce, 'Dorina's dying, Mirella. Do you hear? My wife's going to die.'

'No! Oh dear God, no! There must be something they can do?'

'I told you, she's dying,' the mask repeated.

'Oh, Matty, what can I say?'

'Nothing.'

'Is Arnold with her? Oh, Christ! He's going to take this hard. We all will,' she said, her voice faltering.

Suddenly the mask split from one side to the other as the lips curled and Matty snarled, 'Stop being such a bloody hypocrite, will you? We both know the score. She's been a bad woman – a bad wife and bloody bad mother – but she never deserved this to happen, Mirella. There's no way she deserved this.'

'Of course she didn't, Matty,' Mirella agreed, clearly shocked by his outburst. 'Neither of you deserved it. God knows why such a thing should happen but . . .'

'But you can't help being glad!'

'Matty, don't say that. Of course I'm not glad. I'm very fond of Dorina and so's Levic. He'll be shattered when he finds out.'

'Yes . . . Levic!' Matty spat out the name as if it was poison, before saying, 'You know she's asking for him, don't you?'

'Asking for Levic?' Steffi heard his mother say.

'Yes. That's why I can't stay in there. My wife's lying there dying and it's him she's asking for. Even now.'

Steffi was suddenly overcome by pity for Dorina, finding it quite natural that she should be asking for his father. After all, Levic was her partner and friend so it was obvious she would want to see him. Just as he himself would want to see Rosa and Amy if he thought he was going to die. The fact that his father was too ill to come to Dorina's bedside made him pity her even more.

So, while his heart went out to Matty, Steffi could not understand why he appeared more angry than sad. And above all, he could not understand how Matty could bear to fret time away out here when he could be with his wife, comforting her.

Evidently Mirella was thinking along similar lines.

'Look, Matty,' she murmured, taking hold of his arm, 'I know what you're going through, but you've got to understand that Dorina isn't in her proper mind at the moment. It's the effect of the fever, so you mustn't take any notice of what she says.'

Matty shrugged her away.

'Just remember she loves you,' Mirella persisted.

'Shut up, damn you! It's no good pretending any more. All that's finished now. I don't care if the whole world knows this was Levic's child – it's dead, and they can't save my lovely wife! And . . . and I wish I could hate her for what she's done to me, but I can't. I hate *him*, d'you hear me? I hate his bloody guts, but I still love my wife, Mirella. God help me, I still love . . . her.'

Matty broke down in sobs.

Steffi wanted to help him. Wished he knew what to say and wasn't so dangerously out of his depth. But had to admit he didn't understand what was happening around him.

Matty sobbing because his wife was dying. That made sense.

Mirella, her face drained of all colour, shaking her head compulsively from side to side, as if in some dumb-show.

Steffi gripped her hand.

'Ma, come on. Let's get away from here.'

'No! What he said isn't true. You mustn't believe him, Steffi. It isn't true.'

'I know it isn't, Ma,' Steffi soothed, not sure whether he had heard correctly anyway. Levic's child – dead? What child could Matty have meant? And why did he hate Pa so much? Because Levic had been responsible for Dorina's collapse? But that had been an accident. Besides it didn't explain . . .

'Go away for a minute, Steffi!' Mirella eventually muttered.

He hesitated, reluctant to leave her alone with Matty in this strange mood.

'Go on!' she hissed.

So he went, dragging his feet along the corridor, occasionally glancing back to make sure his mother was all right. Going over and over Matty's words in his mind, trying to squeeze sense from them.

* * *

'Ma?' He rushed to meet her when, after a few minutes, she followed him down the corridor. But although there were so many things he wanted to ask, one glance at her face – stony as a statue – told him now was not the right moment. And, stealing another glance, he doubted whether there would ever be a right moment.

Without saying a word, she gripped his hand so tightly that it hurt, and they started to walk. Down a staircase, along another corridor, through a double door out on to the pavement.

'Ma, what shall I tell Jerry?' he whispered.

'Jerry?' she repeated as if never having heard the name before.

'Yes. He's still holding the cart, remember? Waiting to hear how Dorina is. I ought to tell him something.'

'Yes. Yes, of course you must,' she said, frowning in an obvious effort to pull herself together.

'What should I say?'

She shrugged. 'Tell him it's bad, Steffi. What else can you say?'

'And Pa? Do you want Jerry to wait while we go and see Pa?'

'Oh, no. There's no point in anyone waiting around for that,' she replied vaguely.

Steffi hated being the bearer of such bad news, but at least Jerry quickly grasped the situation and spared him the agony of putting it into many words.

'Okay. I can see how it is, lad. But poor Miss Dorina – I've known her since she was a tot. My God, this is a bad day, a terr'ble day for us all,' he growled, rubbing his sleeve against his eyes before driving off.

Steffi returned to Mirella expecting them both to go directly to see his father. Instead, she strode up the street with scarcely a glance to make sure he was following and walking so fast that he had his work cut out to keep up with her.

'Where are we going, Ma?' he asked, supposing she had just thought of something she needed from the shops.

'Nowhere.'

'But it's beginning to rain,' he urged, thinking she might have failed to notice the fine drizzle already turning the pavements greasy under foot.

'I know, Steffi, but I need to have some air. You go and wait in the hospital, if you like. I shan't be long. Just a few minutes on my own to think.'

He felt wretched as he watched her bedraggled form walk away. His mother so upset that she was walking the streets, getting wet and exhausted – while his father lay sick in hospital with a badly broken leg and concussion. Knowing that people with head injuries could suffer sudden relapses, Steffi was desperately anxious to find out how he was this morning, but dared not go up to the ward on his own in case Levic questioned him about Dorina and triggered him into saying the wrong thing.

By the time Mirella returned nearly half an hour had passed. Her green cape was sodden and the rain dripping off the edge of her hat like a veil of tears.

'All right. I'm going up to see your father now,' she announced very calmly.

'Shall I come with you then?' he asked, jumping up eagerly from the bench where he had been sitting waiting for her.

'No, not this time, Steffi. I shan't be staying long. I don't suppose there'll be much to say once I've told him about Dorina.'

Chapter 13

'What have I done? What have I done?'

Levic shut his eyes and scourged himself over and over again with the words as he began to give way to all the emotion kept in check in front of Mirella.

At first he had been unable to take it in.

Dorina, dying?

Even though, to give Mirella her due, she had forewarned him by suggesting he brace himself for bad news.

'I'm afraid it's Dorina, Levic. She's lost the baby,' she had announced quietly.

And God forgive him for feeling glad when he heard. Relief at a problem solved.

But then Mirella had continued in a voice that was even quieter, 'And she's had a very hard time. It was a big baby and there were complications, you see. A surgeon was called in the middle of the night and did what he could. But she's lost so much blood and . . . Oh, Levic, I hate being the one who has to tell you this, but . . . she's sinking fast. They say there's nothing more they can do.'

'You mean Dorina?' he had said stupidly, immediately conjuring up the image of her in a beautiful white frock, perched securely on the flanks of Black Chieftain. Dorina dying? His beautiful Dorina? Not possible.

Mirella's quiet voice had gone on quietly explaining while he tried to focus on her words, waiting for the moment when he would realise that he had misunderstood. She could not really be saying what he thought she was saying. There had to be some mistake. In fact, he hated her for not disabusing him sooner. Wasn't she supposed to be coming in here to make him feel better? Then what right had she to torture him like this?

Still, at least she seemed to realise, once the truth had sunk in, that all he then wanted was to be left on his own. And went out as quietly as she came in. So quietly, that he could hardly remember her departure later, or even whether she had given him her usual kiss before she left.

Dorina, dying. But she couldn't, she mustn't be allowed to die. What on earth were the people around her doing to allow such a thing? She was young and strong and had everything to live for. They must tell her that. They must force her to make more effort and fight. He would, once he got to her.

He tried to pull himself higher in the bed so that he could put his good leg over the side and struggle to his feet. He must get out of this bed and go to her.

'Aaagh! Eeow! Christ!'

He could not move. As soon as he tried the pain exploded in his leg, sending splinters of agony up his spine and through his whole body until dark clouds swirled down over his eyes threatening to smother his senses. He sank back, for the moment defeated.

'What have I done? What have I done?' he started to moan again. 'If anything happens to her, it will be my fault. But she can't die. Not with so much to live for. Dear God, if there is a God, don't let her die.'

Suddenly he felt ashamed to be lying here so helplessly. Never mind whether there was a God or no. He, Levic, would not let Dorina die. He would climb out of this blasted bed and go to her.

'Nurse! Nurse!' he yelled.

'What is it?'

The big Irish nurse with the face like a bull terrier shambled over to him, her muscular arms akimbo.

'Is it the pan ye'll be wanting now?' she grinned, exposing the last three teeth she had in her head and then leaving them marooned on her fleshy lower lip in the groove they had worn there.

'I want to get up,' Levic declared with as much dignity as he could muster.

'If it's the pan ye'll be wanting, why don't yer say? Sure, there's no call for modesty in this place.' She turned to bustle off to the sluice.

'No. I don't need a pan. But I have to get out of this bed.'

Now she shuffled up so close that her body bulged over him while she peered into his face. She was so fat, her flesh seemed to be held together only by the discipline of the uniform, the ties on her cap keeping her chin lashed in place while her apron served as lagging for her ample lap.

'Now, ye know there's no moving till the bones have chance to set. But you tell me what you want and oi'll do me best to fetch it for yer, that oi will.'

'Look, I've got to get out of here – either on a stretcher or in a Bath chair, I don't care how. I need someone to take me to the other side of the hospital to see a friend who's ill. A woman – a sort of relative – who might be dying.'

'Look, oi'm telling you, it can't be done. The surgeon took a deal of trouble setting that leg, and ye'll undo all the good if ye so much as move an inch before you're ready.'

He remonstrated. He pleaded. He offered her money. She laughed at him.

'Sure and I have me instructions, so it wouldn't be any good if you was to call on the name of the Holy Father to tempt me from me duty. You can't move off that bed, and that's flat.'

He was trapped. He – a grown man, husband and father, artiste of international repute – was forced to lie here helplessly while Dorina died. His whole being rebelled against such a possibility.

It was too much like what happened before. But surely that couldn't happen again. Not now he was a grown man and in control of life. Now it *must* be different.

Before – when he was a little boy – all he wanted to do was run away from what had happened. Run and run. Round the streets, up and down alleys, climbing on walls, shinning up trees and lamp-posts.

'Hel-lo! Here comes little lickety-split again,' folks used to joke. 'Slow down a minute, lad, why don't yer? There's no one chasin'.'

But they were wrong. There was always someone chasing. And he never dared to look back in case he saw her.

God, he needed to get out of this bed. He would go mad if he had to lie here much longer with his thoughts.

But that bloody nurse was right. He couldn't move for the pain. He had suffered injuries before, but never like this. The pain in his head and his back and down his leg kept him on the rack, twisting and mangling his body if he so much as breathed.

Now he wished Mirella had stayed. Wanting her here not to touch him or say anything, just to be with him to hold the

123

demons at bay. He was terrified of being alone – with himself and what he had done all those years ago.

'Mammy! Tell me what I'm supposed to do,' he had stammered, already halfway to the door to fetch someone.

Looking back, he could see her quite clearly again – lying on the bed in the corner of their basement room. Pulled up on one elbow and not like his mammy at all. More like some wild witch with dark hair in tangles round her shrivelled face and eyes staring and enormous.

But then she gave him a little smile and he had felt all right again.

God, the years were rolling back and he was remembering. But he didn't want to. Not now. Especially not now. Except that the memories once they started to come were as remorseless as the pains of childbirth. Nothing could stop them. Here, trapped in a hospital bed, he could not run away any more. His past was catching up with him, leaving him no choice but to turn and face it.

He supposed he must have been about four years old when his mother died, too young to understand what was happening then. But he understood now. Oh, yes. He'd put most of the story together over the years – even if always stopping short of its dreadful climax.

His mother had been expecting a child.

In his youth he had fought against this realisation, not willing to admit that his mother was the sort of woman to bear an illegitimate child. But gradually, when he examined the facts, he knew it must have been so, though who sired the child remained a mystery. Duff, perhaps? Duff was the only man he could remember from his early life, but when he pictured the whiskered red face and white apron bulging over huge stomach Levic had doubts.

Certainly all he knew at the time was that his mother was ill. He seemed to remember her lying for days in her cluttered bed. Long days when he had nothing to do except play on his own on the floor, close by her in that dark stuffy room.

Occasionally one of the other cooks had brought food round in a covered dish for them both and – this he remembered well – he was pleased when his mother ate so little because it meant more for him.

How long she lay on that bed he could not say. In retrospect it seemed like weeks, but then time always seemed tethered to a child kept indoors with little to amuse himself.

He half remembered idling away the hours in the construction of a miniature world on the brick floor, trailing knitting yarn roads around the bed, under the table, round the legs of his mother's chair and up to his own stool. Peopling those roads with screwed up paper horsemen who dashed through the night chasing robbers. And as the time wore on adding more and more features until completely absorbed in his own landscape. Flinching whenever he crawled, galloping his brave horseman before him, to the point halfway between the chair and the stool where he knew lay hidden in the Dark Forest of his mother's cloak a ferocious twisted-paper brigand.

At first his mammy's moans had disturbed him, but she told him to take no notice so he gradually absorbed them into his game, the sounds of her increasing distress becoming no more than the wild beasts in the Dark Forest howling at the moon.

'Aaaagh!'

But he would never forget that moment when her scream became too real to be included in any game, forcing him to leap up off the floor and run to her. Crying.

'Mammy, Mammy, what is it?'

Then standing there, barely able to see over the side of the bed, while her groans got worse.

He had so much wanted to make her feel better like she always made him better when he was not very well. But she pushed him away when he climbed up on to her bed to give her a kiss.

'Fetch Duff, my love,' she said, panting as if finding it difficult to breathe. 'Or one of the women . . . upstairs. Go and fetch someone . . . Tell them . . . they must come.'

And he was glad she asked him to do that, because he was longing to go outside.

So he ran to the door and tugged at the handle. But it wouldn't open. There was a key in the lock, so he knew what he had to do – fetch the chair to stand on so that he could reach up and turn it. So he fetched the chair and climbed up closer to the lock, and turned the key. Then he had to move the chair away before he could twist the handle again.

His mother was moaning all the time now and uttering soft screams.

He tugged at the handle again, but the door still refused to budge. He tried with all his might to turn that handle, this way and that, his hands growing hot and slippery as panic

125

set in. He just couldn't understand why the door would not open.

His mammy's screams were piercing him now and he knew it was up to him to do something for her. He had to fetch help.

The window, then. It gave on to a dark, sunken area below street level, too shallow to provide any sort of view, just enough to give ventilation. And it had bars. Even when standing on the chair he could not reach it. Nevertheless, he stood there and shouted and waved his hands hoping someone would see or hear him.

But no one did.

'Levy. Levy,' he heard his mother calling weakly, as he ran back to the door. 'You must go for help. Go on, my baby. Fetch someone. I need help, my love.'

Then he stood at the door and screamed at the top of his voice for someone to come. And when no one came, he started to kick it with his boots and he fetched his stool and bashed at the handle with it. He splintered the wood and he dented the handle and hurt his toes, and he kept on screaming for help but still no one came. In fact he kept on screaming long after his mammy had gone quite quiet.

Eventually someone had come of course. God knows how long afterwards. But by then it was too late.

He heard their voices outside, but he did not want them to come in and find her. He was frightened what they might do to him when they found out that it was his fault. They would be bound to say that a big boy like him (his mammy was always telling him what a big boy he was now) ought to have been able to open his own door and fetch help for his mammy.

They would know that it was because he had not managed to fetch help when she needed it that his mammy was now lying still and cold on the bed and would never wake up and look after him again.

As Levic lay in the hospital these were the memories that threatened to drive him mad. Every time he closed his eyes it was to see it all happening again. The woman lying screaming on the bed. His own hand locking the door that kept help from her.

Even his precious work, which had hitherto always provided a safe haven for his thoughts, could no longer be relied on to keep demons at bay. For whenever he thought about his act it

126

was inevitably to relive that abortive attempt on the double somersault and the accident. And then – with an agony of self-reproach – to think of Dorina.

When she died in the early hours of the following morning it was as if he were told the sun had gone out and the world grown cold. But at least the darkness settling over his soul provided some sort of cover for his naked self-loathing. And at least he still had access to warmth through Mirella.

Mirella . . . Somehow he assumed she would come as soon as she heard the news. But she didn't.

Arnold came in, straight from seeing Dorina. Laid out. At peace now, he said. All over. So pointless now for anyone to blame themselves.

Then he'd left.

And Levic was left alone.

Waiting.

She came in the evening though, and brought the boy with her. At first Levic hadn't been too pleased about that. Wanting Mirella's attention for himself. Needing her so much.

But he supposed she must have been as shocked about Dorina's death as he was himself – or almost. Or perhaps the events of the last couple of days had caught up with her and left her exhausted. Whatever it was, Mirella was not herself.

There were so many questions he had to ask her – about the funeral arrangements, how folks were managing, what would they themselves do once the show packed up and headed for home?

She answered his questions patiently, assuring him that she had thought everything out and made plans accordingly. And then she rose to go.

'But you've only been here five minutes,' he protested.

'Nearly half an hour,' she said.

'But there's no need for you to hurry away just yet, is there?'

'Not if there's something else you want to say,' she said with an edge to her voice that had him puzzled when he thought about it later.

And every day after that was the same. After looking forward to Mirella's visits so much, he was inevitably disappointed to find her cool and unresponsive when she arrived. Or – what was worse – she sent Steffi in her place and didn't turn up at all.

And if it hadn't been for Steffi being so helpful – bringing him in newspapers and his own shaving tackle – and well, just being there with a sympathetic smile on his face, he would have felt completely forsaken.

Chapter 14
December 1885

When would she come in to say goodbye? Levic wondered as he lay listening to the sounds of their imminent departure – scraping and shuffling of feet, doors thudding shut, trunks and packing cases being hauled along passages and bumped over steps, Mirella shouting.

'Hettie, have you seen that little blue tin I left on the table? The one with the laces and button hook in it?'

Some muffled response from Liddy's servant.

'. . . hat-box, Ma'am . . . already gone out.'

God, how empty this place would be when they'd gone, and how he longed to be going with them. Not that he was not grateful to Liddy, of course, for continuing to extend her hospitality towards him. Indeed, if he had to stay behind – and he realised that in present circumstances he had no choice – there was no one he would rather have look after him than Liddy. Apart from Mirella, of course.

He flinched with the effort of easing himself up on the pillows piled high against the backrest of the chaise-longue.

'Come on, Mirella. Come in and talk to me before you go. Don't leave it to the last minute and then only have time to say goodbye,' he muttered to himself. Though heaven knew, she had enough on her plate with having to organise everything to go up to Apsley's without worrying about him as well.

'Pa? We're nearly ready now,' announced Steffi, peering round the drawing-room door. 'Can I fetch you anything before we go?'

'Yes. Some new bones. Then I could come with you,' Levic grunted, wishing things were that simple.

New bones, or rather a new set of joints in his back and his legs, so that he could jump around as easily as he did two years ago – before that accident triggered off this damned rheumatism.

'I'd be glad to lend you mine, if they'd fit,' Steffi smiled.

At any other time Levic might have accepted the words as an easy expression of sympathy, but at the moment he found them profoundly irritating.

It was all very well for Steffi to joke when he wasn't the one confined to this bloody couch. Besides, wasn't he about to go off to Apsley's to help Mirella settle in ready for the Pantomime season? Taking Levic's place, in other words.

He glowered at his son. Fourteen and just left school. And still without an idea in his head what to do with his life. My God, when he thought back to himself at that age – already out on the road and earning a good living. Was Steffi capable of doing the same? he wondered. Or had the boy been spoilt by too many doting females handing everything to him on a plate all the time?

'Are there any messages you want me to pass on once we get to London?' Steffi was asking.

'Only that I expect to be up there myself before the end of the week.'

'Are you sure?' Steffi looked doubtful. 'But I thought the doctor said . . .'

'You can forget what the doctor said. I shan't lie around here a minute longer than I have to.'

Christ! he hated sounding so peevish, but the effort of turning to talk had given him gyp again and deprived him of all power to be charming. Which was a pity, because he could see the lad was only trying to be helpful. And that was Steffi all over. Always anxious to help others even if he couldn't get his own life organised properly. Still, perhaps Mirella was right and he just needed more time to sort himself out.

Levic began to take stock of the boy, recognising in his features so much of himself at a similar age. Same sort of dark wavy hair and sensitive face. Same slightly hooked nose that Mirella often used to tease him about. Even the same wiry build that made him look taller than his less than average height. So, apart from the blue eyes which had always marked him out from Levic, there was no denying whom he physically took after, even if in temperament, of course, it was a different matter. In temperament Steffi definitely resembled his mother – which was why Levic never knew quite where he stood with him.

He frowned.

It was true. He was no longer sure where he stood with

Mirella. Something had gone badly wrong between them but for the life of him he could not fathom what. All he knew was that for some reason his lovely, warm, responsive Mirella had changed into a cool, remote woman who at times seemed like a stranger to him.

They did not argue. Sometimes he thought it would be better if they did. He missed seeing Mirella – cheeks flaring, dark eyes ablaze – passionately defending her corner. He missed hearing her laughter when he said something deliberately stupid to defuse her fury. Most of all he missed the joy of coming together and making up.

Ah! And that, if he were honest, was probably the source of their difficulties. Nothing had been the same between him and Mirella since they had stopped coming together properly. And whose fault was that? No one's really. That dreadful accident had dealt all their lives a deadly blow. For him the shock of Dorina's death followed by the frustration of lying helpless for so many weeks were the prelude to a period of blank despair in which he had been unwilling to talk about the tragedy but unable to get it out of his mind. Small wonder then that Mirella had taken to distancing herself from him and his misery.

Still, physically he liked to think he was almost completely recovered now apart from these odd bouts of rheumatism which laid him low from time to time. And the great thing was, that by keeping the cause of his grief to himself he had been able to protect Mirella from the ghastly truth. So, even if this was little enough to salvage from the wreck he had made of his life (and Dorina's), it was nevertheless something he was determined to hold on to.

'Has your mother finished packing up the carriage yet?' he asked Steffi, aware how much he and Mirella had come to depend on their son to act as go-between when they stayed at Liddy's house.

'Yes.'

'Where is she then?'

'Just gone upstairs to fetch her cloak, I think.'

'And then I suppose you'll be off.'

'Yes,' Steffi said, biting his lip with concern. 'But I wish you were coming as well, Pa.'

'So do I. But I can't travel in this state, so I'm relying on you to help the driver unpack at the other end. Do you think you'll be able to manage?'

'Oh, yes. I put most of the boxes up by myself anyway, so there shouldn't be any problem.'

'Right. And once you've finished that, I don't want you sloping off on your own somewhere. Remember, you're not going up to London for a joyride. You'll be there to help your mother till I'm fit to join her. Do you understand me, Steffi?'

Steffi shot him a reproachful glance, opened his mouth as if to speak, but changed his mind and simply nodded. Then, after shuffling his feet for a few moments, he mumbled something about having to say goodbye to Liddy and sidled out of the room.

Apsley's – a shiver of excitement and apprehension ran down Steffi's spine. Excitement at the prospect of seeing Rosa and Amy again. Apprehension because so much had happened since they had last met.

Naturally he had written to them after their mother's death to say how sorry he was at their loss. A simple, rather childish letter, he supposed on looking back, so it wasn't surprising that neither of them had replied. Besides, they had probably felt too upset to write letters, and the likelihood was that he would find them both still grief-stricken even now so he must remember to tread carefully if the subject of Dorina came up.

'Well, what do you think?' Mirella asked, drawing Steffi's attention to the freshly-decorated façade as they approached Apsley's after dropping off the luggage at their usual digs in Stangate Street.

'It looks great,' Steffi said, reading aloud the name of the forthcoming production. '"Lady Godiva, or Harlequin St George and the Dragon and the Seven Champions". Phew, what a mouthful!'

'Yes, Arnold never does anything by halves,' she laughed.

The building had two entrances – the grander one being in Westminster Bridge Road where wealthy patrons gained access to their boxes – but it was easier for Steffi and Mirella to go in through the gallery doors in the side street just off Stangate.

'My goodness, what's happening?' The noise made Steffi stop in his tracks as he was making his way through to the arena, a huge cavern of a place echoing with people yelling at each other, banging in nails, carrying tubs and planks and ladders, pulling on ropes and presenting more than a passing resemblance to Bedlam.

'Don't worry, it's always chaos at this stage of rehearsals,' Mirella explained.

'But it looks so different from how I remember it,' he said, gazing around.

'The lights, you mean?'

During performances the arena was brilliantly lit by more than fifty gas chandeliers, but now under just working lamps the guttering shadows reached up no further than the first two rows of curtained boxes, leaving the third tier and the gallery almost in total blackness – as if the Almighty Himself was being kept in the dark about what Arnold Foreman had in store for the public this Christmas.

'Yes, I think that's it. And I'm sure the orchestra's bigger than when I was here last time,' he muttered, trying to spot the bald-headed drummer.

'Probably. I know Arnold's been putting his heart and soul into this place since . . . well, you know . . . the tragedy with his daughter.'

'But that's good, isn't it? I mean, it's good he's found something to take his mind off it, even though . . .'

'What?' Mirella asked, peering at him.

'Well, I'm surprised he doesn't find this place too full of memories for him,' Steffi sighed, himself trying to blot out the image of Dorina riding her horse into this arena last time he was here.

'But I think that's half its attraction for him, Steffi. He doesn't want his memories to die. He wants to give them new life.'

'How?'

'Ah, wait a minute and I think you'll see,' she said, putting her finger to her lips to shush any further remark.

Then Steffi noticed that the orchestra had stopped playing the odd discordant snatches of music that had formed part of the general hubbub and a hush was settling over the auditorium as carpenters and others scrambled up on to the stage to leave the arena clear. Then the bandsmen started up again, this time playing very softly.

'Yes, I thought so,' Mirella whispered. 'I recognised her tune. Now, see if you know who this is.'

Steffi felt the hair prickle on the back of his neck as into the ring rode a rider on a black horse.

'It's Rosa,' he gasped. But he had to stare hard to be sure. She looked so different, so much lovelier than he remembered.

Wearing a short silver and white ballet frock, she sat balanced on the silky black rump of Black Chieftain – side-seated in a way that made her appear to be floating. She sat perfectly balanced, without using either hands or feet to support herself. Then, as Black Chieftain continued to canter round the ring, she swung herself astride, stood upright and eventually started to twirl and leap and pirouette like a ballerina on his bare back.

The effect was magical.

'She's good, isn't she?' Mirella urged.

'Oh, yes!' Steffi sighed, as Rosa sank gracefully down on one knee on Black Chieftain's back, arms and hands outstretched, head erect, and seemed to be smiling directly at him as her horse continued to gallop round before leaving the ring.

'And I suppose you recognised the horse,' Mirella said.

'Black Chieftain, wasn't it?'

'That's right. The grey one Rosa had for her birthday proved useless so Arnold's let her have her mother's horse. See what I mean about keeping the past alive?'

Steffi nodded, but he wasn't really listening. His mind was too full with what he had just seen.

'Do you need me at the moment?' he asked.

'No. You're free to go and say hello to her,' Mirella said, smiling in a way that made him blush.

'Oh, but I didn't mean . . .'

'Of course you did. But don't forget what I used to say!'

'What did you used to say?'

'That no matter where they are, those two little madams spell trouble. They always did and, as far as I know, nothing's changed. So be warned!' she said, wagging her finger at him. And although she was probably only being playful, Steffi was surprised at the sharpness in her voice.

It was not long before he came across Rosa just where he expected to find her – in the stableyard behind the theatre. But seeing her in the flesh, still in her flimsy costume and deep in discussion with one of the grooms, made him feel suddenly shy so he decided to sneak away until later. Before he could do so, however, Rosa caught sight of him and to his delight came bounding up to greet him as if he were her long-lost brother.

'Why, it's Steffi,' she declared, glancing over her shoulder at the groom who looked rather put out at the interruption. 'Did you see me in the ring just now? What did you think? It's the first time I've done the act in my new costume and everyone says it looks gorgeous.'

'Yes, it does,' he agreed wholeheartedly, after which it was just like old times with him talking to her as if they had never been apart.

'And does Amy have her own act?' Steffi asked, looking round for the younger girl.

'Yes. She does a wild apache ride – whirling her pony round the ring. And people seem to like it even though it doesn't look so good as the ballerina act. At least you don't think so, do you, Kenny?' she called to the groom who was still hovering near, presumably waiting for further instructions.

'Eh?'

'I was saying you don't think Amy's act looks as good as mine,' she smiled, preening the flounces on her dress.

'Oh, right. No. Like yours best,' he mumbled incoherently, gazing at her with doglike devotion.

'See?' Rosa said, turning her back on him. 'And what about you, Steffi? Will you be staying with us for long? Ooh, I've really missed you.'

He smiled, delighted by the warmth of her greeting.

'For a week at least. Till my father gets back, I suppose.'

'Yes. I heard Levic wasn't well and that must be awful for you,' she said, her grey eyes large with sympathy. 'But tell you what, now I've finished my practice, I'll get out of this frock and then we'll go somewhere private and have a good old natter. There's so much I've got to tell you.'

She threw a last glance at the groom, presumably to make sure he knew what he had to do, and then skipped off to change.

'Known 'er long, 'ave yer?' Kenny demanded in a tone that Steffi would have found offensive had he not concluded that the chap, although several years older than himself, was simply gauche.

'Yes, I've known Rosa and Amy ever since I was little.'

'Hmm, hardly more'n a sprat now,' the other sneered, drawing himself up to a height a couple of inches taller than Steffi's.

'Ah, but still growing,' Steffi grinned. The groom made no response other than to knit his ginger brows into a dense thicket across his eyes, turn on his heel and lumber back into Black Chieftain's stall.

Left on his own, Steffi decided to make his way up to the

Foreman apartment to say hello to Amy and see if Rosa was ready yet. So he wandered past the workshops, sniffing in the smell of turpentine and paint and glue as if they were old friends, and greeting familiar faces. He was especially pleased when a number of the company recognised him too and called out greetings.

'Hello! Levic's boy, isn't it? How's your father, lad?'

'My goodness, can our little Steffi really have grown up so quickly? Still, glad to see you've kept all that nice wavy hair, young feller!'

Then he clattered up the stone staircase with its wall lined with colourful posters of previous productions, pausing once or twice in front of those boasting the names of Madame Mirella the Miraculous Rope-dancer and Levic, Apsley's own International Clown. He felt in high good humour when he eventually arrived outside the door leading to Mr Foreman's own living-quarters and barely hesitated for a moment to catch breath before giving a loud knock. Then he stood back and waited.

When there was no immediate reply, he moved forward to knock again, but in the very moment that his knuckles connected with the door, it was swung open by Amy.

Her face lit up when she saw it was Steffi. 'Oh, I didn't realise . . .' she started to say.

'Amy!' he smiled – and felt the smile die on his lips as he caught sight of her scar.

Not that he had forgotten it was there. How could he ever forget when that dreadful day still kept coming back to haunt him? – Matty drunk and making a scene in front of everyone, Arnold's striking out with his whip and catching poor Amy across the face. It was just that in this moment his mind was full of other things and he remembered only when he saw the livid scar curving scimitar-like down her forehead across her brow and eyelid.

'Oh, God!' he groaned.

And then, seeing Amy's expression change, was overcome by confusion. 'Oh, I didn't mean . . .'

'It's all right,' she muttered, lowering her head. 'I know what it looks like.'

'Oh, but Amy it wasn't . . . I mean, I'd just forgotten, you see.' But he couldn't think what to say to put the situation right. It was too late. The damage was done.

* * *

Mirella was always complaining about the rooms in Stangate Street and Steffi agreed they were rather small and dingy in comparison with Liddy's comfortable house in Aldershot. On the other hand, as Mirella inevitably finished up saying, they did have the virtue of being within easy walking distance of Apsley's – and with two performances a day as well as long rehearsals it made no sense to go further afield for more agreeable accommodation.

Strolling back with Mirella that evening Steffi took the opportunity to open his heart to her about Amy.

'I could see she was hurt by the way I reacted, but I was caught by surprise and couldn't help myself,' he said.

'What did you do then?'

'Nothing really. She opened the door and I was in the midst of saying hello when I noticed that awful scar and sort of, well . . . I suppose I sort of flinched.'

'And did you say anything?'

'No. What could I say? I was afraid of making the situation worse.'

'Yes. I know what you mean. She was such a pretty little thing before. Well, I suppose she still is – but not in the same way. And one can't help feeling sorry for her.'

'But the thing is, I'm sure I made her feel dreadfully self-conscious about it.'

'Why, what did she say?'

'Nothing. But she kept her face turned away from me after that and hardly said a word.'

'Oh, but that's probably just natural shyness.'

'No, I'm sure it was more than that.'

'Well, even if you're right, she'll soon get over it.'

'I hope so. But should I say something when I see her tomorrow? Tell her I'm sorry or something, and say I didn't mean to hurt her feelings?'

'Oh, I'm not sure that's such a good idea, Steffi,' Mirella said, stopping under a lamp-post to rummage for her key. 'I think this is a case of "least said, soonest mended".'

'So I shouldn't say anything?'

'No. I think, if Amy's sensitive about the scar, she won't like people drawing attention to it.'

'I see what you mean,' Steffi agreed.

Of course his mother was right. Amy would hate to think people took so much notice of her scar as to pass comment on it.

So he would certainly not mention it again. Would make sure she did not even catch him looking at it, in fact, so that she would know it didn't matter to him in the least.

'And how did you find Rosa?' Mirella asked as they went indoors.

'Oh, she was really nice and friendly,' he said, finding it a relief to turn his thoughts to the other sister.

Chapter 15

Apsley's Christmas show had been open almost a week now. But despite playing to packed houses twice a day, the company could tell from the reaction of the audience that it was not up to its usual standard. Not that the sets weren't every bit as exotic or the costumes as splendid, and there were at least as many top-rate artistes on the programme as in former years. No. The trouble was that this year there was no Levic to clown his way between and into each act, sparking the other performers into giving their best.

Each day Steffi found himself beset with enquiries about his father. How was he? When would he be back? Did he think there was any chance of Levic returning before the end of next week? To all these questions he could only shake his head and say that, as far as he knew, Levic was still too ill to leave his bed.

Meanwhile he did what he could to make himself useful behind the scenes, shifting props and helping with the animals.

'Coming upstairs for a drink, Steffi?' Rosa called, as she was dismounting from Black Chieftain and handing him to Kenny who stood waiting to rub him down and put him in his stall.

'I'd like to, but I think I'd better wait till Pepe's finished with the dogs,' he said, watching the dozen little frilly-skirted terriers pushing their striped globes around the arena. 'He likes me to help take them back to the kennels.'

'Oh, leave someone else to do that,' Rosa pleaded, still out of breath from doing her act.

Steffi felt quite breathless himself as he gazed at her – a vision of loveliness in her silver costume.

'I don't think I should. I'm supposed to be making myself useful while I'm here.'

'Well, by coming upstairs you'll make yourself useful to me.'

'How?' he asked, feeling his neck beginning to sweat.

'Oh, just by talking,' she smiled. 'I'm not needed now till the last scene, and if I don't have someone to talk to while I'm waiting I get really nervous.'

Steffi could understand this and was going to suggest she sit with him in the wings to talk, but realised that she deserved a proper sit-down after her strenuous performance.

'Okay, I'll come up for ten minutes then. Kenny, tell Pepe where I've gone, will you?' he called – and was surprised when the groom met his request with a very rude gesture. Still, he put it down to the peculiar sense of humour that many of the stage-hands had in this place and was glad when Rosa appeared not to notice.

Once upstairs, she collapsed on to the chesterfield while Steffi fetched her a tumbler of lemonade.

'Aren't you having some?' she said.

'Hmm, yes. All right.'

'There's beer, if you want it.'

'No, this is fine.' He poured out more lemonade from the jug for himself and began to feel less ill at ease. 'Do you think Mr Foreman would mind us being up here like this?'

'Why should he? It's my home.'

'Yes. But I'm not sure he'd want me up here with you.'

'Oh, don't be silly, Steffi. What harm could we possibly be doing?'

'None, of course, but . . .' It was no good, he could not explain even to himself why he felt so uncomfortable. Unless it was to do with all those warnings his mother used to issue about the girls – warnings which he had long since ceased to take seriously.

'Look, why don't you come and sit down here with your drink?' Rosa smiled, patting the place beside her. 'Then we can talk more easily.'

'Okay,' he said, squeezing up against one arm of the couch and then peering down to examine its upholstery more carefully.

'Did I look all right in the ring today?' she asked.

'Oh, yes. You looked marvellous. But then you always do,' he said, turning in time to notice how his words had brought a pretty blush into her already pink cheeks. 'I mean, you and Black Chieftain go so well together.'

'So it's the horse you admire,' she pouted. 'And I thought you were trying to be nice to me.'

'No, no. I am,' Steffi protested. 'I mean you really look lovely on him.' He sighed. If he had been invited up here to help Rosa control her nerves before her next big scene, he was not making a very good job of it. He must think of something else to re-assure her. 'In fact, I think yours is the best act in the show.'

'Really?'

'Yes, really! So there's no need for you to feel nervous.'

'What makes you think I'm feeling nervous?' she murmured, smiling at him over the rim of her tumbler until he had to look away.

'Nothing, except that I thought you said . . .'

'Oh, Steffi, you are funny,' she interrupted, draining her glass and reaching over to put it on a table. 'Whoops!'

He grabbed at her just as she overbalanced and almost fell on the floor.

'Sorry! I didn't mean to touch them . . . I mean, touch you, there,' he spluttered.

'I know you didn't,' Rosa laughed, 'but it's all right, honestly.' She had a face made for laughter, cheeks that dimpled and eyes that shone with amusement as she pulled her bodice up over her bosom again. 'Amazing, isn't it? I never fall off Chieftain no matter how fast he goes and yet here I am, losing my balance on a silly old couch.'

Steffi seized the chance to fill his thoughts with something less disturbing.

'Yes, I've always wanted to know,' he said quickly, 'how it's done.'

'How's what done?' Rosa asked, her eyes widening.

'Balancing on one flank of a horse when it's bareback and galloping so fast.'

Rosa heaved a sigh. 'Oh, that. That's easy.'

'How do you do it then?'

She settled back into her seat and started to speak in a schoolroom sort of voice. 'Do you know anything about centri-fugal force?'

Steffi nodded.

'Well, you just rely on the centrifugal force set up galloping in a circle together with the rosin rubbed into the horse's back. Oh, and there's a certain amount of friction from his hair, of course.'

'I see,' he said, fascinated by the breadth of her knowledge. She was such an accomplished girl, as well as being pretty, that

141

he felt quite in awe of her. 'And did you learn all that from your grandfather?'

'No. My mother,' she said simply.

And Steffi wished he had bitten off his tongue before asking something so tactless. But there it was, out before he had time to think twice. Just like his thoughtless reaction to Amy. It seemed he was destined to upset both sisters, no matter how hard he tried not to.

'Oh dear, I'm sorry,' he stammered.

'Why? There's nothing to be sorry about. My mother was one of the best equestriennes Apsley's ever had, so I'm glad she taught me so much before she died.'

Relief swept through him with the realisation that Rosa, far from being offended, was looking at him with the same warmth and candour as before. And to be able to speak like that – with such maturity – about something as painful as her mother's death filled Steffi with admiration. Rosa seemed so much more grown-up than Amy. And she was so easy to be with, that he could feel himself losing his old awkwardness and beginning really to enjoy her company.

The sound of a door opening had Steffi on his feet and immediately turning to greet the small dapper man with the balding head and glaring eyes who stood there beating a newspaper against his leg.

'Hello, Mr Foreman.'

'Don't hello me. What the hell are you doing here?'

'I just came to talk to Rosa,' he stuttered.

'Rosa, did you ask him up?' he barked.

She turned pale as she nodded. Steffi was not surprised. Arnold Foreman in his formal frock-coat with jewelled pin glittering in black satin tie, black trousers and elastic-sided boots, looked just like the demon prince out of the pantomime – except that, in his case, rage was not simulated.

'But it was my idea,' Steffi found himself saying in an effort to protect her from her grandfather's wrath.

'I bet it was,' Arnold snarled. 'And why the hell haven't you got changed yet?' he said, turning his attention back to Rosa.

'Because I thought I had plenty of time.'

'What you thought doesn't matter! You know the routine. Go straight to change costume and check make-up and then wait in the green room until it's time to stand by for next cue. How do you think I can run this outfit if I can't even trust my own granddaughter to cooperate?'

'I'm sorry, Grandad. I just felt a bit dizzy so Steffi brought me up here so I could be quiet.'

For a moment Arnold's expression changed into one of concern. 'Dizzy, you say? But all right now, eh? Can't afford to lose another of my stars, especially the way things are.'

'No, I feel better now I've had a rest,' Rosa smiled.

'Good. Well, go down now and get changed. And make sure you tell me if you have any more of them giddy spells,' he called as she made her escape.

'Can't be too careful with them two girls, you see – not after what happened to their mother,' he sighed. 'And especially now their father's buggered off and left me responsible. Not that he ever did 'em a pint of good when he was near. Still . . .' Arnold sighed again before startling Steffi by whacking his furled newspaper against the back of the couch, raising a cloud of dust. 'Still, take each problem as it comes and this—' he whacked the couch again '—this is what could bring us all down.'

Steffi stared, flabbergasted. The couch? The dust? He and Rosa not doing what they should?

It was only when Mr Foreman began to unroll his newspaper and smooth it out so that he could read aloud one particular item that Steffi realised the threat lay within the columns of the *Era*.

'"Apsley's Christmas Pantomime not a patch on previous years" – yes, that's what the buggers have printed. "In recent years the name of Levic has become synonymous with panto-mime at Apsley's, and without his presence the piece, despite the usual lavish spectacle, lacks sparkle. Naturally, there were other clowns on stage last evening, all expertly doing their business, but, commendable as these substitutes were, they remained just that – mere substitutes for the one, indispens-able, irreplaceable Levic." See what I mean?'

Steffi was almost ashamed at feeling such a glow of pride. Levic too would surely be pleased to know how much the public valued him. On the other hand, it did not take much imagina-tion to see how disastrous such a review was for the theatre. It might well lead to a drop in attendances.

'I've had a word with your mother, Steffi, but you know what she's like. Won't hear of me getting in touch with him and

143

suggesting I fetch him up here in my own carriage – not to do his full performance, of course, but just go on and do a couple of turns to keep the customers happy.'

'Oh, but he's not well enough to do even that, Mr Foreman,' Steffi blurted out. 'He's really ill and if he gets up too soon it will only make matters worse. That's what the doctor said.'

'Yes, yes. I just heard the same story from your mother, but . . . Hell! Why'd he have to be ill at a time like this?'

It was on the tip of Steffi's tongue to say that Levic was not laid up by choice, but he kept quiet in case that sounded insolent.

'Still,' Arnold said, going over to pour himself a brandy, 'maybe you could have a word with Mirella, eh? I mean, one word from her and I'm sure he'd be up here even if he had to crawl all the way.'

Steffi nodded, now feeling too angry to speak. Surely Mr Foreman knew Levic well enough to know he would never miss a performance unless he absolutely had to?

'You see,' Arnold concluded, 'it ain't just Levic's antics that people love. I can find others to copy those easy enough, but no one else has got the necessary verve to bring the bloody show to life.'

'Well, I'm sure you can count on my father to get back into action just as soon as he possibly can,' Steffi said stiffly.

'I suppose so. It's just that I was thinking that, if someone were to go down and fetch him, they could make sure he don't overtax himself on the journey.'

Steffi had a suspicion that Arnold's real motives were less philanthropic. Could picture him plucking poor Levic from his bed and carrying him up to London to do the show. And that would be disastrous because, where performing was concerned, Levic was certainly his own worst enemy and would offer no resistance to getting back to work.

'Ma, it's not possible for Mr Foreman to put pressure on Pa to come back to the show before he's ready, is it?' Steffi asked Mirella that evening.

'No, he'd know he'd have me to deal with if he tried a thing like that,' she replied stoutly. 'Not that he hasn't had a good go at me to try my influence.'

'And me.'

'The old devil! I thought he might. But don't take any notice.

I've sent word to Levic that it wouldn't be fair on the rest of the company for him to come back before he's ready to do a full performance. Mind you, I don't know how he's going to react once he sees that damn' review. That's bound to make him fret.'

'Well, I think it's stupid,' Steffi declared.

'What is?'

'Mr Foreman getting so worked up about Pa being ill. I mean, someone's health must be more important than a silly pantomime.'

'Ah, but that's show business for you, Steffi.'

'I still think it's stupid.'

'Yes, but that's because you're not fully involved.'

'And don't intend to be if that's what it takes.'

'Oh, come on,' Mirella chided.

'No, I mean it. I don't care how good an artiste is, there are more important things in life than performing in some show.'

'Possibly. But you can't really know what you're saying until you pit yourself against something seemingly impossible and eventually master it yourself,' Mirella declared. And as she spoke Steffi could almost hear the carriage wheels carrying her away from him so often when he was a little boy and he felt even more certain that he was right.

'Yes, well, that's all right so long as it doesn't hurt other people,' he muttered.

'It's nothing to do with other people. It's to do with the sort of demands you make on yourself.'

'That's not the impression I got from Mr Foreman,' he replied sharply.

Mirella stretched out her arms in a yawn and Steffi could see that her face looked hollow with tiredness and there were dark circles under her eyes.

'I told you not to take any notice of Arnold. He's a showman, not an artiste. Still, if you really feel this is such a bad life, you can always take up something less demanding. Like banking or shop-keeping,' she said, yawning again.

Steffi knew she was trying to be sarcastic, but to him the suggestions sounded perfectly sensible. Not because he wanted an easy life for himself, but because it hurt him to see his mother looking so exhausted and to know that his father might be forced to rise prematurely from his sick bed just for the purpose of entertaining people.

Chapter 16

Levic knew he was behaving badly but found it hard to mask his irritability. He hated being treated like an invalid, hated all this cosseting. What he wanted was to be up and about and back at Apsley's, getting on with his life, not stuck on this blasted couch with Mirella's grandmother fussing over him.

'What's in that stuff?' he asked, biting on the pain as he settled back against his pillows after letting her massage his limbs with liniment.

'Camphor, aconite and oil of hemlock,' Liddy replied. 'It should help reduce the swelling in your joints and relieve the pain.'

'But how long does it take to work, for God's sake?'

'Not long.'

'I seem to have been lying here for weeks not getting any better.'

'I know it must seem like that to you. But your temperature's down and your joints are less inflamed than they were, so be patient and you'll soon be back good as new.'

'Patience has never been my virtue, I'm afraid, Liddy.'

'Come now, that isn't what Mirella says. According to her, there's none more patient than you when it comes to perfecting a new trick.'

'Yes, but that's different.'

'No, it isn't. Not if you look on your own body as a bag of tricks that will only do as you want if you're patient with it.'

'Yes, I know what you're trying to say,' he muttered impatiently, 'but it's not really like that. I don't believe in mollycoddling myself. If I were to give in to every twinge, I'd never do anything.'

'Gracious, what a man of extremes!' she exclaimed, arching her eyebrows and staring hard. 'I'm not saying you should give in to every twinge, Levic. What I'm saying is, for goodness' sake stop punishing your body and take life easier.'

'Take things easier! What, at my age?' he snorted.

'If that's what your body's telling you to do, yes. You're still a young man, Levic, but carry on at this pace and you'll wear yourself out before you're fifty.'

Oh, God, not another lecture, he thought. That wretched quack who came to see him last week had taken the same line, and he'd had to lie here listening to the gloomy advice. Who did they think they were, these people who seemed sure they knew what was best for him? They weren't artistes. How could they possibly understand that a sensible course of action for them was sentence of doom for him?

'You've got to rest,' everyone kept saying. But he would go mad if he was forced to 'rest' much longer.

Still, he was wrong about Liddy, God bless her. Instead of developing her theme she sat herself down in an easy chair and took up her sewing.

He liked her there, sitting quietly, reminding him of Mirella, the only other woman he knew who could fill a room with her presence without bombarding everyone with trivial chatter. The two women did not look so dissimilar either, despite the fact that Liddy's hair had turned grey and she wore it nowadays pulled up under a widow's cap. Her complexion too had faded, but her eyes – they were still just like Mirella's – dark brown and bright with intelligence. So, appraising Liddy's neat, little body and her alertness, it was easy for Levic to imagine how his wife might appear in future years and not find that prospect unwelcome.

'What are you sewing?' he asked at length, trying to make up for his former ill-humour.

'A vapour bath,' she said, smiling at him over the spectacles she wore for close work.

'A what? I thought you said "vapour bath",' he grinned.

'That's right, I did. Although maybe I should have said something to act as a vapour bath.'

'How?'

She held out for his inspection a length of burgundy silk resembling a shroud.

'I shall soak this big piece in oil so you can wrap it round yourself in bed to exclude the air. And these smaller pieces that I've just cut off, I shall turn into sleeves for your waistcoat.

148

There's nothing like thick silk sleeves for keeping rheumatism at bay.'

He must have pulled a face, because the next thing he heard was Liddy's laughter and she was saying: 'You looked just like Steffi then. Now I know where he gets it from.'

'Gets what?'

'That look of determination.'

'Cussedness, you mean.'

'No, determination. Steffi doesn't have any "cussedness" in his nature. He's too eager to please for that.'

'Yes, well, he gets that from his mother. She used to like to please people.'

'But doesn't now?'

Levic felt suddenly uncomfortable.

'No. I mean, yes. What I'm really trying to say is that nowadays she doesn't have to try so hard. People naturally take to Mirella. She doesn't have to work to win affection.'

'Well, that's one of the rewards of a happy marriage,' Liddy observed complacently.

Levic turned his head away in a movement that suggested a wish to go to sleep. Not that he really wanted to doze, because all this enforced rest tended to result in sleepless nights so he tried to keep as alert as possible during the day.

The trouble was he could find no sensible way of channelling his alertness. He had laboured over a couple of letters to Mirella, but what was there to write about when all he was doing all day was lying around? He had tried reading. Had thought up a possible new trick and started to sketch it out, but was daunted by the amount of physical effort it would require in its execution.

But that was stupid. He would soon have his full strength back and then there'd be no holding him. He implicitly believed that. He had to.

God, lying here was agony. It was physical torture when he tried to move and mental torture to lie and be tormented by his thoughts.

All right, she had died. But it wasn't his fault. He couldn't help what happened. He had done his best but couldn't save her. Who? Dorina? His mother? His child? They had all died and there was nothing he could do about it. He was – as he had always been – helpless.

There! He admitted it. All right?

Would they leave him in peace now? He admitted it all.

Not aloud, though. Only to himself. Their deaths were his secret shame. Not something he could possibly share with another living creature. Not even Mirella. Least of all, Mirella. Not now. Not after all this time.

Perhaps at the beginning there had been a moment when he could have told her. Should have. In those first few days after Dorina died, when the knowledge of what he had done hung in the air between them, that was the time he should have told Mirella.

He was aware that Liddy had got up and quietly left the room, leaving him now with nothing else to do except pursue, or be pursued by, his thoughts.

Mirella. He wished she was here now. Nothing ever seemed so bad when Mirella was with him. He wanted her. Wanted to hold her in his arms and kiss her mouth, drawing her delicious warmth into him, and touch her soft breasts and feel . . .

No, stop! It was no good thinking like this. Mirella was nowhere near and such thoughts led only to more frustration.

Think of something else then. Apsley's?

There had been talk of Arnold selling the place after his daughter died, but then he'd put on a brave face and decided to drown his sorrow in work and immersed himself in Apsley's. Refurbishing the building, developing its programme, hiring more artistes, planning and scheming for a future which belonged – if not to Dorina any more – at least to her daughters.

Meanwhile, Levic, eaten up by guilt, had waited day after day in a hospital ward and then here at Linden House for a confrontation that never came. In daily dread of Dorina's father appearing to accuse him. Dreading yet wanting Arnold to come so that he could get the evil hour over – even if it meant losing Mirella in its course. Having by then convinced himself that she would never stay with him once she knew the depth of his duplicity. Even coming to accept that only her loss would be sufficient punishment for his crime.

But Arnold never came. Either he had heard nothing from Matty or decided against dragging his dead daughter's name through the mud and spattering it over his grandchildren. For whatever reason Arnold never came, and gradually Levic's anxiety gave way to dull depression. Life went on, but he was in no mood to pursue it.

Looking back, it was just as well that Mirella refused to

indulge his self-pity and had pursued her career independently last winter. For one thing they had needed the money. For another, although her frequent absences felt like betrayal, they provided the spur he needed to get back into shape.

Ah! He smiled at the next memory.

Ditching his crutches and hobbling out on to the lawn behind Liddy's house and throwing himself into handstands and somersaults and flip-flaps – he had willed his body to obey despite the torture of tissue and tendon being torn apart. Embracing the agony, he had forced himself back into shape. By sheer willpower galvanised himself back into action.

So why couldn't he do that now?

He sighed. Perhaps because of those earlier efforts. Last summer he had desperately drawn on energies he was amazed he possessed. Now when he wanted to do the same, he seemed to have no reserves left. Worn out? What, at forty-three? Nonsense! He was not the sort of man to let a little bout of rheumatism get him down.

Especially when it kept him away from Mirella.

He turned his head at the sound of the door opening and saw Liddy standing with a newspaper in her hand.

'Levic? I hope I didn't wake you,' she murmured.

'No, I wasn't asleep. I was just lying here thinking.'

'You've had a lot of time to do that lately.'

'Too much.'

'Well, Hetty's just been into town and brought this back for you,' she said brightly, handing him the latest copy of the *Era*.

'Thank you. And thank Hetty. That was very kind of her.'

He hauled himself up higher on his pillows and smoothed the paper out over the coverlet. There was little to arrest his attention on a front page which, as usual, contained mostly advertisements, but he still allowed his eyes to wander up and down the close-printed columns to take in the names of artistes and venues. This was his world, his life, and he wanted to savour even this thin connection with it.

Steffi had rushed to answer the door when he heard the knock and was surprised to find a youth standing there dressed in a military-looking uniform with a cap.

'Telegraph despatch for Mrs Levic,' he announced. 'Is she at home?'

'A telegram for me?' Mirella called, emerging from the parlour. 'Lord, what's gone wrong now?'

Steffi immediately picked up her anxiety, although he couldn't imagine who might be sending them a telegram.

'Will there be any reply?' the youth asked as soon as Mirella finished reading.

'No,' she smiled, 'there's no need for a reply, thank you.'

Then, giving the lad a penny for his trouble, she turned to Steffi and announced: 'It's from your father. He must have made a quick recovery because he's on his way up to London and expects to be here in time for the seven o'clock show this evening. Isn't that good?'

'Yes.'

But when he thought about it from his own point of view Steffi was not so sure. He had only come up to Stangate Street to help Mirella while Levic was away. Now, just as he was beginning to feel at home – renew his friendship with the two girls and enjoy life here – he was not so keen on returning to Aldershot to sort out his future.

Although Steffi was delighted to see Levic again, he was dismayed to find him so bad-tempered. Hardly had he come into the house, before he was snapping at Steffi for not keeping the fire sufficiently well-stoked; for not having brought in enough fuel; for letting the door bang behind him as he brought in the cases. In short – for being in the way.

'There's no need to bite Steffi's head off when he's only trying to help,' his mother protested.

Whereupon Levic threw him a look of such irritation that Steffi decided to retreat from the room.

Later, Mirella came in and found him in the scullery.

'What are you doing, Steff?'

'Cleaning the boots.'

'Good lad. I know mine were caked with mud.'

'Well, they're not now,' he murmured proudly, holding out his arm to display the shiny transformation he had achieved.

'That's wonderful, Steff, but come into the parlour and have your tea now. You've earned it.'

'Is . . . is Pa still in there?'

He did not know why he asked really. They had not had a row or anything, but he felt reluctant to go near Levic at the moment.

'No, he's gone round to see Arnold.'

'Is he going to do the show tonight, then?'

'Yes,' she sighed, 'even though he can hardly walk.'

'I thought he was supposed to be better.'

'So did I. But you saw the way he was.'

'He looked all right,' Steffi muttered.

'Yes, I know he looked all right, but he was in agony every time he moved. That's why he was so irritable.'

'Was it?'

Steffi was unconvinced. He had known his father to be bad-tempered before when that had nothing to do with being ill. So it was more likely that Mirella was simply making excuses for him, covering up for the fact that he found his son's presence in their house unwelcome and could not wait to see the back of him.

'Of course it was. He's not usually like that.'

'With me, he is.'

'No, he isn't, my love. You mustn't take it personally. Your father's not well at the moment, that's the only reason he's so short with you.' She threw her arms around his neck and hugged him. 'Don't let it spoil things, Steffi. I've so enjoyed having you here with me and I'll miss you when you go back, you know.'

If her words made him immediately consider prolonging his stay, this idea was scotched once his father returned from the theatre and began to prepare himself for that evening's performance.

'Stefan, are you ready? Come on, can't you? I want you to carry this box for your mother.'

Steffi groaned. It was going to be awful tonight. Usually Apsley's was the highlight of his day. He loved being there, specially when it gave him the chance to see Rosa and talk to Amy. For, by heeding Mirella's advice, Steffi had overcome the difficulty of that first awful meeting with Amy, and simply by keeping his eyes averted from her face found he could talk to her just like old times.

But he doubted whether he would enjoy being at Apsley's tonight, not with his father in this foul mood. He could see Levic was bound to upset everyone and be hopeless in the ring. And what would Rosa and Amy think then? They knew Levic, of course, and were always saying what a good clown he was. Well, perhaps he used to be at one time, when he was younger

153

and less bad-tempered, but now any attempt to make people laugh was bound to end in embarrassment.

For a moment Steffi felt sorry for his father. It must be dreadful to think you were funny when you weren't, terrible to have everyone laughing at you for the wrong reason.

'Come on, old Solemnity, take hold of this.'

Steffi, not sure whether Levic was trying to make a joke or be sarcastic, quickly wound his scarf round his neck and took the box.

'What's in it?'

'Only a few odd bits and pieces.'

'Oh,' Steffi said, curious about the glass he could hear chinking as he lifted the package.

'It's all right. You needn't look so worried. It's just some towels and your father's medicines in there,' Mirella explained as she put on her coat.

'Medicines?' Levic said sharply. 'That makes me sound like an invalid. It's not medicines. Only pills and a bottle of liniment. Lots of performers use those.'

'Of course they do,' she agreed, clutching his arm and walking with him along the pavement, leaving Steffi to bring up the rear.

The rest of the company made a great fuss of Levic when he arrived at Apsley's, but Steffi felt his father could have responded more warmly to their greetings and hoped no one else saw his rude grimace when Madame Elise the Female Samson grabbed him round the shoulders and welcomed him back with her usual bear-hug.

'Steffi, come with me,' Levic ordered, hobbling off to the dressing-room.

'But I have to help with the dogs,' he said, about to rush off to fix on the terriers' frilly skirts.

'Leave that, and come with me,' Levic repeated in a voice which brooked no opposition.

Steffi obeyed, but feeling very resentful. This was exactly what he feared – his father treating him as if he were still a child and spoiling everything for him at Apsley's.

'Look, I want you to stay close by me tonight,' Levic said, lowering himself into a chair and applying enough clown-white to turn his face into a great full moon. 'So stand behind the curtains with the box and be ready to help if I start to seize up. Will you do that for me, son?'

154

'Of course I will,' he said, knowing he'd do anything for his father when asked in that sort of tone.

Then he stood watching Levic's reflection in the mirror as he put carmine round his eyes, on the end of his nose and over the lower part of his face to create an exaggerated smile that bore no relation to his real mouth.

If only, Steffi thought, he would not make himself look so grotesque! There was nothing particularly funny about such a face. It was simply silly, especially as you could easily make out the real eyebrows and lips under their painted counterparts. Still perhaps it would all look better at a distance. He hoped so. He hated the thought of his father being a laughing-stock.

He had to stand aside as Arnold Foreman and other performers came for last-minute discussions about which parts of the programme Levic intended to do, it being decided that he would make only a couple of entrées on this, his first night back in the company. Steffi wondered what they thought of his father's sloppy make-up, but if any of them noticed, they were too polite to comment.

Then the first whistle sounded. People who were not already dressed moved swiftly to lockers or seized costumes off pegs, started tugging on tights, shrugging on tunics, lacing up boots.

'The wet-white! Who's got the wet-white?' someone yelled.

'Over here, by the mirror!'

'Anyone checked the house?' enquired the auguste clown with the big, shiny nose who was busy buttoning up the front of his baggy suit.

'Nope,' a couple of dancers chorused.

'Go and take a look then.'

'We haven't time. Send Steffi.'

'Shall I go?' he asked Levic, anxious not to leave his father's side until the performance was safely over.

'Yes. Nip along to see how full it is.'

Tweaking aside the curtain to get a bird's-eye view of the auditorium, Steffi felt his heart hammering in his chest. He had never been this nervous before, even when about to go into the arena himself, so why tonight? he wondered. Immediately that thin, white face with the grotesque eyes and mouth came into his mind and he knew he was feeling anxious for his father. He was terrified that Levic was going to fail in some way tonight – and, if he did, what would Rosa think? And what would all those people out there think?

He cringed as he put sight to sound and surveyed the source of the din he had been hearing from behind stage. The auditorium was packed with people making their usual cat-calls and hullabaloo. The stalls and most of the boxes, apart from the usual couple next to the stage on the prompt side, were full. As for the gallery, it was so crowded it looked as if some poor folk were in danger of being pitched over its front balcony by those clamouring to climb into the rows behind and already, Steffi noticed, the awning that protected the dress circle was littered with missiles from the gods – sweet papers and orange peel.

What if Levic was a flop tonight and all those people began to hiss him and throw things?

Oh dear! Steffi felt sick at the thought.

There were thousands of them out there and they would not know – and even if they did, probably wouldn't care – that if his father was not on form, it was because he had been so ill.

So what if he, Steffi, told them this? Would it help?

For one moment he pictured himself entering that empty ring of clean white sawdust and trying to make such an announcement, but of course it was madness. No one would hear his puny voice. Besides, one simply did not do that sort of thing in the circus. He already knew enough to know that.

Sounds of the musicians tuning up brought him out of his daydream, especially once he caught sight of the drummer, his bald head gleaming as he leant over and tapped the parchment to test its tension. Any moment now the house-lights would fade ready for the spotlights to come up and the show to start. He must go back quickly in case Levic needed him.

'Well?' asked the auguste as soon as Steffi entered the dressing-room.

'It's a full house,' he admitted with a sinking heart.

'Marvellous. Word's obviously got round that our chief clown's back,' the auguste beamed.

Steffi noticed that, as he turned to acknowledge the remark, Levic's smile stiffened as if in resistance to pain.

Suddenly everything was happening. Outside in the auditorium a bell was ringing to warn latecomers to hurry to their seats.

'Right, folks! Parade positions, please!'

The band struck up with the overture, drowning the noise of jostling bodies, jingling bells and creaking harness as the animals lumbered up the passage and stood fretting to make their entrance.

Instead of taking his usual place with Pepe and the Performing Dogs, Steffi carried a chair for Levic into the wings, fetched the box and, stifling his anxiety, stood next to him to watch the parade.

It took only a few moments for him to be magicked away, for the roll of the drums and blare of pipes, cornets and euphonium shook the arena into a moving kaleidoscope of colours and spectacle. Plumed horses pulling chariots, Roman gladiators carrying banners, elephants with swaying howdahs, veiled girls with tall feathers on their heads dancing and throwing kisses to the audience, the dogs tripping along on their hindlegs.

'Good luck, love.'

Steffi turned to see Mirella stoop to kiss Levic and whisper something in his ear before shaking out the folds of her cloak and sweeping into the arena herself, head erect and smiling regally at the crowd.

She had hardly acknowledged his existence, but he did not mind. He was used to the sort of wrapt concentration that descended on her like a shroud before any performance. Not that she was going on yet. This was only the parade and Mirella's was one of the last scenes to take place in the circle before the start of the pantomime proper.

Now the crowd broke into cheers as the music reached a crescendo for Rosa's entry on her huge black mount, and Steffi felt a warm glow of pleasure spiced by a twist of jealousy to see her response to such adoration.

Then came the acrobats marching in a cohort, and the Female Samson followed by the midgets and an array of exotic beasts which included camels, kangaroos, an ostrich and zebras and then even more gaily caparisoned horses.

Quite suddenly, though, he had had enough.

The noise, the colour, the pageantry, had all combined to drown his senses and leave him gasping. Surely there must be something out there that was more his scale, something for him to identify with in a strange and threatening world?

Then he saw him – the little man with a sad face standing alone in a pool of light in the empty ring.

Steffi sighed with relief. Thank goodness for someone who didn't threaten anyone in the least. In fact this poor chap looked so hopeless that it seemed he had no idea what to do next. Except that now, as he began to look about, his expression was changing from doubt to surprise and delight as he discovered a world full of wonders.

'Levic!'

Steffi's hand shot to his mouth to stifle his shock and at the same time he spun round to find the chair at his side empty. When or how his father had managed to shift himself into the arena he could not imagine. All he knew was that the transition had been made, that the lovable clown he was watching was indeed Levic.

After that he relaxed and forgot his worries. There was nothing wrong with Levic. He was going through his routine as smoothly as ever, rushing from one side of the circle to the other performing stock tricks with as much beaming triumph as if he were doing them for the first time.

What made him so funny Steffi could not understand. It couldn't be what he said, because Levic actually spoke very little in the ring, it being difficult to make himself heard amid all the hurly-burly. On the other hand, he put so much concentrated expression into a few words that he had people rolling in their seats after hearing him mutter just, 'Oh dear!' or 'Nice!' And when he laughed in his own peculiar way, his voice tumbling from top to bottom of a scale of squeaky notes, he had the whole house laughing with him.

He was nearing the end of his first turn, miming some tyrant striding across the ring in four paces and then leaping into the air with as much agility and grace as if his body had no bones. Even when he took a tumble, as Steffi saw him do once, he managed to disguise what was happening by affecting to slip and slide over the surface of the sawdust.

Now, having turned a couple of cartwheels and waving his hand cheerily in the air, Levic was taking his leave. Behind him the crowd, not wanting to let him go, cheered and whistled, stamped their feet and tossed coins and fruit into the ring.

Steffi felt proud and relieved. There had been no need for him to worry after all. Levic had made a complete recovery and was in fine fettle.

'The pills – quick, give me a couple! Aaagh!'

Steffi was horrified to see a bent old man come limping towards him, his face twisted into a grotesque mask.

'The pills in the box, Steffi,' he grunted as he collapsed on to the chair.

Stupefied, Steffi shook out the required tablets and handed them to his father. He could not believe that this stiff, broken figure was the man he had just seen bouncing out of the ring. Surely Levic must be play-acting still.

'And the liniment! Quick, damn you! We haven't got all night.'

Steffi jumped. This was no play-acting. This was his normal bad-tempered father back again. The bringer of such joy in the ring was also this unpleasant, irritable man with whom Steffi and his mother shared their lives. He found such a transition hard to understand – or to forgive.

Chapter 17

'Good. It's from Steffi,' Mirella remarked as she picked up the blue envelope from the mat and took it into the parlour. 'Let's hope he's getting on well in the job.'

'Humph!'

'Come on, Levic. I think he deserves a bit of credit for finding himself such an opening. I mean, there must be lots of youngsters in Aldershot wanting to start work in a bank,' she said proudly.

'But he's only a messenger boy, Mirella, not the bloody manager.'

'Not yet, but who knows? Everyone has to start somewhere.'

'But our son! A messenger boy in a bank when he could be working alongside us in the ring.'

She bit back the first retort which came to mind: 'Yes, and maybe he would be if you had not driven him away.' After all, what boy worth his salt would put up with the ill-tempered jibes that Levic kept making while Steffi was around? For that reason she had been pleased when Steffi quickly found an opening for himself after going back to Aldershot three weeks ago. And for that reason she was still pleased, even though she missed his company. Besides, there was Liddy to consider. Having looked after Steffi for the last fourteen years, it would have seemed ungrateful if he had upped at the first opportunity and found work elsewhere.

She sighed, realising there was no point in thinking about other possibilities. Steffi back at Liddy's was definitely better off than staying here and being subjected to Levic's bad moods. Even if it meant that now she was having to bear the brunt of these herself.

'That's right, my lovely, rein him in hard but remember to keep your back straight,' Arnold Foreman was shouting to his granddaughter as Mirella and Levic arrived at Apsley's early the next morning. He had asked them both to meet him to discuss future plans, but seeing the older man still wrapped up in the business of putting Rosa and her horse through their paces, Levic cursed.

'Typical, isn't it?'

'What is?'

'Arnold. I bet he'll expect us to stand around kicking our heels till he finishes. Well, I have better things to do with my time.'

'Wait a minute!' Mirella clutched his arm to stop him immediately rushing off. 'Arnold,' she called, 'we're ready when you are.'

'Ah, yes, of course. Nine o'clock we said, didn't we?' he muttered, taking out his watch and checking. He was red in the face with exertion and still clearly preoccupied with the business of the girl's practice.

'That's right, but shall we make it another time?' Mirella suggested, trying to ignore Levic's snort.

'No, no. I want to have a chat with you both.'

'What about?'

'About what happens after this lot comes to an end next week,' he said, referring to the fact that the pantomime season was due to finish on the last Saturday in February. 'I don't want you disappearing into the blue without being bloody certain you'll be back next year.'

'That will depend,' Levic murmured, his attention rivetted on the fair-haired girl in the blue riding outfit cantering her horse round the ring.

'On what?' Arnold asked sharply.

'How things go during the summer,' Levic said in a flat voice, still watching the rider.

'I see,' said Arnold, drawing in his breath. 'Expecting an offer from someone else, are you?'

'No,' Mirella interrupted, 'I'm sure Levic doesn't mean that. But can I suggest we go somewhere else if we're going to discuss business? I find it easier to talk sitting down.'

What she really meant was that Levic ought to be sitting down and resting his back, but she knew better than to say so openly. She also felt it would be easier on him if they moved away from sight of the young lass on her black horse.

'Right, well, you go and take a pew then,' Arnold said,

gesturing at the stalls, 'while I give Rosa a little more help. Daren't take my eye off her before she's finished, see?'

'Levic, what did you mean by "depends how things go during the summer"? Don't you want to come back here next winter?' she whispered as they sat down and waited for Arnold to join them.

'I just don't like the way he presumes,' he said testily.

'But what else would we do?'

'I don't know yet.'

'Well, if you've got doubts it's as well we talk about them now, before committing ourselves for next year.'

'Next year! What's the point of talking about "next year"? We might all be dead by then.'

'Please don't say things like that,' she stammered, made anxious by his mood.

Before they had chance to say anything more, Arnold joined them and stood rubbing his hands together as he watched Rosa carrying out his latest instructions.

'Right, now where were we? Ah, yes. Levic was just saying you weren't sure about coming back here next year.'

'Oh no, he didn't say . . .'

'Sh-shush, my dear. If it's a question of money . . .' Arnold glanced around furtively before creasing one side of his face in a wink intended to convey a promise which had to be kept from the rest of the company.

'It has nothing to do with money,' Levic declared.

Arnold ignored the remark.

'I mean, no one can pretend business has been good this year. We had all those poor houses at the start,' he moaned, raising his jet eyebrows at Levic to intimate where responsibility lay for that. 'But, thank God, we've made up for some of it since.'

He smiled a self-congratulatory smile.

'So?' Levic said.

'Well, as you know, I'm not one to cream off profits. They'll all be ploughed back before next season. So, rest assured, that if – and what I really mean is "when" – you two come back, you'll find a very different Apsley's waiting for you.'

'What are you planning to do then, Arnold?' Mirella felt obliged to ask, seeing that Levic was taking so little interest.

'I'm going to improve the bloody safety for a start.'

'Oh dear! I hope you're not going to insist on my using a net.'

'No, no,' he said, patting her hand. 'I never like to interfere with my artistes. They take care of their acts: I take care of my patrons. That's proper division of labour.'

'What do you mean by safety then?'

'Oh, lots of other risks.'

'Like fire, you mean?'

'Yes, fire, of course. You've seen all this stir in the papers about the number of theatres going up in flames – well, that's terrible for business, especially as this place has been burnt down twice already.'

'Will you repair the hydrants, then?' Mirella asked, remembering how an elephant had trodden on one of the celebrated dual-purpose gas pipes almost immediately after they had been installed and put the whole system out of action.

'Better than that. I'm gonner turn the whole bloody lot over to water.'

'And double up with a new set of gas pipes?'

'No. No gas pipes needed because – no gas!' he announced with a flourish.

Mirella surveyed the fifty huge chandeliers that were such a feature of Apsley's.

'No gas?' she repeated.

'Nope. I'm about to install electricity.'

He paused, watching to see what effect this remark would have on Levic, who was still concentrating on the young rider.

'Did you hear that, Levic?' Mirella interposed. 'Arnold's thinking of putting electric lighting into the theatre next winter.'

'That's right,' Arnold continued, now that he had Levic's attention. 'Using electricity to light up the place inside and out.'

'But is that really necessary?'

'What do you mean "necessary"?' Arnold asked him.

'Well, electricity might be all the rage but I still prefer gas. It's more subtle.'

This was clearly not what Arnold wanted to hear. He pursed his lips and his blacked moustache began to quiver.

'More subtle? Who cares about being bloody subtle if there's a danger of the place being blown up or burnt down?' he seethed.

'I care. I'm the artiste, remember – the one who has to look to his performance while you look to your patrons. Proper division of labour,' Levic repeated without smiling.

'But you depend on those patrons as much as I do, and I know when they flock to Apsley's next winter, it will be as much to admire our electric lights as to see the show.'

'A five-minute wonder, then,' Levic sneered.

'Yes, I grant you that. I know many of the big theatres have already changed over. All I'm saying is, Apsley's won't lag far behind the leaders,' he ended smugly.

'Racing headlong towards decadence,' Levic muttered.

'Come off it,' Mirella laughed. 'You can't seriously call electricity decadent. I must say I agree with Arnold. I'm all for making theatres safer. Will you keep the chandeliers, though?'

Arnold nodded before turning with a frown towards Levic.

'I don't understand your attitude, fellow. You should be thrilled with what I'm doing. I mean, even a star needs a heaven to shine in, and what I'm offering you is a better heaven.'

'An electric heaven?' Levic scorned.

'I'm not just talking about the bloody electricity. That stage will hold over a thousand performers next season. There! Can you imagine that? I'm planning a spectacle that will use a cast of more than a thousand people and a hundred animals. What other theatre in London can compete with that?'

If he was expecting Levic to look impressed, he was disappointed.

'Why, Arnold? What virtue is there in scale and numbers? Don't you realise that it's just this sort of cheap extravaganza that's destroying pantomime and circus?'

'Cheap?' Arnold exploded. 'Cheap? Have you any idea what that lot will set me back? And you've got the bloody nerve to call it cheap?'

Mirella cursed Levic's tactlessness. Even if he was hatching different plans for their future, she saw no point in alienating Arnold after all these years. Besides, she would expect Levic to show more consideration to a man whose family he had so wronged. The fact that he was unusually irritable today because his back was playing up was no excuse.

She tried to intervene before their angry discussion erupted into a quarrel, but neither would be deflected.

'I want the biggest and best . . .'

'Big is usually banal . . .'

'. . . crushed if you stand in the way of progress . . .'

'. . . true simplicity of art . . .'

'Apsley's must lead . . .'

'. . . nothing but proprietor's greed . . .'

'If you'll excuse me, gentlemen,' Mirella said with exaggerated politeness as she rose to leave, 'I am in need of some peace and quiet, so shall retire to the basement to watch the lions being fed.'

'You're doing what?' Arnold barked.

Before she finished repeating what she had said, Levic was smiling and Arnold had burst out laughing.

Then he urged her to sit down again so that they could discuss the future sensibly – which, with Levic for the most part remaining silent, they proceeded to do.

'Good,' Arnold concluded, smiling. 'So, once you've finished here next week, you and Levic will set off on a tour of the provinces. But after that you have no firm commitments?'

Mirella nodded.

'Well, there's always an opening for you both here, you know that.'

'Thanks, Arnold.'

'So keep in mind what I've said, and let me know as soon as possible about next year's pantomime. I know it's hard to think that far ahead, but as director I've got to start planning now.'

Mirella congratulated herself that they had managed to stay friends despite such a disagreeable start. Even if she and Levic decided not to return to Apsley's, it made sense to keep their options open at this early stage in the year.

Then Arnold said something which made her change her mind.

'Yes, just look at that lass,' he said, noticing how Levic was staring fixedly at Rosa, who had now drawn her horse to a halt and was sitting awaiting further instruction. 'Isn't she growing into the absolute image of her mother?'

Seeing Levic shut his eyes and slowly nod his head made Mirella realise that it was not just rheumatism that was causing him pain. And she made up her mind there and then to do her utmost to ensure that neither of them came back to Apsley's again.

'Mirella, are you awake? Levic whispered.

He had been lying here for hours trying to straighten out his thoughts. He knew he had behaved badly this morning, sounding off at poor Arnold like that and subjecting Mirella to another of his displays of bad temper. It was not fair on her. Moreover, it was not something he had set out to do. It just happened. And that was the trouble. Losing his temper was the sort of thing that he found "just happening" all the time lately.

'Yes,' came her sleepy voice.

'Did I wake you?'

'Not really,' she mumbled, stifling a yawn.

'I'm sorry.'

'What for? I said I wasn't really asleep.'

He pushed his arm under her head and pulled her towards him.

'I'm sorry for the way I behaved this morning. I didn't mean to make things difficult.'

'You didn't. I know what you mean about Apsley's, but I don't see any point in upsetting Arnold like that.'

'Quite right,' he agreed, sniffing in the fragrance of her hair as he nuzzled it aside to kiss her. 'Ohhh!' he let out a long sigh.

She turned her face so that they could kiss properly and for the first time in ages he felt desire rise in him. Her skin was so soft and warm. He pushed his fingers up under her hair, pushing it back round her ears so that he could kiss the skin of her forehead, brushing his lips gently over her skin.

Yes, he wanted her. He felt the urgency beginning to swell and grow strong. His hands began to probe with more purpose, exploring her, stroking her neck, slithering down her spine, fingering her breasts and lingering there, feeling her nipples harden. Yes, he wanted her all right.

'Mirella, I love you, my darling.'

'Do you, Levic?' she answered.

'Yes, oh, yes.'

There was a pause then, almost as if she were deciding something. But maybe not. In any case, there was no more time for talk before he was kissing her again, smothering her mouth and sucking in her sweet breath. Oh, lovely, lovely, this feel of wanting her again. Like wanting life.

Strong, yes as strong as ever, he leant back and let his organ lead him into her. Oh, Mirella, I love . . . I want . . . I . . . I . . . I . . . I can!

They lay together a long time afterwards entangled in each other's arms, unwilling to spoil the magic.

'It's no good,' she sighed at last.

'Why not?' he whispered, startled.

'My arm's got cramp so I'll have to move.'

'Go on, then, move away from me,' he muttered with mock annoyance, almost crowing inside with relief. 'There, more comfortable now?'

She had shifted until she lay beside him, gazing upward. Although he could not see her expression, the sense he had that she shared his feeling of contentment was confirmed by her words.

'I wish it was always like this, Levic.'

'Hmmm.' He slipped his hand under her head and drew it back against his breast. 'This is how it should be.'

'Why isn't it, then?'

'I don't know, Mirella. I suppose I'm to blame if things haven't been too good between us lately.'

'Well, I know you've had your bad back, but even before that things weren't too brilliant, were they?'

Her tone was not accusing but pensive, and he knew exactly what she meant.

Since the accident – no, before that, ever since Dorina, if he were honest – they had been drifting apart, he and Mirella. This was something he had known without being able to do a thing about it. They had never fallen out, just simply fallen away from each other.

'Don't think about the past, only the future,' he suggested.

She sighed and started to say, 'But don't you think, if we tried to clear the air . . .' when he found himself clutching at her shoulder in a panic, making her cry out: 'Ouch! Why did you do that?'

'I'm sorry, love. I didn't mean to. Just suddenly shuddered like when someone walks over your grave.'

'Ugh!'

Now Mirella was shaken by an involuntary shiver while he searched his mind quickly for something to divert her from the dangerous past.

'You see, I've been thinking,' he began with no clear idea how to continue.

'About what we're going to do after we finish the tour?' she prompted.

'Yes.'

'I hope you're not going to suggest we go abroad.'

'Are you against that, then?'

'Yes, if it means going without Steffi.'

168

'Well, we can't very well take him with us – unless the bank sends him with a message!'

'No, I suppose not.'

'So, if we stay here, I'd better approach the agent and get some bookings lined up.'

He tried to inject enthusiasm into his voice but found it difficult. Normally he would have had the whole season settled by now, but this year it had taken him most of his time to find his feet and then stay on them. Moreover, he had avoided making too many advance commitments after being warned that, even once his acute bout of rheumatism was over, he might still have to face a debilitating chronic phase of the illness.

'I'm not so sure,' Mirella said slowly.

'Not so sure of what?'

'Not so sure we should take on a whole line of bookings.' His spirits drooped. She was echoing his thoughts. Perhaps the doctor had spoken even more frankly to her.

'Nonsense,' he snapped. 'I'm feeling fine now, completely back to my old self.'

'Yes, you've just proved that.' She smiled archly. 'But listen, Levic.'

'Yes?'

'I've a different idea about what we can do. Something that would be hard work but a real challenge. In fact, something I've had at the back of my mind for years . . .'

'Go on.'

'Well, it's only an idea,' she continued doubtfully.

'What is?'

'Putting our own show on the road,' she said in a rush.

'No. I've always been against that kind of thing.'

'Oh, but why?'

'Too much of a tie. I mean, look at Arnold. His life's not his own. It's Apsley's. That huge vulgar building has him pinned down so he can't move. You saw how he is. He's not thinking about the show any more, all he's worried about is installing electricity and how to get the greatest number of people on stage.'

'But it doesn't have to be like that.'

'You mean we could take on a smaller theatre?'

'No. I'm not talking about taking on any theatre. What I'm suggesting is that we start our own tenting circus.'

'Oh.' Her words immediately conjured up a glorious time years ago in the sixties when they had spent one golden summer travelling together with a circus through the southern counties. 'Like Sanger's, you mean?'

'Yes.' She sighed. 'Don't you remember what it used to be like, Levic? That wonderful spirit in the people? I mean, think about it. They weren't just a cast, they were a real *company*, and I think that's because they lived and worked together all the time and knew what they wanted to achieve.'

'I understand what you say, but why start a new circus? Why not simply join a going concern? Go back to Sanger's, for instance? We don't have to go abroad with them, if you prefer not. They've got a section travelling here all through the summer.'

'No, no. That's doing exactly what we've done before.'

'What's wrong with that?'

'Nothing, except it's not what I want, Levic. I told you, I want to start a show of our own, where we can make all the important decisions and take complete charge, you and I.'

'And money? Have you any idea what it would cost to buy a tent, transport, animals, props, costumes? Well, you know for yourself, the list is endless.'

'No, I've no idea. All I know is that what others have done, we can do too – if we really want to.'

'And this is something you want to do?' he asked, twisting round so that he could see her face.

'Yes, if I thought you were keen on the idea as well. Are you?' she urged, the colour rising in her cheeks and her eyes shining. He could not remember when he had last seen her so animated.

'If you had asked me yesterday, Mirella,' he admitted, 'I think the answer would have been no. But today, my love, the answer is: yes.'

Even as he said it, he felt a rush of excitement. In this moment, saying yes to Mirella seemed like saying yes to life, an affirmation which made rheumaticky joints seem of no account. He was back on form and anything – and everything – was possible.

'Right,' she announced. 'So, what I suggest is, we don't rush into things but take our time to look around. See what's on the road already. I mean, there's lots of people we can ask for advice, such as . . .'

'Hey, not so fast! I've said I like the idea, but that doesn't

170

mean to say I want to pursue it to the exclusion of my other interest.'

She looked perplexed.

'What other interest?'

'You,' he murmured, pulling her towards him and covering her mouth with kisses.

Chapter 18

Steffi did not know what to make of this news. His mother and father thinking of starting their own tenting circus? At first dismissing the idea as a mere flight of fancy, he was gradually forced to take it seriously as each of Mirella's letters conveyed more detailed plans.

'You see, Steffi, with your father's health being the way it is, I am hoping (once we get our show on the road) to persuade him to ease up on the performance side of the business when necessary and devote himself to management. Don't you think that makes sense?'

He did. Because through all his mother's letters ran a vein of anxiety about Levic. Not that he was an invalid, she begged to reassure Steffi, but he had to put a lot more effort into his act nowadays and was clearly more often in pain than he was prepared to admit, even to her. Moreover, Levic was tending to fall out with people – theatre managers in particular – over nothing at all, and she attributed this to his stubborn efforts to gloss over his agony.

Hmm. Steffi wondered how long she would go on making excuses for his father's bad temper. Still, in view of the unfortunate reputation Levic was acquiring for being difficult to work with, perhaps becoming proprietor of his own show was a good idea. He could then fall out with others without himself being given the sack! Besides, it was impossible to remain untouched by Mirella's excitement at the project.

Such were Steffi's thoughts as he unfolded the clipping from the *Era* and perused the advertisement for a forthcoming auction at which his parents intended to bid.

'Special Auction Sale of Pindar's Circus Property at Ward's Repository, 407 Edgware Road, London', he read – before running his eye over details such as 'This world-renowned circus possesses the best Performing Ring, Pad, and Hurdle

Horses in the Business, among others Sir Peter, bareback or pad; Gladiateur, bareback or pad; Etty, bareback or jockey; six grey match entire Arabs . . .'

He frowned. Entire? Oh, yes. He remembered how he had blushed when Rosa had explained what the term meant. And quickly read on through a list including Barney the Original Ass (whoever he was), a den of performing lions with brand new cage, eight cases of equestrian pictorial posters, lithographs, etcetera, ten large cases of uniforms, some entirely new, all in first class order and ready for use, five large cases of harness, new trappings for ring horses, new pads, new set of four-horse harness, and . . . ah! here's what his parents would no doubt be most interested in.

'One large hundred foot round-top, fifty foot centre piece, waterproof new side-wallings, never been used.'

Steffi glanced back to the letter.

'Note the big tent. That's the main thing we will try for, although we would like some of the other stuff if we can afford it. Anyway, I have made a list and worked out what each thing should fetch so we won't get too carried away! What do you think, Steffi? Is there anything there that catches your eye? If so, or even if not, do try to come up and join us on the day. Your father and I would appreciate having the services of our own personal banker to hand! Seriously, though, would love to see you if you can make it. Write soonest to let us know . . .'

Steffi looked back at the advertisement to check the date and the time. The auction was due to start at twelve noon on 11 October.

Yes. Why not? It should not be beyond his wits to think up a good reason for his employer to give him the day off. Valuable experience to watch all that money changing hands. And he could drop Mr Sutton a hint that there might be good custom coming the bank's way once his parents' new business venture got off the ground.

Despite an early start, Steffi arrived at the warehouse in Edgware Road well after Mirella and Levic who had allowed themselves plenty of time to view the stock. And since so many people had the same idea, he had quite a job to find them in the crush.

'Hi, Steffi! Over here!'

He caught sight of his mother standing next to one of the

174

animal-cages waving her prospectus in the air to attract his attention. She was looking exceptionally smart, he noticed, taking in her blue costume with its fashionable bustle and matching mauve-trimmed hat. But then so was Levic in his top hat and velvet-collared coat, obviously out to make an impression.

'Hello, Ma. I must say you're both looking tip-top today,' he murmured, greeting her with a kiss.

'Well, we always like to make an effort when seen in public with our son,' she beamed. 'Good journey?'

'Not bad. But I'm amazed to find so many people here,' he said, squeezing in to make room for someone trying to get past.

'We were just saying the same, weren't we, dear?'

'Yes. Everyone who's anyone seems to have turned up here today,' Levic said, peering again at the lions.

'Do you know all these people then?' Steffi asked.

'Yes, most. Those two over there, for instance,' she whispered, gesturing towards two men similarly dressed in top hats and velvet-collared coats who were apparently discussing the finer points of a dark bay tethered nearby. 'That's Fred Ginnett and Bob Fossett and they both own circuses.'

'And what's the betting they'll both go for the Arabs?' Levic muttered. 'I've seen those six horses working together in a liberty act and they were, believe me, magnificent.'

As Steffi surveyed the opposition, his spirits began to sink. Everyone here looked so affluent.

'And there are the Sangers, look,' Levic announced, taking Mirella by the arm to lead her across to say hello to the younger of the two brothers, a particular friend of theirs.

'Good morning, George, might have known you'd be here seeking a bargain,' Steffi heard him say.

'Sure, those Arabs must smell sweet to anyone with a nose for horseflesh. But what about you and your good lady?' He bowed courteously to Mirella before turning back to Levic with narrowed eyes to ask, 'Why are you here then?'

'Just looking around,' Levic smiled.

'At the horses? Not acting for Foreman's, are you?' he demanded.

'No, no. If we were to be tempted on anything, it would be just for our own use.'

'Oh, that's all right then. Have you looked at the Original Ass yet? I could see you putting that old fellow in your clown act.'

175

'Original Ass! My . . . foot!' Levic grimaced as the other showman turned away. 'If he thinks that's all I'm here for, he's in for a shock.'

'Why, isn't the donkey any good?' Steffi asked.

'No idea. We haven't seen it yet.'

Together they moved off in the direction of the donkey as the next item in their systematic inspection. Several people hailed Levic as they progressed round the stock, but he managed to avoid getting into conversation until, having paused in front of a handsome chestnut gelding, he was suddenly accosted by a very familiar voice.

'Hello, fancy seeing you here,' Arnold Foreman called, advancing with one hand outstretched while the other held tightly on to his granddaughter. Not Rosa, but Amy.

'Arnold, this is nice,' Mirella said, shaking hands and offering up her face to be kissed.

'Hello, Amy,' Steffi smiled, glancing round to see if Rosa was with them.

'Rosa's not here,' Amy murmured, picking up on his thoughts. 'She's got a bad cold.'

'Oh dear, I'm sorry to hear that,' he said in complete sincerity. The prospect of meeting her today had been an added inducement to come.

'But she wasn't keen on coming anyway because she's happy with her latest horse.'

'Of course,' he said, thinking of Black Chieftain. 'So why are you here?'

'Grandpa's going to buy me something better so that I can improve my act. Although I don't suppose I shall ever be as good as Rosa,' she added.

Moved by the wistfulness in her voice, Steffi sneaked a glance at her face – so different from her sister's. Not that of an English rose, more a wild meadow daisy – pert and elfin-shaped surrounded by a corolla of gingery curls peeping from her green hat, and with a freckly nose and greenish eyes and . . . At this point, overcome by confusion when he noticed the scar, Steffi dropped his gaze to the floor.

'Oh, I don't know. I'm sure you ride very well,' he said, feeling gauche and uncomfortable and therefore glad when their conversation was interrupted by Mr Foreman suggesting that, if they wanted to get a good view, they should make their way to the main room before it became too crowded.

His advice was well-timed because the place was indeed packed by the time Mr Ward ascended the rostrum at precisely twelve o'clock and, after a few comments about conditions of sale, started the proceedings in earnest.

The atmosphere in the smoke-filled room grew tense as the first horse was led in, and in a loud voice the auctioneer rattled off its age, height, merits and antecedents before starting off the bidding. It was the dark bay and after a slow start there were nods and winks and papers being waved from every quarter until the price shot up so quickly that when the hammer eventually came down, Steffi had no idea who had bought it.

'Sold to Mr Robert Fossett for eighteen guineas,' Mr Ward announced.

'Phew!' Steffi gasped. 'You've got to react pretty fast if you want something, haven't you?'

Mirella nodded, her attention already on the next horse being led in.

'This is the one Arnold said he had his eye on,' Levic muttered. It was the chestnut gelding and Steffi was disappointed on Amy's account when her grandfather dropped out of the bidding so early.

'Oh dear,' Mirella said, 'poor Arnold. He's going to be disappointed.'

'Not at all, the sly old devil,' remarked Levic. 'He's just letting others use up their powder before he comes in for the kill. You watch. I reckon it's the dapple grey he'll really go after.'

'But isn't that the one we wanted?' Steffi asked, at a loss to understand the need for all this subterfuge.

'Yes, and for the same reasons,' his father explained. 'It's short-legged, broad-hipped and the perfect colour to take rosin without it showing. A lovely animal, and steady, too.'

'But I think Mr Foreman wants it for Amy . . .' Steffi began.

His words were interrupted by Levic saying, 'No room for sentiment in business, son.'

Then the next lot of bidding started and three more horses were sold before the dapple grey stallion was led in.

Steffi heard Amy exclaim, 'Oh, isn't he lovely, Gramps?' as the horse was paraded to show to best effect his even gait and fine tail, long enough to sweep the ground.

'Please don't bid against Mr Foreman, if he goes for it,' he pleaded with Levic.

'Why not? I told you, this is business.'

'But it's for Amy.'

'Wrong. It's for our circus,' Levic snapped.

By now the bidding had already risen to the point where those who wanted a bargain were dropping out, leaving the floor to serious contenders such as George Sanger, Arnold Foreman and – no, Steffi could hardly bear it – Levic, who had just entered the fray.

'Nineteen, nineteen guineas I am bid. Nineteen and a half. Twenty. I have twenty,' Mr Ward was chanting dispassionately. 'Twenty-one. Now, twenty-two. What advances on twenty-two?'

Sanger had dropped out. It had become a duel between Levic and Arnold. Steffi looked at Amy's expectant face and felt a sense of shame on his father's behalf.

'Ma, can't you stop him?' he demanded.

And Mirella must have been sharing Steffi's feelings, for her voice immediately rapped out, 'No, Levic, no! It's for Amy, and she's Dorina's daughter, remember!'

It felt as if a hush fell over the room as Levic looked at his wife. His face turned ashen, his dark eyes fading as they suddenly lost their light.

'Of course. I'd almost forgotten,' he mumbled before turning on his heel and walking out.

'Oh Christ!' Mirella moaned, looking as if she were about to follow him.

'But, Ma, if you go now, you'll miss most of the bidding,' he urged, worried by the rate at which lots were being knocked down.

'I know.' She seemed to make up her mind quickly. 'Stay by me, Steffi. I've never done this sort of thing before, but I'm blowed if we're going to lose that tent for want of trying. And if your father doesn't like what I decide to pay for it, then it serves him right for stomping off like that.'

'You bought *what*?' Levic exclaimed later, when he eventually returned and went with them to settle the account and arrange for their purchases to be stored until collected.

'Barney the Original Ass,' Mirella repeated, smiling at him.

'That's what I thought you said, but what on earth possessed you?'

'Sentiment,' she declared. 'Steffi took pity on him. And when I looked at the beast again, I couldn't resist his mulish expression because it reminded me so much of you.'

As the words tripped lightly from her tongue, Steffi could tell his mother was happy. And why not? Even Levic was generous enough to congratulate her on the way she had managed to buy the tent for less than the sum they had set aside for it. And he had sufficiently recovered from the incident with the grey horse to laugh in response to her teasing.

'Fair enough, I deserved that,' he agreed.

As for Steffi he was as delighted that Amy had got something she set her heart on as he was at his mother's success. His only disappointment being that he did not manage to meet up with Amy again to say goodbye. But the crowds were against him and, having peered uselessly around, he made his way out on to the pavement, glad to emerge from the stuffy building into a bright autumn afternoon.

'Fancy a drink to clear all that dust from your throat?' Levic suggested.

'Yes, a drink to celebrate with,' Mirella agreed, 'before Steffi has to go back to Aldershot.'

'By the way, did you hear that the den of lions failed to reach their reserve price?' Levic remarked once they had ensconced themselves in the nearest tavern.

'Yes, Steffi and I were there, remember – the whole time people were bidding.'

Steffi looked anxiously at his father, but he showed no sign of having noticed Mirella's sarcasm.

'So, what figure did they reach?'

'Something pretty high, wasn't it, Steffi?'

'Yes.' He screwed up his eyes in an effort to remember. 'Certainly over nine hundred pounds.'

Levic whistled.

'Then the reserve must have been set at something like a thousand, which is probably what we would have to pay if we wanted an act like that.'

'But you wouldn't, would you?' Steffi asked anxiously, remembering how his mother had told him about seeing her own uncle badly mauled by lions years ago.

'No, we certainly will not,' Mirella declared. 'Horses, yes. The circus was built for horses.'

'Was it?' If he had known the question was about to draw on his head a lecture from Levic on the complete history of circus from ancient to modern times, Steffi might have thought better than to ask.

'. . . So you see, the forty-two foot ring was designed to give equestrians the best chance to keep their balance when galloping round and leaning inwards,' Levic said in conclusion.

'And does it always have to be that exact size?'

'Yes, that's the regulation size and we'll have to make ours to standard otherwise visiting acts could come a cropper.'

'But what made them settle on forty-two feet?' Mirella asked, rejoining the conversation.

'I don't know if there's any mathematical reason. All I know is that when you lean inwards on a horse, the angle your body makes depends on the diameter of the ring and experience proves that a forty-two foot ring is the most suitable.'

'I see,' she said. 'Well, we'll make sure we have the right size ring, but I've just been thinking about all the performers and other workers we're going to need to get this show on the road.'

'Don't worry. I shall start putting out the word after Christmas and, if we don't attract enough suitable chaps, I can always place an ad in the *Era*.'

Goodness! For the first time it dawned on Steffi what a huge step his father was about to take. No longer just a performer, he would be a proprietor like Arnold Foreman. Not working for someone else, but taking his very own show on the road.

'Pa, what will you call yourself?'

'When?'

'When you start your own circus. What will it be called?'

'"Levic's", I suppose. Unless either of you have a better idea?'

'"Levic's". That sounded odd to Steffi. Just as it had always seemed odd for his father to possess only that one name, even signing himself just 'Levic' on official documents. Mirella had explained how this had come about, how Levic being brought up as an orphan had never known any other name and so, even if pressed to supply a forename distinct from his patronymic, simply doubled up and became Lev Levic.

'"Levic's Circus". Hmm, doesn't sound bad,' Mirella was saying. 'But is it a good idea to make it stand or fall by your name?'

'What do you mean by that?' Levic's fiery dark eyes flashed with resentment. Mirella paused before speaking again.

'I don't know exactly. But I've always thought it was a pity you had only one name.'

'Why?'

'Because most performers, especially clowns, have a professional name to sort of protect them. I mean, having a different name on stage must make it easier to revert to being themselves when they take off their greasepaint.'

While she was speaking, Levic sat staring at Mirella as if unsure how to take such a remark. But Steffi understood what she was trying to say. He could see that his father put so much of himself into being Levic the Clown that there was precious little left for any other identity. But would it, he wondered, be any different with Levic the circus proprietor?

'Yes, I suppose you might have a point,' his father muttered. 'Offstage or on, I'm always Levic and maybe that's why I'm wearing out so quickly.'

'Don't talk nonsense. He's not wearing out, is he, Steffi? He's just being made to realise that he's human like the rest of us,' she chafed, burrowing into her bag for a pencil and paper so she could begin to set down their plans. The pencil emerged first but, having been placed on the table, immediately started to roll until it dropped on the floor. Steffi retrieved it and, holding it in his hand, idly read out the name embossed in gold lettering along its side.

'"Minerva".'

'What?'

'"Minerva" – it's the name on the side of this pencil.'

'Minerva,' his father repeated, savouring the sound. 'Yes. "Minerva's Circus" – how about that?'

'"Minerva's"?' Mirella repeated, as if the sound was infectious. 'I like it as a name, but who or what is Minerva when she's at home?'

'Roman goddess of wisdom,' Levic announced, 'so we couldn't do much better than that for a presiding genius, could we?'

'Hmm, "Minerva's". Hand her over, then, Steffi,' she said, stretching out to take the pencil and proceeding to use it to write out 'M-I-N-E-R-V-A'S C-I-R-C-U-S' in bold capitals at the top of her notepaper.

By the time Steffi left them to rush off for his train, both his parents were so absorbed in the task of working out their itinerary for next year that they hardly seemed to notice his departure.

Chapter 19

Steffi often looked back with nostalgia to that sunny day in October – if for no other reason than that it marked the last time he saw his parents that winter. Setting themselves the task of raising as much money as possible for their new venture in the spring, they threw themselves into a succession of engagements in various theatres in the north. So if it had not been for Mirella's frequent letters, he would have felt quite forsaken.

He did hope to visit them at Christmas when they were playing in pantomime at Sheffield, but this plan had to be abandoned when Liddy went down with pneumonia. Nothing could persuade him to leave his great-grandmother when she was so ill – even Mirella's plea that a couple of days would not make any difference, especially as there was plenty of expert help on hand in the person of her own mother, Sadie.

Nor did Steffi regret his decision when, as things turned out, Christmas in Aldershot proved a jovial occasion with his grandparents and two bachelor uncles all spending the holiday at Linden House and, more importantly, Liddy beginning to rally and make a good recovery.

'Thank God, she's turned the corner,' Sadie sighed on Christmas Eve. 'I feared we might have a visit from the Mulo-mush rather than Saint Nich'las this year.'

'Mother means she thought Gran might not make it,' his Uncle Albie explained.

'Yes, I've heard Liddy use that expression. Romany, isn't it? Anyway, I know what it means,' Steffi assured him. 'Now, can I get you another glass of ale? And what about you, Ben?' he said, turning to his mother's younger brother – a man in his late twenties who bore a striking resemblance to Mirella with his delicate features and curly black hair, a contrast to Albie who was fairer and, like their father, heavy-jowled.

183

'I'm surprised our Mirella didn't come running when she heard Liddy was ill,' Albie remarked once all their glasses had been refilled.

'Hmm,' Sadie sniffed, 'shows how little you remember your sister, then! She was never one to run on behalf of anyone other than herself.'

Steffi felt he must come to his mother's defence, even though experience told him it was useless to try to heal the breach between Sadie and her elder daughter. The wound had festered too long. Since his birth, in fact.

'Ma wanted to come, Gran, but it was Liddy who told her not to.'

Sadie sniffed more loudly.

'No, it's true,' Steffi continued. 'Liddy made me write to Ma and tell her not to worry and that she was being well looked after. And, to be honest, I think she would have felt dreadful if she'd upset Ma and Pa's last season because she knows how much they need the money for Minerva's.'

'Money! What's that where flesh and blood's concerned? Blood's thicker than water and worth more than money, I can tell you,' Sadie growled.

Steffi gathered from the way Albie raised his eyebrows at Benjie that this was a familiar refrain. And why not, when Sadie made no bones about the fact that, as far as she was concerned, her family was her life? Seeing herself first and last as a mother, Sadie had no time for someone like Mirella who could pursue a career so obviously at odds with her own son's welfare. And since this was a view Steffi had often been tempted to share, it probably explained why he had always got on so well with his grandmother – even though he could never have written Mirella off in the same way. Black sheep of her family, she might be. And possibly selfish to a fault. Heaven knows, she had let him down enough over the years! But Steffi was not the person to find anything unforgivable in someone he loved.

'Besides,' Sadie was saying in her fussy way, 'it's not just a question of being here for Liddy, I'd have thought your mother owed you at least twenty-four hours of her precious time over Christmas. I mean, Christmas isn't Christmas without family.'

'Don't keep on, Ma. It doesn't make it any easier for Steffi,' Benjie broke in.

'Why? He's big enough to know how shamefully he's been

treated all these years,' she continued relentlessly. 'I mean, what would have happened if she hadn't been able to dump him here with her grandmother to bring up? I'm not saying I wouldn't have been happy to look after you, of course,' she said, turning to Steffi, 'but that don't mean to say I could ever condone my daughter diving headlong into a career when her place is at home with her child. All right, all right, Albie. I know what you're thinking, but I wanted to say my piece. And now it's been said, I'll shut up.'

Steffi breathed a sigh of relief, hoping for the sake of everyone present that that was the last time Sadie would feel the need to 'say her piece' this Christmas. But he rather doubted it. Usually the only person capable of mediating between mother and daughter was Liddy, who had an infallible way of taking the wind out of Sadie's sails.

'I don't care what anyone else thinks,' Liddy would say calmly, 'but I for one have never stopped blessing the day Mirella chose to have her baby in this house and then left him here for me to bring up. Steffi's been a great joy to me and it comes hard to hear you talk about his homelife as if it were some tragedy for him.'

'No, no. Of course I didn't mean . . .' Sadie would then start to backtrack until she had gone far enough to lose her train of thought – whereupon everyone could relax again.

Johnny, Steffi's grandfather, rarely got involved in these conversations but seemed to understand the situation better. He worshipped Mirella, driving over to Aldershot from Windsor to collect her and Steffi and taking them back to his gamekeeper's cottage on the royal estate to stay for several weeks' holiday each summer. So there were some years when Steffi had seen more of his grandparents and uncles than his own parents and felt more like one of their family than the son of Mirella and Levic. And these relationships – together with the dull but secure routine at Linden House – lent stability to his life.

But there were days when this very stability got him down and he found it easy to sympathise with his mother's rebellion against such tedium. How old had she been? Fourteen or fifteen? Certainly no older than himself when she ran away from her kitchen-maid's job and joined a travelling fair. Well, Steffi could only admire her when he thought about it and sometimes he even dreamt of making a similar gesture, especially on days when he received one of Mirella's letters giving details about the latest plans for Minerva's.

Such moods, however, lasted no longer than it took him to remember Liddy and what he owed her. Liddy had brought him up and sent him to a good school. It was Liddy's influence which had secured him his place at the bank where there was already talk of making him up to clerk in the near future.

'Yes, there is such a thing as gratitude,' he chided himself whenever his mind wandered towards an alternative future.

It was unthinkable that he could ever leave Liddy now that she was over seventy and needed from him the support she had so generously given him all his life. Just as he would never wittingly cause pain to someone he loved.

On the other hand once Johnny, Sadie and the uncles disappeared back to Windsor after Christmas, leaving Liddy to continue her convalescence under the supervision of Hettie, her part-time servant, Steffi grew more and more bored at the bank and restless at home.

'I wish you could see your father working his new routine with Barney in the ring,' wrote Mirella. 'He's still too scruffy to call handsome (Barney, I mean!), but he is certainly a character. Do you remember how we were told he had been trained to do hanky-panky – you know, pretending to read people's fortunes and walking round the ring to pick out the biggest villain or the prettiest girl in the audience? Well, though Levic was not too keen on that kind of thing to start with, he has developed a very funny bit of clowning business with Barney which I know you will love when you see it. So our little attempt to bring sentiment into business has paid off!'

Steffi lapped up all these details, laughing at his mother's descriptions of Barney shoving Levic unceremoniously out of the ring at the end of their act. And almost envying the donkey for living so dangerously!

Then, early in March, came Mirella's letter announcing that she intended to make a visit – albeit a fleeting one – the following Sunday. Levic would not be with her because he had an appointment in Portsmouth. Something to do with another circus being sold up – this time by its creditors who might be expected to knock down the stock at bargain prices.

It did occur to Steffi to wonder why, with so many travelling circuses going broke, his parents were so confident that theirs would be a success. But he did not like to say this in his happy

186

reply to Mirella, confining himself to a brief note stating that he would meet her at the station and accompany her back to Linden House to gain precious extra time together.

After all it was nearly five months since he had last seen her and he felt as excited as he had done when he was a little boy expecting her regular visit from Apsley's.

Even when Sunday dawned wet, cold and miserable the weather had no power to dampen his spirits.

'Don't forget to take a brolly!' Liddy cautioned.

'Yes. Thought of that,' he called, buttoning up his mackintosh. Not that he would use the umbrella for himself, but it made him feel good to think of holding it over his mother's head to protect her from the elements. A sign that he had grown up. Just in case she failed to notice the few hairs over his upper lip and round his chin – not enough to shave as yet but definitely growing darker every day.

He left in plenty of time, having looked up the trains in his *Bradshaw* and decided that Mirella would most likely catch the one due to arrive just before nine. There was another about half an hour later, but knowing his mother she would be on the first because she liked to get moving in the morning.

There was an anxious moment when, passing through the booking hall, he caught sight of a special notice alongside the timetable on the wall where the station master always pinned up news of cancellations. His heart sank. But as soon as he drew close enough to read what it said, he realised that it was simply notification of an extra train being put on the line. So that was all right.

Now all he had to do was wait.

Time passed quickly for the first ten minutes or so, his attention being held by an engine shunting waggons into a siding. Then he heard the welcome noise of an approaching train and took up his position on the platform – only to feel foolish when a goods train rattled by. After gazing after it intently to dispel any impression that he had been caught out, he moved back from the edge of the platform and glanced at his watch. Still twelve minutes to go, but now the station was beginning to fill up with people, soldiers for the most part – their red and green uniforms adding a flash of colour to the grey day. About to board? Or, like him, waiting to meet someone? Probably preparing to greet their sweethearts, Steffi surmised.

He walked towards the edge of the platform again, taking no

notice of the rain driving under the canopy into his face. Not long now surely. Five minutes to go. Then four. Then, a long time after deciding not to look at his watch any more, he heard a whistle in the distance and saw the cloud of steamy smoke.

Doors opening, passengers climbing out, throwing themselves into waiting arms, yelling for a porter, struggling to drag heavy luggage from the guard's van. Then people shutting their brollies and climbing into the train, smearing their coatsleeves across misty windows to enable them to see those waving goodbye. The guard blowing his whistle, raising the flag. A latecomer dashing across the platform, wrenching open a door and running alongside until getting up enough speed to leap into the carriage. Then the tail of the guard's van swaying out of the station. And the train had gone. But there was no Mirella.

So she had not caught the first then. Now Steffi had to settle down for another wait. Another half hour, perhaps. Or even an hour. It did not really matter, so long as she got here some time this morning.

He turned up his collar and strode along to examine the weighing machine, wondered whether to buy a newspaper from a shop along the road but decided not, in case the next train was a few minutes early and he missed Mirella.

But he need not have worried because in fact the next train arrived a few minutes late and he could not have missed Mirella – because she was not on it.

He went to check the timetable in the booking hall and then settled down to wait again.

When she had not arrived by eleven o'clock he knew something had gone wrong and began to feel sick with dread. Either his mother was ill, or there had been an accident. She would never have changed her mind and simply not turned up. On the other hand, he supposed there could have been delays the other end, so it was possible she would be on the next. But what if she wasn't?

Damn! It did not matter about him standing around on this platform all morning, but he was worried about Liddy waiting on her own at home wondering what had happened to them. She would have been expecting them to arrive over an hour ago and he could not think how to get a message to her. Damn! The longer he stayed here, the more Liddy would worry. Whereas if he went home, although he would miss meeting Mirella, he could leave a message for her with the porter.

But what a disappointment for her to arrive and not find him here as planned! It was no good. He must wait for at least one more. And if she wasn't on that . . . But, she almost certainly would be.

The drizzle had turned into downpour by the time Steffi set out for home just after mid-day. But he didn't care about the weather. Didn't even bother to put up the umbrella. It would only have slowed him down when all he wanted now was to be back at Linden House as soon as possible.

The trouble was, what would he tell Liddy to allay her fears? For in his heart he felt that only illness or a serious accident would have stopped his mother coming today. Had she fallen from her rope last night? Slipped and fallen with no safety net to catch her. Was she even now lying unconscious in some hospital bed? Or asking for him? Or . . . No, not that other possibility. That he refused to think. After all, it could be that she had only broken a limb or stunned herself.

He broke into a run as he saw Liddy standing behind the front window, obviously looking out for him. Stopped dead when he saw the little piece of buff paper she was holding up in her hand. He knew what that was. A telegram. So he had been right to fear the worst. A telegram. Probably from Levic to tell them.

He steeled himself to walk up to the door. No need to knock. Liddy was already there, of course. Poor distraught Liddy, clutching at his arm to drag him into the dry and wailing how the message had been delivered hours ago but there was no way of letting him know.

Trying to stop himself trembling, he took the paper from her hands and read: REGRET CANT COME STOP URGENT BUSINESS PORTSMOUTH STOP LETTER TO FOLLOW STOP LOVE MOTHER STOP

He read it again. So there had been no accident then. Mirella was perfectly all right, thank God. He closed his eyes. Thank God.

But what had happened? Urgent business in Portsmouth. But how urgent, for heaven's sake? Just how urgent did business have to be to make her change her mind at the last minute and let him and Liddy down like this?

189

He scrunched up the paper in his hand as he made his way into the scullery to take off his wet clothes while Liddy made a fresh pot of tea.

Chapter 20
Summer 1888

Now that he was actually on his way, Steffi was having second thoughts about the wisdom of spending a month with Minerva's. It was all very well going off to visit the circus on odd days at weekends and bank holidays. He was always glad to see his parents, especially his mother. And always happy to make himself useful, even if it was only by manning their ticket office for a few hours and totting up the money afterwards. But the prospect of a whole month was beginning to pall even before he had started.

The trouble was, once Mirella heard that he would be at a loose end for a few weeks before taking up his position at the new bank, she had implored him to spend the time with them rather than accompany Liddy to Windsor on her annual visit. And having been persuaded that anything would make a welcome change from the bank, he had packed a few things and caught a train down to Hastings where Minerva's were open that week in a field conveniently near the station.

Steffi's heart sank as he stood and surveyed the tober. Not because it looked disappointing in any way. The big red and white tent looked grand with its brightly painted showfront and smart wagons drawn all round. But he was suddenly reminded of the similar scene which had greeted him at Oxford four years ago. Not quite thirteen then and come to spend his school holidays with his parents who were working for Foreman's, he could remember how excited he had felt when he arrived. But he could not forget how the holiday had ended in disaster when his father had that fateful accident with the horse.

Still, that was then. Now things were very different. This was not Foreman's but Minerva's. And so long as his father was in a reasonably good humour, Steffi thought he should be able to survive a month with his parents and maybe even enjoy the experience.

'How's Pa been lately?' he asked Mirella as they were seated together in the wagon counting the takings on his first evening.

'Not too bad,' she said guardedly, placing another column of silver coins on the table before looking up. 'I suppose you're talking about his rheumatism?'

'Yes. And his . . . well, his temper. I was wondering if he still got so upset about things?'

'Oh, no,' she said quickly. 'Of course he gets annoyed if things go wrong but that's only natural.' She put another pile of coins on the table but clumsily this time so that they toppled and had to be stacked again.

Steffi felt annoyed that she did not appear to know what he was talking about. Everyone else on the tober was aware of Levic's bad temper. And he himself had only been here minutes before falling foul of it.

'Can't you forget your stomach for once and get out here and help shift this truck?' his father had yelled as Steffi was sinking his teeth into his first bite to eat since leaving Aldershot that morning.

'Give the lad a chance, Levic. I'm sure he'll give you a hand as soon as he's changed his clothes, won't you, Steffi?' Mirella intervened.

'Yes. Of course I will,' he agreed.

'Humph!' Levic grunted. 'I'll find someone else then.'

'That was a nice welcome,' Steffi remarked as his father stomped off.

'Take no notice. He's all right. Just too much on his plate at the moment.' She smiled as if to make up for Levic. But behind her smile, her eyes remained troubled. And it seemed to Steffi that his mother was a lot thinner and more careworn than when he last saw her.

Fortunately they had a bigger wagon than the one they used when travelling with Foreman's but Steffi still found it a squeeze, especially when three adults turned in for the night. He missed his privacy and, try as he might, found it impossible not to overhear his parents' conversations as they droned on into the early hours.

'How were the takings?'

'Up more than six pounds on last night,' Mirella whispered.

'Good, but still not enough.'

'Oh, come on, Levic. We should be able to relax and take it easier now.'

'Not with that blasted horse act still so ragged,' he spluttered.

'Shush! It's not that bad. Anyway, let Hugo worry about it, that's what we pay him for.'

'It was dreadful. The liberties were out of step when they came in,' Levic carried on ranting, 'and I won't tolerate such sloppiness.'

'Sort it out with Hugo in the morning then, but don't fret about it now,' Mirella coaxed in a weary voice.

'Okay, but either he gets it right or he goes.'

And Levic continued to elaborate on what should be done to improve the situation, his voice droning on regardless of Steffi being kept awake at the other end of the wagon, regardless even of how tired Mirella must have been feeling.

Hugo was the equestrian director and ringmaster and, seeing him cut such an imperial figure in the ring, Steffi was at first awestruck. Everyone agreed that in looks he made a perfect ringmaster. A good few years younger than Levic and nearly a head taller, he possessed the sort of fine clear-cut features which, when crowned by the ringmaster's silk top hat, seemed to set him above common humanity.

Outside the ring, though, with his hat off to reveal a mop of tight blond curls above jokey blue eyes and a light-hearted grin, Hugo was a different person. Someone Steffi found so amicable that he chose to ride with him in the rear of the procession when, soon after dawn, the circus took the road to make a fifteen-mile journey to Eastbourne.

Steffi enjoyed the excitement of the move, having thrown himself into the business of dismantling the big top after the last performance the night before and watching the colossal structure sinking down and being reduced to shapeless piles of canvas and poles. But what he did not take so kindly to was being dug out of bed almost as soon as he had gone to sleep, having to drag on his clothes in the dark and stumble out after Levic to help rouse the rest of the company.

Still, thank goodness there was Venie, the snake-lady, to cheer them all up with her cakes and Irish tea – as she called the fiery concoction she dished up in vast quantities on every conceivable occasion. Once more, as far as Steffi was concerned, appearances had been deceptive, because he had been horrified at first sight of this tall, gaunt woman with the fuzz of greyish-ginger hair and fog-horn voice booming, 'Tea-yup! Tea-yup!' But his offer to carry her steaming mugs over to the tentmen was accepted with such a hearty smile that he felt he had found another friend.

In fact they had been deep in conversation when breakfast was suddenly interrupted by his father's whistle telling the drivers to prepare their horses to draw out the loads one by one on to the road – no simple operation when an overnight shower had left the ground so soft, especially near the gate. Eventually it took extra horses, men with lever bars, and even the elephant, Mumbo, with a special harness to shield his eyes, to drag and shove the heaviest loads through.

Once all the wagons were lined up and ready, Mumbo and the two camels went lumbering on ahead while Levic gave the drivers last-minute instructions about where to break the journey. Then came the general signal to be off.

The order on the road, it seemed, was always the same. Levic and Mirella in the front wagon, then the band wagon covered by canvas to protect its gold leaf and glossy paintings. Behind that the other loads, each drawn by three horses and with one or two others tethered. And then Hugo with Steffi beside him bringing up the rear with a beast wagon containing the llama and zebra as well as having several ring horses tethered behind. Although somewhere on the journey the whole procession would catch up and overtake the camels and Mumbo.

'Help yourself.' Once out of the gate, Hugo passed Steffi his cigar case while keeping his attention focussed on the horses.

'No thanks. I don't smoke.'

'Strange chap!' mumbled Hugo, puffing out a small cloud of smoke from the corner of his mouth.

'I know,' Steffi yawned.

'Tired?'

'Yep.'

'Well, you can always join the lampman in the back of the wagon and kip down for a bit ... if you can stand the smell.'

It was a standing joke that the lampman, a funny little man hardly ever seen on the tober without a bent pin in his mouth for pricking out the jets of the burners, always stank of paraffin.

'No, thanks. I don't want to miss anything on the road,' Steffi said, waving at the elephant keeper as they passed.

But despite his words, he was soon nodding off even while sitting on the dickey seat. Being jolted awake by his head rolling dangerously far forward, and then sleeping again until rudely awakened by a cry echoing back along the procession: 'Lope! Lo – ope!'

'What's that?' he asked, trying to shake himself back to his senses.

'It means there's a hill up ahead, so all passengers to walk. But don't you worry, you can be an exception.'

'No, I'd rather get down and walk with the rest,' Steffi muttered, remembering what his father had said about being ready to put a chock behind the wheels if necessary to stop the wagon slipping backwards. Fortunately it was not necessary on this occasion.

Having heard that Eastbourne was famous for its beach, he was disappointed to find that the tober there was in a cricket field some distance from the sea.

'Don't worry, we might have time between the shows to slip down for a swim,' Hugo suggested.

'That would be nice,' Steffi said, his attention now on the line of wagons rattling to a halt, waiting for the first to move on to the tober. He was intrigued to see how his father, who together with several tentmen was already surveying the pitch, would set everything out, for it was hard to imagine how this empty field could ever come to look like the one in Hastings with the big top and all the other tents and wagons drawn into a corral behind it.

Now some of the tentmen were pacing around alternately fixing their gaze on the gate or peering at the sky as if to test wind direction, while others simply stood still and scratched their heads, apparently stupefied by the challenge and about to announce defeat.

Suddenly, Levic made his decision and gestured to two men to start hammering in their stakes.

'Good,' Hugo exclaimed, as an invisible signal flashed back along the waiting column, snapping the drivers into action, 'Now the front door's been settled, everyone can work out for themselves where their particular loads have to stand.'

Steffi prepared to make himself useful. But it was not easy when everyone – apart from him – knew what to do. The

195

grooms fell to assembling their own tent while the tentmen concentrated on the big top and dressing tent. Amid a field of apparent chaos, the air reboant with shouts and hammers clanging, the king pole was raised. After that the canvas quarters, already laced together and attached to the bale ring which formed the neck of the tent, were hauled up. Then, once the canvas had been stretched to its full extent, the side wallings were attached and the big top was ready to receive its interior fittings.

Only then, after the men had measured out the ring, did Steffi find a way to make himself useful by helping to strip turfs from a four-foot-wide track around it and piling them up to form the ring bank. In fact, he was just standing back to admire his handiwork, which really did look splendid once it was covered by a purple curtain draped on the outside from short stakes, when Mirella came in.

'Oh, there you are, Steffi. Found yourself a job, I see.'

'No, this is more like fun,' he grinned.

Mirella looked pleased.

'Right, you can help me now, if you like.'

'Good. What do you want me to do?'

'Well, this is the moment when any performers who use apparatus take over the ring.'

'You mean, you want me to help you put up your tightrope?' he asked doubtfully.

'No, not put it up. That will be done by Storky and Jeff,' she said, pointing to the two tentmen just struggling in carrying a coil of cable between them. 'But I always check everything myself after it's been bolted into place.'

'Don't you trust them?' Steffi whispered.

'It's not so much that,' she whispered back, 'as the fact that I must be able to trust the rope. And I can't do that,' she added, reverting to her normal voice, 'if I don't know everything is exactly as it should be.'

'Not even if they tell you?'

'No. It's not good enough to be told. I have to know. Because a rope's like a person, it can be sick without anyone except its closest friend noticing something's wrong.'

Steffi realised how serious his mother was by the way she proceeded to check everything before it was taken aloft and again after it had been bolted in position.

'How's your head for heights?' she called as she shinned up the rope ladder.

'Not brilliant,' he admitted, hoping she would not expect him to follow her.

'Come on. Try climbing up.'

She mounted as easily as the man who regularly cleaned the windows of Liddy's house, so Steffi waited until she reached the top and then set out after her – only to find that under his body the ladder swayed and twisted so much that he felt it was tying him up in a knot.

He looked down to see if his puny efforts were being witnessed by the property men, but luckily they were too busy stowing away gates, poles, pedestals, and ladders to notice what he was up to. Unluckily, though, they looked awfully far below. So far, in fact, that he felt sick when he imagined how far his body would fall if he slipped off the rope.

'Having trouble, Steffi?' Mirella called.

'No,' he replied mechanically.

'Don't come all the way up if you don't want to,' she said in a low voice that he thought sounded disappointed.

'But I do want to,' he fibbed, resuming the ascent until he stood by her side in the top of the tent.

'There, what do you think of the world from up here?' she asked smiling.

Despite the fact that the air around him was surprisingly warm, he found himself shivering too much to make a sensible reply.

Fortunately, clambering down was not nearly so difficult as climbing up. He felt he was going towards his natural element, sliding gratefully on to the earth just before it was covered with tan bark and sawdust.

'Well, Steffi, does this mean you're going to follow in your mother's footsteps on the tightrope?' Hugo asked, as he sat on the ring bank, gazing up with obvious admiration at Mirella who was still aloft examining the rigging.

'I'm not sure,' Steffi mumbled, finding it impossible to admit the truth – that not for the world could he drag himself so high off the ground again.

After that there was just time to put on a costume and join the parade which Levic was already out front organising. Only then would there be the chance of something to eat – and possibly the quick dip in the sea that Hugo had mentioned – before the start of the show.

Chapter 21

Surprised to find himself so quickly accepted as one of the crew, Steffi began to warm to circus life. He tried to help wherever he could – Hugo on the road, the snake-lady with the teas, even Dai the lampman who normally worked completely on his own filling, cleaning and arranging the hundreds of flare lamps which lit the big tent inside and out.

He also continued to help Mirella check the takings and write up the accounts which, to his practised eye, looked very healthy. So he found it difficult to understand why his parents seemed so bothered about money all the time. Not that either said anything directly to him. It was just the whispered snippets of conversation he picked up in the wagon late at night.

'. . . the loan to pay for the tent . . . everyone's wages . . . food for the animals . . . rent for the tober . . .'

Steffi ws amazed to hear Mirella reciting such an endless list. And to think how he had sometimes gloated over all those tins of coins collected from the ticket office!

He pricked up his ears. Perhaps this explained Levic's bad temper. He was worried about money. Even if that seemed stupid when the circus was doing so well. Played to two full-houses yesterday, for instance.

'. . . blasted interest on the loan . . .'

Ah! Once he heard that, Steffi began to understand. It was not the day-to-day running costs but the money borrowed to buy the tent that was causing the problem, the interest on that initial loan which was putting them under such pressure.

After lying wake worrying about their dilemma, Steffi eventually fell asleep before finding a solution, only to be reminded of the problem afresh the following morning when Mirella announced at breakfast – a meal he took sitting on the caravan steps in the early morning sunshine – that there would be something special happening at Littlehampton when they arrived towards the end of the month.

'What sort of thing?' he mumbled, mouth full of fried bread.

'Did I tell you that we're timing our visit to coincide with a huge fête to celebrate the fiftieth anniversary of one of their friendly societies?'

'Yes.'

'Well, as a special attraction they're going to stretch a rope over the mouth of the river there – the Arun, I think it's called – and I'm going to walk across it.'

'But if it's the Arun, it's awfully wide.'

'Yes. The rope will need to be about two hundred feet, I should think.'

'And how high?'

'Sixty or seventy feet.'

'Phew!'

He was horrified. Unable even to watch his mother on her tightrope since his experience on the ladder at Eastbourne.

'Do you want to do it?' he asked at last.

'Of course,' she said immediately. 'I always like walking outdoors best. I walked on a rope across the Thames once, you know. And at Crystal Palace. And in lots of Pleasure Gardens – Cremorne, Rosherville, Woolwich, Aston Park.'

Her voice had grown so dreamy that Steffi had a vision of her drifting away even as she spoke, gliding along a rope stretching far into the distance. And he suddenly remembered his poor Aunt Cassie who had been a tightrope walker before a fall left her crippled.

'Will it be dangerous?' he blurted out.

'No, my love, not for me.'

Her words failed to reassure.

'But do you *have* to do it?' he asked.

'No, I don't *have* to. But I want to. Besides, there's good money attached to it.'

Then he remembered the conversation overheard the previous night.

His mother, he assumed, was simply putting on a brave face. After all, no one in their right mind would willingly submit to such an ordeal. No, the truth was, the circus needed more money and Mirella was the one who had to risk her neck to obtain it.

It was outrageous. He thought about the miserable sum he

earnt at the bank. That was no use to them. But if desperate measures were needed, why couldn't Levic take it upon himself to do something?

Steffi looked towards the big tent where his father stood talking to Hugo and gesturing at the flags above the showfront, one of which had been ripped by the strong breeze blowing off the sea. People were always going on about Levic being such a great artiste. Well, to give him his due, he was incredibly good in the ring – expert at everything he tackled, hilarious as a clown – but that did not make him as good as Mirella. It was simply that he threw his weight about more.

In fact, behind the scenes, as Steffi knew, Mirella was the one shouldering most responsibility. It was Mirella who handled the business correspondence and accounts. Mirella who acted as peacemaker between Levic and whichever artiste he had just managed to antagonise. And it was probably only Mirella who came up with an idea of how to earn the money they needed to carry on.

While Steffi was thinking these angry thoughts, Levic came across and lowered himself on to a chair next to the trestle table on which Mirella was doing the washing up.

'I've been thinking about that Littlehampton do,' he announced, confuting Steffi's suspicions by going on to say, 'but I still have my doubts about it.'

'Why?' Mirella asked, pushing stray hair from her eyes with the back of her sudsy hand.

'Because of the wind. Just look at those for the effect it can have.'

Mirella glanced quickly up at the flags.

'I see what you mean. But there's over a fortnight to go before I do the walk. It might be calmer by then. After all, it's unusual to get such a run of bad weather in August.'

Steffi had only to think back to last week to know she was right. They had been blessed with a succession of warm sunny days in July. 'Perfect weather for the seaside and circus,' Hugo had observed as they travelled the road to Brighton. In retrospect though his words had been tempting fate, for the sun had disappeared since they arrived and life made difficult by these keen, gusty winds which never ceased to blow off the sea.

'True,' Levic remarked. 'And I suppose we mustn't complain after the fine spell we had last month.'

'No, that's right. We have to take the rough with the smooth in this business, so it's just as well to get the rough over with now and have the weather brighten up for Littlehampton,' she smiled.

Sadly, her confidence proved misplaced.

August continued as it began, each day dawning cold and murky with frequent heavy showers and squally winds which devastated the corn fields. Regardless of conditions, the circus was built up at Worthing and opened for the few spectators brave enough to venture out in their ulsters and waterproofs.

Levic's mood became increasingly gloomy, and Steffi was aware of muttered exchanges from the other end of the wagon at night. Once he heard his mother say, 'But not before Steffi goes back, Levic. I couldn't bear it if we had to take a decision like that now and ruin his holiday.'

A decision like what? He strained his ears but couldn't catch any more. But he knew very well that they were discussing the possibility of disbanding the circus, and he wished they could confide in him and stop treating him like a child.

Next morning he scrutinised Mirella's face for signs of his own torment. Not a bit of it. She was standing over the fire, frying pan in hand, humming the tune that accompanied her act.

'Aren't we lucky, Steffi?'

'Why?'

'Haven't you noticed how the wind's died down? It promises to be a nice day.'

As usual, her enthusiasm was infectious and he forgot his fears.

'Hugo, what are those bushes called?' he asked, as they were driving along the coast to Littlehampton.

'Which ones?'

'The fluffy ones that look like green smoke. I've been noticing them all along the roadside since we left Worthing.'

'Oh, those. They're tamarisk.'

'Tamarisk.' Steffi savoured the word.

'Yes, you see a lot of it growing by the sea.'

'I don't think I've seen any tamarisk before. Are they always that odd shape?'

'Lopsided, you mean? No, that's just the effect of the wind. Haven't you noticed all the trees round here bend the same way?'

'Of course,' Steffi said, spotting a lopsided fir.

'That's because the prevailing wind comes from the south-west.'

'But there aren't many trees, are there? Is that because they can't stand the wind?'

'Probably. But I'll tell you something – the folks living round here like their trees lopsided.'

Steffi looked at Hugo, suspecting some sort of joke.

'Why?' he asked warily.

'Because, if they get lost after dark, they just have to find a tree and gauge its shape to get their bearings.'

'But if it was dark they wouldn't be able to see its shape,' he objected.

'Ah, but they can still feel its bark for lichen.'

'How would that help?'

'Simple. Because of this damned wind, the lichen only grows on the lee side, so it tells the chap when he's facing north-east.'

'Goodness,' Steffi gasped, in his mind peopling the landscape with lost men running their fingers up and down tree trunks to find which direction to walk in. An improbable notion, but that did not matter. He added it to his store of strange and for the most part useless information supplied by Hugo. That's what made these journeys so interesting and why, whenever he had the chance, he chose to drive alongside the talkative ringmaster.

In Littlehampton the circus was pitched on a wide expanse of gorse-covered common close enough to the sea for Steffi and Mirella to be able to stroll down to the harbour once the initial work was done. It was a rare moment of leisure, for there was no show that night, the circus being due to open twice on the morrow. And after that, the really big day – when Mirella did her walk across the River Arun.

'I wish we'd managed to persuade Levic to come down with us,' Mirella murmured as they ambled past a line of wrinkled ruddy-faced fishermen leaning back against the edge of the pier, puffing on their pipes and apparently more interested in all the visitors than watching the little paddle-tug *Jumna* tow a sailing boat out of harbour. 'I'm sure he'd enjoy looking at the boats.'

'Why didn't he come then?' Steffi asked, suspecting that his father would have been keener to accompany Mirella if he could have had her to himself.

'He said he had to run through that comic routine with Barney and Hugo.'

'But it went all right at Worthing.'

'I'm afraid "all right" is never good enough for Levic. He likes everything to be perfect,' she sighed.

'But surely that takes the fun out of running a circus,' Steffi objected.

'Maybe, but that's your father! And neither you nor I will ever change him.'

Biting his lip and looking up at the weathervane spinning on top of the pepperpot lighthouse, Steffi said nothing. Following the line of his gaze, Mirella remarked on how the wind seemed to be getting up again and he felt his former misgivings when he remembered the main reason for their being in Littlehampton at this time.

'Where are you going to do your walk across the river, Ma?' he asked, scanning the horizon from the lighthouse to the windmill with its churning sails and on over the chimneys and rooftops.

'Ah, yes. I thought we might wander that way now and see if they've finished erecting the masts. I gather they're putting them up somewhere close to the chain ferry.'

As they turned to walk in that direction, Mirella explained how she came to be involved in this particular event.

'Actually, the organisers thought they'd managed to get Blondin himself to do the crossing. But his stupid agent didn't realise that their date clashed with one of his previous engagements, so they had to ask me at the last minute instead.'

'Do you mean the famous Blondin who walked a tightrope across Niagara Falls?'

'That's right.'

'And didn't you and Pa used to know him?' Steffi asked, recalling something Liddy had said in the past.

'Oh, yes, we knew him very well. In fact, when I cross the Arun I shall be using a balancing pole that once belonged to him.'

With her mention of the walk Steffi felt the wind blow colder and as if in response to his fears her hand suddenly tightened on his arm.

'Look, there it is,' she breathed, pointing to a black line drawn across the sky. 'And look, Steffi, there's Levic too. What a relief! It must mean he's come round in favour of the venture.'

With a girlish skip, she rushed towards the base of the nearest mast and, together with Levic, ran a series of checks over all the blocks, guys and tackle that had been used.

'Don't you worry, ma'am,' the foreman responsible for erecting the equipment declared, 'these 'ere blocks an' pulleys is the best money can buy.'

'Yes, I'm sure they are,' Mirella agreed, watching as Levic continued with his checks.

'Yep, I derr say six elephants could walk across that lot without coming to grief.'

'I hope not. They'd put me out of business, if they did,' Mirella laughed.

'No, what I'm trying to say is,' the man persisted, 'that little lot won't come down under any amount of weight. But I'll be blessed if I know how you're gonner walk along it without coming a cropper in winds like ours.'

Steffi saw his father's face stiffen as he heard this, but Levic carried on checking the gear and then arranged to return the following day and the day of the fête to check again that everything was secure.

Next morning Steffi was woken by the now familiar cannonade on the roof of the wagon and, when he raised his head from the blankets, his face was spattered by rain being blown through one of the mollycroft skylights that had been left open. He prayed that the downpour would quickly pass and the afternoon be fine enough to attract crowds to the circus.

Then, just as he was about to slide open his shutter and climb out of bed, he heard Mirella's voice raised in anger.

'Levic, please don't keep going on. You've made your point. I know you think the walk's risky, but I'm telling you it's no worse than anything else I've done. And I can handle it.'

'Not if you've got a gale blowing in your face, you can't,' Levic argued.

'There won't be a gale,' she muttered.

'There could be. The fishermen say as much and they know what they're talking about when it comes to weather. I think we should advise the organisers to cancel today, before all the visitors stream in tomorrow and put pressure on us to go ahead regardless.'

'No,' Mirella cried. 'If we do that, I shall forfeit my fee.'

'Forget the damned fee. Your safety's more important.'

There was a silence during which Steffi's heart beat so hard he was afraid it would be heard. Eventually, there came what sounded like a kiss followed by Mirella's voice whispering: 'Trust me, my love. I know what I'm doing and, remember, I shan't want to take risks with Steffi watching. Anyway, if the weather's really bad, I shall expect the organisers to cancel and still pay me my fee.'

Given their financial difficulties, even Steffi could see the sense in that.

The morning of the fête dawned cloudy, but at least it was not raining as it had been unremittingly the day before, causing both shows to be almost literal 'wash-outs'. Moreover, it seemed that further up the coast and inland the weather must have shown more promise, because from ten o'clock onwards people came flooding into town by road, rail and steam boat.

Mirella was jubilant.

'If we can get half this lot into the tent, we'll be able to recoup some of yesterday's losses,' she crowed.

'Never you mind about inside the tent, you just concentrate on what you're going to do outside,' Levic said sharply, before setting off towards the river to check the rope's rigging.

Within a few minutes he was back.

'No, Mirella, it's no good. You can't do it. Believe me, there's a wicked wind getting up and blowing right into the mouth of the river so that even the ferry is being almost jolted out of its chains.'

She raised her eyebrows in clear disbelief.

'Look at the tent, if you don't believe me,' Levic insisted. 'I've just given orders to loosen the guys.'

Mirella peered through the window at the billowing canvas and a look of defeat crossed her face. A moment later, though, and she was jaunty again.

'I don't care. I'm going to earn that fee today if it kills me . . .' Then possibly realising what effect her words were having, she corrected herself. 'I mean, no matter what it costs. Let the officials cancel if they like. They can do what they want, so long as they pay my fee.'

By two o'clock, despite what had now become a sad, overcast day with intermittent blustery showers, crowds had gathered on both banks of the river to await the firing of the cannon which was to signal Mirella's ascent on the east side. Steffi stood below, his attention divided between the gun – he had never been so close to one about to fire before – and his mother who, in obedience to Levic's instructions, was sitting in her carriage till the last moment.

Although Steffi was expecting a loud explosion, the bang when it came seemed to dent his senses and leave him mesmerised as he watched the smoke curl up and be suddenly blown away from the barrel. When he turned back to Mirella it was too late to wish her good luck. She had already clambered halfway up the ladder and was soon alighting on the platform, twisting round to acknowledge the cheers.

Steffi gasped. He couldn't believe that was really his mother up there. Looking so small, like a white bird now she had removed her orange cloak. A little gull which had just landed on the wire before flying out to sea. Except Mirella couldn't fly, she could only fall.

She was standing quite still, just as he had seen her stand so many times in the top of the circus tent, stroking the rope with her foot and holding her pole, minutely shifting the weight from one side to the other until she was happy with its balance. She was smiling happily. But Steffi had seen too much of the performer's smile to be taken in. Neither did he trust the gay wave of her hand as she set out to cross the abyss.

At first things went well and she seemed to be almost skipping along.

Levic was wrong then. The wind, even up there, was not too bad. Although it must be awfully cold, Steffi thought, turning up his jacket collar and twisting his face so that the breeze would blow his hair back rather than into his eyes.

It was the gasp from the crowd which made him look again and see that now, as she approached the centre, Mirella was no longer skipping but clearly struggling against the wind, as if having to push an enormous invisible weight along the rope before her. And the crowd had gasped because at one moment the struggle appeared so unequal that she began to wobble furiously and was even forced into a step backwards.

At that point Steffi could not bear to look any more.

He shut his eyes only to find that the image of Mirella tottering on the rope had so imprinted itself on his retina that he could not banish the sight. Besides, it was only a few seconds before another gasp from the crowd had him looking up again to see her still stepping boldly along the rope, breasting the force of the wind.

This time Steffi determined to watch her every move until she reached the far end.

At last, her progress painfully slow, Mirella got there. She was so far away it was impossible to see the expression on her face, but Steffi, picturing its triumph, jumped up and down and waved his arms with delight. Thank goodness, the ordeal was over and his mother safe.

And his father?

Remembering Levic's anxiety, Steffi glanced around, hoping to share his relief. But he discovered that far from basking in the same emotion, Levic was looking grimly across the river, violently shaking his head at Mirella and gesturing with his hand.

For a moment Steffi thought his father was being churlish and picking fault with the way the difficult walk had been conducted. Only when Hugo, who was standing close by, muttered, 'Surely to God that's enough! She can't be so foolhardy as to attempt more!' did he realise that Levic was in fact signalling her to climb down.

Mirella, however, clearly had other ideas and shook her head decisively in reply before stretching her foot out on the rope again and beginning to walk back.

Chapter 22

Mirella's difficulties increased with every step, especially as she neared the centre.

Once there she stooped to rest her balancing pole across the rope. And made as if to do a headstand.

'Dear God, no! She can't possibly mean to . . .'

While he was struck dumb with terror, all around Steffi in the crowd people exclaimed aloud in horror.

Eventually, though, it became obvious even to Mirella that there was no way the wind would permit her to stand on her head, and she had to content herself with merely lying flat on the rope. In fact, even when after a few moments she carefully stood and took up her pole, she still had a desperate struggle to keep her balance and regain the original platform.

Her achievement was greeted by a storm of clapping, banging, whistling and cheers. By this time, however, Steffi was too stunned to join in or even react when Mirella attempted to bandage her eyes and found the wind to be so strong that twice the fluttering white handkerchief was nearly snatched from her hands. She would not give up. And at length, blindfolded and with a sack pulled over her body, she started to walk out over the river again.

Now the wind had increased so much that the sack was blown against her body to reveal the outline of her face and shape of her limbs in sharp relief. Step by step she cautiously worked her way across and back before making her final descent.

Pulling off the sack and bandana she was exposed – looking perished and blue with cold and – laughing.

'There,' she exclaimed, cutting short Levic's protests, 'that should bring the crowds in!'

Even as she spoke heavy drops of rain started to fall, and it was probably as much to escape them as to embrace the long list of attractions being broadcast through a megaphone by Hugo that people streamed away from the river towards the circus.

Unlike grander, more established companies, everyone in Minerva's circus had to double up and do as many different jobs as they could manage. It was the only way for a small company such as theirs to survive. Even the band suffered a noticeable diminuendo when three of its members had to leave halfway through the programme to do their acrobatic act.

As at Apsley's, being able to do a half-decent flip-flap, somersault and cartwheel meant that Steffi had been quickly seized upon to take part in the opening parade and the charivari – when the clowns all tumbled and bumbled about the ring. So there was no time for him to brood after Mirella's performance. He had to rush back to prepare for the show, and once that started, like everyone else he became too preoccupied with what was happening inside the big tent to be aware of storm clouds piling up outside.

Rain the big top was designed to keep out, but it had not been built to withstand hurricanes. When the performance was about half over, there came one of the most terrific thunderstorms that anyone could have imagined, especially in August.

It crashed overhead and howled under the canvas, causing it to surge to and fro like a ship wrecked at sea, lifting up the poles and sending them flying in all directions. The band carriage was blown over. Venie, caught in the midst of her act, was sent reeling about the ring with pythons apparently clinging to her for dear life. People screamed and rushed for the exits.

Steffi, gaping through the entrance curtains at all this chaos, saw his father and Hugo doing their best to calm the crowd lest they increase the danger by trampling each other in their efforts to get out.

'Stand back! Stand back, everyone! Don't crowd the exits!' the tentmen were shouting, but their voices were lost in the general mayhem. In fact, the only message that was getting through had the effect of causing a worse stampede.

'Lions! The lions have got loose!'

This was the cry, which once heard and taken up by the multitude, sent everyone into panic.

'Get out of the way! There's lions on the loose! They're running amok!'

The warning passed from mouth to mouth and spread like wildfire. When he heard it, even Steffi felt like rushing back through the dressing tent and seeking refuge in the wagon, and would have done so had he not reminded himself that the circus did not possess any lions. Nor tigers. Nor any other big cats.

'Take these and get yourself outside, boyo,' Dai shouted, thrusting three or four unlit lamps into his arms.

Steffi did as he was told. All around him the tentmen and artistes were clutching lamps, props, anything that was easily retrievable before they made their own escape.

Once in the open, although quickly soaked through by rain, he was glad that nearly everyone else was in the process of getting out, some still struggling through the main door while others were wriggling under the canvas like grubs emerging from a chrysalis. And all the while he could hear horses neighing, donkeys braying, birds and people squawking and squealing, poles splintering, and Mumbo trumpeting in the day of judgement.

Dodging the loose poles that were flying around, Steffi rushed to help the men haul down the side-wallings to lessen wind resistance. Once that was done, he caught sight of his father. Still in his clown costume, the wet green satin sticking to his body like shrivelled sea-weed, Levic was standing in what had been the centre of the ring, directing operations.

'Right!' he was yelling, his voice like everything else being carried off by the wind. 'Ready to let her go when I say.'

Drenched by the pelting rain, the men stood by to start lowering the top by means of the ropes attached to the king pole but before Levic had a chance to issue the command, there came an almighty crack.

'Too late! Get back, get back!'

Steffi saw his father look up as the king pole broke and darted forward to help him. As he moved, he could hear all around him the quarter and side poles snapping like crackers under the weight of the sodden canvas before it engulfed him.

Then nothing – no sound or light or air – just heavy darkness smothering him and pressing the breath out of his body. He lay there, underneath it all, assuming his last moments had come. But his bones weren't crushed. He could still move his fingers and arms, stretch his leg, both legs. Feel his toes. By a miracle there seemed no bones broken. In fact, something – he couldn't see what – seemed to be holding the main weight of the canvas

211

off him, providing him with a space in which to draw breath and quickly think.

No doubt the men outside would soon be hurling themselves on the wreckage, trying to cut him free – but what if their movements disturbed his present haven, causing the full weight of the tent to fall and crush him? Or they failed to reach him in time? And what, for heaven's sake, had happened to Levic? Had he managed to escape before the canvas dropped?

Thinking about his father made Steffi desperate to get free. He rummaged for the penknife he knew he had in his pocket, found it and started to slash and rip his way out. But it seemed to take hours before he saw the glimmer above his head that told him just one more layer. Then suddenly he was there, emerging like a salmon after a fly, gulping for air.

A shout went up. He could hear his name. And then a cheer. Felt the rain – such welcome rain – spattering his face. But was overcome by such weakness and trembling in all his limbs that, instead of doing anything sensible, simply waited there, leaning back against the billowy folds until someone arrived to half drag, half carry him off the canvas mountain.

'Steffi! Oh, Steffi. Thank God! Is he all right? Fetch a chair, someone. No, on second thoughts, let's get him over to the wagon and out of this wet.'

'It's all right, Ma,' he said to calm his mother and found that once he managed to smile at her, he could not stop an idiot grin fixing itself over his face. Till he remembered Levic.

'No, leave me.' He shook off whoever it was who was now supporting him. 'Where's Pa, what happened to him?'

'Don't worry. He's okay,' said a voice which Steffi recognised as Storky's.

'No. I saw him. Standing there when the pole collapsed.'

'Shush, Steffi! He's all right,' Mirella interrupted. 'Who do you think carried you out?'

'Was that Pa? But . . . but I thought he was the one . . .'

'No, no. He wasn't in any real danger. He knew which way to leap. Not that he got completely clear but he managed to crawl out under the edge.'

'And he's all right? You're sure?'

'Of course I'm sure. He'll be up here in a minute and then you can see for yourself.'

Although his head had already cleared enough for him to register where his body was bruised, Steffi still felt woozy and

not really in possession of his wits until Venie plied him with
her famous Irish concoction.

'Urrgh!' Too late he realised the drink did not contain its
usual admixture of tea.

'Ah, that's brought you back to life, my lad!' the snake-lady
beamed. 'And teach you for giving us such a nasty shock.'

'Hmm.' When sipped rather than gulped, the medicine was
quite acceptable, sending a warm glow through his body even if
it could not dispel his anxiety about Levic and he wished his
father would come up in the wagon so that he could see he was
all right.

'Stor-ky!'

The tall tentman visibly jumped at the sound of his name.

'That's the boss, so I'd best be off to tell him the lad's all right.'

'Okay. But thanks for helping him over, Storky!' Mirella
murmured, pressing the man's hand as he made to leave.

'Stor-ky! Come on, we need you,' Levic's impatient voice
yelled again.

'What are they doing?' Steffi demanded, making an attempt
to follow but being restrained by his mother and Venie from
going outside again.

'Just salvaging what they can.'

'Then I want to help.'

'Not yet,' Mirella said.

'Is there much damage?'

She nodded her head.

'It couldn't have been worse if we'd been attacked by bloody
Zulus,' Venie groaned.

When he looked outside, Steffi saw immediately what she
meant. The tober resembled nothing so much as a battlefield.
While one or two figures were still picking up stakes and loose
bits of equipment, the rest were standing round the band-
carriage which was lying on its side, wrecked. Furthermore,
the ticket office had been smashed to smithereens and, worst of
all, where the big tent had stood was just a mess of poles, ropes
and shreds of rag blowing in the wind.

'The men tried gathering up the canvas but it was pointless,
the wind's torn it to bits,' Mirella said bitterly.

'Still, at least no lives lost,' Venie muttered.

'No. You're right there.'

And that was the refrain that people used to cheer themselves up. At least no lives had been lost and it was a mercy no

one was badly injured either, they said. Indeed, the only thing that had saved Steffi, it was realised once the debris was cleared, was the fact that he had been knocked to the ground between two of the elephant tubs and these had created a safe igloo round him.

It was also seen as cause for congratulation that the company pulled so well together in such an emergency, leading the animals out of harm's way and everyone rescuing what they could. When the storm finally subsided and the rain stopped, they gathered together around a coke fire outside the mess tent.

'Good old Venie, that's the stuff,' Hugo muttered, smacking his lips in appreciation of the liberal lacing she had given the tea. 'Good for shock.'

'And we've all had a bellyful of that this afternoon,' she hissed.

'Amen to that,' he agreed.

Levic supped his drink without saying a word, his skin and even his moustache looking greenish in the strange rain-soaked light. And he still bore the same expression as when, just seconds before he issued the order to lower the big top, the wind had laughed in his face and brought the whole lot down for him.

Steffi longed to find words to comfort his father. It didn't seem right that all his hard work should just be blown away like this. And it added insult to injury to discover that some felon had even taken advantage of the confusion to make off with the takings from the ticket office. No wonder Levic looked defeated. Minerva's was done for – at least that's what Steffi thought until he overheard Hugo talking with the other artistes and mentioning the word 'insurance'.

'Yes, you can take it from me,' Hugo declared, 'Levic's got his head screwed on all right. Knows all about the hazards of tenting so he'll have made sure this little lot was well covered.'

'That right, Governor?' one of the acrobats asked.

'Is what right?'

'That we'll be able to carry on once you get the insurance?'

'Insurance?' Levic repeated, as if that cheerful thought had not yet occurred to him. 'Oh, yes. We'll be carrying on all right. But I can only deal with one thing at a time. Just been speaking to a policeman about the takings that disappeared and he wasn't very hopeful about our seeing any of that back.'

There were murmurs of sympathy accompanied by blood-curdling suggestions as to what each would like to do to such a mean bastard for whom, apparently, hanging, drawing and quartering was far too good. Levic did not join in this chorus but seemed to be thinking of something else.

Steffi's mind too was working overtime. The insurance, of course. He was trying to visualise the account book. What sort of premium had been paid? He couldn't remember offhand. Nor did he recall Mirella's saying anything to him about the policy, but no doubt they would go through it together this evening and he would be able to help his parents set about making their claim. That was one of the good things about working in a bank – it had given him lots of practice in filling in forms.

'Have you seen your mother?' Levic suddenly asked, drawing Steffi aside.

'Yes, she's gone to lie down.'

'Was she . . . did she look badly upset?'

Steffi winced. Mirella had not been crying or anything, but there had been something about the set of her mouth and her face had seemed to crumple when she tried to smile at him.

'No, not really,' he said, 'just feeling worn out, I think.'

'Of course she is. Who wouldn't be after getting over that bloody rope-walk this afternoon and then having to cope with this . . .'

Levic lifted his arm and wearily gestured at the common. Now that people had finished tidying up there was no more than a circle of trampled grass and sodden sawdust where the big tent had been, whilst the wagons and animal tent seemed to cluster in a sorry huddle once bereft of their focus.

'She'll be all right . . .' Steffi started to say.

'But she didn't deserve this,' Levic moaned. 'Not after all that effort, Steffi. None of us did. It's enough to break anyone's heart.'

It hurt Steffi to see his father so upset. But at least he was talking to him man to man for once, and he was keen to foster that sort of confidence by making some helpful response.

'Look, don't worry, Pa. I'm sure the insurance will cover most of our losses.'

Unfortunately his words did not have the desired effect. No sooner had he spoken than Levic shot at him a look of such fury that Steffi felt his spirit quail within him. And there was no point in saying any more. Now he knew the reason for his parents' despair.

Chapter 23

'It's in the High Street – up at the Arundel Road end,' Steffi announced, trying to keep his excitement in check. 'You can open there from tomorrow onwards, and they'll let you have it free of charge.'

'Steady on,' Levic interrupted. 'Tell us again more slowly. You've found this barn, you say . . .'

'Yes, but it's better than that. A proper theatre barn which is often used by visiting players. And what I thought you could do is this: parade around town tomorrow morning with the band and all the animals and then perform in the barn in the afternoon and evening.'

'But does it have a proper stage, Steffi?' Mirella asked, beginning to show interest.

'Yes, like I told you. It's in constant use as a theatre and I'm sure you could adapt most of your acts to put together a decent show. The acrobats, for example. And Venie with her snakes. And what about your tightrope? You've often used that on a stage.'

'He's right, Levic. And you could do most of your clowning, if you leave out Barney. In fact, if you think about it, it's only the bigger animals we can't use.'

'All right, all right. I see what you're saying, but what's the point?' Levic moaned, running his fingers through his black, wavy hair as if to pull it out at the roots.

'What's the point?' Steffi bridled, his voice rising with exasperation. 'I would have thought that was obvious. The point is, I've found a place where you can put on a performance tomorrow to earn some money.'

He felt like kicking his father for pulling such a face. But at least Mirella was more positive.

'Well, I like the idea,' she declared. 'After all, we must do something. We can't just sit back and not pay these people the wages we owe them, can we? I said, "can we?", Levic!'

Steffi groaned. The last thing he wanted this morning was to cause trouble between Levic and Mirella and now here they were at each other's throats.

'Have you forgotten we have no money?'

'Of course I haven't forgotten,' Levic muttered.

'So we'll try Steffi's idea and get out there tomorrow to put together another show,' Mirella said firmly.

'Okay, but then what?'

Mirella turned to Steffi, shaking her head despairingly.

'Look,' Levic continued, 'there's no point in making all that effort to earn enough for a couple of days. I mean, what do we do then? We can't stay in Littlehampton. We don't have a tent to travel with. We don't have the money to start up again. So all we'll have done is work ourselves into the ground simply to stave off the day of reckoning by forty-eight hours.'

Mirella made a sigh that sounded like a growl.

'What do you suggest we do, then, Levic?'

'Tell the company straightaway that we can't see ourselves getting back on the road – at least for this season. That we can't even pay their wages. And give them the chance to cut their losses and go.'

His father's defeatist tone made Steffi angry.

'But where can Venie go at five minutes' notice? She depends on us. And so do Storky and Jeff. You can't send them away without any money in their pockets!'

'Keep out of this, Steffi. You don't know what you're talking about,' Levic hissed. 'Businesses fail all the time.'

'Not ours, though!' Mirella said. 'We vowed that, you and I – that time we went to Portsmouth to see what had gone wrong with the Myers' circus and its owner took us through all the pitfalls. That was the reason I went, remember? Because you said we shouldn't go into this business unless we had our eyes wide open.'

'I know, I know. And we did. But bloody hell, Mirella, even with my eyes open I couldn't see a storm like yesterday's coming.'

'No. I know, and no one's blaming you, Levic. It's just, just . . .' Mirella started to sob.

Steffi had often seen his mother with tears in her eyes, even tears running down her face. He had seen her cry with rage, but never before heard her sob.

'Don't. Please, don't. I'm sure we're going to get out of this mess,' he pleaded. 'I mean, we're only talking about money.'

'No, not just money. We're talking about all our plans and sacrifices. All our work to get this lot on the road,' she sobbed.

'Then we don't just give up,' Steffi declared with a confidence he was far from feeling.

After all, there was a lot of sense in what Levic said. And perhaps they had a duty to let the company know the true situation. But what if, having been told how things stood, most of them decided to leave immediately? That would settle matters once and for all. Minerva's would be finished. So surely it was better to bluff their way through the next few days by talk of waiting for the insurance money to come through and use this breathing space to try to persuade the company who had advanced their previous loan to put up more funds.

Levic shook his head when Steffi said this, but Mirella's eyes lit up.

'It must be worth a try,' she pleaded.

'I suppose anything's worth a try,' Levic agreed grudgingly.

During the next few days Steffi's mood fluctuated between despair and hope. Lowering grey skies and cold, almost wintry showers did nothing to cheer people up. Their street parade without the glorious bandwagon to lead the way was but a miserable shadow of its former self. On the other hand, for visitors rained off the beach and pier, the barn proved a welcome attraction and was almost full for every show. The townspeople too came up trumps, with a baker making available regular supplies of stale bread for the animals and Nutter's, the greengrocers, delivering a load of damaged fruit and vegetables. The show too was remarkably good considering it was put on at such short notice.

Nevertheless dark clouds (and not just the ones in the sky) glowered over everything.

And to cap it all, Levic was not well. Although he refused to admit as much, it was obvious from the way he moved – and his increasingly bad temper – that his rheumatism had made an unwelcome reappearance. Mirella tried to persuade him to stay in bed, but it was no use. He would not be able to rest until they had heard back from the finance company.

'Not that I'm expecting an ounce of joy from that quarter,' he added in a tone so black that Steffi was glad to leave the wagon and seek the company of his old friend, Venie, who had just finished dishing out the early morning tea.

'Steffi, do us a favour and gather up the cups, will you?' she shouted from under the awning attached to her living-wagon where she tended her urn when the weather was bad.

He did not mind this thin sort of misty shower which tasted salt and was more like sea-spray than proper rain, so he cheerfully went the rounds collecting the crockery and enduring the usual banter from those tentmen who could never resist the chance to pull his leg.

'Hey-up! Let's hope that's good news for the boss,' one of them suddenly said.

Turning to look, Steffi saw a telegraph boy making his way towards his parents' wagon. His heart began to beat furiously. The long-expected reply from the finance company. It had to be. And what would it say? Would it spell the end to Minerva's circus? Or would it be good news, meaning they could quickly purchase another tent and get the show back on the road?

He dumped the loaded tray on Venie's table and, without stopping to say anything, ran over to the wagon. But before he had climbed the steps, another thought had crossed his mind. Who else would send them a telegram? Why, Liddy of course. Perhaps for some reason she had had to delay her return to Aldershot and was wiring to warn Steffi before he went home this weekend. In which case he might try to prolong his stay with his parents, even at the risk of his job, because the idea of turning his back on them in their present fix was almost unthinkable.

Before entering the wagon, he stood aside for the telegraph boy who was already being dismissed with his tip.

'No, thank you. No reply just yet,' Levic murmured.

And it seemed to Steffi that his father's face told him everything. So the message was from the finance company and they had turned the request down! But even expecting this much, Steffi was still shocked to find Mirella collapsed in the chair sobbing her heart out.

It was finished then. He saw the scrap of paper on the floor at her feet where she must have tossed it in despair. There would be no money to bale them out. The circus must go under.

'Ma, don't. It isn't worth it,' Steffi whispered, frightened by the sight of such violent grief. It was not like his mother to keep breaking down like this.

He watched Levic move forward and kneel down by the chair to comfort her.

'Don't torture yourself, my love. It had to happen some time and there was no way you could have known.'

'Yes, yes. I should have seen the signs,' she sobbed. 'I might have seen something was wrong if I hadn't been so wrapped up in my own life. The business – getting this bloody circus on the road – that's taken all my time. Made me blind to everything else.'

'Don't you think Liddy understood that, Mirella? She admired what you were doing and she certainly wouldn't want you to have regrets about it now.'

'But I do regret it, Levic. I regret the whole obsession. She took me in and gave me a home when there was no one else, you know. And she looked after me and then Steffi . . . oh, my God, Steffi!'

Suddenly they both turned and stared bleakly at him, their expressions making him want to run away. Whereas a moment before he had wanted to hug Mirella because she was so unhappy, now he wanted nothing at all to do with her. Wanted nothing to do with anyone. Didn't want anyone to say anything to him. Just wanted to be left on his own. Or go back to Liddy's.

Yes, that was what he wanted. He wanted to be with Liddy again. Liddy, the one person in the world who had never let him down. He desperately wanted to see her again. Strange, how he had spent these last four weeks without sparing her more than a passing thought. Now she filled his mind and all he could think about was her kind brown eyes and sweet smile, the walks they liked to take through the barracks, or along the canal, or over Laffan's plain. He had sent her postcards from Eastbourne and Brighton, but there was so much more he wanted to tell her about. How he'd gone swimming a couple of times with Hugo, about a conversation he'd had with Venie, and about the storm . . . He would tell her . . .

'Steffi . . .' Mirella said, beckoning him to her.

'No.'

'Steffi, please,' she said, tears flowing.

'No,' he growled.

Then there was someone on the steps outside, and a voice called: 'Mr Levic, can I have a word, please?'

Levic went to the door.

'Not at the moment, Jeff, if you don't mind. We've just had

221

some bad news ... No, nothing to do with that. It's just Mirella's grandmother died last night ... Thank you ... Yes, of course I will ... Thanks, I appreciate that, but there's not a lot any of us can do, I'm afraid. I only wish there was.'

Steffi felt his face stiffen and his body grow very cold. He turned and walked out of the wagon. And went down to the jetty to watch the boats putting out to sea.

Chapter 24

'Did you have to wear that red cloak?' Sadie hissed in her ear, after giving Mirella a perfunctory kiss when she arrived at the cottage in Windsor before Liddy's funeral.

'Red's the proper colour for Romany mourning,' she explained, surprised.

'I know that,' Sadie muttered, glancing round to make sure none of her neighbours had overheard. 'But Liddy weren't no gypsy and you should have turned up in decent black.'

'No, Mother, you don't understand. Grandma made me this cloak to wear at Uncle Darkie's funeral, so I know she'd like me to wear it today.'

'But that was years ago and things have changed. Even travellers don't dress in them pagan colours no more. It ain't respectable.'

Mirella felt close to tears. She had not recovered from the shock of Liddy's death, and now to face this tirade from her mother when seeing her for the first time in years was almost too much to bear. On the other hand she refused to be browbeaten.

'Ma, I don't care what's respectable, I . . .'

'No, you never have. That's your trouble,' Sadie snapped, turning her back on Mirella to give Steffi a welcoming hug. 'Ah, here's the one I want to see. Goodness, how you've grown, Steffi! Completely dwarfed me. Now, come along into the kitchen and tell us all what you've been getting up to.'

Mirella watched them go – her son and her busy little sparrow of a mother. She sighed. It had always been the same. The only time she had ever managed to please Sadie was when she gave birth to Steffi.

From the kitchen she could hear a gabble of voices which probably included that of her sister, Cassie, and her Aunt

Phoebe who would certainly be here today. Who else, though? she wondered. Joey, of course. And Tom.

Tom, the middle one of Liddy's three surviving sons. It was funny how his name still had the power to make Mirella flinch. After being so helpful to her when she had first left home, Tom had gone on to treat her very badly. It was the drink that was to blame, of course. She realised that now. The drink, together with the effects of that ghastly mauling he had received from his lions. She found herself shivering at the memory. There were times even now, after all these years, when she closed her eyes at night . . .

'What, lost your way around your old home, my love?'

She spun round and found herself staring into the face of her father as he came through the front door straight into the parlour. As far as she was concerned, this – the moment when her father came in through that door after checking his covers or perhaps mending a fence – had always been the best of the day when she was a little girl. And the remarkable thing was, Johnny seemed hardly to have changed over the years. Although he had put on a bit of weight and there were a few tufts of grey in his beard, his hair remained a lush sandy brown and his eyes as blue as ever.

'Pa,' Mirella whispered. 'Pa, it's so good to see you again.'

'And you, my love,' he said, moving forward to hug her. 'The Lord knows I've missed you. All those times I drove over to see Mother and Steffi, always hoping to bump into you, but never did. But still, Mother would tell us all what you and Levic were getting up to – fetching out her newspapers to show what they'd written. She was so proud of those bits of newspaper, you know. Pasted them all up in a book. And always talking about you, despite poor Sadie not giving her much encouragement.'

As she listened to the warm husky voice once more, Mirella felt the years rolling back. She might even have imagined herself a child again, except that her father was not in the old familiar clothes he had worn then, but in a stiff formal black suit that kept reminding her – if any such reminder was necessary – of the reason for the family gathering here today.

'Did she . . . did Gran know . . . at the end, I mean . . . did she know she was dying?'

Johnny nodded, but took a few moments to put his answer into words.

'Yes, I think she sensed the Mulo-mush was coming near, though she never said anything. He took her in her sleep, you know, and when Sadie found her in the morning, it was as if she was still just sleeping. I mean, I don't think she suffered.' His voice broke and he had to pull a handkerchief from his pocket and brush it under his eyes before he could continue. 'The doctor said it was her heart, and nothing anyone could have done. She might have gone any time, so I think the only way to look at it is, the Lord knew best by taking her while she was here in the bosom of her family and not in that big house with Steffi the one to find her.'

'That's right,' said a quiet voice, which Mirella did not immediately recognise as that of Levic who had come in behind Johnny. 'It was just as well Steffi wasn't there. He's taking it hard enough as it is. But then she was like a mother to him.'

Mirella was surprised to hear Levic sound so moved. He had been fond of Liddy, she knew that, but he had rarely shown such concern for Steffi. She slid her hand into his as he came to stand by her side.

'But you said you thought Gran knew,' she murmured.

Johnny nodded again.

'Yes. I mean, it's hard to be sure, but there were things she said in the days before. I mean, her mind was clear, she wasn't rambling or anything, and yet – she was going over the past and talking about things from way back . . . and then all of a sudden she wasn't talking about the past, she was talking about your Steffi . . . She idolised him, you know . . . and it was obvious who she was talking about but she kept getting his name wrong and calling him . . . Jemmy . . . yes, she definitely kept calling him Jemmy.'

'Confusing him with Grandad, you mean?'

'No, not him. She never called my father Jemmy. He was always Jem. No, she was talking about my older brother. Only she kept getting him muddled up with Steffi . . .'

A shiver ran down Mirella's spine. There seemed something menacing about anyone coupling Steffi with the uncle whose life had, by all accounts, been doomed from the start.

Sensing that he had caused some unease, Johnny changed the subject.

'Have you spoken to Cassie yet? She's with the womenfolk in the kitchen.'

'No, I haven't spoken to anyone except you yet, and Ma, of course.'

'And I expect she was a bit offish,' he sighed. 'I don't know why, but you two have always been the same.'

'And are all the others here?' she asked. 'I mean Phoebe, and Joey, and Tom. Are they all coming?'

'Oh, yes, everyone's here, even Tom who's come on the train from Tewkesbury this morning.'

'Tewkesbury, eh? So where is he now?' she asked, hoping her voice did not sound too apprehensive.

'He's out there,' Johnny said, gesturing towards the garden at the back of the cottage. 'With our Joey. Both paying their last respects to Mother.'

Mirella had not liked to ask about that. It was such a strong tradition in the family for the body to be laid out and a strict vigil kept over it between death and burial, that she was shocked not to find a room set aside for the purpose when she arrived. Knowing Sadie's reluctance to keep up the old Romany traditions, she even suspected that her grandmother's body had been packed off to some impersonal chapel of rest.

It was a relief to discover that this was far from being the case, and that – as she should have realised, knowing her father – Johnny had insisted that his mother be buried with all the proper rites.

'There was no room in here,' he explained, 'so I took your brothers and showed them how to fix up a little bender tent in the garden.'

'Just like you used to live in when you were a boy?'

'That's right. We laid Liddy out there in the open and there's been at least two of us at her side day and night ever since. We haven't left her on her own for a minute.'

Johnny smiled, and Mirella saw that, in the midst of his grief, it was a source of comfort for him to render his mother this last service in a way that he knew would please her.

For most of the hour or so before they had to walk to the church for the funeral service, Mirella and Steffi sat keeping vigil in the death tent. And if Steffi had felt any dismay upon entering, the sight of Liddy lying so peacefully in the candlelight must have reassured him.

'Doesn't she look lovely?' he whispered.

226

'Yes,' Mirella said, gazing at the face which, smooth and white as alabaster, had lost all joy and sadness now.

'And peaceful.'

'Yes.'

She stared at Liddy and at the few ornaments placed with her, objects chosen not for their intrinsic value, but because the family knew how precious they had been to her in life: the silver locket which she had always worn at her throat since her beloved eldest son brought it back from the Crimea, the fine shoe buckles that had belonged to Jem, and her wedding ring. Nothing more.

Mirella was glad when Steffi had offered to come and keep vigil with her – having somehow assumed that he would shy away from any contact with the dead. For he had been reacting very strangely since the news had come. Not only refusing to talk about Liddy, but slinking off on his own like some animal to pine. Perhaps it was her own fault for not breaking the news more gently, but even when she did follow him down to the seashore to try and talk, he had been completely unresponsive. She could not understand why there was no show of emotion, or even much interest in how Liddy had died – just an apparent absorption with the boats leaving the pier.

He was certainly a strange young man, she decided, looking up to see Steffi staring into the coffin, his face tilted on one side, his eyes dark shadowed pools in the candlelight. She watched as he stretched out his hand to touch Liddy's hair and then delicately rested his fingers on hers.

'Do you think she knows what I'm thinking?' he murmured.

'Yes, I'm sure she does,' Mirella said.

His face lit up in a smile.

'That's good. I want her to know.'

The coffin was carried into the church by Liddy's three sons and her son-in-law Joby. Mirella felt too choked by feelings to take much notice of the service, only really coming to when her Uncle Joey played his violin at the graveside. The last time she had heard that piece had been the year Steffi was born when Joey had played at the funeral of Liddy's husband, Captain Cresswall. It was a beautiful piece but made her feel so sad, especially when she thought of the Captain in his lonely grave in the military cemetery at Aldershot.

Still, it was only right that Liddy should be buried here

alongside Jem, the man whose children she had borne and with whom she had shared the greater part of her life. In fact, Johnny said, it was almost as if by dying in Windsor Liddy had declared this wish.

'And trust her to try to make things easier for us all like that,' he concluded.

Afterwards, back in her parents' cottage with so many people all talking at once, Mirella's head began to whirl. First there was her sister Cassie, enthusing about her children. Then Albie and Ben wanting to know how Minerva's was doing. The show had been much praised in the *Era*, she said, trying to respond with some degree of honesty without revealing the dire straits they were in.

'Mirella, *sarishan*.'

She spun round at the Romany greeting and found herself looking into the friendly face of her aunt.

'Hello, Phoebe. It's good to see you again, even if it is on such a sad occasion,' she said, giving her a kiss.

'Yes, it's a sad day for anyone when they lose their mother, but when that mother was someone like Liddy, well . . .' Her eyes filled with tears.

'I know, Phoebe, I know.'

'Our little Mirella, isn't it?' Now it was her turn to be hugged against Joby's ample chest. 'Glad to see you, my love. Nice to see someone else turned out properly,' he whispered, fingering her red cloak. 'All these gloom merchants in black – not at all what Aunt Liddy would want.'

'That's right. That's why I was pleased to see you and so many of the others wearing something red,' Mirella said, looking round at all the scarlet neckerchiefs and rosettes being worn by the travellers.

Suddenly she became aware of a portly, red-faced man in a black suit decked with a massive gold albert bearing down on her, smiling broadly. He looked so familiar, yet for a moment she could not think who it was. Then, almost before she realised what she was saying: 'Why, Tom, I hardly recognised you.'

'Well, things change,' he said, patting his stomach. 'Developed a bit of a corporation, you see.'

'Yes,' chuckled Joby. 'Not so prominent as mine but with a better chain of office.'

'My albert. Yes,' Tom smirked, taking out the appendant

watch from his waistcoat pocket to display its solidity, 'you won't see many of this quality. Engraved, look!' Clicking open its cover, he passed it round for inspection.

Mirella read: 'To my darling Tom on our wedding day, 10 June 1888. Love, Evalina'.

If he had been waiting for her to show surprise, he was not disappointed. She gasped in amazement.

'You've got married, Tom? Is she here?' she asked, looking around the crowded room.

'Of course. As you can see, we only tied the knot last June, so it's too soon for me to be letting her out of my sight just yet.'

'Fancy not telling us,' Phoebe grumbled. 'Where is she, then?'

'Talking to your husband,' he said.

Mirella peered into the dark corner by the inglenook where Levic was standing talking to a well-dressed little woman whose grey hair and faded skin made her look many years older than Tom.

'The lady in the hat with the feathers?' she asked to make sure.

'That's right,' said Tom proudly, 'that's Evalina.'

'How did you meet her?' Mirella asked, observing that the woman was dressed expensively, but not showily, in a costume of black bombasine with a small bustle and simple train, and seemed to be listening rather than talking to Levic.

'Ah, thereby hangs a tale, as they say.'

'A tale you've never told your family,' Phoebe remarked peevishly.

'No, well,' he looked a little sheepish, 'the . . . er, circumstances of our courtship were delicate.'

'You mean she was already married,' Mirella interjected.

'No, no. My goodness, nothing like that.'

She was amused to see that he seemed quite shocked by her suggestion.

'No, no. It's just that Evalina comes from a good family,' Tom continued, implying that most of the folk around him at that moment did not. 'Eldest daughter of a businessman in Tewkesbury and always been the apple of her father's eye and – between you, me and the gatepost,' he said dropping his voice, 'designed to be the support of his old age, so suitors weren't exactly welcome.'

Mirella surveyed his bride in the light of Tom's passion in younger days for more luscious fruit.

'But your persistence was rewarded,' she said, hardly daring to probe further.

He nodded.

'So how did you meet her, Tom?' Phoebe asked.

'Ah, well, amongst his many concerns, Evalina's father happens to be a manufacturer of carts, wagons, roundabouts – all that kind of thing – so, when times were lean a few years back, I took on some painting work for him one backend and made a pretty good job of it.'

As he said this, Mirella found herself no longer able to keep her eyes from his maimed right hand which Tom kept anchored, Napoleon fashion, in the front of his jacket.

'Yes, I bet that surprises you,' he added. 'But I was always a dab hand at painting, and soon found I could manage as well with my left as my right. And, to cut a long story short, my work went down so well the boss took me on full-time and I ended up marrying his daughter. Pretty smart, eh?' He glanced round towards the inglenook before turning back and winking one of his pale blue eyes. 'But now, tell me how things are going with you, Mirella?'

'Pretty well, thanks.'

'And Steffi? How's he taking . . . Liddy?'

'To be honest, I don't think it's really hit him yet, Tom. Or, if it has, he's not letting it show.'

'That sounds more like it, I'm afraid.'

'And what will he do now?' Phoebe asked.

Mirella smiled stiffly.

This was another of those questions she had been fending off all day. People would keep on asking 'How's your circus doing?' and 'Where will Steffi live now that Liddy's gone?' – and she had no answer for either question.

Any reference to Minerva's was painful. For although the news of Liddy's death had in the first instance driven all other griefs from her mind, the arrival on the same day of a letter containing a sharp reminder of the terms of their contract and penalties to be incurred on overdue repayments dashed her spirits still further. Both she and Levic realised that this was the death knell for the show, but by common consent had put the letter away without further discussion and shelved the problem until after the funeral.

'I think your mother wants you,' Joby suddenly remarked.

'Why, where is she?'

'Standing near the foot of the staircase waving at you, look.'

Almost in the same instant, Mirella saw Sadie beckoning her to come up to the bedroom, and with sinking heart followed. She had some idea what was coming. Her mother too would be anxious to hear what plans she and Levic were making for Steffi.

The cottage had only two proper bedrooms and the tiny box room stuck under the eaves which Liddy had been using while staying there as guest. As she ducked under the low lintel of the door, the babble of voices from downstairs died away and the smell of roses came drifting through the open window.

Seeing Liddy's things lying on the bed – her silver-backed hairbrush and comb, a book, a purse, a shawl, and what looked like a little sewing box – and smelling the flowers made Mirella feel as if her grandmother was there in the room with them.

'Come on, sit down for a minute. I want to talk,' Sadie urged, sitting on the bed while gesturing Mirella to the round-backed wooden chair. 'It didn't go off too badly, did it?'

'The funeral? No, you and Pa managed everything beautifully,' she replied, beginning to realise how much her mother's ill-temper was due to anxiety about the arrangements. 'And I am grateful for the way you've looked after Steffi. You've been marvellous with him.'

'Yes, well, that's why I want to have this chat.'

Inwardly Mirella groaned.

'But before I get on to that,' Sadie continued, 'take this in case I forget.'

She handed Mirella the little wooden box.

'Did this belong to Gran?' Mirella asked, puzzled by dim memories of seeing it hidden away in her mother's cupboard.

'Yes. She gave it to me years ago for you. Go on, open it and look.'

Mirella finished examining the decoration on the lid – possibly a rabbit, but the paint was too worn to tell – and then prised it off to reveal some cotton wadding and a curious furry brooch with claws imbedded in it.

'Ugh! This doesn't look like something Gran would wear,' she said, shuddering. 'What is it?'

'It's a haresfoot in a gold mounting, so it's quite valuable. But you're right. I don't remember ever seeing it on Liddy.'

'And she wanted me to have it?'

'Yes. Because it's a family heirloom and you were her first grandchild.'

231

'In that case I shall treasure it,' said Mirella, looking at the brooch with renewed interest, 'if only to pass on to Steffi.'

'Ah, poor Steffi,' Sadie sighed, 'this is a hard blow for him.'

Mirella bit her lip, saying nothing. Of course Liddy's death was a blow for Steffi. It had been a blow for everyone. But it wasn't as if Steffi had been orphaned or anything. He still had a mother to turn to for comfort.

Before Sadie could continue, heavy creaking on the staircase announced the arrival of Johnny whose presence seemed to fill the small room as he entered.

'Have you told her yet?' he beamed.

'No,' said Sadie, frowning at him, 'that side of things has got nothing to do with me. In fact, if I had my way . . . well, you know how I feel about it.'

Johnny's face clouded for a moment.

'Come on, Sadie, you should be pleased for the lad,' he muttered.

Mirella meanwhile sat stroking the silky hair on the haresfoot wondering what on earth they were both talking about.

'Well, of course I am,' Sadie conceded, 'but I still think there's others who ought to have been considered. Our Cassie, for one. And the boys. And Phoebe's lot.'

'But they do all get something.'

'Hmm,' Sadie grunted, 'but Steffi gets the lion's share.'

Mirella heard the words without grasping their meaning. 'Steffi gets the lion's share', repeated itself in her mind. 'Steffi gets the lion's share'.

'What do you mean?' she asked her mother.

'It's not for me to say. Ask him. He's the executor of Liddy's will.'

'Pa?' she queried, turning towards Johnny.

He sat down on the end of the bed nodding, with a smile on his face as big as the moon. 'It's quite right. Mother's left the house to your Steffi. There's money bequests to the others, but the house and contents go to Steffi. That's what she wanted.'

Mirella found herself clutching so convulsively at the haresfoot that its pin drew blood.

'But that's wonderful news!'

'Yes, but before you get too carried away,' her mother said sharply, 'remember this isn't for you. Or Levic. This is for Steffi. Liddy saw her house as Steffi's home and didn't want him suddenly deprived of it. Which is what I've dragged you up here to talk about, 'cept now your father's interrupted me before I could get to it.' She glared at Johnny, who sat clearly unrepentant.

'Well, I wanted Mirella to know before I tell Steffi,' he smiled, 'because he's still under age, remember, so she and Levic will have control till he's twenty-one.'

'I see,' Mirella muttered, while sucking the blood off her finger to prevent it dripping on the brooch and staining its fur. 'And do the others know yet?'

'No. I thought I'd make some sort of announcement once all the neighbours and outsiders have gone. But that needn't stop you telling Steffi straight away, if that's what you'd like to do.'

Steffi – she tried to picture his face when she told him. Good heavens! To think of Steffi inheriting Liddy's house. Houses were worth a lot of money. Enough to buy several circuses. Enough to pay off their existing loan and buy a new tent, so they wouldn't need to disband Minerva's.

Except that the money would not belong to them, of course. It would be Steffi's.

Chapter 25

'Something for you, Steffi,' Hugo called, advancing towards him across the tober, sifting through the pile of mail he had just collected from the local post office.

'For me?'

Steffi took the pale blue envelope and peered at the writing. All the mail he had received in recent weeks had referred in some way to the winding up of Liddy's estate, but this did not look like the usual business letter.

'Well, aren't you going to open it?'

'I suppose so, though I can't think who it's from.'

'Oh, some secret admirer, I shouldn't wonder,' Hugo said, winking as he turned away.

'Small chance of that,' Steffi murmured, at the same time registering a flicker of excitement as a photograph of a pretty girl fell out of the envelope. Quickly he extracted the folded notepaper accompanying it and stared at the top of the page where someone had written in a small, neat hand: Apsley's Amphitheatre, Westminster Bridge Road, London. Then he looked back at the photograph and, recognising it as Rosa, let his gaze rest on her smiling features for several moments before returning to read the letter.

'Dear Steffi,

I am writing to say how sorry I am to hear about the death of your greatgrandmother. I only heard the sad news yesterday when I came home after spending a few months in Suffolk with my father.

Dear Steffi, although I did not know Liddy very well, I remember her as the kind, gentle lady who used to bring you up to Apsley's years ago, and I know from the way you always talked about her that she must have been a very special person and someone you would miss sadly now she

235

has gone. So I wish with all my heart there was something I could say to lessen your sorrow as you tried to lessen mine, for I have never forgotten the kindness you showed me and my sister when our dear mother died.'

Steffi paused and glanced back at the photograph. What a sweet face! How kind of Rosa to have taken the trouble to write. It was good to know that someone with such a generous smile had a heart to match. Then he read the last paragraph.

'By the way, Rosa is sitting by my side as I write and wants me to apologise on her behalf as she would have written too if she had not been so dreadfully upset by the news. She says to remind you that "Time is the Great Healer" and thinks you might like to have this recent photograph of her to remind you of happier days.

With sincere good wishes
from your friend,
Amy.'

Steffi felt slightly cheated when he read the signature at the end. Still, it was clear that the letter really came from both the sisters and it was so good to know they had not forgotten him – just as he could never forget them.

He glanced back over the last paragraph. 'Time is the Great Healer' Rosa said, but at the moment he doubted it. In fact, whenever he thought of Liddy, he felt too sad even to want his hurt to be healed.

'Look, Steffi, no one forced you to leave the bank,' Levic hissed, coming across him while he was still in this dejected mood.

'I know.'

'In fact, I thought you'd soon regret it.'

'But I don't.'

'And you can't say your mother didn't do her best to warn you,' Levic continued, ignoring his protest. 'She knew what suited you.' Steffi winced, sensing that his father was trying to imply that he, Steffi, was probably incapable of making a go of much else. Well, he refused to be goaded; saw no point in arguing with someone who refused to listen.

'I mean, you do realise, don't you? Your mother was prepared to give up all this,' Levic gestured at the brand new striped tent stretched over their heads, 'so that she could stay with you in Aldershot while you took up that new post.'

'But I didn't want to take up the post nor did I want to carry on living in Aldershot. I'm happy with the choice I made,' he said, trying to keep his temper. This was by no means the first scene of its kind and Steffi could not understand why his father must keep accusing him of harbouring resentments that he was far from feeling.

'Ah, so you agree it was your choice to join us on the road?' Levic declared as if scoring a point.

'Yes.'

'Well, that's all right so long as you realise one thing.'

'What's that?'

'Minerva's isn't a passenger train.'

'Meaning?'

'Meaning that no one can just buy a ticket and come aboard for the ride.'

Steffi flinched. That hurt. And again the implication was so unjust, because as far as he could see he worked as hard as anyone else on the tober. He helped build up and pull down, drove one of the beast wagons when they were on the road, took part in the procession and general parades and, to Mirella's intense relief, had taken over responsibility for the bookings and accounts. What more, for heaven's sake, did his father expect him to do?

'I do what I can,' he said stiffly.

'Oh, yes? But what do you propose to contribute in the ring, my son? That's what I'd like to know.'

'I take part in the charivari and processions . . .'

Levic sighed.

'But surely you have more ambition than that, Steffi! I mean, yes, you seem to work hard, but anyone can do the things you're doing. The accounts, for instance. If you'd wanted to be a bloody book-keeper, you might as well have stayed in the bank.'

Steffi breathed in hard. If he had stayed in the bank, if he had not pressed so hard for Linden House to be sold so that he could put the money in his father's circus, then there would be no Minerva's on the road at the moment and his mother and father would be working for someone else. That's what Levic wanted to hear him say – and then to complain about his lot and say he thought his father should be a bit more grateful. But he wouldn't. Because he had no regrets. He had done exactly what

237

he wanted to. And his actions had made Mirella happy. And he himself would be happy if only his father would keep off his back.

'Look, Pa, all this is still pretty new to me, so I need time to find my feet . . .'

'But, Steffi, you're seventeen and by the time I was half your age . . . No, it's no good looking daggers at me. Your trouble is, you don't know how easy you've had everything.'

Oh dear! Levic could hardly believe his own voice. This was not really him, but the pain making itself heard. It was only when the rheumatism was particularly bad that seeing his son prancing round so aimlessly got on his nerves.

Most of the time, thank God, it was different. In fact, these last few weeks had gone like a dream once Steffi had decided he wanted to sell Liddy's house and use the money to set the circus up in style. They had quickly bought another tent, taken on more artistes and put on a spectacular procession and highwire performance to mark their reopening on Southsea Common early in October. And the crowds had flocked in. So, credit where credit was due – at least Steffi had been quick to recognise a sound investment when he saw one! The trouble was, it was probably that very investment that led him to take more interest in the ticket office than in the ring.

'What's wrong, Pa? Have you got a pain or something?'

'No,' Levic snapped, annoyed to find his body letting him down again, especially when he was beginning to think himself over the worst. These last few weeks, for instance, scarcely a twinge – a fact testified by the rave reviews that his clowning received in all the papers.

But now, with the autumn damp beginning to creep into his bones, he felt his joints seizing up again and could not help taking his frustration out on anyone around, especially Steffi.

'I say, you couldn't lend us a hand with the horses, could you, Steffi?' Hugo called out as he carried a saddle through the ring towards the stable tent.

'Yes. Be with you in a minute! If you're sure you're okay,' he murmured, turning back to his father.

'I told you, there's nothing wrong with me. So go and help Hugo.'

'Sorry, did I interrupt?' Hugo asked, stopping.

'No. We weren't doing anything, just talking about this young man's future.'

Hugo looked disconcerted.

'But I thought that was settled. You're not thinking of leaving us already, are you, Steffi?'

'No, of course not.'

'No, he'll stay all the time Minerva's needs a ticket-seller or tentman, won't you, Steffi?' Levic said sarcastically. 'But I had expected rather more from my son than that, so how would you fancy riding bareback in the ring, eh?'

'Why?'

'What do you mean "Why"? Surely that's obvious. This show needs a good horse-act and you need something to do.'

'No, I don't think so. Not after seeing what . . . Well, no, I don't think so.'

Levic waited, but that was all Steffi said.

It was infuriating. After the way Levic had been prepared to help, all his son could find to say was: 'No, I don't think so.'

'You don't think so,' he parroted. 'But that's just the trouble. No matter what anyone suggests, you can't be bothered even to think about their ideas before turning them down.'

Steffi flinched but said nothing more.

So, as far as Levic was concerned, the situation seemed hopeless – the only redeeming feature being that Steffi got on well with the rest of the company, even if it was for the wrong reason. It was easy to take a shine to someone who never said no to carrying buckets of water, feeding and mucking out animals, greasing axles, and who didn't even complain when the men used him as butt for their stupid jokes. Still, if Steffi could not see himself as an aritiste, then there was nothing for it but to leave him to find his own level.

Late that night, after the last show was over, Levic was rehearsing these thoughts to Mirella as they sat outside the wagon – he on a chair and she on the steps, drinking cocoa.

'But I don't think you're necessarily right,' she protested. 'He's actually very good in the charivari.'

'Hmm,' Levic scoffed, 'I'm surprised you could tell. I mean he hardly stands out, does he?'

'Why should he?'

'Well, if that had been me at his age and I had half the

chances he's had . . . But what's the use of saying it? I think Steffi's had it too soft and it's made him idle.'

'No, that's not fair. Steffi's not idle.'

'Well, then he must be stupid . . .' he started to say.

She leapt up.

'It's not him. It's you! For some reason, you've got it in for him and won't let him do a thing right.'

'No, Mirella, you're wrong. I've tried every way I know to teach him what's what in the ring, but he's not interested. In fact, he's happier working with the tentmen.'

'And they don't say he's lazy.'

'No, well, they get a good laugh out of him, don't they?'

'What do you mean?' she snapped, beginning to flush with anger.

'I mean he makes himself fair game. You know how a gang of men like to rib a youngster, especially one as wet behind the ears as our Steffi, I'm ashamed to say.'

'And you let them get away with it?' Mirella demanded, her eyes flashing.

'No, I've tried to discourage him from being too familiar with them, but if he won't grasp the distinction between workmen and performers, he'll have to learn the hard way.'

'Not my son, Levic – I won't have him ridiculed in our own show . . .'

She stopped, peering anxiously towards the big tent where, now that the nights were so much cooler, the company tended to eat their supper round a coke brazier after the last performance. There was obviously some game afoot, because ever since he and Mirella had been talking, regular ripples of laughter had lapped across the field towards them. In this moment, though, the ripples were being engulfed in a flood of screams and guffaws enough to sicken anyone who thought of the poor stooge at the centre of such mockery.

'Come on,' Mirella ordered. 'I won't have Steffi made a fool of. We're going to put a stop to this.'

It was odd how the big tent changed its character, its mood, even its shape, to fit what was taking place inside it. When there was a full house for a show, the tent formed a huge arena: with the ring as the hub of a wheel of concentric tiers of seats stretching out to the canvas walls. Now, as Levic and Mirella entered, the outer rim was in such complete darkness that the tent had shrunk to the size of a crowded homely hearth created round the coke fire on which chestnuts were roasting.

Levic was glad to see the men had raked the sawdust into heaps round the edges beforehand to keep it clean for the next day, and that Dai was still keeping an eye on his precious lamps, knowing that fire was as great a risk after hours as during a show. There was always the danger of an oil lamp being knocked over during practice sessions or when people were using the tent for socialising, as now. In fact, when he looked round, Levic realised there was more danger at the moment not from spilt oil – there were far fewer lamps alight – but from all the smoking. Once the tent hands had put away a few drinks they tended to get careless about where they put out their cigarettes.

So busy was he assessing the hazard, he forgot for a moment why he and Mirella had strode over here, until she whispered, 'Where is he? Can you see him, Levic?'

He surveyed the company – some sitting on upturned boxes leaning their backs against the ring fence, others lounging on sacks of straw or heaps of tan. One or two turned their faces wonderingly towards him – faces still streaked with dried sweat and orange greasepaint – steaming mugs or tankards in their hands.

Once more Levic was struck by this palace of contrasts that was the circus. An hour ago and all was strict routine and order, glitter and smart array. Now that the public had gone, the artistes were like rag dolls who had been tipped out of their toy-chest in a muddle. All had changed out of their costumes, of course, but only to pull on dressing gowns, shawls or long, woollen jerseys over a mismatch of trousers or skirts so that they could sprawl around in comfort while they talked or sang and entertained each other. Like the skinny chap who was singing a comic song at the moment, for instance.

Levic knew the song. He used it regularly in his own performances. Together with the same actions and gestures as this chap was using – cheeky devil! Why, he had even dipped his fingers in the clown-white and used the carmine stick to enhance his imitation of Levic, although he hadn't made a very good job of the make-up. In fact, he looked so pathetic, it was laughable!

Levic turned to say as much to Mirella only to find her clutching both sides of her face as if to stop it splitting with laughter.

'Oh, dear! Oh, dear!' she muttered eventually. 'You can't deny he's got you all right.'

'Yes, and I'll have him, if he's not careful,' Levic warned, 'specially as that's my hat he's purloined.'

Another minute though, and he was forced to chuckle despite himself. The man was trying to copy one of his tricks – throwing the conical white hat in such a way that it spun through the air to land on a special hook. But this joker obviously didn't know enough to adjust the rubber stiffener hidden in the brim and so the hat simply fell splat on the ground. Not that that in itself was very funny. It was the look of utter bewilderment on the skinny chap's face as he went to reclaim his missile and tried again that had everybody in stitches.

'There you are, what did I say?' Mirella chortled. 'I told you he was a chip off the old block.'

'Who?'

Levic need not have asked. He already knew. In fact, he had half-realised that the joker was Steffi as soon as he clapped eyes on him, but for some reason had fought against the recognition. Now, however, he felt a surge of excitement. His head began to throb with ideas. They could do a double act.

Levic and son – between them they could develop that old hat trick into a completely new routine, incorporating Steffi's unconscious humour. It would be so comical! And there was a routine with a mirror that he'd had in mind for months. And the entrée he did with Barney. With Steffi acting as stooge, he could make the ass his ally and add another dimension to that act.

Yes, I should be able to make something of the lad after all, he thought comfortably.

Then the magic was spoilt.

One moment Steffi had the crowd in his hand and was in his element, the next he seemed to shrivel and die under his make-up.

The reason? He had caught sight of Levic among the spectators and with a look of horror immediately snatched off the clown's hat and with the back of his hand wiped the large red grin off his face.

Chapter 26

Steffi was worried. There was no way he could ever emulate his father! Why, Levic was almost a household name when it came to clowning. He had established a reputation on both sides of the Atlantic, had shaken hands with the President of the United States as well as being presented to several crowned heads of Europe. Some people even went so far as to call him the greatest English clown since Grimaldi.

Steffi could never compete with this. Nor did he want to, if it meant having to develop that all-consuming passion for performing that his father had.

'Look, I don't want you to do exactly what I do,' Levic explained. 'There's no point in having two Levics in the same circus, is there?'

'No.'

'So, what I propose is this. You come into the ring as an auguste.'

'A what?'

'An auguste,' Levic repeated. 'You know, the "clumsy idiot" character.'

'Oh, yes. I can do that all right,' Steffi said lightly.

His father immediately bridled.

'No, no. It won't be that easy and you shouldn't approach anything with that attitude.'

'I know. I didn't mean . . .' Steffi started to say, but decided there was no point in trying to explain. Wondered, indeed, whether there was any point in trying to work with his father when they managed to fall out even before they began.

'All right. Down to business,' Levic ordered. 'I want you in the ring not as a normal clown but as a stooge. Get me?'

'You mean you want me to act stupid to make you look clever?'

'Yes,' Levic said.

'And why should that be funny?'

'Ah, that's for you to work out.'

Steffi narrowed his eyes, suspecting that either Levic did not know the answer or he was simply trying to make this clowning business more complicated than he needed to.

'Right,' he said, impatient to move on. 'So tell me what an "auguste" is and I'll have a go.'

'Well, the funny thing is, the first auguste appeared almost by accident. You've heard of the Renz Circus in Berlin?'

Steffi nodded. 'You used to perform there, didn't you?'

'Yes, back in the sixties – when I was younger,' Levic muttered. 'And on one of those occasions I was there with a chap called Belling who'd been employed as part of a troupe of trick-riders. Only he wasn't very good. Always making mistakes. So one evening Herr Renz ordered him out of the ring and told him to stay in the dressing-room as a punishment.'

'That doesn't sound like too bad a punishment.'

'Which shows how little you understand the pride of an artiste, Steffi,' Levic declared, before resuming his story. 'Anyway, it seems Belling got bored and started messing about with some old clothes, putting a jacket on inside out, I remember, and sticking a threadbare wig on his head back to front. And the effect was so comical that, when Herr Renz saw him, he shoved him straight into the ring.'

Levic broke off and, unusually for him when offstage, started to chuckle in such an infectious way that Steffi found himself joining in.

'Oh dear!' he spluttered at last. 'I wish you could have seen him, Steffi. He hadn't a clue that was going to happen, you see. So the shove sent him crashing into the entrance post and then sprawling into the sawdust, and when he sat up looking stupefied, the audience brought the house down.'

'I suppose they thought it was all planned,' Steffi mused.

'They did. And then, when someone in the gallery called out "Auguste!", or "Silly fool!", everyone took up the chant, and poor Belling got so furious, he picked himself up, strode out of the ring and then tripped over one of the ropes and fell flat on his face again. Well, it was by far the funniest thing that happened in the ring that night – even I had to admit that, and I was the official clown!'

'So he put you in the shade?'

'Almost. But as I was coming to the end of my contract

anyway, I didn't mind when Renz signed Belling up to replace me.'

'And that was really the birth of the auguste?' Steffi asked, having enjoyed listening to his father reminisce.

'Yes, that's how the idea of a traditional clown working with a stooge began. So do you understand roughly what I'm asking you to do?'

'I think so.'

After this they practised a few clowning routines which, although they looked simple, Steffi found far from easy. But Levic encouraged him through any difficulties by saying, whenever he made a mistake or suddenly froze and did not know how to carry on, 'That's good. Play it all out, Steffi. Let your feelings show on your face. That's right, let yourself look confused. Good. Remember, you don't have to be anything but yourself.'

Mirella had brought her sewing into the big top so that she could watch Levic and Steffi rehearsing in the ring while she worked. She was making Steffi's costume – a huge, bright-checked suit with a jacket that would droop over his thin shoulders and hang down almost to his knees; an enormous white collar and red tie; overlarge white spats; and a big cloth cap worn askew over a wig-mop of red hair. The effect was going to be charming when Steffi ran into the ring and peered all round the audience before squeaking the time-honoured greeting, 'Here we are!'

'They make a good partnership, don't they?' Hugo observed.

'Yes, surprisingly so,' she agreed, putting out a hand to gather in her skirts as he sank on to the bench beside her.

'Surprising because they're so different, I suppose you mean?' he said, languidly stretching out his legs to ease his muscles. He had just been exercising the horses by galloping them over the common on which the circus was pitched for this, their last series of shows before going into winter quarters, and despite the cold nip in the air, he was bare-armed and still flushed from the exertion.

'Do you think they are that different, then?'

'Oh, yes. Not physically, of course. Steffi's the spit and image of his father in looks. But in temperament they're almost opposites, aren't they?'

She surveyed each in turn, as they engaged in some typical

piece of humpsti-bumpsti involving a chase over various bits of furniture.

'No, I'm not sure what you mean.'

Hugo grinned.

'Well, for a start, Levic's so intense and desperate about everything. I mean, to hear him talk you'd think clowning was some bloody religion. Whereas Steffi – well, to be honest, I think he's a natural.'

'Are you saying that Steffi is better than Levic?' she asked incredulously.

'No, of course not. There can't be anyone better than Levic. He'll make sure of that,' he said easily, bending over to remove a piece of straw from his breeches, his body exuding a disturbing smell of horses and bran and healthy sweat. Mirella laid aside her sewing.

'So you think Levic's greedy about his reputation?'

'Not greedy so much as desperate,' Hugo said, smiling again.

'And you don't think Steffi's the same?'

'No, I'm sure he isn't. Steffi's more – how can I say? – he cares about people more, that's why he'd never get so bound up in his own success.'

To Mirella Hugo's words sounded like a criticism of Levic. And possibly of herself.

'Hugo! Here a minute, will you?'

He leapt up at Levic's shout.

'I thought we might run through the riddle routine once more for Steffi's benefit, so will you come and do your ringmaster bit? And remember, keep as haughty and detached as possible. Ready, Steffi?'

Mirella watched and listened carefully.

First Levic. 'Listen, do you know anyone who is my mother's and father's child, but who isn't my brother or my sister?'

Steffi, utterly baffled, slowly shook his head.

'You don't know the person who isn't my brother or my sister and yet is the child of my mother and father! Why, it's me!'

Steffi, after taking time to think, nodded his head, surprised and delighted with this information.

Then into the ring strode Hugo – and Steffi's thinking was written across his innocent face as he approached the ringmaster and piped up: 'I say, Mr Ringmaster, do you know

246

someone who isn't my brother or my sister and yet is the child of my mother and father?'

'Yes, you,' said Hugo on cue.

'No, not me. Him!' beamed Steffi triumphantly.

It was obvious what was coming, of course, but that did not matter. Steffi acted his part with such artlessness that even Mirella found herself laughing out loud, and she continued to chuckle as Steffi and Hugo staged their quarrel about who should leave the ring first.

'Sir, I go first because I never follow a fool.'

'That's all right because I always do,' observed Steffi, skipping out after the ringmaster.

No sooner had they left than all three reappeared to ask Mirella what she thought.

'It was great, but it will be even better when you're all in costume and there's music to give it more atmosphere.'

Steffi looked doubtful.

'But was it really funny?' he asked. 'I thought I might just sound stupid and not like a proper clown.'

'That's why I say you'll feel better once you've got your costume on. Here, take it. It's practically ready now. Put it on and see what a difference it makes,' Mirella suggested, gathering up all his clobber and handing it to him.

'Good idea,' Levic agreed. 'Get dressed, Steffi, and then we'll sort you out a face.'

That turned out not to be so easy. Poor Steffi had to sit patiently while his skin became parchment which was painted and erased only to be re-painted and rubbed away again before they came up with something that satisfied Levic.

'What do you think?' he asked Mirella, while Steffi moaned that it felt as if they had got down to the bone.

'Yes,' she said, nodding more from fear of her son being flayed alive than enthusiasm for the simple result of all this labour – a face covered in white, with a tiny red button nose and a mouth that was accentuated rather than exaggerated. It was the eyebrows, however, which were the distinctive feature. They had been carefully drawn almost halfway up Steffi's forehead and although the one on the right was the usual shape, the other curled up like the tendril of a plant, giving his face a haunting, questing quality.

'Yes,' she murmured again, 'I think you've got it.'

'Right, let's show the rest of the company and hear their verdict then,' Hugo cried, leading Steffi away.

'I was right, you see, when I said that young man would prove himself valuable in the show,' Levic observed.

'Yes,' Mirella said happily. 'I must say I'm surprised at how good he's turning out to be. And not just in the show either.'

'In what other ways then?' Levic asked sharply.

'In every way,' she countered. 'He's good company and always ready to help anyone, especially me.'

'I hadn't noticed that,' Levic snapped.

'Oh, you must have noticed how well he gets on with people.'

'Yes, but I didn't realise he'd been going out of his way to help you in particular.'

She wanted to shake him. Why must he always have this down on their son? It was perfectly obvious how Steffi helped her by counting the takings every evening.

'Look,' she said, 'what do you think happens up in the wagon after the show every night?'

'He goes up in the wagon with you?' Levic exclaimed.

'Of course he comes up in the wagon with me,' she stammered, trying to work out why Levic was acting so irrationally. 'He lives with us, remember?'

'Yes, but that doesn't mean to say he can take liberties.'

'Wait a minute, wait a minute.' Mirella closed her eyes and thought for a moment before bursting into laughter.

'No, I'm being serious, Mirella. That fellow has a reputation, believe me. And although I was prepared to allow his private life to remain just that, I draw the line . . .'

'Levic,' she giggled, 'I thought you were talking about Steffi.'

'Steffi?' he glared. 'I never mentioned Steffi. I was talking about our resident Romeo – Hugo.'

When Steffi and Hugo returned a few minutes later, Mirella found it impossible to explain why she and Levic were laughing.

That evening, before Steffi made his first appearance in the ring as an auguste, he took another important step in the establishing of his professional identity. He found himself a name.

'You know, if you're going to be a clown, you ought to have a proper clown name,' the snake-lady muttered when she saw him dressed up for the first time.

'What's wrong with Steffi?'

'Nothing, except it's your real name.'

'Well, your real name's Venie, isn't it?'

'Good Lord, no. Venie's my stage name – or Madame Venie, to be exact. You'd never guess what my real name is.'

Steffi stared at her, finding it impossible to imagine her being called anything else.

'Rosa or Rosalina?' he ventured at last.

'Nope. Have another guess.'

'Victoria, Amy, Cassie, Sadie . . .' he chanted, working his way through all the females he knew.

'Nope, you'll never guess. It's Doris.'

He remembered his manners just in time to stop himself laughing out loud. Of course she would have to change her name when joining the circus. Who ever heard of a snake-charmer called Doris? However, surely the same did not apply to Steffi, which was at least as good a name for a clown as 'Levic'.

On the other hand, it might be fun to have another name, he thought; fun to be two separate people. Steffi who always tried to behave well and act responsibly, and . . . well, another self who could enjoy himself more, who would play practical jokes, perform dangerous tricks, take risks. Yes, it could be fun to become this daring other person called . . . What?

Levic?

As 'Levic' he pictured himself able to do all that his father could do: dance along a tightrope forty feet above the ground, fly from one trapeze to another, leap on to the back of a galloping horse, juggle with sharp knives . . . oh, the list was endless. Mirella had told him there was hardly a trick which had been performed in the circus that Levic had not made his own. That was how he was able to hold the whole show together, weaving his clowning in and out of all the other performances – joining Mirella on the high rope, aping Hugo in his equestrian act, making a joke out of the juggler, raising a laugh by imitating the acrobats – and all the while disguising his expertise under a more lovable motley.

It was no good. Steffi was not a Levic – and in any case Minerva's could not have two clowns with the same name – so he must think of something else.

There was always Joey, of course. Circus clowns were often called Joeys – after Joseph Grimaldi, the most famous clown ever. But he had been a pantomime clown, so that wasn't really appropriate.

Grimaldi. Grim-all-day. No. That was no good. I must think up something quite different, thought Steffi as he sat in the dressing tent, already in his costume before the signal to get dressed had even sounded.

'Hello, Steffi, what's up?'

He jumped, too lost in his thoughts to notice that two members of the acrobatic troupe had arrived to get dressed.

'Nothing. I was just thinking.'

'Ooh, never do that before a show. Spoils your timing,' one of them joked, as he dived behind the canvas walling at the end, to reappear a couple of minutes later in singlet and tights. 'Feeling a bit nervous?'

'No, not really. I was just trying to think up another name for myself.'

'In case you need to make an escape?' the fellow ribbed, bending over backwards until his lean face quizzed Steffi from between his knees.

'No, I just thought it would be nice to be someone else when I go in the ring. I mean, like you and Mick and the others become the Dizarellis and Toff becomes Monsieur Henri.'

'Yes, a clown needs a different name,' Mick, the other acrobat, agreed as he too emerged from the men's changing closet. 'What about Bobbo?'

'No, Steffi's not a Bobbo, is he, Toff?' the first acrobat asked the snake-lady's husband as he came in, and then had to explain what they were discussing.

Before long the tent was full of artistes in various states of undress and make-up, scrambling for clothes, wadded cotton, pots of carmine, and shouting out suggestions for Steffi's new name.

'He's an auguste, isn't he? Well, what about calling him September?'

Hugo's suggestion, made as he was pulling tight the laces in his black riding boots, brought a howl of derision which quickly subsided as Levic entered. Steffi had noticed how his father's presence often had this effect, as if the company were always on their guard against upsetting him by behaving in any way that was less than businesslike.

On this occasion, however, he came in smiling and looked put out when silence fell.

'Ah me! Having been attracted here by sounds of levity,' he sighed, 'I seem to have quashed it – which is a pity, because there must always be room for levity in a circus.'

Steffi stepped in to cover the awkward pause which followed: 'I was just asking everyone to think up a good clown's name for me.'

'And did you find one?' Levic asked, gazing round at the company.

'No, but you did,' one of the acrobats said.

'I did?' Levic looked puzzled.

'Yes, "Levity". I thought I heard you say there must always be "Levity" in a circus.'

'Yes, that's the best suggestion yet,' everyone choloused.

'Levity. Levity the Clown. Why not?' Levic murmured.

After that, everywhere Steffi went he seemed to hear the name, his name, being whispered – in the canvas of the tent, the hiss of the lamps, the rustling of animals in the straw. But his best moment came when, while waiting behind the curtain before making his first entrance, he watched Hugo – tall and majestic in silk top hat and tailed coat – command the attention of the audience and announce in stentorian tones: 'And now, ladies and gentlemen, boys and girls . . . introducing . . . tonight . . . for the very first time . . . before the British public . . . Minerva's . . . popular clown duo – LEVIC and . . . LEVITY!'

Chapter 27
1889

Steffi, standing with his head stuck out of the carriage window, was making doubly sure the whole party was on board and that there were no last-minute hitches. They could not afford any mistakes today, not when this train had been specially chartered to take Minerva's Circus to Windsor for a royal command performance.

'Brrrr!'

He turned to see his mother shiver as she plunged her hands deep into her muff. And he himself felt frozen after all the waiting about on Paddington Station, even though, knowing how bitter a February morning could be, Mirella had insisted they all clad themselves in boots and heavy coats before setting out.

'Let me go and fetch you a rug from the baggage wagon, Ma,' he suggested.

'No, I'll be fine in a minute. It's because my feet are thawing out at last that I can feel the cold.'

'If you're sure.'

She smiled happily at him. This venture meant so much to her, he realised that – because Mirella was doing more than just appearing before the Queen, she was returning to the place where she had once worked as a humble scullery-maid, returning in triumph as owner of Minerva's circus and one of its chief performers. That's what made it so vital for everything to go well.

Not that there was any reason why it should not after all the hard work they had put in since receiving the invitation from the Queen's private secretary just over a month ago. The Prince of Wales, it seemed, had personally recommended the show after making a surprise visit one evening around Christmas while they were performing at the Agricultural Hall. As a result Sir Henry Ponsonby wrote asking Levic to select Minerva's twelve best acts to present at the Castle Riding School on the occasion of the birthday of one of the royal grandchildren.

Naturally, a flurry of excitement had ensued and weeks of frantic activity as acts were polished and spruced, new costumes designed, props and fresh hoardings painted. And the only untoward result was that Levic had, as usual, exhausted himself and was now clearly at the end of his tether.

'What about you, Pa – are you warm enough?'

'I would be if you shut that bloody window.'

After a last glance down the platform, Steffi jerked the window shut and sat down beside his father. Levic flinched at the sudden movement – a sure sign that his rheumatism was playing up again, although no one dared ask. For if there was anything guaranteed to make Levic irritable, it was some reference to his infirmity.

Hugo, sitting opposite, raised his eyebrows at Steffi in a gesture of sympathy, while the other two people sharing their compartment – a young married couple who did a perch act in the show – gazed out of the windows pretending not to notice Levic's rudeness.

'They've done us proud with these carriages, haven't they?' Hugo said, biting off the end of his cigar before lighting up.

'Yes, makes you feel like royalty, doesn't it?' Steffi said, trying surreptitiously to stretch his legs without disturbing his father too much. 'I must say, I didn't expect anything so grand.'

'How many wagons are there, Steffi?' Mirella asked.

'Eight horse-boxes, three baggage-wagons, and our first-class coach.'

'Phew! Proves how much they appreciate us,' she observed.

'Let's hope they don't make us walk back, then.'

After that remark from Levic, everyone fell silent again. Steffi returned to his thoughts.

He was feeling uneasy. Not just about the forthcoming show but about his father. There were times when he found him impossible. And even if, as Mirella always pointed out, Levic's temper was but a barometer of his health and should not be taken personally, this was hard for Steffi to accept – especially as Levic held a possible cure in his own hands. For nowadays there was no need for him to take on so much all the time. It would be easy for him to take more of a back seat in the show, especially when it came to performing.

254

And so many people had tried to tell him this! He was a brilliant director and performer, but the show did not need to have him bouncing in and out weaving together every act. He was simply wearing himself out by doing so. Such a fact was obvious to everyone. Except Levic.

And it wouldn't be so bad if it was only himself he was injuring, but to take his frustration out on everyone around him was unforgivable.

It was still early morning when they arrived in Windsor but they drove immediately to the Riding School in the Quadrangle.

'Oh, I remember this,' Mirella exclaimed, as they entered the long, rectangular building with its church-like windows, 'but, do you know, I've never been inside before.'

'Do you think that's where the Queen will be sitting?' Steffi asked her, pointing up to a triple Tudor-arched window over the porch entrance which seemed designed to command the best view of proceedings.

'Yes, I should think so.'

'And the hoi-polloi down here?'

There were about three hundred seats set out in the main body of the building.

'Yes, if that's the right way to refer to the royal household.'

'Well, you know what I mean,' he murmured, turning to survey the space at the far end which had been separated off by a rich, crimson arras-cloth parted in the middle like curtains behind which the artistes, horses and props could be hidden from view. In front of this was the ring covered in tan bark and sawdust ready for the performance, and the rest of the hall had been lined several feet high with gaily-coloured bunting in royal blue and white stripes.

'Where will you put the tightrope?' he asked.

'Across the centre of the ring. There's not enough space to do anything else really,' she said.

Hearing her remark, Levic nodded his head in agreement and set the men to work rigging it up.

Three o'clock and, with surprising punctuality, Her Majesty took her place in the royal box.

'Shows you how desperate she is to see a good circus,' Hugo muttered as the company stood to attention behind the curtain.

'I thought we were here for the children,' Steffi whispered.

'Don't you believe it. The old lady loves circuses. In fact I heard someone say . . .'

'Shush!'

Levic glared along the line as the strains of the National Anthem sounded and the company stood to attention even though they could not be seen by their monarch or the rest of the audience.

Steffi stood peeping through the end of the curtain as Levic bounded out to introduce the first act – a juggler on horseback.

Up in the royal box in front of the distinguished adults, he could make out three or four children with their noses pressed against the glass, their excitement the same as that of children the world over. Which was more than could be said for the rest of the audience – especially the serried ranks of house-servants, grooms and coachmen in their varied liveries, sitting as straight-backed and prim as if in chapel.

He and Levic would have to work hard to get a laugh out of them.

'How do you think it's going?' he whispered to his father as they stood together watching Hugo give his equitation display.

'Hmm,' he grunted, dabbing a towel over his face to mop up sweat without damaging his make-up. 'Hardly a bundle of fun, are they? Like trying to amuse a room full of plump cushions.'

'That's what I thought . . .'

'Still, that's what they're paying us for,' he muttered, swallowing a couple of the little white pills which he was in the habit of taking when his rheumatism was bad. 'And at least they're not throwing things. So, as long as we get through without dire mishap, I shall be happy. Although it would have been nice to see the old lady actually laugh out loud over something.'

Steffi had never known his mother nervous before, but she was today.

'Oh dear, the atmosphere feels so heavy,' she moaned before going on. And the heaviness seemed to permeate her mood and make all her movements stiff so that her performance on the rope lacked its normal zest. Still, the audience appeared satisfied and duly clapped on cue.

'Good luck!' she whispered to Steffi who, dressed in his Levity costume, stood waiting to lead Barney into the ring to go through their famous music lesson routine.

He pulled an anguished face in reply before making his entrance.

There had been some doubt as to whether this particular act was in sufficiently good taste to be presented before the Queen – another reason for Steffi's disquiet. However, the royal children were obviously delighted by the sight of Barney – one of the little princesses clapping her hands with delight as he guided the donkey to his chair and sat him down behind a metal stand bearing a song sheet.

At this point Barney was supposed to turn the music over with his nose and sing, 'Home Sweet Home'.

Instead he suddenly discovered a more urgent interest in the strange tan which had been laid under the sawdust. It clearly possessed a smell he was not sure of, so before Steffi could get him to utter a note he got out of his chair and began to sniff the floor, pausing only to peer at the audience and emit long sighs of satisfaction.

'Come on!' Steffi muttered, trying to coax Barney back on to his chair with the aid of a sugar-lump. But while behind the curtain several members of the company started to giggle and out front the audience roared with laughter, the donkey refused to oblige.

Steffi glared at the animal. Of all the times to play up, none could be more disastrous!

He snatched a quick look up at the royal box – and saw all its occupants convulsed. The Duke and Duchess of Connaught, Prince Christian and his wife, and yes, the Queen herself – all shaking their heads and chortling with glee.

Well, that's what he and Barney were here for – to make them laugh. And if this is what they found amusing, who was he to teach his donkey greater wisdom?

'Come on, Barney, tell me what you've lost,' he asked, entering into the spirit of the new game. 'Lost something in the tan, have you? Well, come back and sing and then I'll help you find it.'

When Barney continued to paw at the ground, Steffi decided he had no choice but to make a virtue of the beast's intransigence. Gazing woefully up at the children in the royal box, he explained how he should never have let Barney persuade him to pay him his wages in advance, because now the donkey had dropped one of his threepenny bits in the sawdust and would not go on until it was recovered.

Meanwhile, even as he was saying this, Steffi was stroking and soothing Barney to the point where he could lead him back to the chair, sit him down, and again instruct him to sing 'Home Sweet Home'. And this time success seemed within reach until, having made a tiny noise, the wretched animal decided he wanted to investigate this strange tan further and promptly got up and went to have another smell.

For a moment Steffi felt like calling it a day and dragging Barney off the stage, but the noise from the audience told him how much they were enjoying themselves – whether because they thought they were seeing a very clever act or simply liked witnessing his own discomfiture, he could not tell. All he knew was how much it was costing him to keep a hold on the situation for, despite the cold day, the sweat was pouring off him as he continued to improvise story after story to account for Barney's behaviour. Then at last, after much persuasion, the donkey brayed and the act was saved.

'Oh, my God, take him away and don't let me see him again,' Steffi groaned when the audience eventually consented to let him and Barney disappear backstage.

'Don't worry, you carried it off marvellously,' Mirella reassured him.

'No, no. It was dreadful,' he moaned. 'After all those times when he's sung on cue, to let me down like that, today of all days . . .'

Although he felt so dejected, there was no time to brood as he helped others get ready to go on. But afterwards, once the show had ended and the memory of his humiliation returned with full force, he dreaded to think what his father would say about the débâcle.

'Levic! Someone here with a message.'

Hearing the shout, Steffi looked up to see his father listening to the footman and then beckoning in his direction.

'You want me?' Steffi asked.

'Yes, it seems Barney has made a conquest, because Her Majesty has sent a special request for the singing donkey to be paraded outside so that they can strike up a closer acquaintance.'

'Good Lord!'

'Quite! But I suppose that just goes to show . . .' muttered Levic without going on to disclose exactly what.

Pulling on a coat over his costume, Steffi joined Levic and

Mirella outside where they lined up alongside Barney to await the royal inspection.

There they stood shivering until, with the aid of a walking stick, the tiny, black-shrouded figure of the Queen descended the three steps from the Riding School. For a fleeting instant Steffi wondered whether he was going to be called to account for the donkey's poor musicianship. But in the event, the Queen was interested in more mundane affairs.

'How old is he? Where did he come from? What does he like to eat?' she asked.

Then, after Steffi had supplied her with appropriate answers, she condescended to touch the animal's back with her stick as if bidding him rise 'Sir Barney'. But Barney, sadly ignorant of the honour being done him, took the gesture as chastisement for previous misconduct and promptly kicked out and broke into an horrendous cacophony of braying which left the Queen aghast.

'Your Majesty,' Steffi quickly interposed, 'Barney sings more readily for you than for me.'

'You call that "singing"?'

'Why, yes. It's his version of "See the Conquering Hero Comes"!'

For a moment Her Majesty surveyed the donkey, seemingly inclined to give him the benefit of the doubt. But after taking stock of Steffi, she changed her mind.

'He can go. I have had enough,' she grumbled, turning on her heel and stumping away.

'Did I say the wrong thing?' Steffi whispered to Mirella as they stood waiting for the rest of the royal party to make their departure.

Mirella seemed to be looking a him with wide-eyed admiration as she answered: 'No, I think you handled a difficult situation beautifully.'

'But the Queen didn't even smile.'

'Perhaps not. But I think she was secretly amused.'

Chapter 28
1890

'I'm not sure I want those girls here.'

'No, Levic. Not girls, young women,' Mirella corrected him.

'Young women, then. It makes no difference. I don't want them here.'

'Don't take them on then,' Mirella snapped.

'It's not that I have anything against them personally, you realise,' Levic said, prevaricating. 'And I'd like to help Arnold but . . .' His voice tailed away.

'But . . . you don't want to see them around. In case they remind you of their mother,' Mirella blurted out.

'No! No, I didn't say that.'

'But it's what you meant.'

Steffi was startled to hear such bitterness in his mother's voice.

'Are you talking about Rosa and Amy?' he asked.

'That's right. Their grandfather's written to ask if they can join us for a few weeks.'

'Come with the others, you mean?' he asked, glowing with pleasure at the thought.

Minerva's had already engaged several members of Mr Foreman's company for the summer season while Apsley's was torn apart in Arnold's latest bid for modernisation.

'That's right. Only your father doesn't like the idea,' Mirella muttered.

'Why ever not?'

He stared, stupefied. The chance to bring Rosa and Amy to Minerva's and Levic not grabbing at it! Why, it wasn't as if the sisters weren't accomplished: their double equestrian act had topped the bill at Apsley's for the last few years and that must make them an asset on any programme. Surely his father knew that.

Rosa and Amy . . . oh, yes, it would be marvellous to have

them in the company, marvellous to meet them again when he hadn't seen them since . . . how long? Steffi thought back. That auction in the Edgware Road where his parents had bought their first tent – he had seen Amy there, of course. He remembered remonstrating with Levic when he had started bidding against Arnold for that horse Amy wanted. But not Rosa, she hadn't been there that day, more's the pity. He clearly remembered how disappointed he had been when Amy told him her sister had a cold.

So it must have been the Christmas before that when he last saw Rosa. Or just after Christmas . . . Now he remembered. He was fourteen, had just left school but not yet entered the bank, and was spending a couple of weeks at Apsley's with Mirella. Rosa had just perfected her bareback ballerina act and . . . oh, yes, she had looked so lovely on her black horse. But that wasn't all. He had talked to her a lot and they had become so friendly that he had dreamed about her for months after going back to Aldershot. In fact, although he didn't care to admit it, he had never really stopped dreaming and daydreaming about her, picturing her lovely bright face and sweet smile, and wanting to see her again.

He turned his attention back to Levic and Mirella, disturbed by the increasing rancour in their voices as they continued to discuss the matter.

'There's no need to adopt that tone,' Levic was ranting. 'I don't think I'm being unreasonable. Those girls – all right, young women – have been strictly brought up and I don't want the responsibility of looking after them.'

'Okay. I've already agreed with you. We won't have them here. I'll write and say they can't come,' Mirella declared with the sort of emphasis one would use when speaking to a dense child.

'But that's stupid!' Steffi declared, entering the fray. 'I mean, you're not talking about children. Rosa's my age and Amy's not much younger, and they're both professional performers so I'm sure they won't need chaperoning.'

He almost regretted his interference when he saw the look which crossed his father's face. Too late he remembered Dorina's death and thought he understood why Levic would not want to be reminded of such a tragedy. On the other hand, there were still the girls to consider and in similar circumstances Steffi felt sure that he himself would put aside personal feelings and do what he could to help them.

'Keep out of this, will you? You don't know what you're talking about,' Levic snarled, in a tone that put Steffi's back up.

'Yes, I do,' he blurted out. 'Rosa and Amy are my friends. And their grandfather has been very kind to me in the past, so I feel we owe him something.'

'I see. Well, that makes all the difference,' said Levic sarcastically. 'Then I must certainly do what he asks, even if it means taking his whole bloody company on to my payroll. So forget what I said, Mirella. Arnold's girls can come and be welcome. I won't discuss it any more.'

He turned and started to walk away.

'No, Levic, that's not good enough . . .' Mirella protested.

'No more talk. Just let them come, if they want,' he said, shooting the words over his shoulder as he stomped off.

If Steffi had thought that Arnold Foreman would allow his precious granddaughters to join a travelling circus without making sure they would be strictly chaperoned, he was mistaken. Half the attraction of Minerva's, Arnold explained when he came down to finalise arrangements, was that he knew Levic ran a tight ship and would soon get rid of any Lothario who tried to sow his wild oats within the company. So he was happy to accept Mirella's assurances that she would keep a motherly eye on the girls and treat them as part of the family during their stay.

Part of the family. Which meant he should look on them as sisters, Steffi thought, feeling rather intimidated as he glanced at the two sophisticated young women sitting side by side on the locker seat in his parents' wagon. Rosa, with her fair hair tucked up under a fashionable red hat and her expression serious as she listened to her grandfather, was still as pretty as he remembered. And once, when she caught Steffi staring, she lowered her head and flashed him a charming smile that reminded him afresh of her grey eyes with their dark, curly lashes and her lovely open face which looked as if it laughed a lot.

Sadly, Amy was less friendly and hardly spared him a glance, let alone a smile. Indeed, compared with her sister, she seemed to have turned into a solemn sort of person whom he might have passed in the street without knowing. Mind you, it wasn't easy to see what she really looked like because she had developed the unfortunate habit of keeping her face turned away all the time. A result of trying to hide her scar, he supposed, feeling pity for the thin twig of a girl with light reddish hair who must realise what a foil she provided for her brilliant sister. And then, recalling the little freckled-faced imp who had been such a merry companion when they were children, he resolved to make a special effort to be kind to Amy while she was here.

'Well, what do you think?'

'Beautiful,' Steffi said, going up to pat the dapple grey which Rosa had just ridden into the ring. 'What is he called?'

'Etty.'

'So that's why he looks so familiar! This is the horse Arnold bought for Amy at the auction,' Steffi exclaimed. 'I remember admiring his long tail.'

'That's right. He was bought for Amy originally, but Grandad persuaded her to hand him over to me when Black Chieftain was put down.'

'Why?'

She shrugged.

'Because he didn't like seeing me upset, I suppose. Besides, I had the biggest part in the act, so he thought I should have the best mount.'

'But didn't Amy mind?'

Again Rosa shrugged.

'Not really. She doesn't feel things strongly like I do.'

'How strange,' Steffi murmured, thinking how he would feel if he had to give up Barney – even though at times he hated the wretched animal.

'Yes, Grandad says Amy's like my father. Nothing ever seems to touch her. Whereas me, I'm more like Mama, always getting carried away by my feelings.'

Steffi stared at Rosa, trying to recall her parents. He could see an immediate resemblance to Dorina – a resemblance that everyone remarked on. Same fair hair and round face – although Rosa's was a lot prettier, of course.

'Do you remember your mother very clearly?' he asked carefully.

'Oh, yes. I shall never forget how I felt when she died.'

'It must have been a terrible shock,' he murmured, remembering how he had felt when Liddy died.

'Oh, yes, dreadful,' Rosa exclaimed. 'I can tell you, I cried night and day for weeks.'

'What about Amy?'

'Oh, I suppose she cried too, but not for long. When Father kept moaning that he couldn't bear to see us crying, she stopped. Just like that. See what I mean? Amy doesn't have nearly such strong feelings as me.'

She swung herself down from the horse and landed lightly next to Steffi, apparently more interested in carrying on their conversation than starting her practice. Which pleased him. For it was nice to have someone other than Hugo as a companion – someone his own age, for once. And, yes, he had to admit it, someone from the fairer sex. For he liked girls, even though they were so difficult to talk to. At least, that had always been his experience until he met Rosa and found her so different from the rest. Different in fact from anyone he had ever known.

'And what happened to your father? He's a juggler, isn't he?'

'*Was* a juggler,' Rosa corrected.

'Oh dear, I'm sorry. You mean to say . . .' Steffi looked at her, horror-struck '. . . he died too?'

Rosa tossed back her mane of fair hair and pealed with laughter.

'Goodness, no. Not him. Matty's still alive and kicking.'

'But you said . . .'

'I just meant he'd given up juggling and doesn't have anything to do with the circus now. Didn't you know? He married again about a year after Mother died. Married a woman whose father kept a pub, more's the pity.'

'So do you still see him?

'Not really. Amy's been down a couple of times to stay with them in Suffolk where they live now. But, well, to be honest, there's been problems that I didn't want to get involved with.'

Steffi would have asked more had it not been obvious from her tone that Rosa disliked talking about her father. Before he could change the subject, however, he was startled by a shout from Amy.

'Rosa, what's wrong? Why haven't you started yet?'

He found himself flinching – and not for the first time – at the sharpness in her voice. For, although he had quickly felt at ease with Rosa, despite several attempts to be friendly he had still not managed to break the ice with Amy. In fact, she had treated him with such disdain ever since arriving here a couple of days ago that he felt most uncomfortable in her presence. At first hurt by her attitude, he had racked his brains for something he might have done in the past to upset her. But once he noticed she treated everyone with the same coldness, he felt a little better, if no less on edge.

'I haven't started because I'm talking to Steffi,' Rosa explained easily.

'I can see that,' Amy snapped. 'But how long do you intend to stand there talking to him?' Striking her whip impatiently against her riding-boot, she addressed the question to her sister, pointedly ignoring Steffi.

'It's all right, I'm just going,' he mumbled.

And, not wishing to cause trouble between them, took himself off – only to find himself at a loose end, because he had actually arrived in the first place to carry out his own practice. Still, he decided, if he had to wait around for the ring to be free, he might as well make himself comfortable in the bandwagon and watch the two girls rehearse.

Having been delighted to find Rosa so affable and light-hearted, now he was surprised to see how quickly she got down to work. How professional she looked when riding round the ring. How she kept her back perfectly straight and moved with such natural grace. He didn't need anyone to tell him what a fine artiste she was.

But what about Amy? he wondered, turning to look at the younger girl as she stood poised in the centre of the ring holding out her whip and shouting instructions to Rosa about keeping the pace even. If anything, she seemed to take the business even more seriously than her sister, but that didn't mean she was such a good horsewoman, of course. It was hard to imagine how anyone could match Rosa.

Which must make life difficult, he mused, before concluding that Amy would scarcely be human if she did not resent having such a talented sister.

He turned his attention back to Rosa who, now that Etty had established a good rhythmic gait, was letting go his reins and clambering first to a kneeling position and then standing upright on his broad back. Even in her rather unattractive short practice tunic, she looked wonderful – like some primitive figurehead on the prow of a ship, her hair streaming backwards as she began to dance.

After this Amy handed her a bamboo hoop decorated with paper flowers – which first she held above her head, and then lowered to a height where she could leap through it. Then she pulled it up over her body and leapt through it again – all the while balancing on the back of a galloping horse.

Steffi was enchanted.

Then it was Amy's turn. But while she went out to fetch her own horse, Rosa stood with her hair almost touching the sawdust as she bent forward filling her lungs and trying to get her breathing back to normal.

Steffi was surprised when Amy led in a smaller horse, brown with a black mane and tail, and urged him into a steady canter before making any effort to mount. In fact, he could not understand what she was up to until he heard a strange half-strangled cry followed by something whirling across the ring. Then he realised. This was Amy and she was leaping on to the back of her horse Cossack-style.

From that moment he was mesmerised.

Not that she showed much grace or finesse. But maybe he wouldn't have noticed if she had. She moved too fast.

Jumping up and down from the horse's back in a way that Steffi had seen only grown men do before, without stirrups or saddle to help her, just a surcingle with a handgrip on either side of the withers and a loop low on the offside.

One moment circling the ring wailing like a banshee, the next flinging herself down, turning a series of cartwheels and somersaults in the sawdust before seizing the handgrips and leaping back to gallop round like a whirlwind again.

One moment facing the horse's head. The next his tail. And back again. Now riding balanced on one knee, with the other leg held straight.

'Oh, bravo! Well done!'

Steffi found himself leaping up and spontaneously clapping his hands as she finished with a backward somersault that landed her on her feet in the centre of the ring ready to take the applause.

Nor was he alone in expressing such enthusiasm. Hugo and several other artistes and tentmen had been standing by the entrance enjoying the performance and most of them broke into cheers.

Not Levic, though.

Standing some way apart from the others, he was staring at the girls with what looked more like horror than appreciation.

'Done your practice, have you?' he barked, turning to glare at Steffi.

'No, I'll do it at lunchtime.'

'I see. And if someone else wants the ring for special rehearsal, they can go hang, I suppose?'

'Of course not. I'm sorry. I know I should have kept to my slot but I got delayed this morning. It won't happen again,' Steffi muttered, knowing he was at fault but wishing his father would have more tact than to dress him down in public.

Levic still glared, his face appearing more pallid than usual in the grey light filtering through the canvas.

'And what are you doing at the moment?' he demanded, letting his gaze drift towards Rosa.

'He's just giving me a hand with Etty,' she smiled.

'We've got grooms to do that,' Levic snapped.

But as she continued to smile blithely at him, his expression softened.

'Still, I'm glad to hear he's making himself useful. And, while I'm here, let me just say what a wonderful display you both gave. It so much reminded me . . . your part especially, Rosa . . . reminded me . . . of your mother. And I know she would have been proud . . .'

Then, in a way that seemed to Steffi completely out of character, Levic faltered, lost for words.

'There you are. I thought so,' Rosa announced once he had gone. 'Your father's quite soft under that grim exterior.'

Steffi snorted.

'Hmph! Well, that's the first time I've seen it. Anyway, I'd better be off. Don't want him to catch me slacking twice in one day.'

'No, wait a minute. There's something I wanted to ask you,' Rosa said, putting out her hand to catch his sleeve.

'What?'

'You know the way your father acts as clown to the rope when your mother's performing?'

'Yes.'

'Well, I wondered if you'd like to do a similar routine in the middle of our performance to give it a bit more interest?'

'I can assure you it doesn't need that,' Steffi offered gallantly.

'But we have someone doing it at Apsley's. Do you know the clown Chico? No? Well, he's worked out a routine that is ever so simple but the audience loves it. Would you consider playing his part while we're here?'

'What does he do exactly?' Steffi asked. And the way Rosa proceeded to explain the thing made it sound fun.

'So, you'll do it for me, then?' she said finally.

'Yes, I don't mind giving it a try, but I'll have to tell my father first just in case he has objections. Although,' he added, 'I can't think that he would, because he's always encouraging me to try out something new.'

'Oh, good! I was hoping you'd do it,' Rosa exclaimed. 'Amy, did you hear? Steffi's going to come into the ring as Levity and go through that funny courtship routine that Chico worked out with me. What do you think?'

Amy gave her a look which made it obvious what she thought.

Chapter 29

'Where's he gone?' Rosa asked, looking around for Levic once she and Steffi finished running through their comic routine for the first time.

'Search me,' he said, equally put out.

He had seen his father sitting in the stalls when they started.

'I thought he promised to help.'

'He did.'

'So why has he beetled off?' Rosa complained.

'I don't know. Perhaps remembered something he had to do.'

'Something more important than helping us?'

'I'm sure it must have been urgent,' Steffi said, fed up with making excuses for Levic when it was clear he just did not want to get involved.

'Okay. So let's run through it once more on our own and then call Hugo over and ask what he thinks.'

'Yes, we could do that,' he agreed half-heartedly. It was so nice working with Rosa on his own that he was reluctant to share her company with someone like Hugo, good friend though he was. On the other hand, this was work not play, he reminded himself, and they needed a second opinion.

Then, glancing around, he saw they were not in fact on their own. There was someone perched in the shadows of the middle row of seats.

'Amy?' he called.

'Yes.'

'Have you been here long enough to see what we did?'

'Yes.'

'Good,' he smiled. 'How did it look?'

'Pretty rubbishy,' she replied.

'Oh, she would say that. Take no notice, Steffi,' Rosa muttered under her breath.

'Wait a minute,' he shushed, gesturing Amy to come down

closer. Then, turning to the younger sister, 'Can you be more specific, Amy? What do you think was no good?'

She darted a quick glance at his face and then, looking at her feet, said, 'I suppose it wasn't that bad really, but it could be a whole lot better.'

'How?'

'If you got the mood right.'

Rosa clicked her tongue impatiently. 'What do you mean, Amy? It's only a simple scene. Why bring mood into it?'

'Because Steffi asked me a question and I was trying to give him a sensible answer.'

Rosa raised her eyebrows at Steffi. 'Shall we forget her and just get on with it?'

'No. I want to hear. Go on, Amy.'

She paused for a moment while the effort of gathering her thoughts puckered the white line over her left eye into rather a quizzical look.

'Well, for a start,' she said, 'you come in all wrong. I mean, you shouldn't run in waving your arms about as if you're trying to flag down a horse-bus.'

Steffi grinned, recognising the truth in what she said.

'But he's only doing what Chico does,' Rosa objected.

'I know. But Chico always looks as if he's trying to catch a bus as well.'

'All right, Miss Expert. You come and show us how it should be done then,' Rosa glared.

'No.'

'Come on. If you're such a bloody expert, you do it.'

'I don't see why I should now I've given you the benefit of my advice.'

'No. I think you're right, Amy,' Steffi said quickly. 'So tell me again, how do you think I should come in?'

He was immediately glad he'd asked, for Amy raised her head and flashed him the first smile he had seen on her lips since she arrived at Minerva's.

'Well,' she began, 'when you first come in, you shouldn't appear so desperate.'

'No?'

'No. To start with, you're simply in love.'

'I know that.'

'Right, so you behave like someone who's fallen in love with something, say like the moon – and at first you're basking in its

272

light, blissfully unaware of the vast distance that separates you from your love.'

'Yes,' he murmured, feeling a delicious warmth suffusing his body as he put himself into such a scene.

'Okay,' she continued in a matter-of-fact sort of voice, 'so what you do is look at Rosa and try to imagine she's the most beautiful thing you've ever seen in your life. Go on, then, *try*!'

For a moment he wondered if Amy was mocking him for making his feelings so obvious.

'Well, are you going to try or not?' she challenged again.

'Yes, I'll have another go if Rosa's willing.'

'Rosa?'

She nodded and Steffi took up his entry position again and on the given signal ran in.

'Wait, wait!' Amy called. 'Hold it there a moment.'

He paused, staring at Rosa, visualising her in her white ballerina dress with its low-cut neckline revealing the softest swelling shape of her bosom. The moon? Oh, yes, and all the stars in the firmament too.

'That's better!' shouted Amy. 'Now, go up to her, Steffi, but keep your gaze fixed on her face. That's right, her face! And you've never seen anything so beautiful in the world, remember!'

Oh, yes. It was easy to go along with that, especially with Rosa fluttering her long eyelashes and dimpling into a smile as she was doing now.

'No, no, no!' rapped Amy's voice.

He jumped.

'Why, what am I doing wrong?'

'You? Nothing. It's Rosa. You shouldn't smile like that, as if thrilled to bits at making another conquest! You're the moon, remember. Beautiful, but cold and distant. You can't be that if you're simpering like a cat all the time.'

Rosa turned towards her sister and scowled.

'So, tell me: how's one supposed to look when accepting adoration?'

'Don't ask me. You're the one to know.'

'What do you mean?' Rosa asked, smiling.

'That you're the one who's had all the practice,' Amy said sweetly. Then, changing her tone: 'Now, if you really want my help, can we move on?'

After that she put them through their paces in a surprisingly

273

efficient way, making perceptive comments on gestures and useful suggestions about how to improve the sketch.

'That's right, no need to pull such a face. Just cock the eyebrow a little. Yes, that says it all, Steffi. And have you thought about giving a little skip just when you're leaving the ring?'

'No,' he replied. 'I wouldn't do that, because that's when I'm supposed to be totally despondent after she's rejected me.'

'You mean you'd completely give up and never, ever try again?' Amy said in a tone which made him realise how facile his judgement had been.

'No, of course I wouldn't.'

'Well, then . . .'

And her next suggestion – that he carry in a bouquet of flowers on his last entrance – made a lot of sense too. Moreover, it was something neither he nor Rosa would have thought to add because it needed an outsider to see the effect, particularly at the end when Rosa took the flowers from him and, once he had disappeared, tossed them carelessly into the audience to win more hearts wherever the blossoms fell.

'Well, what do you think, Steffi?' Hugo said, nudging him in the side as they emerged from the big tent one hot afternoon at Leominster.

'Of what?' he asked, wondering how he could get away. He had caught sight of Rosa stretched out on the grass, sunning herself, and wanted to go and talk to her.

'Of that. What else?' Hugo jerked his head and made a repulsive kissing noise with his lips.

'If you're referring to Rosa, I think you might show a bit more respect.'

'Ho, ho! Like that, is it?' Hugo smirked. 'Another one smitten.'

'I said I think you ought to show more respect,' Steffi repeated, feeling his gut begin to curdle with anger.

It was all very well for circus men to make lewd comments on ordinary girls as they passed them along the road. Steffi had grown used to that and on occasion, in male company, did the same thing himself. But for Hugo – who must be all of thirty, if not beyond – to leer at Rosa in that way was simply disgusting and not to be tolerated.

Still, there was no point in making a fuss about it now.

274

And fortunately Rosa herself had been spared the indignity of witnessing his gesture.

'Well, what do you know? It seems one of us is being summoned. Or does she require the services of . . .' Presumably aware that he was about to overstep the mark, Hugo modified his language. 'I mean, does she want to speak to both of us.'

Steffi looked over to where Rosa was leaning back on one elbow and waving at them.

'I think it's me she wants,' he declared, deciding he must protect her from Hugo's unwelcome attentions. Besides, he could think of no reason why Rosa would want to speak to the ringmaster.

'Hi, Steffi, coming to join me?' she smiled as he approached. 'It's lovely lying here with the sun on your face. And, look, I've rolled up my sleeves as well.'

He had already noticed.

'You're sure you won't get burnt?' he asked solicitously, sinking down beside her.

'No, I've already decided that if I start feeling too hot, I shall go and sit in the shade under one of the wagons. Do you think that's a good idea?'

He nodded.

The thought of Rosa under one of the wagons seemed like an excellent idea, especially if she was sitting there with him. And perhaps they should go there straight away, because there were already tiny beads of sweat glistening on her forehead and where she had unbuttoned her blouse a pinkish arrow pointed the way to her breasts.

He gulped. For heaven's sake! He must get a grip on himself, before he became as bad as Hugo.

'Steffi, did you hear anyone talking about going down to the river for a swim?' Rosa was asking.

'Yes, as a matter of fact Hugo said there's a group of them going before tea. Why, thinking of joining them?'

'Are you going?'

'I'm not sure.'

He wanted to, of course. But, with Levic ill again, there were complications. It would not be so bad if he could be persuaded simply to take to his bed and leave Mirella and Steffi to it, because between them they could manage quite well. But no, he insisted on hobbling around trying to keep tabs on everything, and in the event losing his temper with any member of the company who crossed his path. So, for the sake of harmony, Steffi had taken it upon himself to remain extra vigilant, and the only reason he could sit down now for five minutes was that it was siesta time and most of the people on the tober, including Levic, were resting in their wagons.

Not surprisingly – for yesterday had been gruelling! Having travelled here from Hereford in nigh tropical temperatures, they had then pulled into this meadow, built up, done a street parade, and on top of that a couple of shows in the evening. Then again, tomorrow would be almost as bad. Up for a dawn start with a long journey ahead of them, thirty-odd miles to Ludlow. So today was a comparative haven of rest – with only a couple of shows to do before the pull-down.

'Oh, do come, Steffi! It should be fun.'

'Why, you won't be going into the water, will you?' he asked, trying to imagine Rosa with a wet serge bathing dress drooping over her bosom and thighs.

'I might,' she said, lowering her eyelashes. 'It depends what the others do.'

'What others? You're surely not thinking of going into the water with . . . well, all the men looking on?'

'Oh, Steffi,' she giggled, 'there's no need to look so shocked! There's nothing indecent about men and women bathing together. People do it all the time at the seaside.'

'But there are no bathing machines on the river bank,' he protested.

When Rosa giggled again, he joined in and laughed too. After all, it was pretty stupid to be so concerned about propriety when he himself was already planning to tempt her away from the others and lead her off to a quiet place where they could swim on their own. But then, that would be different because she knew she could trust him to behave with complete decorum.

'Phew!' she sighed, puffing out her cheeks. 'Have you ever known it so hot? But just look at your mother. I don't know where she gets her energy from.'

Across the field Mirella had emerged from her wagon with a bowl of washing which she was in the process of pegging up to dry.

'She's always the same,' Steffi smiled. 'Never happy unless she's busy.'

'I suppose that's what keeps her so thin.'

Looking at his mother's wasp waist, Steffi saw what Rosa meant. His mother was thin, probably too thin. And he was convinced that she did much more than was good for her in the day-to-day running of the business – keeping an eye on the accounts, working out the artistes' contracts, planning the tour, liaising with the advance agent who went ahead to book tobers and organise publicity. All of which used to be Levic's responsibility in the days before he pleaded aches and pains or plain tiredness as frequent excuses to retire to the wagon and neglect his duties.

'How old is she?'

Rosa's question jerked him from his reverie.

'Who?'

'Your mother of course,' she said, screwing up her eyes against the dazzling light to peer at him.

'Thirty-eight,' he replied, doing some quick arithmetic in his head. 'Why?'

'I just wondered. She looks so much younger than your father,' Rosa murmured.

'Well, she is. About ten years younger,' he calculated.

'Do you think it's better for a woman to marry someone older than herself?' she asked dreamily.

'Probably,' Steffi said. Then pulled up short when he remembered that he himself was actually younger than Rosa by a couple of months. 'Although it works equally well the other way,' he added.

'That's what I think,' she enthused. 'In fact, I'm sure it doesn't matter what age people are when they get married so long as they're both truly in love with each other.'

And Steffi loved the way she drew out the word 'tru-ly' while gazing at him with wide, candid eyes that reflected the clear sky.

He felt a trickle of perspiration slide down his spine.

'Look, when we go for a swim, I suggest we leave the others and walk upstream for a bit and perhaps find a place on our own where we can . . . Damn, what does she want?'

'It's only your mother. Finish what you were saying,' Rosa urged.

'Steffi! Can you come here a minute!'

'No, I'd better see what she wants,' he muttered, rising from the grass. He could see Mirella standing talking to Amy who was gesticulating towards the stable-tent. 'Coming?'

Rosa shook her head.

'Okay, but don't go away. I'll be straight back.'

She was obviously put out and he could not blame her. He was as annoyed as Rosa at being interrupted, but there was no way he could refuse his mother when she needed help.

'Do you think we should ask Pa first?' Steffi said, knowing that Levic was bound to dispute any decision made in his absence.

'No. He's asleep and I'd rather not trouble him,' Mirella declared, throwing Steffi a meaningful glance. 'You know what he's like at the moment.'

He did.

'Right then.' Steffi shut his eyes and thought before making a decision. Jeff usually acted as Minerva's horse doctor and he seemed sure about what had to be done. It was just that he was reluctant to take responsibility for treating such a valuable horse in case things went wrong and Levic then blamed him for losing the beast.

'I'll do it,' Jeff repeated, 'so long as you or the missus stands by as I makes the cut. Just so's Mr Levic can't say I acted off my own bat.'

'Of course. No, I'll do this, Ma. You and Amy keep out of the way till it's over.'

'No, I want to stay and help,' Amy murmured.

And there was no arguing with her, especially as it was she who had spotted the swelling on the side of the horse's head and, correctly diagnosing strangles, had alerted Jeff and Mirella to the problem.

'Well then, you find a clean bit of sacking and tear 'un off into strips, miss, while I fetches a bucket of linseed mixture so's we can make a start.'

It was stiflingly hot in the horse-tent even though the grooms had laced back the flaps at both ends to increase air circulation. But fortunately most of the stalls were empty because their occupants had been led down to the river to wade and cool themselves off. Which is what Steffi would have liked to be doing. Except that at the moment he had no choice.

'Be back in a minute,' he promised, rushing off to warn Rosa that he would be delayed.

He hated having to disappoint like this, of course. But being an equestrienne, at least she would understand where his duty lay. In fact, knowing Rosa, once she heard that one of Levic's ring-horses was sick, she would insist on coming over to give a hand as well. And he would not try too hard to dissuade her.

It was a shock not to find her sitting in the sun where he had left her. After all, he hadn't been gone that long and she had promised to wait. But perhaps she, like him, had been suddenly called away. Or maybe the sun had proved too hot and she had moved into the shade.

He glanced towards the nearest wagon. And immediately caught sight of someone, sitting on the other side, with their back against the wheel. But not alone.

Rosa. Yes, he was sure one of them was Rosa. He recognised her pink dress.

'Rosa?' he called, as he strode towards the wagon. 'I'm sorry I was so long but . . .'

He stopped when he saw who was with her.

'Don't worry. She hasn't been lonely,' Hugo drawled, blowing out a puff of blue cigar-smoke. 'Anyway, what was the fuss about?'

Steffi choked with fury as he stared at him. How dare Hugo lie there like that – without his shirt on and sprawled so close as to be virtually rubbing shoulders with Rosa? Did he not realise that it was all very well to strip to the waist when one was working, but quite a different thing to appear that way in front of Rosa?

And it made matters worse when, as if guessing his thoughts, Hugo grinned and sat up, nonchalantly flicking grass off the sunbleached hairs on his chest. Every move he made apparently designed as an insult to Rosa.

'One of the horses has got strangles,' Steffi announced stiffly.

'Not Etty?' Rosa exclaimed, starting to scramble up.

'No, not Etty,' he reassured her. 'Etty's fine. It's Derry, one of the liberties.'

'Thank God. Oh, you did worry me, Steffi!' Rosa moaned.

'Is it bad?' Hugo asked with what seemed like genuine concern. 'I mean, do you want me to come over?'

'No. Jeff's going to try lancing it and I've already agreed to help. But if you want to come . . .' he said, turning to Rosa.

'Me? Oh, no. I couldn't bear it, Steffi. I can't bear to be near anything in pain.'

Seeing her eyes begin to cloud over like the sky spoiling for rain, Steffi could well believe it.

'All right, but it's bound to keep me busy for the next half hour, so if you want to do something else while you're waiting . . .'

'Don't worry about it,' she smiled. 'I'm going down to the river with Hugo and the others so I'll wait for you there.'

Steffi wanted to warn her. She was so innocent, she had no idea how unwise it was to become so familiar with someone like Hugo. Why, he wouldn't put it past the devil to take even greater liberties once they were down on the river bank and he had changed into his bathing drawers. And he hated the thought of Rosa being exposed to any embarrassment without himself there to protect her. Or someone like . . . ah, wait a moment! If Amy could be persuaded to accompany Rosa, that would be different. She could act as chaperone and shield her sister from unwanted attention.

Having decided this, Steffi turned to make his way back to the horse-tent, still so angry with Hugo that he found it difficult to concentrate on the job in hand. Nor was Amy ready to comply with his request.

'But I don't want to go swimming,' she protested.

'You don't have to swim. Just go down to the river with Rosa for the walk.'

'But I've promised to help Jeff.'

'I'll do that. It's more a man's job anyway,' Steffi said, taking the strips of sacking from her hands and dipping them in the linseed oil before handing them one at a time to Jeff, who was too busy muttering reassurance to the horse to interfere.

Amy glared at him, her cheeks flushed pink and her pointed chin quivering with indignation.

'That's nonsense.'

'It's not nonsense,' he snapped.'It's a lovely, sunny day outside and all I'm asking you to do is go down to the river with Rosa, just to keep her company until I can get there. Now, I can't ask you clearer than that, can I?'

'But . . .' she started to protest again.

'Please, Amy, as a special favour to me,' he pleaded.

Fortunately, that did the trick. Which was just as well because it was impossible to explain the reason for his request.

'All right,' she said, frowning until her scar creased into a livid crescent over her hazel eyes. 'I'll go if that's how you want to make use of me.'

'Thanks, Amy. You know I'm only asking you because . . .'

But she flounced off before he could finish.

Chapter 30

Instead of going down, the swelling on the horse's head was growing bigger and bigger, bulging like some dreadful naked belly. Steffi was glad neither of the girls was here to see it, although he could not stop himself straying after them in his thoughts, wondering what they were getting up to on the river bank.

'All right, my beauty. Steady. Right, Steffi. Hold him carefully now,' Jeff urged, dipping his knife into a pan of boiling water before using it to slit the lump right across the middle.

'Ugh!' Steffi's stomach writhed as he watched the old man's bony fingers pressing out all the pus and then bathing the wound.

When at last Jeff announced, 'Ah! That's looking better,' Steffi was relieved to see how much the angry flesh had subsided.

'Well done. You deserve a medal.'

'No, that ain't necessary,' Jeff said before dropping his voice and giving a watery wink. 'But 'alf a bottle might come in 'andy.'

'You shall have it,' Steffi promised, squeezing his arm.

Having gleaned from one of the tentmen that Rosa and Amy were still down by the river, Steffi set off to join them, rushing so that he might have time to take a dip himself.

Despite the current spell of dry weather the ground was so soft that it became almost marsh as he approached the bank and it would have been easy to follow the trail of churned mud and hoof prints marking the animals' passage even if he had failed to pick up the noise of their whooping and yelping attendants up ahead. And soon he saw two more riders ambling towards him, each with a string of horses in tow.

'Off for a swim, Steffi?' yelled one.

He pretended to be startled by the sound of the man's voice. 'Good Lord, it's you, Murph! I didn't recognise you looking so clean.'

'Yes, well, wait till you see the water and you'll tell where I've been,' he grinned.

'Thanks a lot!' Steffi growled, getting his first taste of the river as the passing horses flicked water over him from their damp coats.

More greetings and banter followed as the next party, larger and including some women artistes, rode by. Then another smaller group. But no Rosa, so she must still be there waiting for him, thank goodness. He broke into a trot.

Murph was right. The first part of the river bank he came to was as messy as a cattle-pen. Which was obviously why people had chosen to sit upstream, near the willows. Not that there were many left now. Only three or four, because most people had gone back to snatch a bite to eat before the show.

'Rosa!' He called as soon as he spotted her, so relieved to find her still there that he overlooked the fact that she was sitting with Hugo, sprawled on the bank where it fell gently away towards the water's edge.

'Rosa!' he shouted again.

'Oh, hello, Steffi!' She turned her head to greet him.

'You've been in the water,' he said, staring at her blue bathing dress which had droplets of water still clinging to the fringe around its collar and sleeves.

'Yes, it's a pity you didn't come earlier, then you could have joined us,' she said in a tone that struck home as a reprimand.

'Oh, but I couldn't leave . . .'

'It's all right. I know where you were. It's just a shame you missed everything. It was such fun, wasn't it?' she murmured, turning to share a smile with Hugo.

Steffi knew he had no reason to feel angry. Rosa had a perfect right to go into the water without him. And to sit close to anyone she chose. In fact, he knew he was feeling nothing but pure jealousy. But he still found it hard to stop himself kicking Hugo for sidling up to his girl.

His girl? Yes. He suddenly realised that was how he thought of Rosa. She was his girl. And it made him sick to see her with someone else, even if they were only talking innocently together on a river bank.

He looked at Rosa. She could not have gone far into the water because her hair was not wet even though it had worked loose. Falling like sunshine over her shoulders, curling round her face so that she would have looked like an angel – if an angel could have such dimpled cheeks and a mouth made for kissing.

Oh, Rosa! How could she torment him like this? Surely she must know he loved her.

Except that, looking at her as she smiled down into the grey-green water flowing by, he realised that he was doing her an injustice. She could not possibly know, because he had never said a word to her about how he felt. In truth, had hardly known himself before this moment.

A surge of excitement charged through him. He knew now though. Knew he loved her. Worshipped her. Felt desperate to kiss her and make her his own.

If she would have him. But, oh God, what if she didn't feel the same way? What if, when he tried to say something, she found his words so ridiculous that she laughed in his face?

'Decided not to take the plunge then?' Hugo smirked, as if reading his thoughts. 'Probably wise. The water's a bit chilly.'

'Aren't you going in?' Rosa added.

'Not at the moment.'

'Why not? We've all been in, haven't we, Hugo?'

'Amy as well?' he asked, catching sight of her sitting hunch-shouldered on her own under the willows.

'Yes, even Amy,' Rosa giggled. 'But you know what she's like. So modest she has to walk ten miles upstream before finding enough privacy to take a dip.'

On hearing her name, the younger girl looked up and gestured towards him.

'Steffi,' she muttered when he drew near, 'how did you get on with the horse?'

'Derry? Oh, he's fine. Jeff did a marvellous job. Got out all the poison and reckons he'll be as good as new in a couple of days. Thanks to you,' he added.

'Oh, thank goodness. I thought it must be bad news.'

'Why?'

'You looked so fed-up when you were standing over there.'

'Did I?' Steffi could have kicked himself. He had not meant to let his feelings show.

'I don't blame you, mind. She makes me sick when she goes on like that.'

'Who?'

'Her, of course.' Amy jerked her head.

'But what's she doing?' he asked, following the line of Amy's gaze to where Rosa was holding up her hands and challenging Hugo to haul her to her feet.

'Flirting,' Amy muttered.

Steffi winced.

'No, no,' he protested. 'That's not flirting, Amy. That's, well . . .' But he was lost for words as he watched the clumsy tug-of-war going on between the couple, with Rosa playfully resisting all Hugo's efforts to pull her up, and then Hugo pretending to collapse in a heap once he had succeeded. 'See? They're only messing around,' he said eventually.

'Humph!'

'Oh, come on, Amy – cheer up!'

'Why do you say that?'

'Because now it's you who's looking down in the dumps.'

She sighed by way of reply, a sigh with all the cares of the world wrapped up in it. But that was the trouble with Amy – she was a creature of such changeable moods that it did not pay to probe too closely into their cause.

'Are you two ready?' Hugo called. 'If not, you'll have to excuse my rushing off. I've got things to do before the show.'

Steffi was glad to hear it, especially when, having murmured words which brought a smile to Rosa's lips, Hugo waved his arm and strode off, leaving him to walk back with the girls at a more leisurely pace.

That evening Steffi found Rosa's appearance more enchanting than ever. She was so full of life and gaiety. Looked so pretty perched on her grey horse. And her eyes, when she smiled at him, seemed to know and accept what was in his heart and to promise that, when he plucked up enough courage to speak, she would at least listen.

'Oh, Steffi, that went really well, didn't it?' she gasped, dismounting at the end of the ballerina act and standing bright-eyed and bosom heaving as she tried to regain her breath.

'Yes, wonderful,' he murmured. 'And, Rosa, you looked so beautiful that . . .'

'Yes?'

But he could not bring himself to say it. Not here in the horse-tent with other people milling about. Nor could he do what he wanted to do – kiss her and hold her tight, pressing her

284

body against his. Not here. Not now. That wouldn't be right. But he must find a way soon. Must tell her exactly how he felt even if words spelt the end of all hope.

After a night in which he had twisted in his bunk, alternately bathed in bliss imagining how it would feel to have Rosa in his arms and agony as he pictured her with someone else, Steffi rose early. Silently he slid back the bed shutters and fumbled in the gloom for his trousers and boots. It was easier to dress outside when there was no one about.

He loved being up at this time. Emerging into a meadow where wagons and tents were still sealed against night, their occupants sleeping and unaware of the mysterious world around them. For on a morning like this Steffi found the landscape magically inverted. Trees and hedgerows which the day before had confidently held their ground while above them clouds raced by, were now themselves adrift in a sea of mist.

Having quietly done the rounds checking on animals, ropes and canvas, he retired to sit on a tree trunk, the day's first mug of tea in his hand. Any moment now and the tober would wake up.

As usual he found his attention being drawn to the little yellow wagon parked next to Levic's and Mirella's where Rosa slept. Was she stirring yet? he wondered – in his mind's eye seeing her lovely face light up and her naked limbs start to stretch. And if awake, what was she thinking about? Him? Could she possibly be thinking about him with the same sort of desire he felt for her? Unlikely. But not impossible. After all, they had known each other so long, he and Rosa. And their relationship was special. Surely she realised that? If not, then he must find a way to convince her.

Rosa. Oh, Rosa, I do love you, he was thinking – when the door of the yellow wagon opened and a girl emerged. For one heart-stopping moment she stood on the top step, her back turned, while carefully closing the two halves of the door behind her. But then, once she had leapt down to earth and twisted round to survey the horizon, Steffi saw that it was only Amy.

He waved and, after a show of hesitation, she came towards him.

'Nice to see another early bird.'

'Yes,' she murmured.

'Cup of tea? I've only just made it.'

'Hmm. Sounds nice.' She lifted her head to smile, but then looked quickly away. 'I didn't think anyone else would be up yet.'

'It's too good a morning to stay in bed.'

'Yes. Have you noticed the mist? And how the horses look as if they're cropping at clouds?' she said, handing him her cup to be filled. 'Thanks. That's fine.'

'Is Rosa up?'

'No, not yet.'

'Oh.'

'So that's why you keep looking at the wagon?'

'Do I?' he said, with difficulty bringing his attention back to Amy.

'Of course you do. But she won't be out yet. She was still well away when I got up. Besides, she wouldn't dream of making an appearance before getting properly dressed and doing her hair,' Amy said, defiantly tossing back her own tawny curls.

Her words inevitably triggered Steffi's imagination so that he fell to picturing Rosa in a delectable state of undress with her hair as he had seen it yesterday, flowing down over her shoulders like a shower of golden rain.

'You're really sweet on her, aren't you?' Amy whispered.

'Who?'

'Oh, Steffi, don't pretend. It's so obvious from the way you look at her, but . . . oh dear! I know I shouldn't interfere but . . . I just don't want to see you get hurt.'

'You mean she doesn't like me,' he said slowly.

'Oh, no. I didn't say that. And please don't look so miserable, Steffi. All I meant was . . . Well, you're not the first to fall for Rosa's charms. In fact, there were several at Apsley's and, to be honest . . .'

'No, don't say any more. I don't want to hear,' he muttered angrily.

Amy should know better than to talk about her sister like this. After all, Rosa couldn't help being so attractive, and it was easy for others to criticise her out of envy.

In the silence which followed, his gaze inevitably wandered towards the little yellow wagon again.

'All right, so what are you going to do about it?' Amy challenged.

'I don't know.'

'But you think you love her?'

'Oh, yes. I know I love her,' he declared solemnly. 'And it's not the way you think. Not at all like ... well, any of those others you mentioned. This is real. And I love her so much I think I'd die if there was no hope. Oh, I know that sounds stupid ...' He immediately regretted saying so much, especially to Amy who was peering sidelong at him with such a twisted smile on her lips that he could have hated her.

'So why don't you tell her?'

'How can I?'

'Easy. Just take her aside and say it.'

'What, and then hear her laugh?'

'Why do you say that? Would you laugh if someone said they loved you?' she demanded.

'Yes,' he smiled. 'I'd split my sides.'

'Oh, dear,' she murmured, giving him another sideways glance. 'But seriously, Steffi, if you really think so little of yourself, you're just laying yourself open to hurt.'

He had to strain to catch her words. She spoke so quietly she might have been speaking to herself.

'Okay, so what would you suggest? I can't really take Rosa aside and say it just like that, can I? I mean, not without some leading up to it.'

'Well, then, why not do what Rosa does? Rouse interest by paying attention to someone else. It hardly ever fails.'

The image of Hugo suddenly loomed large. But, detecting the voice of envy speaking, Steffi soon dismissed the spectre.

'Yes. I could do that. Except that there *is* no one else,' he grumbled. 'No one who would look convincing.'

'No. Of course there isn't,' Amy muttered, before sinking into the sort of silence that made him feel uncomfortable.

'Well, this won't get the work done,' he breezed, reaching down for his empty mug.

'No, I s'pose not.' She sounded utterly dejected.

'Come on, Amy. Sun's coming out.'

'Is it?' she said, turning away.

The road leading into Ludlow was always a killer. Steffi, driving the rear wagon, was growing impatient with the number of times he had to pause and wait for those in front to negotiate the hills. Then, during one of these stops, his heart rejoiced to see Rosa making her way back down the line distributing the fruit which Mirella had brought for the journey.

Because of the steep gradient, each wagon had an extra horse harnessed to it. Now the shout came back for everyone to have chocks at the ready to prevent backsliding. Passing the reins to Dai, Steffi jumped down just in time to see the wagon in front beginning to slip back towards an unsuspecting Rosa.

He yelled and leapt towards her, scooping her up and throwing her on to the bank as the wheels rolled past brushing his bootcaps.

'Steffi!' she screamed.

'It's all right. I'm not hurt,' he reassured her, having flattened himself against the bank in a way that would have been impossible for Rosa with her wide skirts. 'No, stay there!' he shouted, signalling for Dai to pass them along the narrow road before he helped her down.

'Oh, my God, Steffi! We could both have been killed,' Rosa stammered.

'But we weren't, and there's no harm done,' he soothed, clutching her round the waist and swinging her down.

'Oh, but when I think what could have happened if you hadn't saved me.' She was trembling, her face white and eyes wide and staring. Even though he threw his arms about her, he could not stop her from shaking. He clutched her tighter, murmuring reassurances and kissing her hair as he would to calm a frightened child. But still her body continued to shake so much that all he could do was press it even more tightly to his to absorb her terror.

Very slowly the shivering began to subside, her limbs to relax and the body under her clothes to yield its tension and melt into his. Until he was standing there still clutching her tight, suffused with warmth, and with no other wish in the world but to remain like this forever.

'Steffi.' As she raised her face to his, he just had time to glimpse the grey light in her eyes before feeling her breath on his and the warmth of her lips as they kissed.

'Rosa, I love you,' he whispered once they had pulled gently apart.

'Oh, Steffi,' she sighed, offering up her lips again.

And this time as they kissed he had never felt so happy in his life.

Chapter 31

Steffi was walking on air this morning. Sky blue above, and everything in the world conspiring in his joy. His heart so full of happiness that it was hard to remember that only yesterday, when he awoke, the world had been a different place, grey and ordinary. Not sparkling and bright as everything was now. And what had brought about this transformation? One kiss.

He shut his eyes so that he could dwell on the honeyed feel of Rosa's mouth. The sweet innocent way in which she had offered her lips to him and, far from pulling back as he feared, responded with all her heart. Freely let him taste his first nectar.

But he had experienced more than just a kiss yesterday. Much more. When their lips had met and he had held Rosa in his arms, pressing her close, he had felt himself harden and grow so excited that he felt shivery at the thought. And at the same time quite sick with wanting her.

And the wonderful, incredible thing was – knowing that Rosa felt the same.

Rosa . . . just to murmur her name was bliss. And to wake up this morning with her name on his lips and then to remember yesterday and know that it was not a dream – well, that was almost too much happiness to bear.

For it had happened. All of it. The kissing. The squeezing. The smiles. His whispered, 'I love you, Rosa.' And her answering, 'Oh, Steffi, do you? I'm so glad.'

And they had both been so engrossed in each other that they did not see Amy and Mirella rushing down the hill.

'Is she all right, Steffi?' his mother was shouting. 'Dai said there'd been an accident.'

Steffi instinctively stepped back and took his arms from Rosa's waist. But before he could answer, Amy, holding her skirts up so that she could run faster, had reached them.

'What happened?' she gasped, white-faced and panicky. 'Rosa, are you hurt?'

She shook her head, but her bright-eyed silence could easily have led her sister to suppose her suffering from shock.

'Are you sure?' Amy persisted. 'Dai said the wagon rolled back on you.'

'It did. But Steffi saved me,' Rosa said dreamily, giving him the most beautiful smile.

'How? What happened?'

By this time Mirella had arrived, and Steffi explained.

'So, thank God, there's no real harm done,' Mirella sighed. And then looked up in surprise when Steffi and Rosa laughed out loud at such comical understatement.

'The fruit doesn't look too healthy,' Amy frowned, picking up the basket and starting to fill it with the apples and plums that had been scattered across the road.

'Well, no one's going to worry about that, so long as Rosa's all right,' Mirella said smiling.

'No. I suppose not,' Amy had muttered, tossing a bruised apple as far into the distance as she could manage.

One thought on his mind all day – Rosa. One instinct, one desire. Passing through the stable-tent where she was rubbing down Etty and pausing to say hello and to smile. And returning five minutes later to smile and say hello to her again. Stumbling through his rehearsal making more mistakes than ever before. And Rosa finding it equally hard to concentrate, especially once he finished the courtship routine and parked himself in the front row to gaze at the rest of her practice. Sitting close to her on the grass to eat lunch – speculating with others about the size of tonight's audience or humour of the Ludlow crowd, but really keeping his attention all the time on Rosa. And she giving all her attention to him.

Steffi was in heaven. And since that was where the best clowns were made, he felt confident that his performance would reflect this fact tonight. In fact, as the overture struck up and the company assembled for the opening procession, he determined that tonight he would excel himself and bring the house down – just to prove that he could. For Rosa.

Besides, there was pressure on everyone to do their best tonight, since the company had been left short-handed when Hugo suddenly collapsed with the sort of sickness that stopped him going into the ring. Levic immediately announced that he himself would double up as ringmaster and although Steffi pleaded with him not to overtax himself in this way, of course Levic being Levic insisted that there was no one else he could trust to do the job properly.

So, with scarcely any consultation, Levic proceeded to drop some of his usual routines and rush to and fro changing from motley to top hat and evening clothes, slipping from one role to another, alternately clowning and directing the performance. It was a magnificent effort and Steffi, if he had been in a less euphoric mood himself, would have realised how much energy it must be costing. As it was, Levic kept up his performer's smile and Steffi had someone other than his father to think about and consequently missed the warning signs.

The tent was crowded with people laughing and cheering and throwing orange peel, the sort of responsive audience that Steffi loved. Levic as ringmaster made a point of being quite unrecognisable as Levic the clown, and therefore strutted in and out of the ring with exaggerated dignity and decorum. All at once Steffi saw the possibility for some comic business and, without a word to Levic, started to follow him around the ring, aping his general mien and every gesture until he had reduced his dignified role to an absurdity.

It worked. The crowd roared its approval. Levic of course quickly guessed what was happening from all the laughter and at another time would no doubt have played along with Levity's antics. But not tonight. Tonight his spirit simply could not stretch that far and he got angry – which added to the fun! Especially when he spun round furiously in an attempt to catch Levity at it and just in that moment, by some peculiar instinct, Levity whirled round too and stood, with his back to Levic, balancing his hat on his nose.

'I suppose you think that was funny,' Levic hissed, when he caught up with Steffi after the show.

'Yes,' Steffi said, grinning. 'I must say it worked better than . . .'

'No, you don't say anything. You just listen,' his father exploded. 'You think you're clever enough to get a laugh by guying me in the ring . . .'

'Oh, come on, Pa. Surely that's what clowning's all about? I mean, you've got to keep your sense of humour going.'

'Not at other artistes' expense,' Levic thundered. 'And certainly not at mine!'

'Oh, come on, Pa. The audience loved it and it's the sort of trick we could do again,' Steffi protested.

'Not without prior consent and proper planning we don't. Do you understand?'

Steffi shook his head.

'Right! Well, let me make it clearer. I know you've put money in this outfit, but that doesn't make you the boss . . .'

'But I never said . . .'

'So when you step into that ring, you're under my orders, right?'

'What, like all your other employees?' Steffi snapped, beginning to lose his temper.

'Exactly.'

'Then why don't I get paid like everyone else?'

'Paid?' Levic repeated, as if payment was a concept new to him.

'Yes, paid. It may have escaped your notice but I don't get a penny for all the work I do.'

'No, but you get fed and clothed and there's nothing you go without.'

'That's not the same as having proper wages.'

'Maybe you're not worth proper wages,' Levic sneered.

Steffi felt his eyes grow hot but was determined not to row. His father was tired and speaking out of bad temper, he knew that, but still the injustice hurt.

'"Any man is worthy of his hire",' Steffi murmured through tight lips. 'And remember, you're talking to a man now, not a boy. And I don't like being insulted.'

Levic snorted.

'A man, is it? So is that why you're hanging round the girls like a love-sick moon-calf?'

'What?' Steffi was taken by surprise at this sharp turn in the conversation.

'You heard me. I suppose you think I don't know how you behaved yesterday? You and that girl making a public exhibition of yourselves on the highway. Well, I won't have it. Not that sort of behaviour. Not in my show.'

Levic's words left Steffi speechless. To say he felt angry was an understatement. That his father should dare to refer to that precious exchange between him and Rosa in such a tone was intolerable. But before he had found the right words to convey his outrage, worse followed.

'Yes, you might well look shame-faced, Steffi. There's no excuse for that sort of conduct even if, as I can well believe, the girl in question's no better than she should be.'

Rosa! Levic was actually talking about Rosa in that cold, sneering way he had. Denigrating the girl he loved. Steffi clenched his fists.

'You'd better not say any more,' he growled.

'No, perhaps not,' Levic said, sounding suddenly so weary that Steffi, had he not been angry, would have felt sorry for him. As it was, he did no more than register the fact that his father's dark eyes, normally so fiery, at that moment looked like dead cinders in an ashen face. Even his moustache drooped dispiritedly.

And there the confrontation might have ended had not some devil been stirring the embers and poked another into life.

'But I mean it, Steffi,' Levic said, a malicious gleam returning to his eyes. 'You'll stay away from that girl if you know what's good for you.'

'You're not by any chance talking about Rosa, are you?'

'Of course I am. Unless you're carrying on with half a dozen others behind my back.'

Steffi could do nothing but smile contemptuously at that remark.

'I mean,' Levic continued, 'it doesn't take much to attract girls if you happen to be a circus-owner's son. Which brings me back to my point – you are my son and I expect you to behave responsibly and not take advantage of your privileges.'

'Privileges!' Steffi snorted, looking hard at his father to see if he intended this as a joke.

Levic stared back grimly, giving Steffi to understand that, as far as he was concerned, Steffi was and always would be completely in the wrong. And there was nothing to be gained from further discussion.

After that the situation went from bad to worse, every day bringing further cause for father and son to be at loggerheads.

Even the glowing review of Minerva's show which appeared in the columns of the *Era* that week seemed to fuel Levic's resentment. Under a banner headline MINERVA'S CIRCUS AT LUDLOW – ACCLAIMED AS BEST EVER there followed a detailed description of each act, with the greatest praise being reserved for the clown Levity: 'who had the audience eating out of his hand from the moment he bounced into the ring, squeaking his greeting "Hello! Here we are again!" to his final fond farewell'.

At first Steffi could not believe what he was reading. Then assumed that the reviewer had confused the two names and written 'Levity' instead of 'Levic'. But when he read on, he knew there had been no mistake.

'Of course one must not – in passing – neglect to pay tribute to that other institution of Minerva's, the venerable clown Levic, whose admirable presence (one might indeed say "omni-presence") continues to hold the show together. However, on this occasion he seemed to be struggling too hard to find the right pitch for his comic business – which is probably why it was to the more endearing character of the silly auguste that this audience gave their hearts.'

'Steffi, you can't imagine how proud that makes me feel!' Mirella enthused as, having just read the report out loud, she put the paper down and hugged him. 'Do you realise how much people are beginning to appreciate our brilliant son?' she then asked Levic, clumsily overlooking the fact that Steffi's triumph had been achieved at his father's expense.

'Humph! And what did he call me? "Venerable"? What's that supposed to mean? That I'm getting past it, I suppose.'

'No, no. Of course not,' she hastened to soothe his ruffled feathers. '"Venerable" is "very much respected", isn't it? You shouldn't complain at someone calling you that.'

But Levic would not be mollified.

'No, I think it's criminal when some young whipper-snapper just about able to hold a pen is paid to write that kind of rubbish. "Struggling to find the right pitch!" What the hell does he know about clowning? And how would he like it if I approached him and . . .'

Steffi did not stay to hear more. He had come to accept his father's irascibility, but these ranting moods were something different and he could not understand how his mother put up with them. There were times when Levic raved for hours over something so trivial that it warranted no more than a passing comment. And then complained about being exhausted, took some pills and retired to bed leaving others – particularly Mirella or Steffi – to handle the situation as they thought best.

Still, no need to brood on that now, he decided, tucking the newspaper down the front of his waistcoat, ready to produce it with a flourish once he found Rosa. For his first thought on reading the review had been: Won't Rosa be pleased when she sees this!

'Rosa!' he called from the bottom step of the girls' wagon.

'Yes? Come on up, Steffi,' she called back, without troubling to open the door.

He pushed the top half slightly ajar, having decided not to go in because of Amy who, since the incident on the road outside Ludlow, had begun to treat him most oddly. Shunning him as if he had offended her in some way. Naturally he had asked Rosa what was wrong, but she had been unable to suggest anything beyond the fact that Amy was probably suffering from jealousy – as usual.

'Rosa, will you come out for a few minutes? There's something I want to show you,' he explained. Then leapt back down the steps and stood whistling while he waited.

After about five minutes she emerged from the wagon looking so pretty as to take his breath away and he found himself sliding down from his last note.

'Phe-e-e-eow!'

'Do you like it? It's my new blouse,' she smiled.

'Yes, pink suits you,' he said, admiring the way the material tucked tightly into the waist of her mauve skirt emphasising her soft figure. And noticing that she had done something different with her hair today, tying part of it up in a red ribbon while the rest was left flowing over her shoulders.

'So what did you want to show me?' she murmured.

'Not here. Let's go for a little walk,' he suggested on impulse, 'and I'll tell you about it as we go along.'

'A walk? Shall I fetch my hat then?'

'No. There's no need. We won't go far. Just up the lane a little way towards the fields.'

The track was rough and rutted but, because of the prolonged dry spell, happily free from mud, enabling them to walk comfortably side by side. Steffi waited till they were beyond sight of the tober before he slipped his arm around Rosa's waist and pulled her towards him.

'Did I say how lovely you look this morning?' he whispered, pushing back her hair and kissing her cheek. She turned her face towards him so that he could kiss her properly on

295

the mouth, sucking again at the familiar sweetness.

'Oh, Rosa, I do love you,' he breathed.

'So do I. Oh, no. I didn't really mean that,' she started to giggle. 'I meant to say, I love you too, Steffi.'

She said it so naturally and her gaiety was so infectious that Steffi chuckled too. Then they kissed again and walked further up the track until they came to a wooden bridge crossing a dried-up stream.

'Tell you what, let's go and sit over there,' Steffi said, pointing towards the remains of an old hayrick in the sunniest corner of the meadow they were just entering.

For a moment Rosa stared doubtfully.

'Just so we can talk,' he urged. 'Nothing more.' Then grew embarrassed at what his words implied and rushed to cover up by pulling the newspaper out from the front of his waistcoat. 'Look! I've brought this week's *Era* for you to see.'

'Oh.'

'There's a really good review of Minerva's in it.'

'Oh,' Rosa said again, looking bemused.

But she followed him readily enough and helped him pile up the loose hay into a nest where they could sit quite comfortably secluded from the world.

After that he quickly found and smoothed out the relevant page and tried to hand it to Rosa.

'No, I'd rather you read it to me,' she murmured.

So that's what he set out to do – despite the difficulties of trying to concentrate on such tiny print while someone was tickling his ear with a length of grass all the time.

'"For all those drawn to the castle field last Wednesday Minerva's circus offered a treat not to be missed",' he read. 'Oooh! don't, Rosa. That tickles! . . . "And as for the young clown, such was his magnetism that he drew the author of this review back" . . . oooh, Rosa. Don't!'

However, he obviously did not sound convincing because she did not stop. And eventually there was nothing for it but to put the paper down and grapple with his tormentress. After all, eager as he was for her reaction to the review, he could glean that later. Whereas at the moment, with the drowsy warmth of the morning sun bearing down on them and the sweet-smelling softness of the hay underneath, there were better ways to enjoy being in a hayrick.

'Isn't it hot?' Rosa sighed, unbuttoning the top of her blouse as she leant back in their bower. 'Phew! That's better. Why don't you get rid of that wesket, Steffi? You don't need it at the moment.'

Of course she was right. He took it off immediately and loosened his shirt.

'This is nice, isn't it?' he said, putting his arm round her.

'Yes.'

She snuggled her face up close for a kiss and he found his hands wandering down her back, then pressing her body into his. And he loved it when she responded by pushing her hands up under his shirt and stroking his bare flesh.

'Hmm, you've got ever such strong muscles,' she said, 'even though you are thin.'

'Am I?'

'Yes. A lot thinner than Hugo.' As if aware he might be taking this as criticism, she added. 'But I think that's good. I hate fat people. That's why I try not to eat too much.'

'But you don't have to worry about getting fat,' he reassured her.

'Oh, I do. Look!' She pulled back, squeezing her dimpled hands round her own waist and frowning. 'You see? It ought to be at least an inch smaller.'

'Nonsense. It's perfect the way it is. I think everything about you is perfect,' he averred. 'Your lovely grey eyes.' She shut them so that he could stroke his fingers gently along their lids. 'Your nose.' He ran his fingers down its length. 'Your lips.' He kissed her again and they sank back together into the hay.

Then she broke the spell by uttering a little squeal. 'Ow! Oh, Steffi, I think something's got down my blouse. Oooh! Yes, I can feel it. Some sort of creepy-crawly. Oooh! You must help me get it out.'

He peered down her collar.

'I can't see anything,' he said, feeling a cold trickle of sweat slide down his spine. 'But perhaps if you undid some more buttons . . .'

She quickly obliged. Stripping off until she sat in just her bodice, a pure white garment which just failed to cover her modesty. Then she shook her blouse.

'Funny! Whatever it was must have dropped out. Probably an earwig,' she decided, laying the blouse carefully to one side.

'Well, don't worry about it. Just come back here,' Steffi mumbled, pulling her down beside him and burying his face in her bosom. The firm whiteness of her breasts, her hair – so sweetly scented – as it fell over him, her breath, her warmth, her yielding softness all drew him to her. He felt himself swelling and growing hard. Knew he had the power, the power to take whatever he wanted. And in this moment wanted only one thing in the world. And that was Rosa.

Afterwards Steffi lay in a happy daze, his arms round her, their bodies still entwined. Reluctant to speak in case he spoilt the magic. But then doubts began to crowd his mind. This was not the way he had intended it to happen. He loved Rosa and would never have set out to take advantage of her. It was just that things had happened more quickly than he had bargained for. Still, that was no problem, so long as he and Rosa felt the same way about each other.

'Rosa, are you all right?' he whispered.

'Yes.'

'Are you sure?'

'Yes.'

'I love you, you know.'

'Do you?'

'Of course. And I want you to know, well – that I'd never let you down. That I want you to marry me. If you want to, that is. Because I love you, Rosa. And I think I've always loved you ever since the first time we met. Do you remember that? Oh, Rosa, you will marry me, won't you?'

Instead of answering, she stared up into the sky, her brow creased in a frown.

'Rosa, don't you want to marry me?'

She sat up abruptly and reached for her blouse.

'Of course I do. In fact, I was just thinking about how I'd be able to tell all the others. Especially Amy. I can't wait to see her face when she hears.'

'Will she be pleased, do you think?' Steffi asked, suddenly uneasy.

'No, she'll be jealous as hell. But that can't be helped. But then there's Grandpa, of course. I wonder what he'll say? And your folks. I suppose we'll have a big wedding, won't we?'

Steffi breathed a sigh of relief. Thank God, it was settled then. Rosa had agreed to marry him. His darling girl, accepting him just like that. No fuss. No argument. He must certainly be the luckiest man in the world.

As they walked back hand-in-hand to the tober, he swinging

his waistcoat over his shoulder, they decided it would be best to wait a few days before announcing their engagement.

'Time to prepare the ground with my parents,' Steffi explained.

'Why? Are you afraid they won't approve?'

'No. Not at all. I'm sure they'll both be delighted.'

He spoke the words confidently in an effort to reassure her, but he had a feeling there would be trouble.

Still, what did that matter? he asked himself. So long as he and Rosa loved each other, they would get married no matter what obstacles anyone tried to put in their way.

Chapter 32

'What do you think, Steffi? Is it worth bothering with Bromshurst, or shall we give it a miss?'

The advance agent, a thick-set man with smooth black hair and big muscular throat, popped a toffee in his mouth while sitting alongside Steffi in the pony trap waiting for an answer. Minerva's seldom visited towns of fewer than three thousand people unless it was to break a journey.

'What's its population?' Steffi asked.

Tad consulted his Railway Guide.

'Two thousand five hundred plus.'

'Hmm. Hardly worth it then, is it? So let's forget it and head straight for home.'

'Suits me,' Tad agreed, settling to chew his sweet.

It was not hard for Steffi to justify his decision. The town was small. No certainty of finding a suitable tober. They could make better use of the time by putting up more advertising posters in the villages on their return journey.

But, if he was honest, his real motive was to get back to Rosa. For though living cheek by jowl, they had spent hardly any time alone together during the last few days. Which was frustrating in more ways than one when there were so many things to sort out. The date of their marriage. Where they would live. What they would live on.

It was this last which particularly vexed him. For he knew the time had come for him to establish his independence. He would not go on living off hand-outs. He was entitled to a proper salary. And that's what he would demand – at the first opportunity.

'You did what?' Levic thundered at him after he arrived back on the tober later that day.

'Decided to give Bromshurst a miss.'

'But it was on my list. I told Tad exactly what places to try.'

Steffi cursed Tad. This sort of thing was always happening. Members of the company wringing a decision from him that they knew might upset Levic.

'We thought it was too small to bother with,' he mumbled.

'Oh, I see. *You* thought that.'

'Yes. Besides, it was already getting late.'

'And you wanted to get back here – for obvious reasons,' Levic said sarcastically.

'What's that supposed to mean?'

'You know bloody well what I mean. You didn't take a blind bit of notice of me, did you?'

'I don't know what you're talking about,' Steffi said, about to walk away to avoid another row.

'Don't go before I've finished,' Levic snarled. 'I'm talking about you and that girl. Don't you realise the whole place is buzzing with your carryings-on?'

This was news to Steffi who thought that he and Rosa had been amazingly discreet. But, in any case, since they were about to make an announcement it surely did not matter what people were saying.

'So?'

'So, do you think it's fair? Because I don't. Those girls came here under my protection. I didn't want them, remember. But you and your mother twisted my arm and now look what's happening!'

'But I don't see why you're getting so upset,' Steffi murmured, wondering if this was the moment to speak of his engagement.

Levic snorted. 'Then you're more stupid than I thought.'

'I mean, if it's Rosa you're worried about, perhaps I . . .'

'No, it's not Rosa. It's you. You ought to have more sense than to get mixed up with a . . . a . . .'

'Look, Pa, I won't stand here listening to you insult Rosa. It's not her fault if I made a wrong decision on the road today. Not that I think I did, as a matter of fact. I just think you're looking for someone to row with as usual.'

'And I think you're someone who's got too big for his boots all of a sudden.'

'Then I'll buy myself a new pair.'

'But you won't wear them round here, my lad. Not all the time I'm boss. Nor will I have you playing fast and loose with members of my staff, do you hear me?' he shouted.

'So I'm telling you once and for all, leave that girl alone.'

Steffi felt his face growing red. Everyone knew that tents had ears yet here was Levic, after warning him against causing scandal, making what amounted to a public proclamation of his personal affairs. And what if Rosa got to hear how she was being spoken of?

In a quiet voice Steffi said, 'You may be my father, but you can't dictate to me who . . .'

'Oh, can't I?' Levic interrupted. 'And I suppose I can't send that girl packing if I decide she's more trouble than she's worth?'

'Yes, I suppose you can,' Steffi said. 'But before you do, I'd better tell you that I've asked "that girl" to be my wife.'

'You haven't! Not Rosa?' Levic spluttered.

'Yes, Rosa. And, incredible as it may seem, she has done me the honour of accepting. So, although this isn't the way I planned to break the news, please understand that Rosa and I intend to get married. As soon as we can make proper arrangements,' Steffi added.

'You idiot! You bloody idiot,' his father groaned.

'But why did you have to tell him like that?' Rosa sniffed, her face red and puffy from crying. 'I thought we'd agreed on how we'd do it.'

'It wouldn't have made any difference.'

'Oh, but it would. If you'd left me to tell them, I'd have done my hair up special and put on my good dress and made them see what a good match we are.'

'Look, you mustn't take this personally. It's not you, they object to,' Steffi hastened to reassure her. 'They – or rather my father – would oppose any marriage I wanted to make. And why? First, because he's cussed. And second, he's afraid of losing a good unpaid worker.'

'But I'm sure I can get round him if you let me try. I'm very good at that sort of thing,' she said with a watery smile.

'No. I don't want to placate him. I think everything's happening for the best.'

'How?'

'By forcing me to leave Minerva's.'

'But I thought you loved Minerva's. And, anyway, it actually belongs to you.'

'But all that's beside the point. It's time I spread my wings.'

'And flew to London?' It was as if she had suddenly seen the light.

'Exactly. There's plenty of theatres in London and, after the kind of reviews I've had recently, plenty of managements who'd take me on.'

'But Steffi, you wouldn't have to ask anyone else. Grandad would give anything to have you at Apsley's.'

'Yes, except that I'm not sure . . .' Steffi began to say, not wanting to find his wings clipped by Arnold Foreman so soon after starting to fly.

'No, no. It's obviously the best plan. You come back with me and Amy. I'll tell Grandad we want to get married – oh, I'm sure he'll be pleased when he hears that – and then I'll tell him that you need a job. And after that, well – Bob's your uncle! He'll bend over backwards to keep you at Apsley's, you can bank on that.'

Rosa proved more accurate in her prediction than he could have imagined.

Having telegraphed ahead to let Arnold know they were coming, she and Steffi were given a royal welcome when they reached Apsley's. And when, within minutes of mounting the stairs to the family's living quarters, Rosa nudged Steffi into explaining why they had come, the old man stroked his black whiskers and declared that no news could have given him greater pleasure.

'Not that I wasn't expecting something of the sort,' he twinkled.

'And I do have prospects, Mr Foreman. Shares in Minerva's,' Steffi explained, reluctant to lay any greater claim than that on his father's business.

'Tush!' said Arnold disparagingly, waving his hand as if to brush aside a gnat. 'No offence meant, but Minerva's is nothing. Nothing. The main thing is, knowing you're the right stock and that Rosa's brought me someone I can work with. So don't even think about a paltry concern like Minerva's any more. You're in for the big time here, Steffi. Put yourself in my hands and I'll make something of you.'

'Oh, but that's not why I came,' he protested. 'It's very generous of you, Mr Foreman, but I'm here to ask for your permission to marry Rosa, nothing else. We certainly don't expect you to provide for us once we're married.'

'Shush! Don't worry, I shall see you're all right,' Arnold insisted, squinting into the corner of the room as if afraid of eavesdroppers. 'And, you take my word for it, Steffi – you did better than you knew the day you landed little Rosa. Isn't that right, my treasure?' He smiled benignly at her.

For some reason Steffi felt threatened, as if the bars of a cage were beginning to close in on him. And he had not flown free of Minerva's only to be confined elsewhere. Especially as, heaven knows, it had cost him dear to leave.

When Mirella heard he was going, she had been distraught.

'Please, Steffi,' she begged, 'don't do anything rash. I know how you feel, but you and Rosa are young, and there's plenty of time before you need think about marriage.'

'But I love her, Ma. And she loves me,' he said.

'All right, I accept that. But that doesn't mean you have to rush into marriage.'

'But I want to marry Rosa. Don't you understand? I want to marry her because I can't bear to live without her.'

'But you don't have to rush,' she repeated. 'You could stay here when she goes back and take time to think it over.'

'No!'

'But why, Steffi? What are you afraid of?'

'I'm not afraid. I just don't want to stay here. I can't stand it any longer.'

'I see.' As Mirella dabbed her eyes with the corner of her pinafore, she muttered, 'I suppose that's because of your father.'

'Partly. It's true I can't stand the rows, Ma. And to be honest I don't see why . . .'

'No. That's right, Steffi. You don't see . . . I mean, you don't realise what . . . Oh, dear! I don't know any more. So perhaps you should go away, even if it's with that . . . No, no. I won't speak ill of her. But, oh, Steffi! You've got so much to offer, don't throw it all away on the first one to come along.'

Which was the sort of stupid remark any mother might have made, but he was disappointed to hear it from Mirella. Disappointed to receive no more than icy disdain from his father as he set about packing his bags. Disappointed in Amy's reaction when he and Rosa told her they were planning to wed.

'No, no! You can't,' she cried, her face puckering into a frown that made her scar turn livid. 'Not you and Rosa. It wouldn't be right. You mustn't do it, Steffi. Oh, please, you mustn't.'

'Well, that's nice,' moaned Rosa. 'I introduce my husband-to-be and my sister tries to put him off. Still, I suppose I should have known better than to expect anything like congratulations from you.'

Appalled at seeing them both so upset, Steffi rushed to restore harmony. 'Please, Amy don't upset yourself. Rosa was bound to get married some day and it doesn't mean I'll be taking her away from you, you know.'

But his words worked no magic. During the rest of their stay at Minerva's Amy had made it obvious that she bitterly resented his relationship with Rosa and did not welcome the prospect of his returning with them to Apsley's.

Even today, as soon as she had arrived and greeted her grandfather, Amy had taken herself off to inspect the animals and not been seen since. Which meant that Steffi's pleasure at being back here was spoilt. Arnold may have given him a warm welcome. Rosa beamed with happiness as she regaled Apsley's staff with her news. But Steffi found it hard to forget that, amidst all the rejoicing, Amy was somewhere in the building unhappy and alone.

'"Mazeppa" – that's what we're going to put on this autumn,' Arnold announced. 'The most exciting equestrian drama ever staged.'

'"Mazeppa"? Isn't that the one that caused all the scandal?' Steffi asked, bringing to mind some scantily-clad female strapped to a bareback horse that he had once seen on a poster.

'Ah, but that was years ago, when Menken rode in it.'

'Who was Menken?'

'Adah Isaacs Menken, a young American who made her name over here by riding half-naked in the halls.'

'And that's what you're proposing to stage at Apsley's?' Steffi protested.

'Oh, yes. Nobody turns a hair about that sort of thing nowadays. Besides, even Menken was never as shocking in the flesh as on the hoardings – and that's the way it'll be with us. Well within the confines of decency,' said Arnold, watching the smoke curl up from his cigar.

'And who will play Mazeppa?'

'Ah, of that I'm not sure. Which of the girls would do it best, do you think?'

'Girls?'

'Yes. Rosa or Amy? Naturally I shall give one of them the title role.'

'Oh, yes. Of course. I suppose that's obvious,' Steffi muttered, trying to disguise his dismay at the thought of Rosa as Mazeppa. Not that she wouldn't be good in the part. And she would certainly relish doing it, but . . . Oh, dear! Perhaps it was jealousy on his part, but he just did not like the thought of seeing Rosa disport her charms to thousands of people in that way. Whereas Amy . . . well, she could pull it off without making such an exhibition of herself.

But if Steffi had any ideas about having a quiet word with Rosa and telling her how he felt about the situation, he was baulked by the fact that Arnold had already told the girls and provoked them into heated rivalry.

'Ah, Steffi!' Rosa rushed up and seized his arm to drag him into the fray as soon as he entered the stable where a moment before the two sisters had stood glaring at each other across one of the partitions dividing the stalls. 'I want you to tell Amy she's not suitable to do Mazeppa.'

'Why isn't she?'

As he glanced at Amy, her eyes lit up and she almost smiled.

'Because . . . well, I would have thought that was obvious,' Rosa declared.

At which remark, her sister's smile evaporated and her hand rose to cover the scar above her eye.

'It's not at all obvious to me,' Steffi said quickly. 'In fact, as far as I'm concerned I think Amy would make an excellent . . .'

'No, no. She'd look stupid,' Rosa interrupted. 'She just hasn't got the right . . . you know.'

'If you mean I'm not curvy enough, why don't you say so?' Amy exploded.

'All right. You're not curvy enough to look good tied half-naked to a horse. There! I've said it.'

Steffi hung his head in embarrassment. What Rosa had just said summed up his own reservations about her taking on the part.

'And I suppose you think you'd look so much better?' Amy retorted.

'Yes, if you want to know the truth, I think I would,' Rosa murmured, running her hands down over her bodice and waist as if to prove the point, throwing Steffi's thoughts into further turmoil.

'But aren't you forgetting Mazeppa's supposed to be a *boy*?' Amy challenged.

'That's got nothing to do with it. You know as well as I do that nowadays people always expect it to be done by a girl. And the bit they like best is when she's tied naked to the horse and rides over the mountains.'

'Well, I could do that,' Amy muttered, glowering at her sister. 'In fact, I'd do it far better than you because I wouldn't be posing on my horse like a bloomin' ballet dancer!'

'Nor would I. I'd do it properly, like Menken. What do you think, Steffi?' Rosa asked, turning back to him for support. 'It's got to be me in the part, hasn't it? Because you can't have a weedy Mazeppa wooing someone a couple of inches taller than him, can you?'

Steffi shrank himself by bending his knees and slowly raised his eyes to look up at her in a gesture that exaggerated her height.

'I don't know. I think it could still work.'

Now it was Rosa's turn to look put out, especially when Amy started to chuckle.

'I can see there's no point in trying to talk seriously to either of you,' she said, flouncing off to make her views known to her Grandfather.

Chapter 33

Arnold cast two Mazeppas, each to play the character of the Tartar chief on alternate nights while the other took on the less exacting role of Olinska. And since Olinska was the betrothed of Count Palatine, the character whom Steffi himself played, the result was most strange – the sisters bringing such opposite qualities to their parts that it affected the whole mood of the piece and left Steffi with the feeling that he was taking part in more than one drama.

Take the fight scenes, for instance.

When the curtain rose to reveal Amy as the Tartar prince who had disguised himself as a page in order to pay court to Olinska, her fighting spirit bristled forth like lightning. And when it fell to Steffi as Count Palatine to challenge this fiery Mazeppa, he found he had a real battle on his hands.

Not that Amy was any physical match for him, of course. But in the face of such hostility it was easy for him to feign being beaten back and vanquished. And when he eventually collapsed at her feet, seeing her green eyes narrow into tigerish slits and gleam with triumph was disturbing. Still, at least it made for an exciting performance – as he could tell from the mood of the house.

In fact, after a while, Steffi wished he could provoke some more genuine emotion from her sister.

'Come on, Rosa! Remember you're a wild Tartar and thrust!' he kept urging in rehearsal. But she simply smiled and went limp all the time.

'Don't be silly,' she murmured. 'We're too far away for anyone to see what's happening.'

'But it still matters.'

'No, it doesn't. As long as we wave our swords around and you fall down at the right time, the audience will get the message.'

'No, I want us to do it properly, Rosa.'

'But there's really no need,' she said comfortably. 'Grandad would soon say if there was.'

Steffi found there was nothing he could do in the face of such complacency, but it irked him – especially as Rosa then proceeded to ham it up in the following scene when she knew everyone's eyes were on her. For this was the scene most of the audience had come for, the scene in which poor Mazeppa was stripped and bound with thongs to his horse's back, then turned out on the Steppes to perish.

And if people came expecting to see what the posters promised, then as far as Rosa was concerned it was not going to be her fault if they went away disappointed. So, although both she and Amy wore the same tight fleshings and white linen tunics reaching towards their knees, in Rosa's case the material always managed to slide up and reveal a long, pink length of thigh.

Kenny, promoted from stableyard to prop-man with the job of simulating the wolf who snapped at Mazeppa's horse as it travelled up the various slopes on the stage, had what he kept scurrilously referring to as the best view in the house. Until Steffi put a stop to the joke by taking over the job himself.

'Here you are, Steffi! Time to go and be wolf,' Kenny would grin as he handed over the carved wooden head with its movable jaws. Then Steffi would have to crouch below the canvas parapet of the highest platform ready to crawl along behind Etty and snap at his hooves as he reached it. After that Mazeppa 'himself' would disappear off stage and be replaced by a series of cardboard figures gradually diminishing in size until one of those passed out of sight over the horizon. At which point the curtain fell.

Steffi was not needed in the next act – which revealed Mazeppa safe among his father's Tartars in a snowclad landscape, slowly recovering from his dreadful ordeal before marshalling his troops and riding off to effect the rescue of Olinska. But after that he had to be ready for his last entrance – the scene in which he was sadly slain by a now respectably attired Mazeppa who then went on to bring the whole affair to a happy conclusion by marrying the fair Olinska.

It was during one of Mazeppa's passages of flight across the wild Steppes that the wretched zig-zagging inclines claimed a casualty after the 'wolf' tripped into one of the supports and practically wrecked the platform. Amy, playing Mazeppa at

310

the time, did her best to manoeuvre Etty round the abyss which suddenly gaped before them, but without success. And while Steffi stood horrified, trying to hold the remaining struts steady, both horse and rider tumbled towards him.

There was no time to think. No time to feel fear. Or anything. Only time to try to jump clear as he realised that there was a mound of horseflesh falling towards him. Then the breath being knocked from his body as he fell and just lay there waiting for chaos to subside. Waited for Etty's grey limbs to stop threshing about before he dared raise his own head to assess what damage had been done.

And then, once the horse had struggled to its feet, shaken itself and stumbled towards the wings, pulling himself up – and seeing Amy lying motionless just a few feet from him. Perfectly still.

'Amy! Amy!'

He was kneeling at her side, his face next to hers to make sure she was still breathing, his hand on her heart to feel its beat.

'Amy! Say something,' he pleaded. 'Tell me you're all right.'

And nothing so welcome in the world as the tiny movement of her lashes as she started to open her eyes.

'What happened?' She was clearly dazed, her skin deathly white except where the pink thread-like scar twisted above her eye.

'You tumbled off the platform. With Etty. Oh, Amy, I'm sorry,' he stammered. 'It was all my fault!'

'No. No. I'm sure you couldn't help it.' She managed a little smile, before her eyes clouded over like jade and creased with pain.

'What is it? Where are you hurt?'

'Just my shoulder and – ow! Yes, my back. But don't worry, Steffi. It's not bad, honestly. No more than bruised, I think. But what's happened to Etty? Is he all right?' She craned her head round and started to get up.

'He's fine. It's only you I'm worried about.' He stretched out his arm to hold her still while at the same time stroking her hair back from her face and begging her not to move until they were sure nothing was broken.

By now an anxious crowd of artistes had gathered and Arnold came bustling up.

'Okay, let's get this mess cleared. No time to stand staring.

311

You there, get a move on. We're in the middle of a show, remember.' And only then did Steffi realise that the world had not stopped while he had been kneeling here next to Amy fearing that she was hurt. The audience had in fact accepted her unorthodox exit as part of the script once their attention was caught by the cardboard figure which took her place and continued its hapless journey over the horizon. And nobody seemed to notice the demise of the wolf.

'She all right?' Arnold barked.

'No, she caught her back . . .' Steffi started to say.

'No, it's okay, Gramps. I'm fine really,' Amy protested, making an effort to scramble to her feet despite Steffi's efforts to restrain her.

'Right. But will you be fit for the next scene? That's what I need to know. Or shall we do a swap? Thank God,' he murmured, mopping his brow and turning to Steffi, 'I had the sense to cast the pair of them. Must have known they'd be bloody accident prone.'

Steffi found it hard to believe Arnold could be so heartless. But assuming that her grandfather would show Amy more sympathy once he realised the facts, Steffi started to explain how it was he who had caused the accident. He did not get far.

'No, Steffi. It was no one's fault. Really it wasn't. Etty stumbled and . . .' Amy interrupted. Then caught in her breath sharply as she tried to ease her elbow and shoulder in a circular motion backwards.

'That's right. What's done's done – so long as it don't happen again,' Arnold agreed. 'So what do you think, Amy? Can you go on with Mazeppa? Or shall I tell Rosa to take over?'

'No. I'd rather carry on,' she said quickly.

Steffi knew she was in pain and felt he ought to put his foot down but one look at her face told him he would be wasting his time. She was clearly determined. So he helped her go backstage to get changed, full of admiration for her pluck. But at the same time strangely disturbed by the whole incident.

Naturally he hated the thought of Amy being hurt, especially when he himself was so much to blame. But there was something else. The way he had felt when she looked at him. It was odd, that. When he thought he knew her so well. Would have said everything about her was completely familiar. Then to look at her and suddenly discover that she had such beautiful eyes. Like malachite – green with tiny flecks of amber.

Eyes that contained an expression so soft and limpid that he could not withdraw his gaze from them.

Yes, that's what had disturbed him. That moment when Amy first opened her eyes and looked unguardedly into his. As they had looked at each other, something happened. Some silent exchange. Some mysterious declaration. Something dangerously like love.

Except that he loved Rosa. And Rosa loved him. And nobody was going to come in between them and spoil that. Nobody. Certainly not her sister.

And, having said that to himself, he felt almost angry with Amy for posing such a threat.

So, once the initial shock was over, Steffi tried to put the whole incident behind him. After all, no great harm had been done. Amy was tough and seemed to recover within a couple of days. She, thank God, seemed oblivious of the emotional tumult she had caused. And as for his own feelings, so long as he was careful to keep them concealed, they would do no harm.

Except that, as each day threw him into situations where he worked closely with Amy, so each day he found it increasingly difficult to hold his feelings in check.

He told himself it was madness. That you could not love two women at once. And he loved Rosa. Moreover, he had always loved Rosa who represented everything he ever wanted from life. So what could he be thinking of when he went to bed at night and dreamed of Amy – longing to feel the touch of her lips, to stroke the sandy strands of her hair aside and plant a kiss on her neck, to hold her in his arms and tell her how much he loved her?

What could he be thinking of?

'Humph! Thought that fall might have knocked her off her high horse!' Rosa scowled, as they stood together watching Amy on stage as Mazeppa a week or so later.

'I'm glad it didn't,' Steffi declared, fastening on the sword he wore as Count Palatine.

'Why? You don't think she's any good, do you?'

He started at her question. 'Good?'

'Yes, as Mazeppa? Because I don't think she is. She's got no idea how to make herself look . . . well, you know . . . provocative when she's tied to that horse. She just looks scared.'

'No, not just scared,' Steffi said, staring at Amy. 'She looks defiant. Which is what you'd expect from a Tartar chief.'

Rosa glanced at Amy, then turned, narrowing her gaze as she took stock of Steffi.

'Maybe. But it's not what the audience likes . . .'

'Perhaps not.'

'Anyway,' Rosa sidled up close and took hold of his arm, 'don't let's talk about Amy. Let's talk about us, Steffi. Grandad thinks an Easter wedding would be a good idea. What do you think?'

'Easter?'

'Yes, I know it sounds a long way off, but there's so much to do. You've no idea – we've got to get my dress made, work out the guest list, plan the wedding breakfast. And I'd like our rooms redecorated before we move in.'

'What rooms?'

'The rooms we'll live in, of course. My parents had them refurbished but there hasn't been much done since.'

'But I don't want to carry on living here once we're married.'

'Why ever not?'

'Because I want us to have our own home, of course.'

'But that's stupid. It's obvious that Grandad will expect us to live here at Apsley's – especially as he sees you as its owner one day. You do realise that, don't you?' she said, as if that settled the matter.

Steffi stared at Rosa in her pink and lavender Olinska costume with its low-cut neck revealing an expanse of porcelain flesh and her fair hair hanging on either side of her face in formal ringlets while her eyes had been dramatically made up so that she looked like a china doll. And his heart lurched as he remembered the day he had lain with her in the hay and loved her. As he still loved her, he quickly told himself. Except that for some reason things had seemed different then. Rosa had seemed different.

'Steffi, is it waiting so long that's worrying you?' she whispered, squeezing his hand. 'I mean, if you'd rather we brought the wedding forward . . .'

'No. Easter. Easter should be all right,' he murmured, turning his head to kiss her.

'Good. I knew you'd agree,' she smiled back as she skipped off to answer her cue.

He shut his eyes, feeling slightly sick. Rosa seemed to think they were in agreement about everything, but they clearly were not. They still had not settled the question of where they would live, for instance. Nor could they unless one was prepared to give way to the other.

But how different from that former day when they had lain together in the hay and he would have lived anywhere, done anything, given everything for the chance to be with Rosa. There had been no possibility of falling out over such an issue then.

So what was going wrong? he asked himself. And how could he put it right? For it was obviously his problem and nothing to do with Rosa. After all, she was still the same. And her feelings remained the same. It was only he who was unreliable; he who apparently enjoyed the chase more than winning the prize.

Still, now that he realised his own weakness, he would do something about it. And whatever happened, certainly not let Rosa down. That much he owed her for the way she had so trustingly given herself that day. Yes, put like that, he had no option. Besides – he shook himself – there was no need for him to be considering other options, because of course he loved Rosa and would marry her once they had sorted out all the practical details. And after that? Oh, after that, he would make sure things worked out – if only for Rosa's sake.

And having made this resolve, he greeted Amy with a brotherly smile as she came off stage – and was immediately reduced to jelly when she half-smiled back.

'Amy, I need to talk to you,' he stuttered, later that evening after going into the stables to find her.

'Ye-es?' She looked up with a troubled expression.

'I . . . Look, I don't know how to say this. I suppose what I really want is your advice.'

'I see.'

'No, I don't think you do. It's about Rosa.'

'I thought it might be,' she said slowly, biting her lip.

'Why?'

'Because I guessed you'd start worrying once we got back here. But, look Steffi – I don't think I'm the right person for you to confide in. I'd like to help, but being Rosa's sister, I know I mustn't take sides.'

He stared at her, nonplussed.

'What do you mean "take sides"?'

She peered up at him in that lopsided way that he had grown used to over the years. 'Well, forgive me if I'm wrong, but I imagined you two must have fallen out, or that you were worried because you'd seen . . . Oh, I don't know. I've obviously misunderstood, so . . .' She began to sound very flustered. 'Oh, just forget what I said,' she muttered, stopping abruptly and biting her lip again.

'No, wait a minute, Amy. Finish what you were saying. Why did you think being at Apsley's would worry me?'

'I said, just forget it, Steffi. I was wrong to open my mouth. It was just that I misunderstood what you were going to say.' As she gathered up the bridle she had come for and turned to leave, Steffi grabbed her arm.

'No, don't go.'

At his touch, she twisted violently round, her eyes flashing.

'Look, I can guess what you think of me, but you're wrong. I'm not like that.'

'Like what?'

'Like the sort of person who would cause trouble between you and Rosa.'

'Of course you aren't,' Steffi murmured, keeping his hand on her arm and instinctively drawing her closer. 'I never thought you were.'

She looked up at him, obviously troubled, and he wanted to reassure her. He squeezed her arm and was pleased when she responded by looking up into his face with a smile. Without pausing for thought, he leant forward and kissed her.

In the next instant she had sprung back, her eyes so wild they startled him.

'I'm sorry, Amy. I didn't mean . . .'

'I know you didn't. But, oh Steffi, you mustn't. I just can't stand that sort of thing,' she growled, turning and running away.

After that Steffi felt so ashamed he found it hard to hold his head erect, let alone look Amy in the eyes. So he took to avoiding her – a tactic which worked to some extent during the day but let him down lamentably on stage each evening when the tension of appearing together was painful.

Somehow the situation had to be resolved, he knew that. But he felt too confused to see the way forward and feared taking any steps which might cause Amy worse embarrassment. On

316

the other hand, he was quick to blame himself when he realised how his inaction had forced her to take matters into her own hands.

'Have you heard what my sister's done?'

When Rosa greeted him with this question one morning towards the end of 'Mazeppa's' run, Steffi's heart lurched with fear.

'Not hurt herself?' he cried.

'No. But she's handed in her notice.'

'Her notice?' he echoed as if never having heard of such a thing.

'That's right. Told Grandad she won't be available for the pantomime. Have you ever heard anything so ridiculous?'

'But why? What will she do?' Steffi demanded, haunted by a vision of Amy sitting depressed in some corner of Apsley's, sewing costumes or doing anything, no matter how menial, so long as it enabled her to avoid him. 'I mean, she can't give up performing!'

'Oh, she's not doing that,' Rosa said. 'She's going up north to join a circus for their Christmas season.'

He was shocked.

'But she can't do that!'

'Why not?'

'She can't go on her own. Not to strangers,' Steffi protested.

'Oh, but she's not going to strangers. She's going to Minerva's,' Rosa explained. 'She said she's written to your mother and got it all arranged. They're expecting her to join them at Manchester.'

'Minerva's,' Steffi repeated, still trying to come to terms with the news.

'Yes. I know it's a shock and I told her just what I thought about her pulling such a trick at a time like this,' Rosa complained. 'After all, she's supposed to be our chief bridesmaid.'

'Of course. I'd forgotten the wedding,' Steffi mumbled, unable to grasp anything beyond the fact that Amy was going away.

'Hmm, seems she did too. But don't worry, I've reminded her now and made her promise to be back for that.'

Chapter 34

Steffi cursed himself. Fancy upsetting Arnold when that was the last thing he wanted to do! But no matter what he did, he seemed to find himself treading on someone's toes lately. First Amy. He could not forgive himself for the way he had behaved and still blamed himself for her sudden departure from Apsley's. Then there was Rosa who, while still as affectionate as ever, seemed oddly distracted yet reluctant to tell him what was on her mind.

And now he had made some thoughtless remark about Levic and Dorina working together in the past and opened up that old wound for Arnold.

'Yes,' the old man sighed, mournfully shaking his head, 'those two were sensational – sensational, I tell you. Well, would have been, barring the accident.'

'I know. I was there,' Steffi murmured, recalling the scene for the first time in years.

'Were you? I'd forgotten. But then, I've forgotten nearly everything from that time. Put it all out of my mind, if you understand me. It was the only way.'

'Yes. I can imagine. It must have been so dreadful. Still,' Steffi said in a brighter voice, 'you carried on, that's the main thing.'

'Yes,' Arnold heaved another sigh. 'Carried on. For the girls' sake I had to, but it wasn't easy. Not on my own. Remembering all the time what I'd lost. But, yes, I carried on.' He pulled a coloured handkerchief out of his pocket and blew his nose.

Then, as Steffi made a move to walk away, he found himself grabbed by the sleeve while Arnold muttered, 'I know you were there at the end, but I bet you hardly remember my Dorina, do you? What she looked like, I mean?'

Steffi shook his head.

'Well, come with me and I'll show you.'

They set off along the dark passage leading from backstage to the grand staircase and up to the private suite over the main entrance. Passed through the kitchen and sitting-room which Steffi was by now familiar with and on into Arnold's own bedroom – a room which, despite two large windows, was rendered dark by its deep red curtains and heavily patterned wallpaper. Steffi had never been in here before – nor had many others, to judge by the musty smell of tobacco and dust that lay thick on the tables and wardrobe and marble-topped washstand.

Most of the space was taken up by a big, brass bedstead covered by a damask quilt.

'Here we are! Come in and shut the door behind you, my lad!' Arnold commanded, striding to a window and pulling back the curtains as far as they would go.

As he did so, daylight fell on a portrait in a gilded frame hung high on the wall above the mantelpiece – a life-size painting of a lovely young woman sitting side-saddle on a black horse. She was wearing a blue riding-costume, her flaxen hair flowing loosely down over one shoulder.

And the mantelpiece, Steffi noticed, was arranged like a shrine – with vases, and candlesticks, and wax flowers under a glass dome.

'There!' Arnold whispered. 'That's my Dorina. What do you think, Steffi? Didn't I tell you she was beautiful?'

'Yes,' Steffi stammered, shocked to find himself gazing at the face of someone he at first took for Rosa.

'You see? She was an angel – a beautiful, talented angel who had everything to live for. All this,' Arnold swept out his arm to indicate Apsley's and some indeterminate space beyond, 'would have been hers one day. That's what I was working for. I was building it up for Dorina and her son.'

'Her son?'

Steffi thought he must have misheard.

'Yes, her son – if she had lived to give him birth. But, there you are, it wasn't to be. Still, at least she left me the two girls to carry on working for – and I thank God for that.'

Arnold took a cigar from the box on his bedside table and sniffed it before lighting up. Steffi could not move his gaze from the girl in the picture.

'I didn't realise how closely Rosa resembles her mother,' he murmured at last, studying the sea-grey eyes and lips set slightly apart.

'Oh, yes, she's her very image.'

'And yet Amy's completely different,' Steffi observed, searching in vain for any trace of the younger girl's features.

'Yes. Apart from her talent with horses which she must get from Dorina, that one takes from the father, more's the pity.'

'I gather you don't have much time for Matty.'

Arnold snorted. 'Nor would you if you could see him now.' He made a gesture of someone lifting a glass and knocking back its contents. 'A wastrel. Supposed to have conquered the demon, but I doubt it. Once it gets that sort of hold on a man . . .' He shook his head disparagingly.

'Drink, you mean?'

'Yes. That's why I stopped the girls going there. They used to visit when they were younger, of course. And Amy spent nearly a year with him and his new wife when she was fifteen, but in the end I put my foot down and insisted she came home.'

'I didn't know that.'

'What, that Matty drank?'

'No, that Amy stayed there so long.'

'Well, it's like I said. She takes after that side, you see – which I suppose is why I've always favoured her sister. I know where I am with Rosa, you see. I look at her and see my Dorina.'

As Steffi glanced back at the painting, he felt a shiver run down his spine.

Afterwards, when turning the conversation over in his mind, he still felt uneasy. Was it all those references Arnold kept making to Dorina that unsettled him, reminding him of a tragedy he preferred to forget? Or was it the fact that Rosa looked so much like her mother that worried him, connected with an episode which he had never fully understood?

Whatever the reason, Steffi found himself beginning to brood on the past. Began to feel the weight of Apsley's – the place that had cast its shadow on his childhood – looming over him again. Apsley's . . . the way Arnold talked made it sound like some dark god ravening after sacrifice, with Steffi and Rosa being lined up as victims.

Still, at least Amy had made her escape. In his present gloomy mood that gave Steffi comfort. And he was gratified to discover how well Minerva's was doing on their tour.

'Packed houses for Minerva's at Pontefract'; 'Wakefield woken up by Minerva's sensational show'; 'All of Huddersfield hurries along to Minerva's', he read each week in the pages of the *Era*.

And of course there were always letters from Mirella.

Hurt letters after he had left – full of regret that he should attach his fortunes to Apsley's rather than Minerva's, the show that the Levics had worked together as a family to create. But letters that were also full of love and his mother's efforts to come to terms with the fact that he had his own life to lead.

He used to open those early letters with such mixed feelings. Happy to hear that she was well and the show enjoying such success wherever it went. But unable to ignore the creeping anxiety just under the surface of her words.

'Your father sends his love,' she once wrote, 'and thanks to the help of a friendly apothecary, his health better of late. He still has the pains but keeps them under check with medication, taking the pills whenever the rheumatism threatens so bad as to keep him out of the ring, and pleased to say in this respect manages much better than before. His temper is not always improved as much as his body, but there, we can't have everything, and I'm only grateful to see him out of so much pain at least.'

Naturally Steffi wrote back immediately to ask if she was sure everything was all right and should they not try a London physician if Levic's rheumatism was that much worse?

But the next letter was frosty as she told him that he had misunderstood and what she had intended to convey was that his father was in better health than he had been for years.

From which he inferred that his father had taken umbrage at the way Steffi, having chosen to leave, was still trying to poke his nose into what Levic would regard as his private affairs. And it was noticeable that after that Mirella's letters became less personal – avoiding any reference to Levic's health, speaking only of the weather and suchlike things.

Steffi hated to find himself excluded in this way. But at least he and Mirella had kept writing to each other, and now he was particularly glad to have this channel of communication.

'P.S. Please to tell Arnold Amy arrived here safe and sound Tuesday. Picked her up from the railway station at half-past four, and not to worry as she is well and already settled in like family' was his mother's scribbled postscript on the first letter to reach him after Amy left to join Minerva's.

* * *

'Not another bloody letter from Steffi. Can't that boy find anything better to do than sit around writing letters all day?' Levic snapped.

Mirella drew in a sharp breath, prepared to say anything for a peaceful life. 'But this one's quite amusing, Levic. Here, read it!'

'No, I'm not interested in anything he's got to say,' Levic growled, shoving the letter aside when she tried to put it in his hand.

Mirella drew in another sharp breath. She dreaded it turning into another of those days. For although it was bad enough dealing with Levic on her own, the prospect of having a witness to the way he treated her was worse.

She turned and smiled apologetically at Amy as the girl looked up from her book, and was grateful to receive an understanding smile in return. Perhaps, after all, Levic's mood was not as bad as she feared. And it was rather reassuring to have Amy there, quietly sitting in the corner of the wagon, like Steffi used to sit when absorbed in his own thoughts.

Not that she had been at all keen for Amy to join Minerva's when she first applied. It seemed like inviting trouble to step over the doormat to have one of Arnold's family joining them again. But then, Minerva's did need a good horsewoman and Amy's was the only suitable application that came in response to their advertisement. Besides, Mirella had grown quite fond of her last summer.

'Ah, here's a message for you, Amy,' she announced.

'Yes?' Amy looked up quickly, her eyes bright with expectation.

'Steffi says to tell you everyone at Apsley's misses you and sends their love.'

'Oh, I see,' she muttered, looking more pained than pleased.

Which confirmed Mirella's suspicions that there had been more to Amy's departure from Apsley's than the reason given. No one left a London theatre just before Christmas in order to widen their experience by touring the provinces! Still, at least if Amy was running away from some unhappy love affair, she was not wasting her time mooning about. She was bright and lively most of the time, a perfect companion. It was only in unguarded moments that she let her sadness show.

'And is that all he says? No more sarcastic remarks about my health, I hope,' Levic said testily.

'No, nothing like that. Most of it's about the new show. And there's a bit about the weather – everyone coughing because of the fog – and, oh yes, he wants to know how Amy's getting on so that he can tell Arnold. That's all.'

'Hardly worth the bloody stamp then,' Levic grunted.

'Maybe not. But it's nice to keep in touch,' Mirella said, thinking how she might send Steffi a cutting from the *Huddersfield News* with the photo of Mumbo leading Minerva's parade into town. He would like that.

'Mirella, can I ask you something?'

They were on their own, she and Amy. In the wagon sewing spangles on to costumes -- a fiddly, time-consuming job which was good to do in company.

'Depends what it is,' she replied lightly.

'Ah.'

Amy's sigh led Mirella to expect something quite different from what she went on to say.

'It's about Levic.'

'Oh, that.' Mirella dug her needle into the cloth. She had not been expecting that, because most people knew better than to ask questions about Levic. In fact, most people pretended not to notice that there was anything wrong. Still, if Amy was finding his moods unbearable, who could blame her? 'I'm sorry, love. I should have warned you.'

'His moods are pretty bad, aren't they?'

'Yes,' Mirella said defensively. 'But don't worry about it. I'll have a word with Venie and you can move in with her. She's got a spare bed in her wagon and will make you welcome. I'm just sorry I didn't warn you, Amy. But you're right to complain. You shouldn't have to put up with this atmosphere.'

'But I'm not complaining. I just wanted us to talk about it so I can understand what's happening.'

'Talk about it?'

Mirella thought Amy's words made it sound so simple. Talk about what? About Levic's moods? About the way he would one minute be talking to her quietly and the next, for no reason at all, erupt into a destructive fury? Talk about how he was becoming so irrational that she was sometimes afraid he was losing his mind?

'Yes. I mean, do you know what causes his moods?' Amy asked, putting down her sewing and gazing at her earnestly.

'No.'

'But you realise they're getting worse?'

'Are they?'

'Oh, yes. I don't like saying it, but he wasn't nearly so bad last summer, was he? And he's looking dreadful.'

Mirella sighed. Amy was presenting her with a truth she had no wish to hear.

'That's because the pain's never so bad in the summer.'

'His rheumatism, you mean? And how long has he had that?' Amy asked.

'I don't know. I suppose it started with the accident.'

'That bad fall he had just before my mother died,' Amy said softly.

And suddenly, for the first time in years, Mirella found herself looking back and talking about the past.

'That's right. I think all Levic's problems started then. He was . . . well, very fond of your mother, you know. They had a very good partnership and, although he'd never admit it, he's never really got over her death.'

'No. I can believe that,' Amy said.

'I mean, anyone would be upset by a tragedy like that,' Mirella said hastily. 'But Levic was particularly laid low because of his injuries.'

'His broken leg?'

'Yes, that and his rheumatic attacks which started soon after. Oh, my God, he used to be in such pain, Amy. Crippled by it for days on end so that it would make you weep to see him trying to hobble around.'

'And is that the trouble now?'

'What?'

'That he's in so much pain?'

'No. Not exactly.'

'You mean he takes something,' Amy said slowly.

Mirella nodded her head.

And who, having seen Levic struggling against such pain, could blame him? For a man as active as he had always been, and so proud – a man whose whole life had been dedicated to developing his prowess and pitting himself against the impossible – for him to be struck down and prevented from doing the things which gave meaning to his existence was intolerable.

So he had started taking the little pills containing a confection of opium and was more than happy when they did the trick – allowed him to harness his resources and bound into the ring with something like his old grace and dexterity.

Allowed him to indulge in the sort of drastic exercise which wreaked such havoc in his body that he needed ever larger doses of the drug to dull the pain thereafter.

That's how it had started.

'Does he use laudanum?' Amy asked.

'Laudanum or pills, and sometimes both together if the pain's bad.'

'But doesn't he realise what it's doing to him?'

Mirella shook her head. 'I don't think so. To be honest, I've only just started realising it myself. But, my God, if I'd known earlier, I'd have done something to stop it reaching this state.'

'Such as?'

'Oh, I don't know. Anyway, what's the good of talking about it now, when it's too late and the harm's done?'

Mirella stopped speaking for several minutes and lowered her head over her work until she had regained composure.

Then, keeping her voice calm, she began to explain how at first Levic's deterioration had been so gradual as to be hardly noticeable. Irritability drifting towards irascibility, periods of violent activity succeeded by days of nervous exhaustion, his moods swinging from depths of despair to feverish heights of elation. But then, since he had always been prone to extremes, these excesses had not seemed so extraordinary. And, as always, it was not his moods but his performances that attracted attention and these distracted people from the way he was behaving betweenwhiles.

And so the destructive pattern had been established. Levic's performances, though wonderful, left him mentally and physically exhausted, and exposed him further to the effects of the drug. Until one day he woke up to the fact that he had become . . . addicted.

'But why didn't he seek help?' Amy demanded.

'You know Levic. At first he thought he could handle it himself. So, not saying a word to me, he poured every damn' drop of the stuff away and scattered all his pills to the winds. And . . .' Mirella felt her eyes pricking with tears at the memory '. . . twenty-four hours later he was reduced to a writhing mass of pain worse than anything he'd had before.'

'My goodness, I never knew any of this. Steffi's never said a word.'

'That's because he doesn't know. And, Amy, this is important: I want you to promise that you'll never tell him any of this.'

'Why?'

'Because it's the way Levic wants it. It's hard to explain, but despite all appearances Levic is very fond of Steffi and proud of what he's achieved. And rightly or wrongly he attaches importance to what Steffi thinks of him and is terrified of losing his respect.'

'Yes. I can understand that,' Amy murmured. 'And of course I won't say anything if you don't want me to. Although I'm surprised he hasn't realised.'

'Oh, Steffi knows his father takes pills but he doesn't realise that they've become the problem. You see, he never knew Levic well enough before, and that's another part of the tragedy – that father and son have remained such strangers to one another and probably always will.'

Mirella rose to make some tea while Amy sat, patiently continuing with her sewing and asking questions, until the whole story came out.

Levic had not abandoned his efforts to break the habit, but every experiment had ended in disastrous failure when, the pains having increased to a point where he was forced to give in, he then had to pay the penalty for trying to escape from the drug's clutches by actually increasing his daily intake. At which stage the pain would recede, leaving his mind an open house for any dark notion or nightmare to inhabit.

'But what I don't understand is why he didn't go to a doctor,' Amy remarked, taking her cup and placing it carefully on the locker. 'I mean, surely a doctor would have helped?' Without knowing it, she had touched a raw nerve.

'Humph! You think so? Well, let me tell you, I went to a doctor – behind Levic's back, of course – and I told him what was happening, and do you know what the gentleman said?'

'No.'

'He said the drug was one he often prescribed himself because it was efficacious when used in proper quantities. But if someone had been silly enough to exceed the dose, then there wasn't much he could do beyond suggesting possible programmes of detoxification. But it was his opinion that in the end any cure would depend on simple will-power and that was something only the patient himself could supply.'

'How ridiculous!' Amy expostulated, her cheeks flushing with anger. 'I can't think of anyone with greater will-power than Levic but that's no match for opium once it's got a hold.'

'Exactly.'

'So what are you going to do about it now?'

'I don't know, Amy. I really don't know.'

'Another doctor?'

'I don't think so. Because what I didn't say was that Levic went to another quack without telling me and got exactly the same response. "A self-inflicted ill, Mr Levic," he said, "something you must wean yourself off like a baby leaving the breast."'

'So? That doesn't sound impossible,' Amy urged. 'Especially if other people have tried and succeeded. Anyway, it's worth another try.'

'Shush!' Mirella leapt to her feet, spilling her tea as she did so. 'Here he is. For God's sake, don't let on we've been talking about him.'

'Oh, God!' Levic groaned, letting his head sink forward and shaking it from side to side as if to negate everything in life. 'It wouldn't do any good, Mirella. I've tried. You know how I've tried. But it's too late.'

He sat in a huddle of misery and despair, covering his face with his hands, refusing to meet her eyes. Not self-pitying, though – she must grant him that. Even in his darkest moments he had never sunk into self-pity. Quite the reverse. He was riddled with self-reproach and always proclaiming that his sufferings were no more than he deserved.

Which made Mirella angry. Especially when she remembered the man she had married. Levic, with eyes bright as ebony and full of enthusiasm for life. Not this miserable wreck, wracked by fears and deliriums, waking out of wild dreams to seek comfort like a child.

She felt enraged at such waste.

'Nothing's ever too late,' she declared. 'Even young Amy said that.'

'What the hell's she got to do with it?'

'It was her idea. She thinks you ought to stop everything and get a cure. Put a couple of months aside and . . .'

'You discussed this with her!' Levic stormed. 'After all we said!'

'Levic, Amy was already aware of the situation. And that's the trouble. Things are getting to a point where it's impossible to hide what's happening.'

'But I won't have you talking about me to a young slip of a girl. Why, the next thing you know it will be all round the tober and back at Apsley's. Did you think of that?'

'No, Amy won't say anything.'

'How can you be sure?'

'Because talking to her made me realise what an extraordinary young woman she is. Quite different from how you'd imagine. And, although she's so young, she understands what we're up against.'

'How can she?'

'Because of Matty.'

A name which stopped Levic in his tracks.

'Matty?' he said, blenching.

'Yes. Not laudanum with him, though. Just drink. But with the same devastating effect on those around him, including Amy. It seems there were many times she saw him writhing in the pit when she stayed at his house, but luckily she was also there to see his second wife take him in hand and help him climb out.'

'Yes, but it's easier with drink,' Levic muttered.

'Okay, so it won't be easy, but we can make it work,' Mirella insisted. 'At least we can if you'll give it a really good try.'

'No, it wouldn't work, Mirella. I've told you, it's much too late for that sort of thing,' he moaned, shaking his head again.

But with Amy there to fire her determination, Mirella refused to be put off and together the women planned their campaign.

To start with, there would be no going back to London at the end of the tour. For although there was an empty yard waiting for Minerva's in Tottenham and enough in the kitty to tide them over to spring, it would be putting temptation in Levic's way to have his circus paraphernalia and practice arena so close at hand.

Instead they would rent a house in Sheffield or Leeds – somewhere near a theatre where Mirella and Amy could get work if they wished while Levic enjoyed a complete rest. Then, at the same time as he was resting his body and building up his strength, they would encourage him gradually to cut back on the number of pills he had been taking.

'Look, if it was that simple, don't you think I'd have done it years ago?' he objected when the women announced their plans.

'Yes, but the point is, you've always rushed everything before,' Mirella explained. 'But what you're going to do now is cut back gradually on the pills. Do you hear what I say, Levic? *Gradually!* Everything gradually.'

'Yes, I hear what you say. Gradually,' he repeated, smiling sadly at her as if to humour a child.

Chapter 35

Being brought up at Apsley's Amy was used to being surrounded by a busy theatre company, so it felt strange to be
left on her own with Mirella and Levic. As if her world began
to slither to a halt once fellow artistes dispersed to their
Christmas engagements and the tentmen left for Tottenham
with Minerva's animals and living-carriages.

As it happened, the theatre Mirella had suggested in Sheffield
had just been gutted by fire, so they considered themselves lucky
to secure a joint engagement at the Alhambra in Leeds – Mirella
to walk her tightrope and Amy the globe. And lucky to find a
pleasantly spacious house on the outskirts of the city where they
could set up home for the next couple of months.

Not a happy home, though. For Levic's moods hung over the
place like black stormclouds once he started trying to wean
himself off the drug. And Mirella, despite her apparent com-
mitment to his efforts, at times showed surprisingly little
sympathy. Or perhaps she just lacked patience. Whatever the
reason, Amy found herself increasingly acting as peace-maker
between the couple.

'I knew this would happen, and I tried to tell her. But would she
listen? No. And that's the trouble, she never listens to anything
I say,' Levic thundered, after Mirella rushed from the house in
a fury one afternoon, threatening not to come back.

Looking at his glittering eyes, Amy felt like running away as
well. Except that she felt so sorry for him.

Besides, where could she go? Certainly not back to Apsley's,
for although her grandfather had made it clear she was welcome to return whenever she wished, she could not bear the
thought of going back to resume her role of unwelcome guest at
the feast. Her sister's wedding feast.

Not that she begrudged Rosa her happiness. Nor Steffi his.

She wanted them both to be happy, she really did. It was just that she could not control her feelings when Steffi was near. Could not see him or hear his voice without aching for his touch. And when he touched her – if only to stroke the hair from her face after she fell – then she was filled with unbounded joy and left with unbearable yearning.

So she certainly would not go back to Apsley's, and in the absence of joy would at least try to bring about what healing she could.

She was startled by the sudden thin, creaking sound that passed as Levic's attempt at laughter.

'I'm sorry?' she said, thinking she must have missed the joke.

'It's all right. You wouldn't understand.'

'What?'

He made an impatient gesture.

'Are you in pain, Levic?'

'Yes, it's torture today,' he muttered, screwing up his eyes against the pale light filtering through the blinds. And her heart went out to him. Poor man. Pains in his joints and fiery stomach cramps, ulcers in his mouth and his jaw all swollen – no wonder he was irritable. 'But a couple of drops would fix it. Fetch them for me, will you, Amy?'

'No. I'm sorry Levic. You know you mustn't,' she said, feeling like a criminal for denying such an apparently reasonable request.

'Christ! What do you know about pain?' he exploded. 'It's all very well for you to stand there saying no. But that bitch is cutting it down too fast. I'm used to having three hundred drops and all she's giving me is half. I can't get through on that.'

'Come on, be fair,' she chided him. 'It's not right to blame Mirella when she's only trying to help.'

'Help? She's not trying to help. She just likes to nag and bully people all the time.'

'No, Levic. Mirella's doing her best to help. You must know that really.'

'Then why the bloody hell isn't she here when I need her?' he screeched.

She instinctively backed away from his couch, frightened by his wild, staring eyes and violent reaction – and wishing for a moment she had gone out with Mirella. After all, if Levic became obsessed with the desire for more laudanum, there would be little she could do on her own to restrain him. And if she did not relish the thought of a physical struggle, then she must give in to his wishes or take herself off and leave him to his own devices.

Except that . . . She had a sudden thought: I wonder what Steffi would do if he were here now? Not abandon his father, I'm sure of that.

She recalled his gentle touch on her face and his tender concern. Dear Steffi, he would be so hurt if he saw his father in this state. Which was another reason why she must help Levic over this crisis.

But how?

'Levic, I'm going to fetch our coats so that we can go for a walk,' she announced brightly, as if by walking through the front door he might leave the torment behind.

'No. I'm better off in here by myself. I'm sick of people,' he muttered, 'and the cold air gets on my nerves.'

'Please come. I need a walk but I don't feel safe on my own,' she lied.

He continued to object even after she had fetched his coat, muffler and gloves. Nevertheless he put them on and, still grumbling, followed her out. And she was gratified when, after a further ten minutes or so, he was congratulating her.

'You know, Amy, I didn't want to come, but you were right to force me out because I'm already feeling so much better for the exercise.'

'Good,' she said, smiling with relief.

'And the thing is, I must keep myself in shape if I'm to get back into the ring next season.'

'Of course,' she agreed, wondering if he realised how little chance he had of making such a come-back.

'Which is why,' he continued, 'I make myself walk round and round the garden when you and Mirella aren't there.'

'Yes, I've noticed the circle made by your feet on the lawn – almost exactly forty-two feet in diameter, if I'm not mistaken,' she joked. But she did not let on that she and Mirella had once watched him pace that circle for more than an hour on end, head down and looking like some lost soul from Bedlam.

'Atchoo! Atchoo! A-a-a-tchoo!'

'Oh, dear? Is it a cold?' she asked him.

'No, just another kind of reaction. I'm afraid it often takes me like this in a bout of sneezing,' he said, wiping his eyes which had gone watery.

'So would you rather go home now?' she asked.

'No. I'm enjoying this. Good for morale to have a pretty young woman on my arm,' he said, clearly perking up. 'So let's go as far as the park and back, if you can stand my company that long.'

'Of course I can. I'm enjoying this too,' she said, glad to hear him sounding so cheerful.

'Sorry about leaving you in the lurch like that this afternoon,' Mirella muttered.

'It didn't matter,' Amy said, happy to find Mirella already home when she and Levic returned from their walk.

'You do understand, though, don't you? Why I just had to get away from him for a while?'

'Yes. I know it's a strain, but I'm sure it's worth it. He was quite cheerful while we were out on our walk just now. And if you and I chivvy him along for a bit, I think we'll see a huge improvement.'

'Do you?' Mirella challenged, picking up a breadknife and hacking into the loaf she had bought for supper. 'Well, I wonder.'

'Shush! For goodness' sake don't let Levic hear you say that,' Amy cautioned, glancing towards the door. 'The last thing he needs at the moment is other people's doubts.'

'Yes, well, it's easy for you to say that when you haven't lived with this problem as long as I have. And to tell you the truth, I'm sick of it.'

'Sick of what? Me?' Levic asked, coming into the kitchen.

'No, sick of this damn' weather,' Mirella replied, trying to cover up.

But she wasn't very convincing and in the awkward silence which followed Levic's spirits seemed visibly to droop.

'No, I shan't be coming round to the theatre with you tonight,' he declared after they had all shared a subdued meal.

'Why not?' Amy asked.

'Because you don't need me there.'

'Oh, but we do,' she said, glancing anxiously at Mirella.

'Yes, come on, Levic,' Mirella said briskly. 'You know what we agreed. That you don't stay moping in the house on your own.'

'Shut up, Mirella. I won't have you treating me like a child,' he muttered, looking daggers at her.

'Well, then, don't . . . Okay, I'm sorry. But we did agree . . .'

'I know what we agreed, but I'm sick of going into that theatre like some superannuated artiste whose days are over. I mean, can you imagine how it makes me feel – smelling the greasepaint and hearing the orchestra strike up? Rubs salt into the wound every time.'

Of course, Amy tried pleading with him.

'Oh, please come, Levic. You don't know what a support it is for me and Mirella to see you sitting in the wings. Besides, I want your advice on my second entrance – whether to come in from prompt or my right,' she gabbled.

But either he saw through her ruse or was too entrenched in his attitude to be moved.

'No. I must stay here,' he insisted in a weary voice.

'Well, if you must, you must, I suppose,' Mirella agreed, buttoning up her cloak and rushing to the door at the sound of their cab.

It was with great misgivings that Amy took her leave.

'You're sure you'll be all right, Levic? I mean, one of us could easily stay . . .'

'Bless you, child, but no. You go with Mirella. I'll be fine,' he smiled. But in the yellow lamplight his face was full of shadows.

Mirella smiled to herself, feeling more at home in this second part of her programme when she performed on the horizontal rope. But she must not let herself get too confident, because although she was only six feet off the ground, a slip could still result in injury.

She had acknowledged the cheers of the crowd, taken off her fur-edged cloak and handed it to Amy who deposited it in the wings. Now she stood rubbing her shoes against the rosin pad, and then stroking her left foot along the rope before stepping on to it.

The next part would be straightforward – one step, and then another, and another – keeping her eye on the marker and not wavering too much to left or right until she reached her goal. Which was how she liked things to be. Straightforward. Not complicated and devious, like Levic.

She paused in the middle of the rope and reached to take hold of the hoop that Amy was handing up to her. Swung it aloft, and in time with the music passed it down over her body before stepping out of it and smilingly waving it at the audience.

Why should Levic put her through the hoop like this? Hadn't he already made her suffer enough? And Amy. Why, when she thought how Levic had abused that poor girl's family, she felt incensed to see him imposing on her good nature now. Except that she had to confess to being a broken reed herself these past few weeks when, if truth were told, there had been times when she felt like giving up the struggle to help him.

Hey! Concentrate! Tempo growing faster. She stepped into the hoop again and pulled it up over her body – and again and again, speeding up with the music, skipping through the hoop faster and faster until it spun over her body so fast she lost sense of whether it was she who was spinning or the hoop.

Ah, standing still now. After all the frenzied activity, breathing out slowly and taking stock. Just the backward somersault and headstand and then she would be finished. Another performance over.

And then? She groaned. And then she must change her clothes and go home to Levic.

'Mirella, I've got your outdoor cloak and all our things, so shall we go?'

It was incredible. Here she was, hardly down from her rope before Amy was urging her to leave.

'Not yet. He wants me to take another curtain,' she hissed, smiling at the manager who was gesturing her back.

'Do you have to? I really think we ought to go,' Amy said, clearly agitated.

'All right,' she agreed, noticing how anxiety made the girl's scar stand out in a bright crescent. Yelling back to the manager, 'Sorry, not tonight. I've got to rush,' she quickly changed shoes and threw the cloak over her costume.

'But why the panic, Amy?' she gasped as they flew along the corridor towards the exit.

'I don't know. I just feel we should get home.'

'Because of Levic?'

'Yes. I have this awful feeling he needs us.'

336

Now it was Mirella's turn to feel panic-stricken. And guilt-ridden too, because of those disloyal thoughts she had entertained tonight. Not that she had meant to be disloyal to Levic. She would never be that, because she loved him and had always loved him. Loved him and wanted to be with him, no matter what he had done.

God! She found herself clutching at Amy's hand, so scared all of a sudden.

Chapter 36

Steffi stood next to Arnold in the street outside Apsley's, watching workmen bricking up a small door.

'Bloody officials! If they can't find anything that needs to be done, they go away and invent something.'

'I must say it seems stupid to get rid of that door. What possible harm was it doing?' Steffi asked.

'No harm. But that's the Board of Works for you – ordering works to be done just to justify their own existence.'

'But surely they gave you some reason?'

As Arnold opened his mouth to speak, his breath hung white in the frosty air.

'Reason? That lot don't need reasons. They just send you a lot of twaddle about building regulations, fire precautions, unauthorised entry points and God knows what.'

'I see. Well, it could have been worse.'

'How?'

'They could have told you to brick up the main entrance,' Steffi laughed.

'Shush! Not so loud! I wouldn't put anything past these buggers,' Arnold muttered, turning to go back into Apsley's.

After a last glance at what remained of the door, Steffi followed, his mood gloomy when he recalled the letter he had received that morning from Mirella. His parents, it seemed, had changed their plans and instead of coming back to London this winter had taken a house in Leeds where they would be performing at the local theatre over Christmas. And, what was worse, Amy had decided to stay on with them.

Despondently he made his way up to the tiny room which served as an office and found Arnold puffing on a cigar, waiting to talk business.

'Come along in, my boy. That's right. Shift that rubbish and sit yourself down,' he mumbled from the side of his mouth, gesturing to a chair buried under a heap of posters. 'That's right. Cigar? No, of course you don't. Sensible chap. Filthy bloody habit.'

Steffi moved the paper and perched on the seat.

'Now, what do you think of this one?' Arnold shoved a script across his desk towards him.

'"Harlequin Cinderella And The Little Glass Slipper; or The Kitchen Maid That Became a Princess"', Steffi read aloud. 'Haven't you done this one before?'

'We have,' Arnold said, puffing out his cheeks to exhale a cloud of blue smoke, 'and it went down a treat.'

'Yes, sounds just the thing for Christmas,' Steffi observed. 'With Rosa in the title role, I suppose?' He could just see her sweeping into the ballroom on the arm of the Prince. In her element.

'Yes, probably. But that's not important. Any pretty girl can play Cinderella, but it's Clown who has to carry the piece.'

'Yes, I realise that. So who played it last time?'

'Last year, Chico. But he was hopeless, so I shan't have him again. But do you know who played Clown in our last production of Cinderella?'

'No?'

'Your father,' Arnold said, almost drooling at the memory. 'And believe me, Steffi, he was mag – nificent.'

'Yes,' Steffi sighed, wondering whether he was harbouring some fond notion of calling on Levic again. 'But that was then.'

'Quite. So that's why I want *you* to take it on this time.'

'*Me?*' he squeaked. 'But I'm only a circus clown. I've never done pantomime before.'

'So?'

'So I wouldn't know how.'

'So it'll be a challenge,' Arnold urged. 'Besides, some clowns find pantomime a lot easier than circus because they can use all that stage machinery for comic effects.'

'Ye-es,' Steffi said dubiously, remembering how Levic always stressed that a real clown needed no complicated props. 'But it's the traditional gestures and antics I shall have to work hard at, if I'm to get them right.'

'Good. So you'll do it,' Arnold declared, puffing out another cloud of smoke.

'Yes, I'd like to try,' Steffi agreed with mounting enthusiasm.

So, leaving behind his identity as silly auguste, he found

himself putting on Grimaldi's motley, sticking scarlet patches on his cheeks, assuming an inane grin and standing with his toes turned in. The time-honoured image, but scarcely flattering! And there were times when Steffi looked enviously at the dashing figure cut by Harlequin – especially in the scenes where this egregious young gentleman made off with Rosa in her guise as Columbine.

But it was only a passing feeling. There was no time for him really to worry about such things. He was too busy. They were all too busy. Especially once they were halfway through rehearsals and confronting the usual problem of how to fit a gallon into a pint pot, or a full day's entertainment into four hours – Apsley's being notorious for over-running its programme. In fact, once there had been a riot in the street as ticket-holders clamoured to take their seats for the next showing.

'So what are we going to do?' Arnold demanded, knocking his ash on to the floor.

'Cut back on the "Scenes in the Circus"?' Steffi suggested, but he might as well have saved his breath.

The programme always started with 'Scenes in the Circus'. It was part of the pantomime tradition and therefore sacrosanct. Just as were all the following scenes: 'Great Kitchen of Bombast Castle', 'Grand Ballroom of the Prince's Palace', the interlude featuring Boudicca in 'A Vision of England's Greatness', and the long, concluding 'Harlequinade'.

'Or we could try to shorten the "Harlequinade",' Steffi added, starting to cough.

'No, we can't do that. People will complain if we change anything.'

Again, it was true. Year after year the old series of jokes had to be repeated: Clown had to steal his strings of sausages and legs of mutton, and make a slide out of butter to topple irate shopkeepers and policemen. And against a backdrop of shops there had to be a long chase where babies were kidnapped, and mounds of vegetables thrown, and a red-hot poker applied to any unsuspecting bottom.

'So what do we do?' Steffi said, coughing again as he threw the question back at Arnold.

'Haven't caught a chill, have you?'

'No, just the smoke getting at my throat,' he said hoarsely.

'I see what you mean. Bit of a fug, I'm afraid,' Arnold

muttered, brushing his hand in front of his face to disperse the cigar haze. 'Want to open the window?'

'Yes. I think I'd better.'

It took quite an effort because the sash was so stiff. After wrenching it open, Steffi stood for a few moments drawing fresh air into his lungs. And then, while listening to Arnold's voice running through various other ways they might cut the programme, he continued to stand and stare out of the window down into the stableyard behind the theatre where folk often came for a breather between rehearsals. And where at this moment Rosa was sitting on a bench next to Kenny, who despite the cold day was in shirtsleeves.

'Can't take the dogs out of the procession because the kiddies love them,' Arnold muttered.

'No. Mustn't do that,' Steffi murmured, wondering what Kenny had just said to bring such a coy smile to Rosa's lips and wishing she would look less coquettish. Not that she meant anything by it, he realised that. It was just her natural way. But still, when she lowered her head and peered at someone through her lashes as she was doing now, it could have a devastating effect – as he well knew.

'What about the acrobats then?'

'Eh?'

'Shall we get rid of them?'

'We could,' Steffi replied, hardly aware of what he was saying.

Down in the stableyard Rosa had put up her hand to Kenny's chin, apparently to stroke his bristles.

'What, scrap the whole act?'

'Yes,' Steffi snarled, digging his nails into his palms as he watched Rosa stretching out her hand to rumple up Kenny's shirt and start running her fingers over his bare flesh.

It was only horseplay. Of course he knew that. But not the kind of behaviour one would expect from a young woman of twenty, especially one engaged to be married, he thought primly. And immediately despised himself for being such a prude. After all, Rosa's high spirits were one of her most endearing qualities and he would hate to see them curbed.

Nevertheless, he would still have a word with her. Choosing his time and approaching the matter tactfully, he thought, turning away from the window after he had seen Kenny stand up, tuck his shirt inside his trousers and saunter back to the stables.

'Good. Well, let's hope that solves our problem,' Arnold said. 'Mind you, I don't relish telling the acrobats.'

'Telling them what?' Steffi asked.

He was conscious of a building which was throbbing with activity as he left Arnold and went in search of Rosa. A score of sewing machines clattered away in the wardrobe room, a monstrous pumpkin and masks were being made up by the papier mâché experts and a gilded coach assembled by carpenters and wheelwrights. The air was heavy with the smell of glue, paint and turpentine, and blue with the sound of tempers exploding. Everyone was complaining that there wasn't enough time to do everything and yet everyone knew that somehow everything would get done.

Rosa, when Steffi eventually found her, was seated in a little haven of calm in one of the green rooms buffing her nails.

'You *what*?' she stormed, when he started to mention the little scene with Kenny that he had witnessed earlier. 'You mean to say you were spying on me?'

'Of course not. I just happened to be glancing out of the office window and I couldn't help . . .'

'Hmph! Well, I don't like being spied on,' she pouted. 'And nor was I flirting, if that's what you're thinking.'

'I didn't say you were,' Steffi said – although that sounded a pretty fair description of what he had seen.

'The fact is, I've known Kenny for years.'

'I don't see what difference that makes,' Steffi protested. 'He could still get the wrong idea.'

'You could, you mean.'

'Oh, come on, Rosa. Look, I don't want to quarrel, but I think it's important for you to know how I feel, because we don't want to start off on the wrong foot, do we?'

Having spoken in a tone which he considered altogether reasonable, Steffi was amazed at the outburst which followed.

'*Your* feelings: Why do men always go on about *their* feelings? What about *mine*?' She glared at him, cheeks flaming and her eyes shrinking with fury. 'I mean, why shouldn't I have some fun? I bet you do.'

'Oh, but I wouldn't, Rosa. Not like that.' Suddenly he thought he saw what was troubling her. 'You don't really think I'd let you down, do you? I mean, tell me – is that what this is all about?' It made sense. He had taken advantage of her, persuaded her to yield too soon. And if she was now feeling vulnerable, it was up to him to reassure her. 'Rosa, my love, I've told you I won't let you down. You can rest assured of that.'

She tossed back her hair, chin quivering.

'So why have you gone so cold towards me?'

'But I haven't. Of course I still feel the same about you. I just think we should wait till we're married before . . . well, coming together again.' And surely that was right, he argued with himself, trying to ignore the niggling fact that he had found it surprisingly easy to keep his distance. 'Anyway, I thought that was what we agreed?'

'All right,' she mumbled. 'So long as that's all it is and you're not having a fling somewhere else.'

'Rosa!'

'Okay, Steffi. You needn't sound so shocked. I don't think anyone would be surprised if you turned out to be a chip off the old block where women are concerned.'

'Good lord, what do you mean by that?'

'You know damn' well what I mean. You're like your father in so many other ways – in the ring, for example – it would hardly be surprising if you had his wandering eye for women.'

'But he hasn't! I mean, my father's not like that. Levic's never looked at another woman all the time he's been married.'

At which Rosa started to laugh. First no more than a snigger as she sat shaking her head and making him feel like some kind of idiot. Then lifting up her face and braying like a horse.

'For Christ's sake, stop it, Rosa. And tell me what you mean.'

It seemed to take her several minutes before she managed to control her mirth sufficiently to tell him.

'No.' That's all he could say when he first heard. 'No. I don't believe it, Rosa. Not Levic and your mother.'

But even as he whispered the words, the scene in the hospital all those years ago came back to him. 'My wife is lying there dying and asking for Levic,' Matty had snarled. 'Asking for Levic?' his mother had said. And then there had been those other mysterious words, 'This was Levic's child and it's dead.' Yes. Something like that. Words which made no sense yet continued to haunt him even after Mirella had dismissed them as the ravings of a sick woman.

Those words had been said and he had heard them. And his poor mother had known and had to cope with the knowledge. And Matty had known. And he had told Rosa. So – oh, my God!

344

'And does Amy know as well?'

'Of course.'

'My God.'

Steffi sat covering his face with his hands.

'Come on, Steffi. Don't make such a drama of things,' Rosa said, squeezing his thigh. 'I don't care what your father did. It's all over now. And it's not as if he was really to blame for my mother's death.'

'No. Of course not. Why, did anyone say he was?'

'Yes.'

'Who?'

'Well, my father for one. And you can't really blame him. I mean, imagine how you'd feel if that happened to your wife,' she said. But under her wide-eyed gaze, Steffi found the challenge impossible.

'But what about your grandfather, Rosa? That's something I don't understand. Why didn't Arnold throw Levic out? Why have him back at Apsley's after the accident when it must have been like rubbing salt into the wound every time he saw him?'

'Because Grandad never knew,' Rosa said simply.

'Your father didn't tell him?'

'No. He didn't mean to tell us, either. But it just slipped out one day when Amy and I were staying at his place and, as usual, he'd had too much to drink.'

'What a terrible shock for you both,' Steffi said.

'Oh, I didn't care very much. Like I said, it was all over and done with by that time and I've never seen any point in crying about the past. No, it was Amy who made all the fuss.'

'Amy?' His heart lurched at the thought of how hurt she must have been when she heard such things about her mother.

'Yes. She took Dad's side and blamed Levic for everything. But then, she's always put Ma on a pedestal.'

'Has she?' Steffi asked, surprised.

'Oh, yes. That's why she'll never forgive your father for what he did.'

'And yet she chose to go and work with him and Mirella rather than stay here,' Steffi observed, even more intrigued.

'Yes, I didn't understand why she did that, I must say. But don't let's talk about her any more, Steffi. Let's talk about us,' Rosa pleaded, squeezing his thigh again.

* * *

Tension at Apsley's had reached a peak by the final dress rehearsal on Christmas Day. By starting at six everyone hoped they might be finished at lunch-time and then have the afternoon free. But no such luck. By the end of the morning they had still rehearsed only half the programme and even that was massively over-running.

So, the company was given exactly two hours off to eat their festive dinners and then had to report back on the dot for further rehearsals.

'Phew! There's got to be an easier way to earn a living,' Steffi groaned as he eventually climbed into bed in the not-so-early hours of Boxing Day.

His body ached with tiredness so he expected to fall asleep immediately. Instead he found himself lying wide awake worrying. Was he going to be able to carry off his part in the pantomime when it opened tomorrow? The Press would be there, so if he failed in any way he would not only be letting down Arnold and the company, but the whole world – his parents and Amy – would get to read about it too. And he would hate that.

Then, reminding himself that he always had these fears before a first night, he pushed them to the back of his mind and started to think about something else – the thing that was always there waiting to pounce: his marriage to Rosa.

She had accused him of growing cooler towards her of late and naturally he had rebutted the charge. Moreover since then he had tried to show her more affection, because he *was* fond of her, and in truth would rather die than hurt her feelings. But in his heart he knew that what she said was true: he no longer felt the same about her.

But, hell, he could never tell her so! Not now that they had lain together and he had promised to be true. And how many times had he vowed never to let her down? Then he must keep his word. To do otherwise would be cruel. And too much like his father, he thought bitterly.

So there was no point in thinking about it any more. It was settled. He must not only go through with the marriage, he must make it work – no matter what the cost.

'Well, what does it say about us?' Arnold barked on seeing a new copy of the *Era* in Steffi's hands. 'Go on, read it out.'

Steffi folded the newspaper so that he could focus on the relevant column.

'"Apsley's was literally besieged when we reached it last Thursday. It seemed as if everybody who had seen the show had gone about telling everybody else what a wonderful production it was,"' Steffi read, before pausing to breathe a sigh of relief. The review was obviously favourable.

After that he read the rest, dwelling on the points he thought Arnold would most appreciate.

'"There is little doubt that the secret of the favour which has attended this production lies in the magnificent surroundings which the enormous resources of this unique establishment boasts. What other pantomime could with any hope of success attempt to rival such a spectacle as we get here in the 'Vision of England's Greatness'? In the 'Harlequinade' Levity, in the character of Clown, exhibits extraordinary powers in jumping, and from beginning to end the fun proves fast and furious."'

'Ah, good, good! That's just what I want to hear,' Arnold grunted. 'Is there anything else?'

Steffi read on.

'"During the first performance a sensational report was current as to some alarm caused by an incident involving fire. However, we have it on the best authority that this was the result of a false rumour and at no time were any of Mr Foreman's patrons in the slightest danger. Indeed, the theatre having recently undergone extensive, and one might add expensive, works to render it safe in this respect, its management can boast with confidence that it has now been rendered virtually proof against any such scourge."'

'Bloody fool, fancy putting that in,' Arnold stormed. 'We can do without that sort of publicity.'

'At least they were good enough to point out it was a false alarm,' Steffi observed, scanning the piece again.

'Yeah, but you know what people say – "No smoke without fire!" And in this case there was only a little wire smoking and that was soon dealt with.'

'I shouldn't worry. When you read it through again, Apsley's comes out of it quite well.'

'I still wish they'd never mentioned it.'

Steffi only understood the reason for Arnold's concern a week later when two inspectors arrived at the theatre to carry out further checks in connection with fire hazards.

'My God, I don't believe it!' Arnold spluttered, hammering his fist against the side of his head with rage after they left. 'I took them round, showing them everything they wanted to see, including all the bloody work I had done recently. And when they spotted that little door the other idiots told me to brick up – you're never going to believe this, Steffi – they ordered me to *unblock* it again and fix a bloody spring on the inside!'

Chapter 37

'My God, the place is in darkness,' Mirella muttered as the hansom cab pulled up outside the house.

'Don't worry. I expect Levic's gone to bed. He said he wanted an early night,' Amy said, keeping her tone light to mask her anxiety. For there was something about the dark, silent house that gave substance to her fears.

After throwing the fare at the cabby she ran up to the front door where Mirella stood waiting, key in hand.

'Do you know, Amy – I'm not sure I want to go in.'

'Why not?'

'I don't know. But see how I'm trembling.'

'Here, let me do it then,' Amy said, taking the key from her and fitting it into the lock.

Quite what to expect she had no idea. Except that she knew beyond doubt that something was wrong, something waiting ahead of them in the black silence. Until, as they stepped into the tiled hall, that silence was suddenly pierced by a thin shriek.

'Oh, my God!' Mirella stuttered, grabbing her hand as if clutching at life itself. 'What the hell is it?'

'From the parlour,' Amy whispered.

'But what would make a noise like that?'

'I think it was . . . but maybe not. It didn't sound like a person.'

'No, I'm sure it wasn't.'

They were still whispering, but by this time Amy had her hand on the parlour door and was about to turn it – when the piercing shriek came again. And this time, the sound which sobbed and ebbed away into the darkness was all too recognisably human. As if someone behind that door was in mortal terror.

Amy twisted the handle so that she could rush in. But the

handle would not turn. And as she and Mirella stood helplessly by, the person on the other side started to scream: 'Help! Let me out! Let me out!'

'It's Levic,' they said, turning to look at each other in disbelief.

Amy immediately guessed what had happened. That once she and Mirella had left, Levic had taken – by accident or design – a large enough dose of opium to leave himself stupefied. But how much had he taken? that was the question. And they could not find out until he opened the door.

She tugged again at the handle but it would not budge.

'Why won't it open, Amy?'

'It's jammed.'

'Here. Let me try,' Mirella said, tugging and pulling at the handle in a panic before admitting defeat. 'I can't understand it. Unless . . . Wait a minute. I think I know what's wrong. The idiot's holding on to the handle.'

'Of course.'

'Levic?' Mirella shouted. 'Levic, let go of the handle if you want us to come in.'

There was silence.

'Levic, don't be an idiot. You must let it go on your side otherwise we can't open the door.'

He obviously did not understand because he responded by shaking the handle more violently.

Now Amy tried, taking her time to explain the problem to him. But to no avail. There was no way she could persuade him to release his hold.

'Oh, this is nonsense! What are we going to do? LEVIC – LET GO OF THE HANDLE!' Mirella screamed.

'Wait a minute. I've got an idea. Levic? Levic, there's a key on the dresser,' Amy called. 'Could you fetch it, Levic? Go on. Get the key from the dresser.'

It worked. He must have turned and relaxed his grip, enabling her to twist the handle from her side and easily open the door.

The nightmare, however, was far from over.

On entering the room they found Levic in a dreadful state. Standing cowering by the sofa, shirt hanging loose over his trousers, his face grey and haunted – he looked like someone in a madhouse. And he was shaking from head to foot.

'Oh, Levic, my love, what have you done?'

While Mirella rushed to comfort him, Amy tried to think what to do.

He was almost in a stupor yet she knew it was vital not to let him fall asleep. So she went to the kitchen and, having made strong coffee, laced it with a teaspoonful of sal volatile before taking it back and helping Mirella to force it down his throat.

It helped, but still left him drowsy.

'Let's try lemon juice. That's supposed to be good against laudanum,' Mirella suggested. 'Mix it with plenty of warm water and we'll give him that.'

So they tried that, giving Levic the mixture every fifteen minutes and all the time talking to him and trying to get him to talk back – talking and talking about anything that entered their heads.

'So tell me again, love,' Mirella urged, 'why couldn't you open that door?'

'Don't know,' he muttered, still half-asleep. 'Don't know. She must've shut it.'

'Who? Come on, Levic. Wake up and tell us what you're talking about,' she ordered, stroking his face as he sat slumped on the settee beside her, his eyes glazed.

But then he started to ramble on about incidents apparently related to his past, incidents which – to judge by his shudders and groans – seemed more real to him than the present. And at one point, to Amy's intense distress, broke down and started to sob like a little child.

'What is it, Levic? Come on, please tell me, my love,' Mirella murmured, cradling his head in her hands and smoothing back his dark hair.

'It's the door,' he sobbed. 'I must get it open.'

'But it is open,' she soothed.

'No, no. You don't understand,' he cried. 'The door's locked and can't open.'

Poor Mirella, she was looking at her husband as if he were demented. And no matter what she said, Levic remained inconsolable and must have it that the door was still locked.

'God, I don't know how to deal with this.'

'Why not try playing along with his notions?' Amy whispered. 'Then he might show you what he's got in his mind.'

Mirella looked doubtful but gave it a try.

'All right, Levic, the door *is* locked. But why does it matter? Why do you have to get it open?'

351

'To fetch help,' he replied immediately. 'I must get her some help.'

'Who for? Who must you get help for, Levic?' Mirella persisted.

'My m-m-mammy,' he sobbed, becoming quite frenzied.

'I don't think we should probe any further,' Amy whispered in alarm. 'Let me talk about something ordinary that he won't find upsetting.'

Whereupon, in an attempt to divert his mind back to normality, she launched into a conversation about Steffi – in a quiet voice mentioning how proud he must be to have his son playing Clown in the Apsley's pantomime. And, to her relief, Levic took the bait.

'Mind you, it's a waste of the boy's talents,' he was soon declaring. 'Steffi's too good to be playing pantomime Clown. All those gimmicks and machinery – you don't need a proper clown to get laughs from that stuff, all you need is a mechanic.'

'Good girl,' Mirella muttered to her. 'Once he starts being quarrelsome, I know he's getting back to his old self.' However, just as they thought things were returning to normal, Levic became agitated again.

Mirella had risen to go into the kitchen for some more hot water.

'No! Don't let her close the door!' he screeched in a panic.

'It's all right. Look, we'll place this stool in front of it so it can't slam shut,' Amy said to placate him. Then, when they were all three drinking more coffee to keep themselves awake, Mirella asked, 'Levic, what do you remember about your mother?'

'Why do you ask?' He sounded quite calm now.

'Because a little while back when you were . . .' Amy guessed she was searching for some word other than 'raving' '. . . in a sort of delirium, you kept going on about a locked door and something to do with your mother. And I was wondering, did she ever lock you in on your own or anything?'

'No, of course not. Never,' he declared.

'But something must have happened, Levic. Why else would you be . . .'

'Oh, yes,' he sighed. 'Something happened.'

'So won't you tell us about it?' she coaxed.

'I'd like to. But, to be honest, it was all so long ago I don't think I know any more what was real and what was nightmare. Except . . . except . . .' He broke off, shuddering.

352

'Except what?'

'Except for what I did.' He paused before announcing in a strangely impersonal voice, 'I killed my mother, you know. It was I who was responsible for her death.'

'Oh, Levic, you couldn't have been. You told me you were only four years old when she died.'

Then, in the same emotionless voice, he described what had happened. And Amy listened, horrified, feeling that she should not be there to overhear but afraid of interrupting his flow by leaving. And he spoke so graphically that he made her see the dingy, dark basement room where he had lived as a boy, smell the damp, and hear the moans of his mother lying on her bed. Made her see Levic himself – a thin, little boy playing on the brick floor. And felt his terror as he realised his mother was in danger and needed help.

'It was all my fault, you see,' his voice went on remorselessly. 'That door hadn't been locked until I turned the key, and then I must have panicked and kept on trying to turn it the wrong way, while my mother lay there dying. Can you imagine that? All I had to do was open the door and fetch help. Only I was too stupid and let her die.'

'And have been blaming yourself ever since,' Mirella chided. 'Punishing yourself for something that wasn't your fault, Levic.'

'But it was my fault.'

'No. You were just a child. You did the best you could.'

'But it wasn't good enough.'

'So?'

'So I've never been able to forgive myself.'

'Then let me do it for you,' Mirella said, leaning over to kiss him.

Amy crept out of the room and, now that it was getting light, out of the house and into the garden.

Low in the sky, just clearing the roof-tops, the merest sliver of the old moon glimmered. But no lamps had yet been lit in neighbouring houses. So the world and his wife are still asleep, she thought. And it pleased her to see that, while they slept, a sharp frost was covering the ground with silver.

Towards the end of the morning Mirella woke and, recalling the scenes of the night before, turned towards Levic with dread – only to find him sleeping beside her peacefully as a babe. She gazed as if seeing him for the first time in years.

Though the flesh on his face had fallen away and he was pale, his skin was clear and healthy-looking, his moustache silky and black – in contrast to the silvery waves of hair that swept back from his forehead.

Seeing him sleeping so peacefully, she sighed with a sense of crisis past. Yet she would not make the mistake of leaving him on his own again. If he refused to come to the theatre this evening, then she would send word that she was unwell and hand in her notice so that she could devote all her time to him. Which was what she should have done in the first place, she realised. Amy was right. It had been stupid to leave him on his own.

And what a tower of strength that girl had been last night. Mirella smiled. A tower? Not an appropriate image for a slender, little thing like Amy! Which made it all the more surprising to see her take over – seeming to know exactly what to do when Mirella herself gave way to panic.

'All right, then. I shall quit,' she declared in the face of Levic's resistance to the idea of accompanying her to the theatre that evening.

'But what about Amy? You can't let her down,' he objected, his face full of concern.

'And I don't want to, but I'm putting you first.'

'All right, I'll come,' he agreed, after a brief moment to consider.

He was back on the laudanum, of course, but only the reduced dosage he had been taking before yesterday's wild spree, so his mood was calm and he appeared almost back to his old self.

Stepping out on to her rope over the stage, she caught sight of him sitting in the wings, looking up at her, his eyes once more alive with interest. Just like old times.

It was only after they arrived home and Amy had retired for a much-needed early night that his mood changed again.

He had insisted that Mirella sit in the parlour while he brought them in some cocoa. But there was something so strangely distant about him as he carefully poured the liquid into their cups that she grew disturbed. Surely he had not taken something while he was in the kitchen?

She watched him anxiously. And when he started to pace up and down the room, clearly agitated, her fears were confirmed.

354

But she could not bring herself to challenge him. She was too tired. Too tired, after last night, to care much any more. Especially if his reformation were to last such a brief time. She felt she really could not cope with any further crisis.

'Mirella,' Levic said – making her name sound, as he always did, like a caress.

'What is it, Levic? Won't you sit down and take it easy?'

'No. I don't want to sit down at the moment.'

He continued pacing up and down, until suddenly coming to a halt with his arm resting against the mantelpiece.

'It's no good, Mirella. I don't want to go on like this.'

Almost too tired to respond, she summoned up the last of her energy to say, 'Stop thinking like that, Levic. You mustn't think of giving up, not now you've come this far.'

'No, Mirella. When I say I don't want to go on, I mean I can't carry on living this lie. Especially after watching you tonight.'

Now she was totally confused.

'Why? What was I doing?'

'What you always do – walking your own straight line,' he replied, meeting her gaze. 'I watched you and it made me want to weep, the way you moved along that straight path. You always do, you know. I've never known you waver.'

'Well, a wavering tightrope walker doesn't get far,' she smiled, at a loss to see where his remarks were leading.

'Don't make a joke of what I'm saying.'

'I'm sorry, Levic, but I'm very tired.'

'Look, what I'm trying to say . . . to tell you . . . Oh, it's no use. I can't say it.'

'What?' she yawned.

'Mirella, I don't want to hurt you, but I've got to get this off my chest.'

'What?' she asked. 'Something else you've remembered about your mother?'

'Not my mother. Someone else.'

'Someone else?'

'Dorina,' he said simply.

She braced herself for what she now guessed was coming. And to think there had been all those years when she had longed for him to clear the air and re-establish the old trust between them. Yet now, when he was about to tell her, she did not want to hear. Did not want to listen to him talk about his love for Dorina.

'You don't have to say anything,' she muttered.

'No, I have to say everything,' he said. 'I've lived with the lies too long. The fact is, the child Dorina was carrying when she died was . . . mine.'

She knew. Of course she knew. But she could not bring herself to admit knowing. Too tired to react in any way, she sat mute.

'I realise it's no good saying I'm sorry. But by God I've paid for what happened, believe me. No, Mirella, let me finish! I don't expect you to forgive me, but I want you to know this: I never meant to hurt you. You believe that, don't you?'

She mustered just sufficient voice to whisper: 'Tell me, Levic, did you love her very much?'

He seemed to choose his words carefully. 'I loved her as a friend, but our friendship got stupidly mixed up with something else.'

'For how long?' she asked.

'What?'

'How long did it last, this friendship which got mixed up with something else?' she repeated, unable to keep the bitterness out of her voice. She was shivering and the room had turned suddenly very cold.

'Mirella, I don't think you understand. Dorina and I were never really in love with each other. We just gave way to temptation, that's all. And that only once.'

'Just once?'

He must have read the incredulity on her face.

'Why are you looking at me like that? My God, Mirella, you must believe me. I only betrayed you once.'

'All right. I believe you, but I wish you'd told me sooner,' she said.

'I know, and I'm not offering excuses. But I promise things will be different from now on. No more lies or subterfuge – not even with the drug. Everything in the open from now on. A fresh start.'

She felt emptiness. Or perhaps lightness. She wasn't sure which. Like dancing along a rope which stretched in the sky among stars that danced with her.

'Mirella, are you all right? Shall I take you to bed?'

'Oh, yes, Levic. To bed. Together. And don't worry. I feel fine,' she smiled.

Chapter 38

Amy took up her pen reluctantly. She had not written to Steffi for years and was only doing so now at Mirella's request.

'I think he'd want to know what's happening, don't you?'

'Yes,' Amy had agreed.

'But you see why I can't tell him. I promised Levic never to breathe a word.'

'I see.'

'But luckily *you* haven't made any promise,' Mirella observed.

'No, but I don't like the thought of interfering,' Amy protested.

'Oh, but you wouldn't be. All you need do is give a hint, and if I know my Steffi, he'll be up here like a shot to see what's wrong.'

'Yes, I think you're right,' Amy said, heart beginning to pound.

And that was the trouble. How could she in all conscience write anything designed to bring Steffi up to Leeds? She might tell herself it was just to please his mother, but she would know what her real motives were. She wanted to see him herself. And to drag him away from Rosa, if only for one day. For presumably he would not be able to spare more until the pantomime season finished.

'Dear Steffi,' she wrote. Not 'Dearest' nor 'Darling' nor 'My beloved'. Then stopped and chewed her pen. No, it was impossible. There was no way she could write without giving herself away. No way she could hint that he should come to see his parents without her own plea being heard through the words. And how, having left London to get away from him, could she bear to be here when he arrived? See him again without throwing herself into his arms?

She put down the pen. It was no good. She could not do it. So if Mirella wanted Steffi to come and see his father, she would have to write to him herself.

After all, it wasn't as if there was the same urgency any more. For although Levic still had good days and bad days, his condition had steadily improved since that dreadful crisis before Christmas and the future was looking far brighter. In fact, the only real problem she and Mirella had now was how to restrain him from being too ambitious. For it was clear that he would never be able to give up the drug entirely, but must concentrate on reducing the dose in small, steady steps until able to manage on something like twenty-five drops taken on alternate days.

And since it was only to be expected that his temper would be, to say the least, uneven during such a period of adjustment, Amy and Mirella had worked out strategies to help him – and themselves – cope: Mirella always prepared to read to Levic at night when he could not sleep, and Amy to accompany him on walks when he was restless during the day.

And when, on one of their walks one bright Sunday morning, he announced, 'Do you know, my dear, I've just had a wonderful idea,' and began to enthuse about some new routine for Minerva's, it seemed clear to Amy that he was well on the road to recovery.

'Hello, who's that, I wonder?' he said, interrupting his own flow and gesturing towards the house with his stick. 'Not expecting a visitor, are we?'

A hansom was just pulling away from the door having deposited a smartly-dressed stranger – a slim young gentleman in a glossy top hat and double-breasted overcoat.

'Oh, no,' Amy gasped.

'You know him?' Levic asked, looking at her puzzled.

'Yes, of course. It's Steffi,' she said, instinctively glancing around for means of escape. Steffi arriving here out of the blue – why hadn't she prepared herself for this possibility?

'My Steffi?' Levic was repeating, his eyes brightening. 'But that's marvellous! His mother will be so pleased!' And dragging her along with him, he raced to greet his son.

'My God, Steffi! I didn't recognise you,' he exclaimed, throwing his arms around him and clapping him on the back.

'Hello, Pa. Thought I'd give you a surprise,' he said brightly enough. But Amy had seen the look of pain that flashed across Steffi's face as he took stock of his father. 'Yes, that's right. Just

358

up here for the day. But got to be back tomorrow in time for the show.'

Amy's heart dropped. Only a few hours then.

'Amy?' His voice stopped her in her tracks as she turned to go into the house. 'Aren't you going to say hello?'

'Of course. Hello, Steffi,' she murmured, glancing into his face and then down to the ground. A very quick glance, but enough to show her he was looking well – a little strained after the journey, perhaps, but clear-eyed and well. And his smile as lovable as ever. But at the sight of that smile, she found herself wishing he hadn't come – and wishing even more that he didn't have to go away again. 'You'll excuse me, won't you? I'd better go and warn Mirella you're here,' she said, diving into the house.

After that she busied herself in the kitchen, preparing food and keeping out of the way. Which was obviously the best thing to do.

'No Rosa with you?' Amy had heard his mother say as they entered the parlour.

'No. I wanted her to come, but she doesn't like train journeys.'
'I see.'

'Anyway, she had a dress-fitting today.'

'Dress-fitting? Oh, for her wedding dress, I suppose?'

'That's right.'

'Not long now,' Mirella was crooning as Amy shut the door so that she could not hear any more.

There was no way of avoiding Steffi at lunch but, once that was over, Amy made a headache the excuse to retire to her room and leave the family to talk among themselves. It was almost dark before someone tapped on her door.

'Who is it?' she called, starting up from the armchair, where she had been sitting staring out over the back lawn.

'Me. Steffi. Are you all right?'

'Of course.'

'Then can I come in for a minute? There's something I want to ask you.'

'Okay, but I was just coming down actually,' she lied.

'Amy, I was hoping for a chance to speak to you on your own,' he said, sitting down on the trunk under the window facing her, so that there was no way of avoiding his scrutiny.

'Why?' she asked, gazing down intently at the plum-coloured

plush on her chair-arm and stroking it first one way and then another.

'I want to thank you.'

'Whatever for?'

'I think you know. Ma wrote and told me how marvellous you've been, helping Pa over this crisis.'

'That was nothing.'

'She said there've been times she couldn't have managed without you. But why didn't you write and tell me things were so bad, Amy?'

'How could I? Your father would have gone up in the air. He was so difficult then. Not at all like he is now. Anyway, there was nothing you could do.'

'No, probably not. I've never been much help to him, I suppose. But then . . .' Steffi stopped short. 'And how about you, Amy? You must have found it a terrible strain.'

She nodded, while thinking that nothing during the last few weeks had been such a strain as sitting here now, so close to Steffi.

Then he leant over and put his hand on hers.

'Don't,' he said.

'What?'

'Pull out all that velvet.'

'Oh dear!' Her agitation increased at his touch. 'I didn't realise what I was doing.'

'It's all right,' he soothed. 'Thanks to you the worst is over now.'

It was no good. She couldn't stand it any longer. She tugged her hand away from his.

'What is it, Amy? What have I done?' Steffi cried. 'I know it should have been me who bore the brunt of all this, but I didn't know. Honestly, I had no idea things were so bad.'

'Oh, it's not that.'

'What is it, then? I know I must have done something to upset you. You've hardly looked at me since I arrived. And part of my reason for coming was to see you,' he added.

'Why?' When he didn't answer, she looked up and found herself gazing into eyes that seemed to be pleading with her. 'Why?' she asked again.

'I don't know. I just needed to see you, Amy. I want to know why you left Apsley's so suddenly,' he said rather lamely.

'But you know why. I wanted to join Minerva's. Strike out on my own for a change.'

'But that can't have been the only reason,' he said, his eyes still pleading.

'Well, it was. And stop looking at me like that, will you? What do you want me to say, Steffi?' she demanded, lowering her head so that he could not see her face.

'Rosa seemed to think it might be something to do with our getting married,' he said hesitantly.

'But that's ridiculous. What the hell's your marriage got to do with me?' she retorted.

'Well, nothing. But I realise you and Rosa have always been close and . . . No, that's not what I wanted to say. Oh, Amy, look at me. You remember that time when you fell?'

'In the middle of "Mazeppa"?'

'That's right. And I thought you were badly hurt.'

'Yes.' She tried to look away but found her attention held by his gaze.

'Amy, I don't know how to say this, but since then I haven't been able to get you out of my mind,' he said slowly. 'Even though, God knows, it's the last thing I wanted to happen.'

She didn't know whether she understood him properly or not, but her heart was pounding painfully.

'Don't, Steffi. Don't say any more,' she begged.

'But I have to, Amy. Don't you understand? I've got to be sure. For everyone's sake.'

'Sure of what?' she cried, springing out of her chair to bring the conversation to an end.

Almost in the same moment it seemed, Steffi had risen too, and seized her in his arms.

'No, Steffi. We mustn't,' she started to say – until the first touch of his lips melted all her resistance. Then they stood in the darkness, holding each other so close it was impossible to imagine how anything could come between them.

But he's going to marry Rosa, Amy told herself sternly that night as she lay in bed trying not to think of Steffi lying just the other side of the wall. Trying not to remember the soft warmth of his lips, nor to imagine how it might feel to be loved by him. It's all arranged. And he's very fond of Rosa. He told me so himself.

361

Put like that, what she was thinking was shameful.

But then this evening he seemed to be saying he was in love with me, she reminded herself. And for a moment bathed in the glow of that possibility.

But he can't be in love with us both, can he? The glow was immediately extinguished.

So, thinking about it rationally, is it likely that he could prefer me to Rosa? She conjured up a picture of Rosa – with her fair hair and pretty face – and compared it with an image of herself – sandy hair and that awful scar that had marked her out since childhood. How could anyone be seriously attracted by that?

So what had Steffi meant by his behaviour? Knowing him, he had been swamped by his finer feelings and then swept away by pity for her. And if that was so, then it was up to her to throw him some sort of life-raft.

So, tomorrow morning that's what I'll do, she vowed, praying for strength to carry it through.

Knowing that Steffi had to catch the early train, her normal instincts bade her rush downstairs to prepare breakfast as soon as she heard him stir. This morning she resisted any such temptation. And instead, having washed and dressed, sat in her armchair and listened to the sounds of his imminent departure.

A door slammed. She heard feet clattering on the stairs. Someone riddling the boiler. Soon Mirella's voice urging Steffi to hurry down if he wanted time to eat. Levic calling that he was strolling up to the cab-rank at the end of the road. The front door being unlocked and opened.

And she could almost hear her own name being whispered. No Amy yet? Where's Amy this morning then? I'd have thought she'd be up to say goodbye. Perhaps I'll go and tell her I'm off.

His footsteps on the stairs as he mounted towards her. Her heart beginning to pound. But she was ready. This time she was ready. And waiting for the tap on her door.

'Hello, Amy. Just come to say goodbye, I'm afraid,' he murmured as she opened it.

'Oh, it's you, Steffi. Well, goodbye,' she said abruptly, refusing to meet his gaze.

'Amy, I wish I didn't have to go. I don't want to leave you. But I'll write as soon as I get back to London, I promise.'

'Don't bother,' she snapped.

'Amy, what's wrong? Of course I'll write,' he started to protest.

'But I don't want to hear from you.'

She sensed a smile had disappeared from his face.

'Why not? What's wrong, Amy? Why are you acting so strangely this morning?'

'Strangely?'

'Yes, treating me like a stranger.' He put out his hand to touch her arm, but she backed away.

'Don't! I don't like you touching me.'

'You don't? But, Amy, you know how I feel about you. And I thought . . .' He hesitated. 'I'm sure you feel the same about me.'

'Well, you're mistaken, Steffi,' she said coldly. 'I don't feel anything towards you. I don't even particularly like you and never have done.'

'But yesterday when I held you in my arms and we kissed and you said you loved me . . .'

'Oh, that,' she said in an offhand way. 'I thought you realised! That was only playing.'

'No,' he whispered, 'I can't believe that.'

'Well, it was,' she declared. 'Just playing.'

'But why, Amy?'

'Just to see how far you'd go, I suppose.'

'No. I don't believe that,' he said faintly.

'Well, it's true. I wondered if you were the same as all the rest and you showed you are. Exactly the same.'

'The same as my father, you mean,' he muttered.

'If you like,' she said, scarcely aware what she was saying, only longing to bring the interview to an end. 'Anyway, I suggest you go back to Rosa now. And don't worry. I shan't say a word about this.'

'But, Amy, I can't go back to Rosa after what happened between us. You may have been playing. I certainly wasn't.'

'Oh, for goodness' sake, stop it, Steffi! Nothing happened between us. And I don't want you making trouble between me and my sister by suggesting otherwise, do you understand?'

At which point Mirella's voice came echoing up the stairs to announce that Levic had a cab at the door waiting to take Steffi to the railway station.

'But, Amy, I love you,' he whispered, trying again to put his arm round her.

'No, Steffi. Leave me alone,' she snapped, breaking free. 'I've told you what the situation is, and you've no right . . .'

'I'm sorry. But surely you . . .'

'Steffi! You'll miss that train!' Mirella called.

Amy glanced at him then. And, for a moment, seeing such pain and confusion in his eyes, she faltered in her resolve.

But before she could say anything, Steffi had turned and, with bowed head, was walking away.

And she was left to shut her door and fling herself on her bed to sob her heart out.

Chapter 39

Steffi was expecting his first visitors. Apart from Rosa, that is. And she had so far come only once to see him in his new lodgings.

'I just don't see why you had to move out of Apsley's,' she complained, wrinkling her nose when he welcomed her into the admittedly shabby room. 'Surely it doesn't make sense to give up free board and lodging in order to move round the corner and pay good money for this?' She waved her still-gloved hand to indicate the dingy furnishings.

'I told you, I wanted to be more independent,' he declared, lighting his little paraffin stove so that he could boil the kettle.

'But you only had to say, and Grandad would have given you all the independence you wanted at Apsley's.'

He sighed. It was no good. She would never understand how he had felt when he came back from Leeds – so confused and in need of time and space to work things out. Neither of which was in plentiful supply at Apsley's.

'And I hope you'd never expect me to live in a place like this, because I couldn't, Steffi.'

'No. I wouldn't expect you to live anywhere you didn't want to,' he said.

'That's all right, then. Because Grandad expects us to take over Apsley's once we're married and I for one would hate to disappoint him. It's been understood that the place would be mine since Ma died.'

Steffi flinched. He still felt a raw nerve where Dorina was concerned, especially in the light of Amy's remarks. Just like his father in his treatment of women – that's what she had said. And in some ways it was true. He had mistreated Rosa. Declared undying love for her one moment and then grown cool the next. Lulling the poor girl into a false sense of security and then betraying her.

Except that he had not betrayed Rosa. Not really. And after Amy's little homily he would make sure he did not. After all, Rosa had not changed and it was not her fault if his own passions had proved fickle, he reminded himself for the hundredth time.

As soon as he heard the knock on the street door he rushed down to greet them – Levic who, though as thin as ever and leaning heavily on his stick, smiled cheerfully enough, and Mirella in a cherry-coloured bonnet and clutching a hamper of food.

'No Amy?' he queried, peering over their shoulders.

'No. Just us,' Mirella said.

'But she did come back from Leeds?' he said as he showed them up the stairs and into his room.

'Oh, yes. She came back to Tottenham with us, but went off to see her grandfather this afternoon.'

'At Apsley's?' Steffi asked, hoping that meant he would see her at the theatre later.

'That's right,' Levic replied. 'Hugo offered to drive her over there to pick up some tackle Arnold's letting her have.'

'I see,' Steffi said, feeling a stab of jealousy at the thought of Hugo and Amy driving anywhere together. 'And how's Minerva's new programme coming on?'

'Really well,' Levic enthused. 'Most of the company are back and the way things are going I reckon we'll have the best show that's ever opened on the Heath at Easter.'

Mirella, sitting next to the fire fixing a muffin on to a toasting fork, raised her eyes towards heaven in a gesture of despair. From which Steffi deduced that she was still afraid that Levic would overtax his strength and set himself back to square one.

'So what time do we have to leave, Steffi?' she asked.

'Well, I shall have to go at about six, but you can both stay as long as you like,' he grinned. 'Unless you fancy seeing the pantomime round the corner. I've heard it's rather good.'

'A panto? No, I don't fancy all that Cinderella nonsense. Give me a good circus any day!' Levic chaffed.

'Well, it has circus scenes as well. And even if it's not up to Minerva's standard, at least the horses are good,' Steffi said, sucking the butter off his fingers after dropping a muffin on to his father's plate.

'Never mind the horses, what about the Clown? Is he any good?' Levic demanded.

'Oh, yes. He's excellent this year,' Steffi said modestly.

'Well, in that case I shall take my notebook and write down his name for future reference. Minerva's is always on the lookout for talent.'

'Ah, but better not get too keen,' Steffi said with a sense of regret.

'Why not?'

'Because I'm afraid Arnold Foreman has him under a long contract.'

'Here we are. Come along in.' Arnold smiled, ushering Levic and Mirella into his living-room after the show. 'And you, Steffi. Well, this is nice. Quite like old times, eh?'

'Yes,' Levic agreed, lowering himself into a chair, 'and I must congratulate you on the show, Arnold. Certainly up to Apsley's standard.'

'Yep, not bad – though I say it myself. Here, take this,' he said, tossing Levic a cushion. 'Back still giving you gyp, I see. Bloody shame,' he added, shaking his head in commiseration. 'Slows you down, I bet.'

'Not so's you'd notice,' Mirella broke in, knowing how Levic hated attention being drawn to his infirmity.

'So what will you have to drink – a drop of port wine, Mirella? After all, we've something to celebrate, eh?' Arnold said, eyes sparkling. 'Speaking of which, does Rosa know your parents are here, Steffi?'

'Yes, she spoke to them in the interval.'

'So where is she now? And where's Amy? I've hardly clapped eyes on her since she came in with that blond chap this afternoon.'

'I don't know,' Steffi said, trying not to sound too tight-lipped.

'I bet I do,' Mirella chuckled. 'If Rosa and Amy are anything like me and my sister, they'll have tucked themselves away in a corner to have a good old gossip.'

'Well, if that's the case, go and dig them out, will you, Steffi? There'll be plenty of time for that sort of thing later.'

He was glad to comply with Arnold's request, for so far this evening he had caught no more than a glimpse of Amy as she sat with Hugo in the prompt box to watch the show. And he did

367

not want her to slip off to Tottenham before they at least had chance to say hello.

Remembering what Levic had said about Amy and Hugo coming to pick up some riding tackle, he made his way to the stables to see if they were there. But the place seemed deserted, a lamp in the courtyard casting a yellow pool of light in front of the dark entrances to the stalls where the horses were beginning to settle for the night. For a moment he stood listening to their fidgeting, sniffing in the warm scents of bran and horse-sweat, before turning to go back into the theatre.

Then something else caught his attention – a sound of scuffling and voices whispering up in the hayloft.

A couple of the stable lads messing about? Well, he hoped they had not chosen such a place to have a quiet smoke after all this recent fuss about fire hazard. Perhaps he ought to have a word, Steffi thought. And was about to call out when he heard someone giggle.

A girl up there then. With one of the stable lads? Steffi smiled – a smile that died on his lips when it occurred to him that perhaps she wasn't with one of the stable lads. Perhaps she was with Hugo.

He felt sick at the thought.

What was it Amy had said? 'I was only playing. Just wanting to see how far you'd go. To know if you were like all the rest.'

He shut his eyes. But not with Hugo, Amy. Anyone getting involved with Hugo would soon find themselves playing with fire. Everyone knew that.

And Steffi's thoughts turned murderous as he pictured Amy with the man who, besides being old enough to be her father, made lewd remarks about every girl he passed in the street.

Not that Amy would realise, of course. She would not see that side of him, only the suave ringmaster who presided over Minerva's. That's what Hugo would trade on – if someone didn't stop him.

'Hugo!' he shouted. 'Come down here a minute.'

A silence fell over the stableyard as even the horses responded to the urgency in his voice.

'Hugo! I want a word with you.'

The silence grew heavier.

'Look, you might as well come down, because if you don't I'll be up there to fetch you.'

That had some effect. The whispering started up again and

there was some panicky shuffling overhead before a pair of boots made their appearance on the steps followed by brown corduroyed legs and the rest of a man's body crowned by – not a fair, but a ginger thatch of hair.

'Kenny!' Steffi exclaimed as the other turned on him a sheepish grin. 'I'm sorry, I thought you were Hugo.'

'Naw. He's gone. They loaded up the cart and left as soon as the show finished.'

'They?'

'Yeah. Him and Amy.'

'I see.' He felt foolish. Of course it wouldn't be Hugo and Amy. If only he had stopped to think before letting his imagination run riot, he would have guessed it was someone who worked here. 'Okay. Sorry I disturbed you,' he muttered, feeling embarrassed and beginning to move away.

Then Etty made a whinnying noise so he stopped to give the beast a reassuring pat and it was only when he finally turned to leave the stableyard that the other occupant of the hayloft started her descent.

'Has he gone?' he heard her whisper. 'Golly, that was a close shave!'

Then, as her slippered foot touched the ground, she turned towards Steffi and he found himself looking straight into her eyes.

He had a fleeting impression of the girl he had lain with in the haystack last summer – the grey eyes and flaxen hair and pretty dimpled face. But this Rosa was like a parody of that former self. With straw in her hair and traces of stage make-up still plastered on her face – blurry blue around her eyes and a smudge of rouge on each cheek.

'Steffi!' she gasped. 'It's all right, honestly. We haven't been . . .'

But there was nothing he could say as he stood there watching her button up her blouse. There was nothing to say. It was all over.

'Please don't be angry, Steffi,' Rosa said.

And he wasn't. That was the strange thing. He did not feel in the least bit angry. Only relieved.

There was so much to do before Minerva's new season opened on Hampstead Heath that neither Amy nor Mirella had time to visit Apsley's. But Levic and Hugo had to drive over to the theatre on business several times.

'Did you see Steffi?' Mirella asked when Levic returned from the first trip.

'Yes. He was there,' Levic said, grinning with pleasure. 'Helped us load those benches into the cart.'

'And is he well? I hoped he might be over to see us soon,' Mirella sighed.

'He's fine, but very busy at the moment otherwise I'm sure he'd be over.'

'And Rosa, is she all right?'

'As far as I know.'

'And Arnold?' Mirella persisted.

'Ah, there I'm not so sure?'

'Why, is Grandad ill?' Amy butted in, feeling guilty about not making more effort to visit him.

'No, no. Nothing like that. Just having to deal with some problem or other connected with the theatre,' Levic said vaguely.

As Easter approached, the last members of Minerva's company came straggling into the yard in Tottenham which was already humming and clanging with activity. There was too little space for them to erect the main tent, so rehearsals took place in a makeshift ring set up in a nearby warehouse. And it was here that Amy was standing with Mirella watching the new troupe of jugglers when Levic hobbled in – and collapsed right in front of them!

'It's all right. It's all right. Don't make a fuss,' he hissed as they rushed to help him up. 'It's nothing serious. Only a cramp.'

But for days now Amy had seen him hobbling about on his stick and suddenly putting his hand to his hip, and she knew it was more than that. The trouble was, he would insist on trying to limber up so that he could do his old routine – flip-flaps and throwing himself into a series of backward somersaults. The sort of thing which, if persisted in, would leave him crippled.

'Mirella,' she whispered, 'don't you think he ought to give himself a rest?'

'Of course I do. But you try telling him and see if he takes any notice.'

'All right,' she said, going first to fetch a chair.

'Thanks,' he muttered, easing himself on to it. But he quickly brushed aside her concern. 'Don't worry, I was only trying one or two tricks. Mustn't let myself stiffen up completely, you know.'

'But if you're like this now,' Amy started to protest, 'think what you'll be like a week or two into the tour.'

'Ah, but I'm only like this because I'm out of condition,' he muttered. 'I'll be better once I've limbered up.'

Nothing she said could make him see the folly of what he was doing. And when Mirella added her voice to the argument, he showed disturbing signs of his old irritability.

'Look, I know how you feel,' he declared, grabbing her arm and staring up into her face. 'You've told me clearly enough.'

'I just don't want you to cripple yourself,' Mirella said.

'Don't! Don't go through it all again, either of you. I know what I'm doing. Okay?'

'Okay,' Mirella shrugged.

After which there seemed nothing more Amy could do.

Yet it grieved her to see Levic changing before her eyes. The calm philosophical man of these past few weeks effervescing into the possessed artiste as soon as he picked up the smell of horses and sawdust and the blare of brazen music from the band. It occurred to her that his son was probably the only person who had the power to make Levic see sense. But she failed to warn Steffi because she dared not let herself get involved with him again.

371

Chapter 40

Amy was sitting on the wagon steps watching a dozen shadowy figures circle round throwing down poles, hammering in stakes and hauling on ropes. She was waiting for the magical moment when the king-pole would rise for the first time that year.

'Here he comes!' she breathed, feeling as if she were welcoming the return of spring. A feeling which grew stronger as each bulky grey cocoon was dragged on to the tober to lie in the damp grass until, with the sun climbing the sky, the canvas was ready to be shaken out and stretched like the wings of some bright butterfly.

'We're lucky with the weather,' Mirella observed. 'I was dreading a wet build-up.'

'Well, let's hope it lasts till lunchtime. There's nothing like a sunshine parade to bring the people in.'

Amy tried to sound cheerful, because she knew Mirella was still fretting about Levic. And, looking at him now, she could not blame her. After being up nearly all night solving last-minute hitches, he had driven their wagon over to Hampstead and been rushing around ever since, hardly allowing himself time to swallow breakfast. And it was no good for anyone to remind him that, with a street parade after lunch and two performances this evening, it was going to be a very long day. He knew all that, and he did not care. Nor did he seem to care about the pains in his joints which, to judge from his awkward movements and sudden grimaces, had certainly not gone away.

Poor Mirella, she must know more than anyone what this effort was costing Levic. And she – like Amy – had to stand by and watch him pit himself against the odds and simply pray that he would not resort to the old drug when he found he could not cope.

* * *

'Ladies and gentlemen, boys and girls ... it is now my ... very great pleasure ... to introduce ... the internationally ... renowned ... clown of our show ... the one and only ... inimitable ... Levic!' came Hugo's familiar announcement. But as Levic made his entrance, the thunderous applause which greeted him sounded to Amy like a challenge to mortal combat.

From behind a curtain she watched him carefully. Whilst it was noticeable that he did not throw himself around with quite the old abandon, at the end of the humpsti-bumpsti he hobbled from the ring with such a stupefied smile on his face that her fears about the drug returned with a vengeance.

She looked to see if her fears were shared by Mirella, who was standing in her fur-lined cloak waiting to go on next. But Mirella, wreathed in her performer's smile, had already risen above such mundane problems. So, deciding there was nothing she could do, Amy gave herself up to watching her.

When the music changed, Mirella skipped into the ring, cast her cloak into the arms of an attendant and started to climb. Up and up. Pausing now to wave and then climbing again until she reached her high wire and perched there like a dove. Forty feet above the ground now and dancing along that thin wire, stopping to kneel on it and swing on it and even stand on her head. And all the while making it seem as easy as playing in the park.

Amy was held so spellbound that she forgot everything else until, while the audience was still applauding what the ringmaster described as this death-defying act, she saw Levic come bounding in. This time his movements were so spry that she felt sure he had doped himself. For there was no other way he could sustain such a dynamic performance – a flip-flap, cartwheel, flip-flap, and then silently standing in the centre of the ring and staring at the audience in a way that made them howl with delight.

He was back on form all right, but at a cost she could not bear to calculate.

Now the audience was screaming out loud in their efforts to warn him of the whereabouts of an invisible mosquito which he was twisting himself into a corkscrew trying to catch.

Would they laugh, she wondered, if they knew what agony those movements were causing? And yet, as she watched, his mimicry was so good, she found herself chuckling despite

374

herself. She had seen him do this routine many times before, but never so well as this. Rarely had she known the crowd so happy. Why, it was almost worth . . .

Except that nothing was worth what Levic had gone through last winter and would doubtless go through again if he persisted in this madness. Nothing was worth that sort of hell.

'Bravo! Bravo!' Even the tentmen standing next to the ring entrance were cheering.

At last he had finished and was somersaulting round the ring before bounding out. No, he wasn't. The crowd had called him back and were refusing to let him go. My God! he must be so exhausted, Amy thought, turning her back on the ring to make sure there was a chair near the exit in case he collapsed again.

'Bravo! Bravo!' shouted a man next to Mirella in tones that were ecstatic. A man who looked just like Levic.

My God! Now Amy felt she was going mad. That man! He not only looked like Levic, it surely *was* Levic! Levic standing there cheering and clapping the clown in the ring who was – she spun round to look back – who was . . . also Levic!

But that was not possible. So if the clown in the ring was not Levic, then who was it under the greasepaint?

It did not take her long to guess. But how he had managed to get away from Apsley's on the day that Arnold was due to open with his new production she could not imagine. Especially as he was supposed to be playing the lead.

'Do you see who it is? Steffi!' Mirella beamed, coming up to her with the news.

'Yes. I realised that. But how? Surely he hasn't walked out on Grandad. Oh, he couldn't, could he? Not at the last minute?'

'You know Steffi. He wouldn't leave anyone in the lurch,' Mirella smiled. 'But I've no idea what's happened. All I know is that when Levic talked to him a few weeks ago Steffi said that, much as he'd like to come back to Minerva's, he'd committed himself to Apsley's for the season and couldn't see any honourable way out of his contract.'

'So what's changed? Has Grandad put back the opening a day or two, I wonder,' Amy said, her heart a battlefield of emotions.

'I've no idea. But here's Steffi so you can ask him yourself.'

Amy hardly noticed his motley – the sea-green satin costume and ridiculous wig and bizarre red mouth – because in this moment she was not interested in that image of a clown he had painted on his face. She did not care whether he was in the guise

375

of Levic or Levity, she was seeing only Steffi. Her Steffi. Coming smiling towards her.

'Amy, I know this isn't the right time, but we've got to talk,' he gasped, still panting to catch his breath after his antics in the ring.

'Why? Is there something wrong, Steffi?' she cried.

'Not as far as I'm concerned. For me everything's come right. At least, nearly everything. And I'm working on the rest,' he murmured, blue eyes beginning to sparkle.

'So why are you here and not at the theatre?'

'Because Arnold has just been ordered to close the place down,' he said baldly.

'Apsley's? But why?'

'Because of fire risk.'

'But the authorities have been on about that for years.'

'Exactly. And up till now Arnold's always managed to fob them off with piecemeal alterations. But yesterday they turned the heat on by confronting him with a list of requirements that would mean practically rebuilding the place.'

'Oh, no!' she groaned. 'Poor Grandad, will he do that?'

'No. Apparently not. He says he's had enough and wants to sell up.'

'But will anyone buy?'

'Yes. The ground landlords have already offered a good price because they're keen to build something else on the site. So there's no need to worry about your grandad,' he said, looking at her anxiously. 'He's happy to retire in style.'

'I see.' Amy frowned trying to assimilate all the news. 'And this means you're free to join Minerva's?'

'Completely and wholeheartedly,' he smiled.

'And Rosa?' she whispered, looking towards the stable-tent expecting her sister to make an appearance too.

'No. Definitely not Rosa. We've both realised that was a dreadful mistake.'

'Oh, but Steffi . . .' Amy started to say, her hand instinctively flying up to cover her scar – only to find that he immediately pulled it away to kiss her.

'And remember,' he whispered into her hair, 'I've come back not because I want to be at Minerva's, but because I want to be with you. And whether you accept my love or not, it will always be yours, Amy. Because that's the way it is, even if it's taken me a hell of a time to realise it.'

'A hell of a time with Rosa?'

'No. A hell of a time without you,' he murmured, clasping her tight until someone yelled, 'Hey up, you two! Mind your backs!' and ushered them aside to let the elephant through.

Steffi had been warned what to expect when he was formally introduced to the audience at the start of the second half of the programme.

'Today, ladies and gentlemen, boys and girls,' Levic was announcing from the centre of the ring, 'it is my very great pleasure – and privilege – to introduce to you the clown who in the guise of Levic slipped in earlier and stole our hearts. Now I want you to give a very warm welcome to him in his own right. A big hand, ladies and gentlemen, please, to welcome my son and new star of our show – Levity!'

Peeping through the curtain, Steffi could see the bright circle of faces and blur of hands clapping and the ring empty of all except his father who was standing there, one arm upraised, looking expectantly at the entrance.

And the applause was thunderous at first. Echoing through his head right down his body until it reached his boots. Everyone out there was clapping. But for how long? He knew they could not keep it up forever. So he waited until slowly but inevitably the clapping grew less. The audience, beginning to lose faith as he failed to appear, letting their applause trickle away like water from a leaky bucket.

Steffi grinned. All those people thinking that they knew what they were waiting for – the audience, and Levic, even Amy. He could almost hear them thinking: Good lord, where is he? What's happened? What's gone wrong?

Well, they were in for a surprise.

Now in his own costume as Levity, the silly auguste, he made a different sort of entrance from the one he made as Levic, the traditional clown. Rushing into the ring pell-mell, full of joy and confidence – before tripping himself up and falling over the suitcase he was carrying!

He rubbed his head. Surely someone must have pushed him over? But who? He peered behind himself and one by one carefully surveyed the audience, reducing them to helpless laughter at the sight of his bewilderment. Then he smiled at them, reassured that there were no enemies out there.

Dusted himself down and scratched his head, trying to

remember what had brought him into the ring in the first place.

Then dear old Levic came to his rescue by pointing and mouthing loudly: 'Come on, Levity. Show us what you've got in there!'

Of course! Now he remembered. It was something to do with the suitcase.

The trouble was, that suitcase proved to be one of those very tricky cases to open even after he had sat himself down on top of it and curled his legs round its edge to get a better purchase. Still, after a great deal of kerfuffle, he eventually managed to wrench it open and pull out – a smart top hat and frock coat.

'For you, Levity?' Levic asked.

He shook his head vigorously and shyly pointed one finger.

'For *me*, Levity?' Levic cried, clearly touched by the gesture.

Levity, beaming, nodded his head.

Peeling off his old jacket, Levic tried on the handsome new frock coat which all could see fitted him perfectly. Then Levity handed him the top hat which he carefully placed on his head.

But Steffi had not finished yet. He stooped to lift another object from the suitcase.

'Something else for me?' Levic asked, surprised.

'Most certainly.' And with a flourish Steffi presented his father with a director's baton before joining the audience in their generous applause.

The applause continued long after Levic had limped from the ring. But slowly it faded and the light dimmed and drew back into one bright pool at the centre of which stood Steffi on his own. And as he stood there he became aware of a hush so intense that for a moment his heart shrank within him.

But only for a moment. For in the next instant the orchestra had struck up with a polka by Strauss and on to the brightening scene hurtled a young woman on horseback who proceeded to circle round him like a whirlwind. Flinging herself down to spin cartwheels and somersaults. Leaping back to continue her gallop. Flushed and radiant. And irresistible.

In a gesture that was unrehearsed Steffi doffed his baggy clown suit, turned, ran across thc arena and leapt up behind Amy with an ecstatic yell. Their horse gave no sign of slowing its pace as, with arms raised in a joyful salute, they circled the ring together.

378